WINTER INTO SPRING

LIZ UNSER

ISBN 978-1-910652-03-9

Winter into Spring is a work of fiction. Names, characters, places, and incidents either are the product of the author's imagination or are used fictitiously. Any resemblance to actual events, locales or persons, living or dead, is entirely coincidental.

Edited by The Oxford Editors, www.theoxfordeditors.co.uk

Typesetting by Prepare to Publish, www.preparetopublish.com

For all members of the SGI worldwide especially those in SGI-UK and SGI-USA.

1

That Saturday began as a cheerful sort of day. Elin Petersen hummed as she entered the kitchen, washing basket on her hip. She nuzzled a kiss on the back of her husband's neck as he lounged at the central island, pulling his collar back gently, finding the soft skin below his thick brown hair. He twisted round to grab her around her waist, but she had already danced out of his reach. He acknowledged the teasing with a shrug, and his eyes, a deep hazelly green with sweeping black lashes, softened before they returned to the screen on his phone.

Elin made a pile of whites and a pile of coloureds, content with her lot – thirty and happily married, lovely home, pedigree dog and two of the cutest cats in Cardiff. She could hear the dog snuffling at the back door and the cats were wailing hungrily at her feet. She opened a pouch of food and shared it between their bowls, wrinkling her nose at the strong, fishy smell and rinsing her hands before returning to the laundry. She glanced through the window, saw the morning sunshine reflected off the broad camellia leaves and hoped there would be no need for the dryer today. Elin resumed humming as she bent to stuff underwear and shirts into the washing machine.

Suddenly she gasped and fell silent, her heart thudding in her ears. Her left hand groped for support, freshly painted nails clicking against the enamel as she pushed herself upright, her right hand clutching a shirt. She glanced down at the gleaming floor tiles, trying to shake off the feeling that she'd stepped off an unseen kerb and left her stomach behind. The warmth of the under-floor heating reassured her, she straightened, brushed her hair away from her eyes and examined the shirt, her brain buzzing. Her mouth was dry and her heartbeat too fast. Elin didn't trust her legs to carry her across the room. Her voice quavered.

"Joe, come and look at this."

She could see that he was in no hurry to move. His legs were folded, giraffe-like, around a tall kitchen stool as he flipped screens and sipped coffee amid toast crumbs and scattered weekend supplements. Earlier, they had pored over the travel section, tossing around ideas for their next big holiday, his arm draped casually over her shoulders.

Joe acknowledged her request with a nod, but didn't move. Elin studied the shirt and the pink streak next to the top button, bringing it closer, scratching it with her nail and giving it a quick sniff. She waited, holding the shirt, as Joe pushed back the stool and wandered over, mug in hand.

"Look at this. What is it?" Elin succeeded in keeping her voice neutral.

Joe glanced down. "It'll come off won't it? That's my favourite shirt."

"I asked what it was?" An edge crept into Elin's voice.

Joe dutifully examined the shirt. "Looks like lipstick to me. Not the first time, and probably won't be the last!" He grinned at her and took a mouthful of coffee. "Ugh, that's cold." He walked to the new, all bells and whistles, coffee maker, a Christmas gift from his parents. "Want a latte?"

"No thanks." Elin followed Joe, shirt in hand. She stuck it in front of him again and her voice trembled as she insisted. "I know it's lipstick, that's obvious: it isn't my lipstick. Whose is it?"

Joe sighed. "It has to be yours. There's no other explanation." He measured coffee beans into the machine, pressed some buttons and as the smell of dark roast Colombian filled the air he gave her his full attention. "It's not like you to be upset over nothing."

"I'm not upset about nothing. I want you to answer my question." Espresso trickled, steam belched and Elin felt her cheeks flush. Her voice rose a full octave. "Just listen to me Joe! I'm absolutely certain that's not my lipstick."

Joe's eyes held hers and a half smile hovered as he reached for her hand. "Elin, you're being silly. There's nothing to explain." Elin's hand lay inert in his but he persevered, lifted it to his lips and kissed her fingers. "C'mon, *cara mia*, smile, there's no mystery."

Elin snatched her hand away, holding his gaze as she yelled, "You wore this shirt last night... out with the boys... one of them's wearing lipstick now, is he?" She stalked away, studied the mark one last time and shoved the shirt into the washing machine. She closed the door with a bang and jabbed buttons until the machine purred into life.

Joe frowned. "Now you're being paranoid. The pub with Ricky and Bob is hardly a wild night out."

"We've had this conversation too many times, Joe, and nothing changes," Elin snorted. "I know you work hard and a Friday night drink is reasonable – but lipstick on your shirt?"

She stared at Joe as he took off his glasses and polished

them absent-mindedly on the hem of his cashmere sweater. Steam hissed through milk and Joe slowly assembled a latte to his liking. As he took an appreciative sip, Elin burst out, voice shaking, "That's it? Aren't you going to say any more?"

"There's no need to shriek. There's nothing more to say. It's your lipstick, I'm certain. If there's any problem it's in your head." Joe shrugged, exuding total confidence, and carried his drink into the home office and closed the door.

Elin fought the sting in her eyes and sniffed in frustration. She could picture him at the computer: he'd have forgotten their row already. As the youngest professor of Astrophysics at Cardiff University, one of the leading research universities in the UK, she envied his ability to bury himself in his work. His hopes of travelling in space and his obsession with becoming one of a handful of British chess grandmasters had impressed her when they met, and he was far too sexy to be a nerd. The way he held himself, the authority in his voice, made it impossible for him not to be the centre of attention. He worked hard, and an enormous legacy from his great-aunt cushioned their life. Everything was picture perfect. She had Joe, short for Giovanni, the quirky, handsome only child of an Italian fashion model mother and a Norwegian businessman father; an ultra-modern home and just enough work as a supply secondary school science teacher to keep boredom at bay. Elin was living the life of her dreams.

But, it was not her lipstick, and that was a problem.

The sound of water draining brought Elin back to the present and the debris of breakfast. She hauled herself up, put the dishes into the dishwasher and wiped the grey marble countertop. The clatter alerted the dog and he threw himself against the back door, yelping for attention. Mutt was a year-old Afghan Hound, as elegant as he was crazy, and impossible to ignore. He was Joe's dog: she had been content with her two rescue cats, Alley and Tom; but Joe's enthusiasm and promises of taking care of him had worn her down so here Mutt was. A wave of resentment hit her so strongly that she wanted to pull Joe out of the office, scream blue murder, pummel his chest and get the truth out of him. She knew that wouldn't work, and she would end up feeling foolish and apologising in the face of his implacable self-control. She might as well work off her anger and resentment with a long walk on the beach.

Hours later, Elin turned into a cul-de-sac and slowed her Mercedes to a halt in front of a sprawling detached house. The house looked welcoming in spite of its pebbledash walls and ageing roof. A stone Buddha, pots of fading freesias and abandoned boots fought for space in the porch, and the front door had been painted purple. She switched off the engine, but made no attempt to get out. Elin could see movement in the kitchen, which ran full length from the front to back of the house. It was probably her good friend Hilary, cooking as usual. She sat for a few moments gathering her thoughts, noticing that the garage door was open with just one car, Hilary's, inside. There were no skateboards or bikes left on the pavement and no music could be heard. In spite of her affection for Hilary's two teenagers, Elin felt a surge of relief. She wanted, no, needed, Hilary's full attention. She angled the mirror in the sun visor towards her and wrinkled her nose, unhappy with her reflection. She raked her fingers through her chin-length, chestnut hair until it regained some of its customary sleekness. Leaving the dog in the car, she got out, brushed sand, acquired during the bracing beach walk, from her designer jeans, and made her way to the front door.

"In the kitchen, Elin," Hilary yelled. Elin left her sandy

trainers in the porch, made her way through the familiar spacious hall and pushed open the kitchen door. Hilary looked up and gasped, "Oh, Elin, what's happened?"

"No one's died, don't worry!" Elin's light-hearted response fell flat. She halted in the doorway. "Do you have time to talk? You look busy." Elin looked around at the chopping boards and empty tins of tomatoes littering the granite-topped centre island.

Abandoning what looked like a lasagne, Hilary strode across the kitchen and enveloped Elin in a warm hug. "Of course I've got time. Sit down. Tea? Coffee? Something stronger? Just let me get this in the oven then I'm all yours." Hilary put two mugs on the table saying, "Tell me what's going on. I've got all afternoon; the kids are out with friends and Ricky's playing golf."

Elin sniffed. Hilary tore off several pieces of kitchen roll and handed them to her. "Take your time. Is this about Joe?"

Elin's eyebrows suddenly became visible over the top of her makeshift handkerchief. "Why do you think it's Joe?"

"Well, he's not exactly in contention for husband of the year, is he? I know what a selfish bastard he can be at times."

Hilary's tone was direct and forceful. Elin knew Hilary's bluntness was tempered by a big heart, but she struggled to continue. Hilary bustled around the kitchen. "Have you had lunch yet? I know it's late, but I haven't eaten, too busy cooking for the Scouts' fundraiser tonight. I was just going to make myself a sandwich, do you want one?"

Nodding, Elin took a couple of deep breaths and wiped her already sore nose on the harsh surface of the kitchen towel as Hilary filled the mugs then busied herself making sandwiches. "There was something this morning, it's so trite, such a cliché, that I can hardly believe it. Like something out of a soap opera."

A phone began to ring; Elin hesitated and took a sip of tea. Hilary ignored the phone and indicated that Elin should continue. Elin put down the mug and took a deep breath.

"I was loading the washing machine when I saw lipstick on Joe's shirt. It wasn't mine! He was right there so I asked him, hoping for a simple explanation, messing about at work, you know, birthday jollies, something like that, but no, he insisted it was mine!"

"Possibly it was?" Hilary enquired mildly.

"Good God, no, it was pink! I don't even own a pink lipstick. It definitely wasn't mine."

"There wasn't a simple explanation?"

Elin exploded. "That's what I was trying to find out, don't you see? But no, he was so obnoxiously calm, Hilary, he insisted I was mistaken! I felt I was going crazy. I'm certain that it wasn't mine. I began to hate him for making me feel like that. He said it was all in my head. It wasn't, I know it wasn't!" Elin paused for breath. "Then there was last weekend as well, that was probably my fault... you know how I like to plan things in my head... I shouldn't get upset when Joe can't read my mind..."

"It's alright Elin, slow down, just tell me."

Elin sniffed again. Hilary left the kitchen and came back with a box of tissues.

"Thanks. Sorry, I'll try again. You know Joe."

Hilary nodded and was grim-faced as she responded, "Indeed, I do. I'm surprised you haven't been over here to cry on my shoulder before."

"He was out late again, a week ago, the usual Friday night at the pub and on to a club. I'd spent the evening wondering about our marriage, feeling as if we were getting in a bit of a rut, maybe? Not unhappy, just, you know, I used to wait up for him..." Elin's voice trailed away.

Hilary nodded encouragingly.

"I wanted to make the next morning special, I had it all planned." Elin's green eyes filled with tears and she squeezed them tight closed. "He came home as I was drifting off to sleep. He took a shower and I felt him slide into bed. We cuddled and fell asleep. I had lovely plans for the morning so that was enough. OK, this sounds silly now, but when I woke up I got out of bed quietly, crept downstairs and when I came back up with warm croissants and coffee he was getting dressed!"

Hilary's expression remained enigmatic.

"I thought we'd stay in bed, have wonderful sex and everything would be like it used to be. You know what I mean." Elin's voice rose as she delivered the *coup de grace*, "He insisted he'd mentioned he had to go out, even though it was Saturday. He didn't notice I was disappointed. He kept saying I'd forgotten, but he hadn't told me. I definitely hadn't forgotten."

Hilary opened her mouth, closed it again and paused before speaking. "But surely there must be more than that to upset you so much?"

"It's the combination of nine years of marriage, my worries about the late nights, the lipstick..." Elin frowned, searching for words, "... most of all it's the occasions when he twists it around, makes it all my fault. Other times he's wonderful, most of the time we're really happy."

Hilary topped up their mugs and settled back down opposite Elin. "You poor thing, no wonder you're upset. Look at all you've done, moving here for his career and now you're stuck with supply teaching."

"Oh no, it was my idea not to look for a job when we moved here. The money from his aunt meant we could buy the house outright and still have plenty in the bank. I wanted more time to design the house and garden. The supply job at Beechwood High suits me down to the ground. I shouldn't get so upset: he's generous and never complains about my clothes habit, the good stuff doesn't come cheap, you know."

"Complain? Why should he complain?" Now Hilary was incandescent, unable to keep her temper under control any longer. "He spends more than you do on clothes! I've never seen him look scruffy — why, he was wearing that gorgeous sweater you bought him in John Lewis just to clean the car last weekend! And the cars! Did you ever ask for a Mercedes?"

Hilary's outburst shocked Elin. Tea and sympathy were turning into a wake-up call. Hilary's tone became softer. "I don't know how to say this Elin, but do you think things might be different if you and Joe had kids?" She leaned forward, closer to Elin, anticipating another flood of tears.

Elin smiled her first genuine smile of the day. "God, no! Neither of us wanted children. It's one of the things we have in common. I thought I told you that I had a burst appendix as a teenager, peritonitis, then complications. As if that wasn't enough, I had an ovary removed because of a huge cyst a year later and the other one didn't look too good. Having children wasn't on the cards, and I've always accepted that. I think I missed out on the maternal gene. I love teaching, but babies and little kids, sorry, no, that's not me at all. Definitely not."

'What about Joe, does he feel the same?"

"He's adamant that he doesn't want to be a father."

There was a long pause before Hilary spoke again. She closed her eyes briefly, debating her words. Her indignation had evaporated and she smiled wanly. "I've given up on 'happily ever after'. Let it go soon after Jemmie was born."

Jemmie was Hilary and Ricky's daughter, born just eleven months after her brother Finn.

"What do you mean, given up?"

"No one's life is perfect you know Elin, no matter how it might look. I finally realised Ricky wouldn't give up any of his interests, said he needed time to de-stress after work, and as I was home all day I obviously had time to do what I wanted!" Hilary shook her head in disbelief. "I was basically on my own. I could either choose to be totally on my own, and there were times that seemed attractive, you know how independent I am."

Elin smiled an acknowledgement uneasily. This was a side of her friend she had not seen before.

"I knew how hard it was to look after two little ones on my own, and was it fair to the children? I decided that some help from Ricky was better than none. After all, if he was slumped in front of the TV in the evenings I didn't have to get a babysitter. I could see that once they got older and interested in sport he'd be more helpful. We both love our kids in our own ways."

"What about you and Ricky, you're happy, aren't you?"

"Happy enough I suppose." Suddenly Hilary grinned and added, "Come on girl, life's not over yet. Do you want me to come over tonight and talk some more?"

Elin sat up straight. "I'll be OK, but thanks anyway. I need time to ponder. You've made me think I've been too idealistic. One minute I'm sad and hurt, next minute I'm angry as hell."

"Don't worry too much, you'll work things out, I'm sure."

Hilary's very definite views were often overwhelming, and Elin wanted to be alone. It was a short drive to her own spacious home with its sweeping drive and double garage, terraced front garden and huge picture windows glinting in the pale late-afternoon sun. It was as modern in style as Elin herself and she loved every inch of the place. She had selected each cushion, curtain and lamp with loving attention to detail, and the overall theme was simple and relaxed.

However, this time, as she walked around the back to put the dog out in the grassy rear garden and entered through the kitchen door, she didn't feel the frisson of pleasure that usually accompanied her return. She was relieved to be greeted only by her two tabby cats as they competed for space around her ankles and meowed as though she had been gone for days. Joe was nowhere to be seen.

2

The following week, Elin reflected on how attentive Joe had been since the lipstick incident. He surprised her with a dinner out and then, as they ate, suggested a holiday to India in September. Elin had hoped to be teaching then but, once she had accepted Joe's plan, India became an enticing prospect and Elin started to get excited.

"It all sounds wonderful, Joe, the holiday of a lifetime." She'd reached for his hand and they'd picked up their wine glasses and clinked them together.

Slightly tipsy, they'd taken a taxi home. Joe's touch had thrilled Elin and they made love with all the intensity of the early days. Afterwards, as Joe lay snoring gently at her side, Elin had gazed at his outline under the duvet and a niggle of doubt about his charm offensive had grown stronger as she'd struggled to fall asleep. With his lanky frame and heavy rimmed glasses, Joe had made her think of Clark Kent when they first met but now the Superman effect was fading fast.

There were times in the week when she felt that she

hated Joe for making a fool of her, and other days when he acted like the perfect husband. Elin wondered about the choice of the verb "acted" even in her thoughts.

Beechwood High School was an oasis. She felt an ever-growing camaraderie with the staff, renewing connections made during a three-week stint teaching Chemistry there the previous year. This time she was covering Years 7, 8 and 9 Biology for the summer. The previous term, Elin had developed a comfortable relationship with Mia, another supply teacher, but nobody knew where Mia was anymore. Elin remembered many of the staff by name. Aaron, the P.E. teacher, was gregarious by nature, always deep in animated conversation. Elin noted his easy command of his powerfully built body, his blue eyes that crinkled with laughter and his wide, engaging grin. A friendship with Fiona, a gentle, soft-spoken English and Drama teacher, was developing slowly. Still she wished Mia were there.

Elin wondered how Mia's relationship karma was playing out these days; a recent relationship had been with a Zen Buddhist who had disappeared to a retreat. Then she had met an accountant-turned-carpenter whose lack of success in his new business might have been because he actually wasn't a very good carpenter.

Another Monday morning, and another week at Beechwood as April crept towards May. Entering the staff room with its aging armchairs and smell of stale coffee, Elin felt the familiar lift in her spirits in response to the buzz of conversation, and smiled.

"Hey, Elin, guess who I bumped into at the supermarket last night?" The question came from Aaron who had been watching the door, coffee in hand, wearing his tracksuit ready for first lesson. Not waiting for a reply, he carried on, "Our mutual good friend, Mia!"

Elin smiled even wider. "That is wonderful, how was she?"

"You can ask her yourself, I got her new number for you."

"I'm thrilled, thanks so much," Elin said, truly grateful.

At that moment the bell rang. Aaron caught his breath in frustration as he moved towards the door.

"Give me your mobile number?" he urged, phone in hand, "I'll text you her details."

Aaron was as good as his word, and by the end of the day Elin had received the promised text.

"Always happy to be of assistance," he had said with a smile that lit up his face and highlighted his intense blue eyes as Elin thanked him before leaving that evening.

Once home, Elin tried phoning Mia, then left a text and a message. Much later, she tried again but only got voicemail. How frustrating. Perhaps Mia didn't value her friendship the way she valued Mia's? Elin felt her spirits gradually sink.

Still no response from Mia by the end of the week. Elin tried hard to rationalise. Mia might have lost her phone, but Elin still felt rejected. She threw herself into school activities and found herself volunteering to help Fiona with the summer show as a general assistant with the dance group.

"Some of them are pretty hopeless, Elin," Fiona confided. "Michael Jackson has a lot to answer for! They probably dance along with *Thriller* but getting them to follow the steps for the show is a different kettle of fish."

"How I can help? I'm no dancer either."

"Oh, don't worry, I'm glad to have help. They're not very fit; could you take some of the practices? I copied the routine from one on YouTube and I'm afraid to tinker with it. The theme is Children Protecting the Environment. That's just up your street, isn't it?"

"Yes, it is, but I've no clue how that translates into a dance. I'll do what I can. Perhaps I'll get fitter myself?"

When Joe left for the pub on Friday evening, Elin settled down to watch the YouTube version. After one viewing she had the basics, after the second she'd figured out the moves and on the third she tried to join in. Out of breath, she flopped on to the sofa, disturbing Alley and Tom, who sniffed, yawned and moved away. Just then her phone rang.

"Is that you Elin? It's Mia. I only just got your messages!"

Elin couldn't help smiling. Her doubts about her ability to sustain a friendship fell away at the sound of Mia's voice. "Yes, it's me, a bit out of puff."

"You do sound breathless, what *are* you doing? It's Friday, you're supposed to be relaxing!"

This was ironic coming from someone who was always on the go.

"You don't want to know! Where are you these days? I'm back at Beechwood."

"Good for you. I'm just back from a week volunteering with Wild Places. It's a small green charity. They had us clearing a whole hillside of rhododendrons. My hands are blistered and my back aches — I can't wait to get into a hot bath."

"Aah! That's why you were incommunicado, I thought you didn't want to speak to me!"

"Don't be silly, sister, I've always got time for you. What's up?"

"I just wondered if we could get together?"

"Absolutely! The problem is I don't have a car at the moment; I'm trying to be green and manage without one. I'll be riding a bike as soon as I get my old one from home –

would you believe my parents still have it in their shed! Why don't you come here?"

They made plans for the next day. Elin took down directions to Mia's house, which was not too far away – funny that she'd not known that before. Elin broke into tuneless singing as she got ready for bed. She drifted off into sleep and didn't hear Joe creep in at gone three in the morning.

Joe was so groggy when Elin woke that she felt sorry for him. She showered, dressed in jeans and a rugby shirt and strolled around the garden carrying her morning tea. It was a cloud-filled day, but that didn't matter as she looked for green shoots to confirm that spring was on its way. Elin decided to spend the next day working outside; she loved the natural look even though perennials took longer to mature. Patience was one of her virtues; being willing to wait for what she really wanted. Perhaps her patience with Joe had caused him to think that the way he led his life was perfectly fine with her.

Elin fed the cats then allowed Mutt to drag her around the park for twenty minutes before she jotted a note for Joe saying she'd be at Mia's. She left it on the counter top, having no desire to kiss a stale, unshaven, half asleep Joe goodbye.

Mia's house was smallish and mid-terrace. Elin parked and walked briskly to the door.

"At last I've discovered where you live, how long have you been here?"

"Bought it last year, joined the ranks of respectable house owners," Mia laughed. "I never quite saw myself with a mortgage on my precarious income, but Dad kept nagging me. He wasn't impressed with the footloose and fancy-free argument. He felt that I should have a firm base, economically anyway!"

"That's impressive, buying a house on your own."

"Well, Dad helped me with the deposit, I couldn't have done it otherwise. The furniture and decorating, well, as you can see, that's going to take a while."

A faint hint of incense floated around the living room, a couple of brightly coloured rugs warmed the scuffed wooden floorboards, and the seating was an old sofa covered with a blanket and a multi-coloured throw. Magazines spilled down from two packed bookcases. The shiny taupe curtains were evidently hand-me-downs from an exceedingly elderly relative or a charity shop find. The rest of the furnishings comprised of an ancient lamp, a couple of floor cushions and some mismatched coffee tables. A world away from Elin's carefully decorated sitting room, but comfortable and totally non-threatening.

"Let's have some tea, would you like Earl Grey or builders? Or I think I've got some coffee here somewhere. Sorry, no milk, I haven't been to the shops yet." Mia chattered on as she disappeared into the kitchen.

Elin leaned against the doorway, observing the kitchen, which was small and contained the necessary basics, sink, stove and fridge, but there was nothing streamlined about it. The units looked like hangovers from the seventies or eighties and a small table with an assortment of chairs completed the décor.

"Not exactly *Ideal Home* is it?" Mia grinned. "It's going to be ages until I can afford to spruce it up. Did you say which tea?"

"I'll go for Earl Grey, I prefer that without milk anyway."

They made space amid the clutter for their mugs and a

biscuit tin and settled in. "So, what've you been up to, Mia? What are your plans?"

"To tell the truth, I'm drifting. I want to retrain, but I can't decide what to do. I guess I'll have to do some supply teaching to pay the bills now that I'm a home owner... thanks Dad, but other than that, I've no idea," responded Mia ruefully.

"Wow, that's exciting! Good for you. Any ideas what line of work?" Elin asked.

"No, not really. Maybe environmental protection or I quite fancy conservation in museums. I'm going to check out what qualifications are needed. What's happening with you?"

Maybe Mia could put a fresh slant on the Joe situation. She took a deep breath and catalogued how things had changed with Joe. Mia didn't interrupt and Elin was grateful. "I don't know what to do." Elin complained finally. "I've tried the obvious things; look good, show him you love him... all that crap. It's not working and it makes me more resentful while Joe stays just the same!"

"Have you talked to him?"

Elin delved into her handbag for a tissue, "Talk is hardly what you'd call it. I try, he evades the issue. He's right. I'm wrong. End of story."

Mia refilled the kettle ready to top up their mugs and absent-mindedly munched on the last biscuit. Elin waited.

"I really don't know what to say. I'm not an expert on the joys of togetherness: look at me, thirty-four and not a single long-term relationship to my name."

"So, what happens? You don't have any difficulty attracting men!"

Mia was slim with long, dark brown hair that hung almost to her waist. Her face was always totally devoid of makeup, but her pale skin and even features made a lasting impression. Mia admitted that fashion was something of a mystery to her – a mystery that she couldn't be bothered to solve. She could look stunning, but more by accident than design. She could be a walking disaster, style-wise, or closely resemble a runway model. Whichever it was, Mia never lacked for male attention.

"Don't know really. I enjoy being part of a couple, but the single state does have a lot of advantages."

"What about the last one? Jack, wasn't it? Anyone could see that he doted on you."

"That was the problem! Can't stand a know-it-all and can't stand a door-mat either."

A rueful expression crossed Mia's face and Elin thought for a moment that it would be tough to be Mia's partner. Mia was stoic, "What's the rush? I definitely don't want children."

"Well, we have the no children thing in common: we're quite a rare species, women without the biological clock, or if we have, it's not ticking. I thought that would be the glue that held Joe and me together."

They stared ahead at nothing much for a moment or two. Elin broke the silence with a sigh.

"To think I freely chose my situation and now I'm unhappy. He's changed; he's not the Joe I signed up for."

Elin dabbed her nose with the balled-up tissue and moved to the window. Mia watched until Elin broke the silence, "Time's getting on, do you have plans or shall we pop down the road and get some lunch?"

Mia jumped up, "Great idea, I can go food shopping afterwards."

Leaving their mugs unwashed in the kitchen sink, they picked up their bags — Elin's the latest candy-coloured patent leather, Mia's a battered canvas satchel — and sauntered off arm in arm. They didn't talk about Joe again.

Mia laid her fork down with a contented sigh, "I've gotta go, let's get together soon. Next week, same time?"

They agreed and as Elin walked back to her car she wondered what, if anything, would be different by the following Saturday. The greyness clouding her thoughts of Joe and the familiar churning of resentment in her stomach had not gone away.

Joe was occupied cleaning the MG, car radio blaring, when Elin returned. He greeted her with a tentative smile.

She went inside and threw the ingredients together for a chicken casserole, stuck it in the oven, kicked off her shoes and flopped onto an armchair. She glanced at the clock, still only four, a bit early for vodka and tonic, Better to hold off the alcohol; she intended having a serious discussion with Joe that evening.

Joe came to the doorway, mobile phone in hand. "Ricky's on the phone, he says Hilary wants to know if we'd like to go over for a few drinks tonight and maybe a takeaway? Gina and Bobby will be there. I said we didn't have any other plans, so how about it?"

She felt a prickle of irritation. Ricky was still on the line, now aware that they had no plans. She didn't want to risk offending Hilary so the serious discussion with Joe would have to wait.

Then Joe made mojitos with the fresh mint she'd bought to serve with roast lamb the next day. He had a flair for getting cocktails just right. The casserole could go in the freezer. An hour later, and well into her second mojito, Elin lay back in the bath, thinking. Joe certainly did have some excellent qualities, maybe she was being just a little paranoid? She dressed in new jeans and a ruffled top, choosing her accessories with care. As she descended the stairs, Joe showed his approval with a low whistle — "*Sei belissima!*" — but he knew better than to smudge her lipstick.

Elin and Joe sat together in an oversized armchair as the evening wound down, Joe's arm resting companionably on Elin's shoulders. Walking home after midnight, the clear sky, the stars and mild night air conspired to cast a spell. Joe and Elin held hands, the old electricity flowing between them again. Later, with arms still wrapped around each other they fell into a blissful oblivion. Neither one had checked their phones.

Next morning Elin smiled to herself as she waited for the kettle to boil, wondering what on earth she'd been getting worked up about. She and Joe were OK. She wasn't the slightest bit fazed when she listened to the message from Mia that she wouldn't be able to make their planned lunch date, as she was joining another conservation crew. The genuine regret evident in Mia's voice made up for any residual disappointment. Mia said that she wouldn't be able to use her mobile up in the mountains. Elin noticed that Mia hadn't said how long she'd be away, but the urgency she'd felt about seeing her again wasn't there anymore.

A few weeks later a postcard of Snowdon arrived for Elin.

"Decided to stay for a month. Hard work, beautiful scenery. Hope all is well with you. Love, Mia."

3

The dance troupe were truly terrible, but Fiona and Elin wanted the children to stay positive so what was to be done? It might have worked as a comedy act, but what about the damage to those fragile egos if the audience laughed uproariously on performance night? Costumes were being made, parents, cousins and friends were sewing away; there was no Plan B.

Elin and Fiona felt increasingly anxious. At a staff room strategy meeting, they decided to divide the group into two and increase the practices to daily. Aaron overheard the discussion and drew up his chair next to Elin.

"How are their fitness levels? It must be hard for them if they're out of puff."

Fiona frowned in agreement, "That's true but it doesn't help."

Aaron looked at Elin first, his glance a tad longer than necessary, then turned to Fiona, "Can I do anything?"

"Thanks, Aaron, all help accepted! We need fresh ideas," Fiona said, sounding desperate.

The three of them sat glumly. Just then Elin's phone beeped to announce a new text message.

"Back in town, how r things? Action Men at Barn Theatre on Sat, want 2 come?"

Elin almost leapt from her chair. She turned to Fiona, face aglow. "Wow, why on earth didn't I think of Chrissie before? Oh Fiona, this is wonderful, let me explain...." Elin couldn't wait to share her brainwave.

"Mia has this friend, Chrissie, I've only met her once. She's a choreographer and she has a show on Saturday at the Barn Theatre." Elin was almost babbling in her haste. "Why don't we go? We can talk to Chrissie, she'll be able to help. Can we do that?"

Fiona looked doubtful and not nearly as excited as Elin.

"Wouldn't it be a bit pushy to expect help from a professional?"

Elin's face fell, "You may be right, but she's a really nice person, it wouldn't hurt to ask."

Aaron leaned in, his arm on the back of Elin's chair, and said, "Why don't we go on Saturday? Elin, you find out details from Mia and we can meet the choreographer afterwards that way we'll be a paying audience and, as you say, we've got nothing to lose!"

Elin's beam of relief matched Aaron's grin. "OK, I'll contact Mia tonight. I'll ask Joe if he wants to come. Would your husband come, Fiona? And your wife, Aaron? We could get a group together, some of the other staff might be interested too, who knows?"

Once home and changed into her leisure clothes for the evening, Elin made a huge bowl of salad, using the first lettuce of the season from her vegetable garden, while organic chicken breasts were cooking under the grill. She put oil and vinegar on the table before dialling Mia's number. She settled down at the kitchen table with a glass of Sauvignon Blanc. The number was busy. Elin munched her way through a small bowl of salad. She tried again, still no luck, so she fed the cats then strolled around the garden. At her third attempt, Mia picked up on the first ring.

"It's me, Elin, how are you? When did you get back? What's up?"

"Oh, we've had a great time. Got back earlier today. The place was so basic, we had to buy supplies for the week when they took the van to town on Saturdays, so it's nice to cook again, I'm fed up with Pot Noodles and sandwiches!"

Elin probed, "What's this 'we' business? Sounds as if there's something you're not telling me."

"Well, uh, yes. He's called Daniel, he's a volunteer too. I met him last time and we've always got on well. Things heated up this time. He's between jobs so we were both there for the whole month. He's quite a bit younger than me, but who cares? We're just having fun, *carpe diem* and all that."

"Wonderful, I can't wait to hear more! Will he be going on Saturday?"

"No, he's going back to Manchester to pick up his stuff."

"Bringing it to your house? Wow, things are moving fast! But you're going? Can we get tickets at the door? Some people from Beechwood are interested."

"Great! Chrissie will be pleased; men's dance doesn't draw big crowds and the name doesn't help, people expect them to be parachuting down from the ceiling! Getting tickets on the night will be fine. Who's coming?"

"Fiona and Aaron and maybe some others."

Mia sounded puzzled, "Fiona and Aaron are coming?"

"Our dance group are dreadful and we've only got four

weeks left. Truthfully, we're desperate and are hoping for advice from Chrissie. It'll be fun even if Chrissie can't help."

Mia reassured her, "I'll explain to Chrissie and we'll get together for a drink at the bar afterwards."

Elin let out a sigh of relief, "Mia, you are a life saver!"

Mia chuckled, "I'll see you and your gang in the foyer at 7.15."

"Great, thanks so much, we owe you, big time!"

Elin swirled her wine and savoured its smoothness; she was still smiling when she heard Mutt going crazy. She put the ready-to-bake rolls into the oven and the plates on the table as Joe came through the door.

"Hello *pulcino*, had a good day?" Joe gave her a quick peck and launched straight into his plans for a minibreak in France. "We're not going to India 'til September and I saw an offer online, the Loire Valley, you and Mickey's wife would get on like a house on fire. Mickey and I might set up a few chess games, there's a local chess club, I found that on the internet too."

"Slow down, this is all news to me," Elin laughed, mellow from the wine, talking to Mia and the relief of having access to a real choreographer. "When is this happening? I've never been to the Loire Valley and I'm not sure I've even met Mickey's wife? If I have, I don't remember anything about her."

"It's this coming weekend! That's why it's such a good deal, I was lucky to see it when Mickey was right next to me, it's so cheap they're practically paying us to go!"

Elin's good mood evaporated in an instant, "Oh, no! I can't go this weekend, it's too sudden and I have important plans..."

"Too sudden?" Looking at her in trim workout trousers and top, Joe put his head on one side and gave his designer stubble a rub. "*Amore mio*, you look great just as you are, you could come along exactly like that and just bring a toothbrush."

"I can't even remember Mickey's wife's name for goodness' sake! Why would I want a weekend away with someone I hardly know? Saturday is a big opportunity. I haven't had a chance to tell you, you just came charging in and threw this at me!" Elin voice rose shrilly.

Joe remained calm, "What do you mean Saturday? Since when do you work on Saturdays?"

Elin struggled to keep her voice level as she explained how the planned night out would be fun and would help her work.

"Whatever made you think that I would want to see... men... dancing?" asked Joe disdainfully. Elin could feel his good mood follow hers and vanish.

"Because it's important to me! I need to go to this show, and it has to be this Saturday. They're terrific, vibrant and athletic as well as beautiful. If you've never been, how would you know?"

"Let me see, couple of hours spent just down the road in the Barn Theatre or a weekend in the Loire Valley? Let me think about this for a moment, which sounds more enticing?" Joe was getting into his sarcastic stride, ignoring Elin's stricken expression.

Suddenly the dam burst. "Go to hell, Joe. When did you ever think of what I want? Cooped up in a hotel with someone I don't know and probably won't even like sounds just great! You're not fooling me. You're pretending you're giving me a treat to salve your conscience about yet another few days devoted to your precious chess. Go on your own if you want to, if it's that cheap what does it matter? I'm not going. I'm staying here and doing what I want for once."

Elin had shocked herself. Joe's face flushed and he was shouting something about ingratitude as she rushed out of the room and upstairs to the bathroom, locking the door behind her and turning on the taps.

Elin's anger faded. Joe had made no attempt to follow her and she felt foolish sitting on the edge of the bath with the door locked. She smelled warm bread and remembered the rolls in the oven. She turned off the taps and let the water drain away.

Putting the rolls on the table, Elin called out that dinner was ready. She didn't feel like continuing the row, but she didn't feel like apologizing either. Joe wasted no time coming into the kitchen. "Seems we have a problem with plans for this weekend?"

"Seems as if we do." Elin busied herself tossing the salad.

"Well, actually, Mickey and I have already booked the trip. We thought that you and Sophie would be pleased."

"You know, Joe, Sophie may well be pleased but I'm not. I have plans, I'm not just being awkward."

"How are we going to work this out, then?" Joe looked suitably contrite.

"If it's that cheap, why don't you go with Mickey and Sophie? You can play all the chess you like and Sophie would probably appreciate the peace and quiet."

"Are you sure you wouldn't mind?" Joe hugged Elin and she sighed with relief.

On Friday morning, the house was a flurry of activity with Joe checking tickets, credit cards and passport while Elin calmly prepared for school.

Friday's abysmal dance practice did not dampen Fiona and Elin's spirits. Everything felt different.

Saturday came. Elin took Mutt to the beach, using the time and space to think about her flare-up of anger. Her ability to carry on as usual surprised her and Joe had made an effort too. A feeling of release had stolen over her when Joe had driven off yesterday. Should she be worried about that? The last few months had been OK. She sometimes shared a grouch with Hilary and Gina about Joe's Friday nights and interminable chess matches, but she had her friends, her yoga and her garden. Mutt was still an irritation: she couldn't bear to see him moping and Joe's good intentions seldom materialized into dog walking action. Elin decided to stop complaining about Joe.

Elin dressed for the evening in new, navy-blue linen trousers, choosing her blue animal print top rather than the stripes. She didn't feel much like a breezy sailor right now; so much was resting on her tenuous connection with Chrissie. She sat for a few minutes to calm herself with Alley and Tom snuggled up close.

"Hello Elin, we're over here!" Elin found Mia as she made her way through the throng in the theatre foyer. What on earth was Mia wearing? She looked as if she was still dressed for field work in Snowdonia – faded trousers and baggy shirt blending in well with the young man standing close to her side who was wearing an equally battered pair of jeans topped by a shrunken sweater. Elin exchanged a hug with Mia before standing back and looking expectantly at Mia's companion.

"This is Daniel. He got back from Manchester early. Daniel, this is Elin."

"Hello Elin, Mia's told me about you." Hand extended, Daniel seemed happy to be there. He had a cute smile and curly blond hair, which together with muscular shoulders, outlined through his slightly-too-small sweater, presented a very attractive picture. No wonder Mia was seizing the day.

Fiona appeared next, "Hi Elin, this is my husband John."

She didn't wait for handshakes before introducing the knot of people, some neighbours as well as teachers from Beechwood. "Oh, there's the bell! Have we all got our tickets?" Fiona fussed around chivvying people to finish their drinks and get moving. "What should I do with Aaron's ticket, Elin? He phoned earlier and asked me to get one as he might be late. Perhaps I should have left it at the Ticket Office?"

Elin looked around as the crowd thinned but Fiona was the first to spot Aaron rushing through the door. "Oh, there he is, in the nick of time." Fiona hurried him forward, questioning him as they moved along, "Just you, Aaron, I thought your wife was coming?"

Elin was often surprised when she met staff members outside the school gates. Out of context, Aaron looked older, although his casual jacket and well-cut jeans certainly suited him. His dirty blond hair had just the right degree of mussed-up-ness. He flashed a smile at her and she felt his glance slide down to her toes and back up. She took in a deep breath, surprised by her sudden acute awareness of his presence.

"Babysitter let us down at the last minute. Sorry I'm late, Fiona, hope we don't miss the start."

"Not late, just perfect timing, let's go." Fiona ushered them through, the last of their group. Elin found herself seated between Aaron and Fiona. The lights dimmed and with an explosion of sound and energy the ensemble burst into action. Elin was riveted to every move, regretting that by focusing on one part of the stage she was missing action in another. The applause was rapturous when the lights came on for the interval.

"Anyone for a drink?" John looked enquiringly along the row.

"Not for me," replied Fiona. "I'm going to sit here and reflect on that amazing performance."

The others shuffled down the row and towards the bar, leaving Elin and Aaron with Fiona who turned to Elin. "Wow, Elin, your friend certainly knows her stuff, that was spectacular! Oh, my goodness, I do hope she can help us."

"She's Mia's friend really, I've only met her once, but I was impressed. I'm sure she'll help if she can."

Aaron joined in, "Well, she'll be feeling good after that performance."

Elin hoped he was right. "We'll soon find out. Mia's already arranged for us to meet in the bar afterwards.

They discussed the performance until their friends squeezed passed them, heading back towards their seats for the second half. After the finale the ensemble took curtain call after curtain call until the audience began to leave. Eventually, just Mia, Daniel, Fiona, John, Aaron and Elin were left to make their way to the bar. The place was packed and loud with excited conversation. John, Aaron and Daniel fought their way to get drinks while Elin, Fiona and Mia tried to make some space to call their own. There was no chance of a table, but before long they were standing in a compact circle clutching their drinks.

"Any idea how long it'll be before Chrissie joins us?" Elin wondered aloud to Mia. "I expect they'll all be in the dressing rooms revelling in their success for quite a while."

"I wonder how she got such a talented group together?" mused Fiona.

"We can ask her; look, there she is!" Mia gestured behind them. They turned towards the door as Chrissie entered, smiling broadly. She stopped to acknowledge the congratulations of friends then joined their small group. Kisses of congratulation and general hubbub ensued. Elin stood quietly while Fiona asked technical questions, fascinated by Chrissie's boundless energy. Chrissie was as she remembered, quite small, wiry, with a shock of untidy chestnut curls; dressed all in black, she looked every inch a dancer.

"How long have you been rehearsing Action Men, Chrissie?" Aaron's interest was on the hard work required.

"About three months in all, though it feels like three weeks to me," responded Chrissie with a laugh. "I love all aspects of dance, not just the final performance."

Here was the opening Elin had been waiting for. "Funny you should say that, Chrissie, we wanted to ask you about our dance project at school..." With a quick glance at Aaron and Fiona, Elin launched into their story, finishing with a doubt-filled appeal.

"So, we were wondering if, by any remote chance, you could help us?" continued Elin, adding hastily, "Of course we know that you're probably very busy... there are only four weeks before the end of term... but we're at our wits end and any advice would be fantastic..."

Elin trailed into silence. Maybe she'd overstated the situation and upset Fiona. Aaron gave her hand a squeeze of support before giving more details to Chrissie. Fiona soon made it three. Chrissie stopped them with a grin, "Enough already folks, I'm convinced! I've got a month free before rehearsals for the next show so the timing's perfect. Shall I come to a practice? Are you sure it's OK with the head teacher?"

Fiona assured her that she'd clear it with the Head on Monday. Chrissie agreed to come in for the Wednesday practice, giving Fiona time to explain what was happening to the kids.

The crowd thinned out; they found seats and just as Elin

was leaning forward to catch something Aaron said, she felt a tap on her shoulder.

"Elin, I thought it was you! Wasn't it a fabulous performance?" There stood Hilary with Ricky, both smiling. "Ricky knows one of the dancers. Small world, isn't it? We've got to get back; can't give Jemmie and Finn too much rope. Give me a ring, though, it's been ages since we caught up."

"Yes, it was wonderful! Hey, save a phone call, why don't you come over tomorrow? Joe's away, so I'd be glad of the company."

Mia and Daniel had great stories to tell about their time in Snowdonia. Chrissie regaled them with stories of the difficulties that had cropped up right until minutes before this evening's performance. She confessed it was a miracle the show had gone so well. Aaron caught Elin looking at him and his blue eyes held her gaze. He touched her arm lightly.

"Let's hope we get a miracle too!" he whispered.

Elin was confused by the quickening of her pulse, her sudden acute awareness of Aaron's presence. She frowned, looked at her watch and decided it was late enough for her. The bar staff were already gathering up the empty glasses, so she made her farewells and drove home, elated and relieved in equal measure.

The phone rang early the next morning. Elin guessed it would be Hilary, but pleaded the need to exercise Mutt and managed to put her off until later. Hilary insisted she would bring bread, courtesy of her new bread-maker. Elin threw on some old clothes and her scruffiest trainers, pausing only to get homemade soup out of the freezer before setting out for the only park within close range where she could let Mutt off the lead.

Mutt's behaviour was improving ever so slightly and she

hoped he'd check in with her at various times as she walked the perimeter of the park. She'd found that giving him total freedom resulted in a much-improved chance of them leaving for home together. There had been times when this plan had failed and she'd left without him, returning hours later to find Mutt waiting in the car park. Even Mutt didn't care to be abandoned.

Elin was just putting the soup on the stove to warm when she heard Hilary arrive. "Hi, I hope you like leek and potato soup, if not you'll have to forage for cheese and salad in the fridge, should be some Brie and a heel of mousetrap in there."

Hilary pulled a face, "You make that sound so inviting, Elin, just as well my favourite soup is leek and potato." She unwrapped her bread and placed it on the table.

Elin inhaled the fresh yeasty smell as she turned the heat up under the soup. "I'm looking forward to trying your bread. I'm glad you phoned early this morning so I didn't eat that second piece of toast at breakfast."

Hilary shrugged, "Sorry I phoned so early, I couldn't wait to talk to you, find out what's going on. I forget you don't have to get up early for kids. Do tell, where's Joe, and who was that gorgeous guy you were with last night?"

"Joe is in the Loire Valley. I stayed home because I wanted to see if we could recruit Chrissie, last night's choreographer, to help us with the kids' dance routine, you know, the one I've been worried about."

Elin laughed at the expression on Hilary's face and continued equably, "I wasn't WITH anybody last night. We went out as a group and I came home on my own."

"Don't give me that, you're talking to Hilary now, don't forget. Whoever the hunk was, he certainly was taken with you, I saw him practically drooling."

Elin's brow furrowed in disbelief, "Don't be silly, Hilary, if you're talking about Aaron, he wasn't drooling. He's the P.E. teacher at Beechwood and he was there for the same reason as me. He's married, his wife wasn't there because they couldn't get a babysitter."

"OK, I'll believe you, thousands wouldn't. What's up with you and Joe? I thought you were love's young dream again?"

"Not so young, I'm thirty years old, thirty-one soon."

Elin wasn't sure how she could describe her marriage these days. "We had a bit of a disagreement earlier in the week, but it was my fault. I wouldn't go along with his plan for a weekend in the Loire valley."

"The Loire Valley, wine tasting and wonderful meals! How come you didn't want to go?" persisted Hilary, hot on the scent of something amiss.

"It wasn't that I didn't want to go, any other time it'd have been great. The problem was he'd already booked to go with Mickey and Sophie. I got a bit mad because I'd committed to going to see Action Men."

"No wonder you weren't happy, Mickey and Sophie aren't the liveliest couple either. But the wine tasting, the food!"

"Hmm, not sure how much wine tasting there would have been. It was a package deal, meals at the hotel with a chess tournament thrown in."

"Now I get it, making out a chess tournament was a treat for you! Men! Typical!"

Elin had always found Hilary's jaundiced view of men amusing in the past. Secure in her relationship with Joe, it had been fun to listen to Hilary's outrageous stories. She and Ricky were polar opposites. Ricky wanted a quiet life, hated to argue, loved routine; Hilary thrived on challenges, debated everything and could even make the weather a contentious topic if she felt like it.

"Do you think Joe is that selfish? We've had good times on last minute getaways, so it was a pretty natural assumption that I would enjoy it. Don't know about Sophie though...."

"Oh Elin, grow up! Concentrate on that dishy P.E. teacher. Let Joe enjoy his chess time away. At least he doesn't come home from soccer trips with bags full of stinky kit like Ricky – though he does wash it himself."

Hilary acknowledged Ricky's good points with a sigh. They continued to analyse Joe's behaviour as the soup disappeared and they plastered the freshly baked bread with butter. Then they got to the topic of Mia.

"They met at a conservation project back in March. Then she took off to Snowdonia, and turned out he was there too. Romance blossomed during the cold nights on the mountain."

"Good for her, she knows what she wants and goes for it, my kind of girl!"

"Daniel's a social worker; he was taking a break. Mia was there and the rest is history."

"Sounds like a nice guy, she should hang on to him, there aren't many about these days." responded Hilary with a derisive sniff. "I wonder what Joe'll get up to this weekend?"

"There you go again Hilary, we're OK, a comfortable life, good jobs..."

"He's got his dream job, granted, but what about you? You're happier now you've been at Beechwood for months, joking about the P.E. teacher aside, you're getting involved. Supply teaching is OK as a stopgap, but as a career? You know you want more."

Elin was silent; Hilary had hit a nerve. Maybe she was right; her dissatisfaction with life could be more to do with her job than Joe. She'd had less time to concentrate on his perceived shortcomings since she'd been at Beechwood full-time, even if it was temporary.

"But it was my choice not to look for a full-time job, even though it's out there somewhere in my life plan. I wanted to have time for the house and garden."

"Elin, Elin, sometimes I despair of you. Just because you wanted it then, doesn't mean you want it now. Things change, people change! Wake up girl!"

4

I mmediately after the rehearsal, Chrissie bounded forwards and clapped her hands, a huge smile on her face. "Thank you, girls and boys, I really enjoyed that! You have some wonderful material, and an inspiring message about conservation to share."

The kids nodded. Fiona and Elin were stunned. How could they have lost sight of the purpose of the dance?

Chrissie continued addressing the children, "I'd like to help, is that OK with you?"

Murmurs of assent echoed around the room.

"Wow, you're so keen, I love your energy! We've got four weeks left. It'll be hard work. Are you ready to work hard?"

Resounding yeses filled the air. After the children had left, Fiona hugged Chrissie. "You miracle worker!"

Aaron chipped in, "But there's only a month to go?"

Elin faced Chrissie, "You're the expert, Chrissie, you have the experience: can Fiona and I do this? It's an enormous challenge."

Chrissie responded with a huge grin, "Absolutely, the kids can do this. The question is.... do you believe they can?

Your job is to keep the kids enthused, get them engaged with the subject."

"You made it look easy, Chrissie. How can we do that?" begged Elin.

"With children it's best to focus on movement. Swaying like a tree in the wind, floating like a leaf, help them to remember why they are moving."

Eventually Elin walked Chrissie back to her car. Chrissie stood, car keys in hand, and repeated. "Keep believing in the kids, Elin, and make sure it shows. Your belief will be contagious. A bit of tweaking the action and we'll have a great performance. See you soon." Chrissie jumped into her battered Mini and drove off, leaving Elin relieved and happy. At the end of the day, Fiona caught Elin just as she was leaving. Fiona was grinning from ear to ear.

"I think Chrissie's going to save the day! Do we have a schedule worked out with her? Can we get together with Aaron before we forget anything? How about tomorrow lunchtime?"

"Sounds good, between the three of us we should remember everything."

Elin drove home humming the dance music; the sun was still strong and she was reluctant to go inside. She wondered what time Joe would get home; perhaps they could take Mutt for a walk together and have a pub meal. She changed and took her yoga mat outside instead of preparing dinner. Just as she finished savasana, she heard Joe's car and smiled to herself at the excellent timing. She reached up on tiptoe to give Joe a kiss but was distracted by Mutt's yelping and barking.

"How about us giving Mutt a good run, then eat out afterwards?"

"Sorry, *amore mio*, not tonight." Joe dumped papers on

the kitchen table. "We could have a drink here in the sun, get a takeaway?"

Mutt was still going crazy. Elin's good mood prevailed. "Why don't you sit outside while I take Mutt for a quick run? You order the food."

Joe looked relieved and Elin reminded herself that his job was stressful too. She gathered Mutt's lead and filled her water bottle. It was so much better when they didn't argue. "See you later. The takeaway menus are in the middle drawer."

Once back home, Mutt subsided on the grass after siphoning up gallons of water from his enormous bowl. Joe looked the picture of relaxation on the patio: glass of beer in his hand, Alley on his lap and Tom at his feet. Elin joined him and they waited for the delivery of another Indian meal.

The next morning Fiona bounced over. "Aaron can't meet at lunchtime, how about after school? I want to review Chrissie's advice ASAP."

"Best not to delay, after school's fine."

"I'll confirm later. Thanks for bringing Chrissie in, Elin, this has changed everything."

At lunchtime Elin was reheating her leftover curry in the ancient microwave when Fiona caught up with her again.

"Something smells good!" Fiona was clearly still in a buoyant mood. "We're all set, meeting at the Yelverton, just down the road, is 4.30 OK?"

The microwave gave a weak ping and Elin removed her plate, uncovered it and took it over to her seat.

"The Yelverton? That's fine, thanks for sorting it out."

"We've had after-school meetings there before and it's always dead quiet. We've got to keep the momentum going."

Just before half past four, Elin pulled into the car park of the Yelverton. She could see Fiona's car – she must have arrived only seconds earlier and was still in the driving seat. Elin parked alongside and switched off the engine. As she groped around on the floor for her handbag, Aaron's old Land Rover roared in and took the parking space on the other side of Fiona. Elin watched him get out, then noticed that Fiona was still in her car, talking on her mobile phone, frowning. As Elin locked the car, but before she had time to speak, Fiona lowered her window.

"Elin, Aaron, I'm so sorry. That was my older son James. Harry, that's the younger one, managed to crash his bike into a parked car. He's OK but his front teeth are loose and he's covered in blood. I've got to go home."

"Go on, Fiona," Aaron cut in, "make sure he's OK. We'll go ahead and fill you in first thing tomorrow morning, won't we, Elin?"

"Of course. I hope he's OK."

"Thanks a million, both of you. I really appreciate this. I'll get him to A&E. Perhaps we can meet early tomorrow?"

Aaron interrupted, "We'll work it out, don't worry. Off you go!"

Immediately, Elin backed him up, echoing his words, "Don't worry about the meeting. Make sure Harry's OK."

Fiona nodded her thanks, reversed, then drove the car out of the car park, leaving Elin and Aaron standing awkwardly side-by-side. Elin set off towards the entrance, saying as she went, "We'd better carry on while our memories are fresh."

Aaron rubbed his chin and sighed, "Let's hope this is the last thing to go wrong, Fiona has enough on her plate already."

The Yelverton was not the old traditional pub suggested by its name. The lounge had been renovated into boring beigeness, all faux leather armchairs and sporting memorabilia. The smell of lunchtime chips was overlaid with a whiff of air freshener from the toilets. Elin registered this in an instant, but what made far more impact was that the place was completely and utterly empty, not a soul, not even a barman, in sight. It looked abandoned and the small seating groups failed to give out an inviting ambience. It was extremely odd. Being alone with Aaron for the first time and the large unoccupied space combined with Fiona's hasty disappearance, felt surreal. Elin felt removed from reality, in another dimension.

"What would you like?" Aaron's voice brought her abruptly back to the present.

"I'd really like a cup of coffee if possible, if not, a J2O, please."

Elin made her way slowly to a far corner of the room, steadying herself on the backs of chairs as she went. She chose an upright chair with its back to the wall and sat down, relieved to merge with the background. The room was silent. Aaron made his way to the bar and the barman appeared, looking surly and unwelcoming. She observed Aaron's physique. She'd never been attracted to men who were into physical fitness, but as he gave their order she had to admire his strong shoulders, compact, muscular body and long legs. He did seem to have a pleasant personality with some interests other than rugby and football. As if watching a film in slow motion, she saw Aaron pick up the drinks and turn towards her with that engaging smile. She was reminded that he was handsome too; nothing too rugged about his face, but the brightest of blue eyes, dirty blond short spiky hair and such an expression of optimism and fun it was hard not to be drawn into his orbit.

"No coffee, machine's broken, so it's a J2O." He put her juice and his half of shandy on the table and slid into the chair opposite, subsiding into it with a sigh of relief as he stretched out his legs and turned a questioning gaze towards Elin. She thanked him as the barman switched the music on. She felt dizzy, disoriented. As Aaron pulled his chair closer she picked up her juice and took a steadying sip before speaking again. There was a break in the music and her voice rang out clearly in the ensuing lull.

"I'm glad there's plenty of room to spread my legs."

There was complete silence. Her words screamed in her brain, repeating and repeating. Every blood cell in her body rushed to her cheeks and promptly morphed into red hot coals. She covered her face with her hands, but her embarrassment was too obvious to disguise. She felt a hysterical giggle bubble up and she bent her head and started to laugh. The music started up again, this time The Beatles warbling *All You Need Is Love*. She heard Aaron cover up his snort of laughter with a strangled cough. When she dared peep between her fingers she detected a sympathetic softness in his eyes as he struggled to regain control of his expression. Elin reached for her drink. Humiliation converted the waves of heat in her cheeks to a flush that encompassed her whole body. She blurted, "Oops! Did I just say what I think I said?" She blew out a long slow breath and fanned her face with her hands. "What I really meant to say was 'plenty of room to stretch your legs ... because you've got such long legs... but the words came out wrong!" She trailed off, now she'd made things worse by telling him she was aware of his long legs.

Aaron rescued her. He cleared his throat, lips twitching in an effort to disguise his grin and his eyes still held vestiges of laughter as he searched for an appropriate response. He managed to mumble, "Whatever you say, Elin," before giving in and emitting a deep belly laugh, giving her a look of disbelief and repeating, "Whatever you say." He picked up his glass and held it out towards her. "That was quite a surprise!" He tilted his head, "Cheers, Elin."

She touched her glass to his, aware that her slip had changed the dynamic between them, then drank a cooling gulp of juice. She pulled her expression back into business mode. "Shall we get on with Chrissie's suggestions?"

Within minutes of leaving the Yelverton, Elin sent text messages to Mia and Hilary, imploring them to contact her as soon as was humanly possible.

Hilary was the first to reply: she was on her way home and she'd only had time to fill the kettle when she heard Elin at the front door.

"Hi Elin, give me five minutes to say hello to Jemmie, then I'm all yours." Hilary smiled in welcome, noting that her friend did not look her usual composed self. "There's a bottle of Chardonnay opened in the fridge, help yourself or make yourself a cup of tea and I won't be long." Hilary ran upstairs, and finding Jemmie revising for a French test, came back down straight away. Elin was pacing up and down the kitchen, gulping at the full glass of wine in her hand.

"What's happened? Want to tell me over dinner?"

Elin shook her head and tapped her glass nervously with her nail.

Hilary gave Elin a quick hug before turning to the fridge. "Well, I need to eat, so sit at the kitchen table and calm down."

Hilary poured herself a glass of wine and put together a plate of cold ham with potato salad before pulling up a chair. Elin covered her face with her hands, shuddered and flushed bright pink, all at the same time. "Oh Hilary, I'm so embarrassed, I don't know how I'm going to go into school tomorrow."

"I haven't got a clue what you're talking about, take a deep breath and explain."

Elin tried to unknot her shoulders, inhaled deeply and exhaled slowly.

"Do you remember the guy you thought had his eye on me? Aaron, the P.E. teacher?"

Hilary couldn't resist interrupting. "Oh yes, Elin, the guy with his eyes glued to you at the Barn Theatre."

Elin rolled her eyes and Hilary clamped her mouth firmly shut.

"We were meeting with Fiona after school but Fiona got called away, Aaron and I were sitting in the pub..."

"Wait a minute, how did you get to the pub?"

"We couldn't coordinate a meeting in school time so we decided to meet at the Yelverton, it's by the school. Fiona got the phone call from home and she had to leave."

"Why didn't you reschedule the meeting?" Hilary broke in.

"I wish we had! Now I don't want to go back to Beechwood tomorrow."

Hilary frowned, head on one side, "I'm not getting this."

Elin buried her face in her hands again; this time she was half laughing and half crying. She cleared her throat and made a huge effort to speak slowly. "Fiona didn't even get out of her car, she took a call from her son then left. Aaron and I went inside. The room was completely empty. It felt bizarre, alone with Aaron. It threw me. I felt weird."

Hilary chose a mouthful of potato salad and munched with concentration. Elin continued.

"I don't understand why it felt so peculiar, but it did. Like an out of body experience. Aaron went to get the drinks and I was watching him. It's hard to explain, even to you, Hilary."

Elin stopped and gulped some more wine. Hilary leaned forward.

"Oh, for goodness' sake, Elin, I'm dying to hear what happened so get on with it!"

Elin squared her shoulders. "OK. Well, you know what a Freudian slip is, right? Imagine Aaron coming towards me with a big smile on his face. All I could think of was being the only people there. Aaron pulls out a chair and sinks into it. I'm thinking that his long legs wouldn't be all cramped up and do you know what I said?"

"Go on!"

"I meant to comment on the empty room but what came out of my mouth was 'Nice that there's plenty of room to SPREAD MY LEGS!'."

Hilary paused for only a second before breaking into peals of laughter. "That's hysterical! What happened next?"

"I didn't say any more. I felt as if I'd suggested sex."

"Well, you had, really," Hilary clapped her hands together, still laughing, "What did he say?"

"Nothing. There was utter silence. I started to giggle and luckily, he laughed too. We basically ignored it and discussed the dance group. We didn't refer to it again."

Elin took a small sip of wine, tasting it for the first time. Hilary was fixated on the chemistry between the two, but Elin wanted advice.

"Hilary, I don't want to think about any attraction. Fiona's going to text later to confirm us meeting tomorrow and I'm dreading it."

"Aaron won't say anything. If he did he'd scupper any chance with you. If he tells anybody you're well out of it. You win either way."

"It's not a game, Hilary. Joe and I are back on course. Just don't go there, OK?"

Hilary raised her eyebrows. "Joe doesn't deserve your loyalty. He seems to have enough secrets of his own."

Elin stiffened, "What do you mean, secrets?"

Hilary put her knife and fork down on the plate with a clatter and stood up, then moved towards the dishwasher. "Forget it, Joe's out a lot, that's all. Don't listen to me, I'm jaded and cynical." Hilary put the plate in the dishwasher then turned back to Elin with a wry grin. "But I don't want you to miss an opportunity you might regret!"

Elin began to feel a lot better. Soon they heard Ricky bringing Finn home and at the sound of the car Jemmie emerged from her bedroom.

"We brought ice-cream, who wants some?" Finn burst in waving a carrier bag.

Elin suddenly felt hungry. Maybe a huge bowl of ice cream was not normally regarded as a healthy dinner, but it had not been a normal day and ice cream makes everything better.

Eventually, Elin made her way home, feeling very full. It had been good to listen to everyday chat from Finn and Jemmie; she felt more grounded and less filled with paranoid anticipation. Her phone beeped again: two new messages. The first was Mia, suggesting a Sunday get together. The second was from Fiona saying that James was fine apart from a swollen face and three stitches in his upper lip. She'd be at school and hoped to meet with Aaron and Elin at 7.30 am.

5

On Friday evening, happy after a wonderful dance practice with Chrissie, Elin walked the dog, fed the cats and was starting to prepare dinner when Joe rang to say that he was delayed at work and not to expect him home until very late. She was about to tell him about her day when the hum of light conversation could be heard in the background, as if a door had been opened and allowed the sound to escape. Joe hastened the call to a close, "Gotta go. Don't wait up." A click and he was gone.

"Mobile phones," thought Elin, "he could be anywhere, but I'm not going to start checking up on him, we're supposed to trust each other." She stopped chopping vegetables and made tea. She sat, hands around the mug and mused on the topic of marriage: the glitz surrounding weddings; celebrity weddings, royal weddings, even local weddings with all the drama and fuss. What about the fairy tales fed to little girls? Cinderella, Snow White and Rapunzel, all ending with them living happily ever after with their fairy tale prince. Magazines were full of articles about ways to keep a marriage happy, but at the moment working on her marriage seemed contrived, cold and technical, like resuscitating a dead body.

It was all too much to think about now. She dumped her mug in the sink, went to the drinks cupboard and poured herself a large vodka and tonic, added ice and wandered up the stairs, automatically running a deep warm bath. Tension was making her shoulders rigid. She pushed the thought of what Joe was doing to the back of her mind and thought about school.

The next few weeks flew by, filled with end of year exams and dance rehearsals. The performance came to life. Home for Elin became a place where the minimum of effort was expended. The priority was marking papers in the evening to the point of exhaustion. It was busy for Joe too; the degree results could make or mar budding careers. Joe took his responsibilities seriously and was totally preoccupied.

Elin thought about Aaron. Sometimes Elin wondered if the incident at the Yelverton had actually taken place, he was behaving so normally. She pictured his face, crinkled with laughter; she remembered the frisson of excitement that had run through her even while she was in the throes of embarrassment. Her memories brought the same buzz. If he felt the same, he didn't show it. She resolved to put such thoughts out of her mind and concentrate on Joe. She would put more energy into their relationship. When he came home that evening she noticed the dark shadows under his eyes and a rare tightness in his jaw. She felt a surge of compassion. She kissed him welcome and ran her fingers through his hair, then massaged his knotted shoulders. He barely responded, but he did say he was starving and could they eat very soon, please? She had prepared his favourite paella and had laid the table with care, adding fresh flowers from the garden. Joe had already opened the bottle of wine and poured himself a generous glassful as she put the finishing touches to the dish. He filled her glass, but before she sat down, Joe was on to his second. As they ate he answered her questions monosyllabically then switched on the TV. Elin took the hint and ate silently opposite him, only enquiring about his day during the commercial break. He brushed off her enquiry, saying that there was a meeting to finalise grades the following day. From his grim expression, it seemed he was anticipating trouble. He topped up his glass, pushed back his chair and headed straight off to his computer, oblivious of Elin's expression and the sound of Mutt leaping at the door, reminding them of his urgent need to go out for a walk.

"So much for that effort!" Elin thought, still trying to feel positive as she cleared the table, loaded the dishwasher and wondered what to do next. The obvious thing would be to take Mutt out and leave Joe in peace, but perhaps Joe would enjoy a walk; it might clear his head and help him relax before tomorrow's stressful meeting. She stuck her head into the office.

"Fancy coming with me to give Mutt a run? We needn't be long. It might make you feel better?"

"Don't worry about Mutt, he'll be OK, just ignore him," Joe said, not taking his eyes off the screen – but it seemed to Elin that he'd clicked quickly to another site when she'd opened the door.

Elin changed her shoes and went out with just Mutt for company. She set off at quite a pace and was getting out of breath when she heard her mobile and dug it out of her jacket pocket.

It was Fiona. "You sound strange, perhaps this isn't a good time to talk?"

"It's fine, I'm walking the dog."

"I've been thinking about all the help we've had from Chrissie. It's a bit awkward to give her flowers at the curtain call, as she's not on the staff. How about a party at our house after the show? If the weather holds we could do a barbecue, if not we can all bring food to share. What do you think?"

"That's a great idea!

"There'd be you and Aaron and your other halves, Mia, some staff, some friends and Chrissie would be the guest of honour." Elin's stomach did a quick flip at mention of Aaron.

"We'd better check that Chrissie would be available."

"I was wondering if you'd do that?"

"Sure, I'll call her when I get home and I'll let you know what she says, OK?"

"Thanks Elin, I thought you'd be up for it. Let me know tomorrow."

Joe was still in the study when Elin got home; he must have heard her greeting but there was no audible response. She sat at the kitchen table and made the call to Chrissie. Afterwards she leaned forward on the table and closed her eyes for several seconds before gathering her thoughts and leaving a message for Mia and Daniel, inviting them to the party. She flopped on the sofa with her faithful feline friends and switched on the TV, channel-surfing mindlessly.

AFTER THE CONCERT, Elin watched Fiona chatting with parents. Chrissie was still backstage, congratulating the children. As the crowd thinned Fiona looked around.

"What happened to Aaron?" she asked, "I saw him with his wife earlier, but they've both disappeared. He should have been here with us."

"Maybe they had babysitter problems?" Elin was trying

to fend off a gathering disappointment that had started when she noticed Aaron and Rachel slipping out of the hall early.

"I hope they're coming back for the party," muttered Fiona. "I didn't ask many and we'll miss them if they don't turn up. Plus, Rachel said she'd bring a green salad."

Elin had persuaded Joe to attend the concert and the party; he hadn't been too keen but he hadn't refused. He was talking to the head of the Maths department, enjoying himself more than he had at any time during the concert. It helped that she was a stunning brunette, only a few years older than Joe. Elin wanted to be in full command of her feelings about Aaron so had insisted on driving so she had an excuse not to drink. She needed to be sober and in control. Now it seemed this subterfuge had been unnecessary.

Fiona continued, "Let's round up our guests. John is at home lighting the barbecue. Thanks goodness it's a lovely evening."

Elin didn't care much about the party anymore, not even about the chocolate cake with caramel filling she had spent hours preparing the night before.

Fiona's garden was transformed as the last of the daylight disappeared. Straggly bushes mellowed in the glow of large candles in glass jars and one fake antique streetlight brightened the patio. The light from the kitchen window illuminated the barbecue, loaded with kebabs and burgers. Once everyone had a large drink, Fiona turned her attention to the garlic bread, producing enough to feed a small army, then arranging the guests' contributions. There was no green salad to be seen.

Fiona presented Chrissie with a gift voucher and flowers. Elin led the applause then moved away, standing back in the shadows with a white wine spritzer in her hand. Music filled the air as she watched Joe downing a large vodka then helping himself to an equally large second. She noticed Gina and Bobby arriving and idly wondered how Fiona knew them. Joe seemed to be enjoying himself. He had attached himself to couple of attractive young women and had topped up his drink again. Elin watched how easy he was around people and wondered if he really was enjoying himself or whether he'd want to go home before too long; either way was OK with her.

Elin froze; she couldn't believe her eyes; Aaron stood framed in the kitchen doorway, looking awkward, a large bowl in his hands. Her diaphragm contracted, her breath shortened and she felt a flush creep over her cheeks. Thank goodness, she was hidden in the shadows. She stayed rooted to the spot. Fiona went forward to take the bowl from his hands. Fiona's voice was louder than usual after a few glasses of wine, as she said, "I'm sorry Rachel's not feeling well. Let's hope she'll feel better after an early night. Thank her for the salad, just what we needed. Help yourself, there's loads of food and the drinks are in the kitchen."

Elin still hung back. Every hint of tiredness had evaporated and she felt ready to party all night. She shivered slightly in her light cotton dress and pulled her cashmere cardigan more closely round her shoulders. An almost forgotten, magical feeling crept over her. She watched Aaron's every move as he filled his plate and stood on the edge of a chattering group. Every now and again he looked around, checking out the other guests and his surroundings. She glanced in Joe's direction; he had subsided into a luxurious garden lounger, glass in hand, and was listening to Ricky and Bobby sitting in matching chairs, making a small semicircle. They were probably talking about cricket, which would account for Joe's half-closed eyes. It looked as if he might give up the fight to stay awake in a few minutes, so Elin elected to stay where she was. She really had no idea how the evening would progress, but felt an overwhelming need to be close to Aaron, whether they spoke or not, whether they touched or not, she just had to be where she could see him and he could see her. Elin watched and waited until Joe appeared to be dozing, before venturing out into the throng. Hilary noticed her and called out, "Where've you been hiding Elin? Come and join us!"

Elin murmured something about taking a walk around the garden, but nobody was listening. Laughter filled the air as she merged into the crowd. She drained her glass and strolled into the empty kitchen to get some more soda water with just a splash of wine. The ice bucket was empty, so Elin was refilling it when the sound of footsteps made her turn around. Aaron stood there, empty glass in hand. He came towards her, holding her gaze, and put his hand on her shoulder. Electricity shot through her whole body; she jumped back as if burned.

Just then, Hilary came bustling in, two empty glasses in her hands. The look on her face and her reaction when she saw Aaron and Elin alone together were exactly what Elin had been hoping to avoid.

"Oh sorry, am I interrupting? I just wanted to get more wine."

"Don't be silly, Hilary, I was just filling the ice bucket and Aaron came in looking for another drink like you. I'm not sure that you two have met. Hilary this is Aaron, he teaches P.E."

"Of course, we've met before at the Barn Theatre! Nice to see you again Aaron. Let's start a new bottle of white, I can only see red opened. Where's the corkscrew?"

The three of them fussed with ice and refills. Hilary moved back out to the garden and Elin followed reluctantly.

Joe had given up his fight to stay awake and was snoozing quietly on the lounger. Elin was grateful for his simultaneous presence and absence as she moved towards Mia, Daniel and Ricky. Some particularly inviting dance music began and Ricky put his arm around her waist and drew her into a small space on the patio to dance. They kept stumbling over the uneven paving and abandoned the attempt. The barbecue still sent out a relaxing warmth, but gradually the crowd thinned out. Joe was still asleep and Elin was carrying a tray of empty glasses to the kitchen when Aaron sought her out again. He moved close to her and took the tray. She breathed in his scent of woody aftershave and a tingle ran down her spine.

"I'll text you later," he muttered under his breath, "I have to see you alone." Elin smiled an acknowledgement. She continued tidying up, aware that in that instant they had crossed over a line and they both knew it.

By the time she'd helped Fiona clear the worst of the mess and filled the dishwasher with its second load, she and Joe were the only guests left. She shook him none too gently by the arm.

"Joe, wake up, it's time to go. Fiona and John are tired, we need to leave."

"What, what? Oh, OK, was I asleep long? Sorry, I didn't realise how tired I was, couldn't keep my eyes open." Joe rubbed his eyes and struggled upright.

The distance she felt from Joe at that moment shocked Elin. He could have been a complete stranger for all the affection she felt for him. For two pins, she would have driven home alone and left him there. She helped him to his feet and they made their way to the car, showering thanks over their shoulders. Joe dozed again. Was she only capable of responding to events as they unfurled around her, like a fallen leaf being tossed along on the surface of a fast running stream? There were times when she felt reasonably content in her marriage, convinced of its rightness, wanting to avoid any complications, but a whisper from Aaron had propelled her helplessly in a different direction. The excitement and anticipation made her feel fully alive.

6

E lin was sitting in Hilary's enormous back garden idly watching Ricky hacking back shrubs in the distance. Hilary, who had phoned earlier eager to be updated on Aaron, came out with a tray bearing two mugs of coffee.

Elin waited as they made themselves comfortable, knowing that the important part of their conversation was yet to come. Hilary launched into her interrogation. "What's going to happen now, Elin? Summer holidays, no more Beechwood, no seeing Aaron every day."

Elin spoke slowly, "I don't know, I've just been reacting. I wasn't on the lookout for a flirtation. I certainly set a match to dry tinder with that slip of the tongue in the Yelverton."

"Not Freud's fault, that's for sure, he only observed human nature," responded Hilary settling deeper into her chair. "The question is what are you going to do?"

Elin felt very uncomfortable, how could she respond when she didn't know the answer herself? Despite being a totally modern woman, she had married Joe in a picturesque church, making the traditional vows. "It might sound weird, Hilary, but I honestly don't know. I know I shouldn't do anything to affect my marriage or Aaron's. Then the strength of feeling comes over me and I forget everything. I truly don't know what the future holds. You know Aaron and I haven't contacted each other, no phone calls, no texts and no secret assignations."

Hilary shrugged, "OK, it's your business; just remember you only live once."

They watched as Ricky dragged a lawnmower out of the shed and tried to start the engine. It sputtered a few times, then died.

"Does it need petrol?" shouted Hilary.

"That's definitely not the problem, I filled it up last week and a tankful lasts a month at least. Dammit, I wanted to get the lawn done today."

"He's going on a golf trip and leaving the garden neat and tidy was part of the deal," Hilary confided to Elin, "so he'd better work something out pretty soon."

His solution was to borrow Joe's lawnmower, so he followed Elin as she drove home. She was surprised to see that Joe's car wasn't in the drive and the garage door was open, which was strange, he was usually meticulous about security. As she checked indoors, she heard Ricky shout from the kitchen.

"Is it OK if I help myself to the lawnmower, I can see it there at the back of the garage?"

"Sure, go ahead. Do you need the extension cord?"

"I forgot yours is electric, yes I'd better take it." Ricky had found what he needed by the time Elin came downstairs. He appeared in the doorway still red-faced and somewhat breathless. "Thanks Elin. Joe doesn't usually go in on Saturdays, does he?"

"It's a bit unusual. You look hot; would you like a drink? Water, beer, fruit juice?" Elin opened the fridge.

"A beer sounds wonderful, Elin. You're too good for Joe you know."

She handed Ricky a cold can from the fridge and looked quizzically at him. "What do you mean, too good for him? You make me sound like some kind of saint!"

"I just wondered if you were getting your own back, I saw you looking at that fella last night, same one that was in the bar at the Barn Theatre, and I saw him watching you." Ricky concentrated on opening the can, not looking at Elin.

Elin was mortified. The inference was plain. She took a glass from the cupboard and poured herself some fruit juice as slowly as she could, trying to give the impression of being relaxed, aware that her hands had developed a sudden tendency to shake. "What do you mean about Joe?" Elin asked as she pulled out two chairs and sank down, looking expectantly at Ricky.

Ricky ran his hand through his thinning hair and took a gulp of beer. "I just assumed you knew..." he trailed off in confusion.

Elin pressed home her advantage, "Knew what? About Friday nights?"

"Let's leave it, I shouldn't have said anything." Ricky took refuge in his beer again, taking a long pull then wiping his mouth with the back of his hand.

Everything fell into place. Now she understood why Hilary had been so vitriolic about Joe when Elin had run to her in distress. Hilary knew from Ricky that Fridays weren't as Joe portrayed. No wonder Joe had dug his heels in about the lipstick, using force of will to persuade her she was paranoid. How could she have been so stupid, so trusting?

It explained why Hilary was encouraging her to have an

affair. She knew that Ricky would be loyal to Joe, so she embarked on damage limitation, summoning up all the dignity she could muster. "I know Joe's not perfect but let's set the record straight. Aaron and I are work colleagues and that's all." Elin drained her glass and put it down on the table with a decided thud.

Ricky stood up to leave, squeezing her shoulder lightly, "OK, gotta lawn to mow. Thanks for the beer. Take care of yourself Elin."

As soon as she heard the clunk of Ricky's car door, Elin put her head in her hands and closed her eyes. She felt sick and shaky. Whatever her suspicions about Joe had been, they had always been just that, suspicions. Ricky's evasiveness meant no more denial. Joe had succeeded in making her feel that the problem was in her mind, but not anymore. Whatever he was doing it was public knowledge, and she felt betrayed and foolish. How could she have been so gullible? She felt Tom jump on to her lap and Alley rub himself against her leg. She nuzzled her head on Tom's back and bent over to stroke Alley, finding consolation in their soft fur and simple demands.

Her phone buzzed announcing the arrival of a text. Was this the message that she had been waiting for?

"Plz phone in next 30 mins if u can. A."

Elin held her breath; she had been undecided about her response, but a whole lot had changed in the last ten minutes. Her stomach churned. She wanted to run away and hide, she wanted to run towards Aaron, she wanted to run away from Joe; and why did she have to phone in the next half hour? She sat up suddenly, grabbed a warm sweater and Mutt's lead, then bundled the surprised dog into the car and swung out of the driveway much faster than usual.

Once away from the house, Elin felt more in control.

She wasn't the person she had been yesterday – or even that morning. There had been a radical change after Ricky's throwaway comment. Where was she going, literally at this moment and, more importantly, with her life? She glanced at the clock on the dashboard and noted that fifteen of the thirty minutes had already gone. Would she make the phone call? If her hands had not been clutching the steering wheel she knew they would be shaking uncontrollably. Glancing in the mirror, she indicated and pulled in. She took some deep breaths. She took her phone out of her pocket and stared at it for several minutes. How could she prepare herself for this conversation with Aaron when she had no idea what he was going to say?

"It's me."

"Elin, I was afraid you weren't going to phone." She could hear the relief in his voice, he spoke quickly, "I've been waiting for an opportunity to contact you all day."

The word opportunity jarred, but she ignored her brain's message because her whole body ached to be near him. She said nothing.

Aaron continued, "I don't know how you're going to feel about this. I'm looking after Oliver all day; he's only ten months and he can't talk yet so I was wondering if I could bring him with me and we could walk somewhere and talk?"

This was not what Elin had expected; she bit her lip, hesitated. Aaron spoke urgently, "Please, Elin. We can talk, it'll be OK. It's just a walk."

"I've got the dog, he can't talk either..." That she could joke in these circumstances surprised both of them, "Do you know Rest Point? It'll take half an hour to get there, but it'll be quiet and the dog can run wild."

"Good idea, I'll see you there in half an hour."

Elin sat dumbfounded. She hadn't expected a walk on the beach with a baby and a dog.

There were only a few cars in the car park when Elin arrived. She supposed that the darkening clouds had sent most beach-goers home. Mutt yelped excitedly, working himself up into a frenzy. She stayed in the car, ignoring the dog, wondering how long it would take Aaron to arrive. Minutes later, an old Volvo estate drew up beside her. Aaron jumped out and Elin did the same. Their eyes locked. Elin went to him and let him pull her into his arms, burying her face in his chest, feeling his warmth through his soft wool sweater. At that moment it was exactly where she wanted to be.

Seconds later Elin stepped back hurriedly and whispered, "You never know who's around. Let's pretend we met accidentally and start walking." Raising her voice, she turned back to the car, where Mutt was flinging himself at the window and barking furiously. "Mutt, calm down, I'm coming as fast as I can."

Elin opened the door attached Mutt's lead with clumsy hands. She felt her life unfold in slow motion; half of her behaving instinctively, the other half observing, like a film critic assessing the part she was playing in her own movie. Each small action was part of a whole, happening in reality, not just in her mind. She knew how serious her decisions were but was unable to ignore her desire to be physically close to this man. Aaron must feel the same, otherwise why would he have taken the risky step of meeting her in broad daylight in a public place? Elin turned and watched in silence as Aaron expertly removed his son from the car seat, settled him into a baby carrier then hoisted it on to his back in a fluid set of movements. The baby gazed around with wide eyes, taking in the expanse of shore and the waves pounding in the distance. Seagulls wheeled overhead and Oliver pointed at them laughing and babbling delightedly.

"Told you he couldn't talk, didn't I?" Aaron smiled as he looked across at Elin who was almost being pulled off her feet as she hung on to Mutt's lead. "Looks like we need to get started. Which way shall we go?"

Elin indicated the direction and Mutt set off as if a starting gun had been fired.

"I'll let him off the lead as soon as we're away from the cars," Elin gasped over her shoulder, hoping Mutt would cooperate. Very soon, Elin decided to give up the battle, dragged Mutt to a halt and unfastened the lead. He took off like an arrow from a bow, long hair streaming behind him, the picture of elegance and grace.

"Beautiful creature! What's his name?" Aaron caught up with her and they stood for a moment watching the dog run.

"He's called Mutt, he might look great but he's quite a handful. I'm never sure he's going to come back when I call him."

Elin set off in Mutt's general direction. She felt she should say something to acknowledge the baby but she had no experience with babies and had no idea what to say. Aaron appeared to be ignoring him completely, and he seemed content as Aaron walked by Elin's side. She was acutely conscious of their close proximity but told herself that, at this point, nothing was irreversible. They were just two friends who happened to meet near the beach.

Elin glanced at her watch. "It's half past two already. How long before you have to leave?" She felt uncomfortable bringing up the topic yet she desperately needed to know.

"Oliver will probably drop off to sleep, but if he doesn't I'll have to get him home by about four thirty. I forgot to bring anything for him to eat, I wasn't thinking straight."

Aaron looked at Elin, he seemed as surprised by what was happening as she was. She groped around for a suitable comment, "Mutt will probably wear himself out and find us again by then. Shall we go towards the cliffs?"

"Sounds good. I forgot coats, I hope it doesn't rain," Aaron said, looking anxiously at the sky.

Elin felt tension and lightness simultaneously. She wanted nothing more than for time to stand still. The next hour could change her life forever or change nothing at all.

Elin caught a glimpse of gold in the distance as Mutt started to gallop back towards them. They watched together as he ate up the space effortlessly and Oliver crowed with delight once Mutt returned and circled them.

"Let's hurry, those clouds look ominous," Aaron reached out to take Elin's hand, hesitated, then returned it to his pocket. He looked at her closely, then quipped, "Don't worry, it may never happen!" His remark jarred and he lapsed into silence.

They trudged on over the firm damp sand leaving a trail of footprints in parallel, one large set and one small, with Mutt's messy trail everywhere. Suddenly the dog took off again, tearing away into the distance. Elin's body was knotted with tension. The clouds loomed darker and drops of rain began to fall. Aaron gestured towards the cliffs.

"Do you think there's any shelter over there? If Oliver gets soaked I'll have to take him straight home. He's only just recovered from a bad cough so I can't risk him getting cold."

They broke into a run, Oliver being jolted with every step but loving it and gurgling with glee. Mutt sensed the change of plan and returned, yelping and making smaller circles around them. The scattered raindrops became light rain and Elin struggled to keep going. Aaron finally grabbed her hand and his touch galvanised her into finding a reserve of energy. They reached the cliffs just as Elin felt her lungs would burst. A quick glance around showed a small sheltered spot with a rocky overhang. They reached it quickly and saw that it led to a small cave with just enough room for the two of them to stand upright side by side.

Elin felt that the heavens had conspired to throw them together. They struggled to regain their breath. Aaron's arms circled Elin's shoulders and she lay her head on his chest. They stood unmoving. Elin noticed his unfamiliar aftershave and the smell of his damp sweater; she felt the strength of his arms, his height and his muscular broadness. She relished this unknown entity that was Aaron.

Aaron took one arm away from Elin's shoulders and gently tipped her chin up towards his face. He kissed her softly, his lips warm and slightly salty. Elin gave herself up to the moment, nothing else mattered, she had no defences left. Just as the pressure of their lips was building and Elin, eyes closed, could only hear the pounding of her heart another sound intruded into her bubble, a happy cooing noise. How could she have forgotten about little Oliver? She had no right to be here, she had no right to be kissing Aaron; he was Oliver's father and Rachel's husband. Aaron kept her firmly close to him with one arm, lifting his other hand to reach back and touch his son reassuringly.

"Don't say anything, Elin. Let's stay 'til the rain stops." They stood still and silent, their breathing synchronised. Oliver babbled on. His tone gradually changed to complaint and Aaron scrabbled in a pocket with one hand searching for something to amuse his son, but found nothing.

"Elin, can we meet again? We can work something out, nobody need know."

Thoughts of Joe came rushing back; Ricky's comments had changed everything.

Oliver raised his complaints a notch, the rain eased off and they ventured out. Elin's thoughts were in turmoil. She hadn't responded to Aaron's appeal. Mutt appeared, wet, sandy and bedraggled; his presence distracted Oliver who reverted to making happy noises as the dog loped alongside.

"Why so quiet, Elin? Say you'll meet me again?"

Elin heard his desperation and looked at him. The urgent enquiry in his expression mirrored the questioning in her own mind. "A lot has happened today. It's complicated."

They reached the now deserted car park. Elin called Mutt who jumped into the car at the first request. Aaron deftly returned Oliver to his car seat despite his loud complaints.

"I've gotta go," Aaron glanced at the unhappy baby. "He'll give me no peace now. Please Elin, meet me again? We have to talk this over." He looked at her with mute appeal.

"We do have to talk, but I'm not used to this, what can we do?" Elin stood by her car.

"We can't use mobile phones or email." Oliver's wails grew louder, adding more stress to the situation.

Elin gestured towards Mutt. "I can always take the dog for a walk. Do you have time now it's the summer holidays?"

"Sometimes, but it's hard to know in advance."

Elin couldn't respond, her mind wasn't functioning. Aaron spoke over his shoulder as he tucked a blanket round the baby. "We bump into each other somewhere? A coffee shop, the park?"

Elin managed to find her voice, "The coffee shop on Oak Street? How about Monday at 11? Maybe, maybe if one of us doesn't make it we can try Tuesday at 11? And keep going until we meet? I can't think of anything else." The conversation felt unreal; the noise of the surf and the seagulls and the crying baby.

Aaron nodded, "OK, let's do it." He gave her a quick hug and jumped into his car. Oliver's cries had developed into screams of frustration. Aaron wound the window down.

"Do you mind if I go first? Sorry, it seems wrong, I should make sure you're safely on your way."

"Don't be silly, I've been here on my own many times."

"See you Monday at 11."

The old Volvo spluttered into life. Elin got into the Mercedes slowly and sat for a few minutes before starting the car. She drove in the direction of home, her body on fire, her mind a cacophony of conflict.

7

Joe's car was in the drive. Elin had to go inside and act normally. She towelled Mutt dry, refilled his water dish, gave him food then headed upstairs to take off her damp clothes and dry her hair. The door to the office was closed and Joe didn't acknowledge her return.

Warm and dry again, Elin opened the study door, "I'm making tea, would you like a cup?"

Startled, Joe looked up, "Sure, that would be nice, thanks." He gave her a quick smile then looked back at the screen. Elin turned and walked back to the kitchen. Was Joe always this self-centred? She made tea and took a mug into Joe, putting it down on the side table. He looked up, "By the way, Gina phoned about half an hour ago, she and Bobby are having a party tonight and invited us. She wants you to phone her back."

"Any idea what brought that on?"

"They have friends staying, apparently you've met them before. Their names didn't ring any bells for me."

"I'll phone her, you OK about going?"

"Sure, why not? We can walk, both of us can have a drink."

With the hurdle of her first communication with Joe safely negotiated, Elin was grateful for the respite of a predictable evening ahead. Two hours later, Elin was starting her makeup as Joe finally tore himself away from the computer. When he emerged from the shower there was no time for conversation as he selected jeans, shirt and sweater then dressed quickly before putting the finishing touches to his hair. She observed his appearance dispassionately. A good-looking man, but not in the typical Hollywood style, his appeal was more subtle than that and she knew that the *je ne sais quoi* that had attracted her was no longer working. She completed her short makeup routine and then chose a light jacket from the wardrobe.

"Are you nearly ready?" Elin asked.

Joe turned and smiled when he saw her, "*Sei belissima, tesoro mio.*"

Elin put red sandals into her bag and slipped on ballerina flats. Joe resumed choosing their wine contribution.

"Shall we take two bottles?" he asked, "I don't suppose Bobby's salary runs to much decent wine."

"Sounds good to me." She didn't say so, but she had the feeling she'd be consuming more than her fair share tonight.

Hours later she accepted, giggling, yet another top up from Bobby. Joe seemed to be finding Jaya, the visitor, quite fascinating. Her Indian heritage had granted her flawless skin, enormous dark eyes, flowing black hair and a figure that was simultaneously voluptuous and regal. Elin was glad that Joe was otherwise occupied.

"We meet again!" Hilary appeared at her side.

"Isn't it wonderful to see Neal and Jaya again?" Elin deflected the conversation away from herself and signalled that she was fine with Joe's spellbound appreciation of Jaya.

"Yes, she's great, so successful, earning a bomb in the City," offered Gina as she joined them and the three women squished together on the comfortable sofa. Most of the men had ended up close to the makeshift bar in the kitchen. Elin began to feel very sleepy, perhaps it would be just as well to make a move now before it became too much of a struggle. She heaved herself out of the upholstered comfort and staggered slightly as she made her way to the kitchen in search of Joe.

"Oops. Sorry, looking for Joe," Elin made a big effort and opened her eyes wide in apology as she bumped into Ricky. Her words were slurred and he snapped to attention.

"Don't worry, Elin, just stay here a moment and I'll find him for you."

"Oh, thanks Ricky, you're so sweet." Elin supported herself on the doorjamb and surveyed the scene. All the faces were flushed and most were grinning broadly. Elin hoped she looked as unconcerned as she felt about Joe's whereabouts. The men looked embarrassed. Elin wondered if they were embarrassed because she was clearly drunk or whether they had some idea of where Joe was and didn't want her to know. Jaya, of course! Ricky didn't want Elin to find Joe with Jaya after his gaffe earlier in the day. Well, today was certainly turning out to be action-packed. Elin decided to get a glass of water and made her way to the sink carefully.

"Here he is, Elin," Ricky's voice was tinged with relief. Joe made his way across the room and put his arm round her shoulders.

"You OK, *cara*, can I get you anything?" Joe was full of

concern. Quite possibly she looked pale and there had been times when she'd felt better. She downed the water and turned towards Joe.

"I'm OK, just a tad too much wine. Maybe we should go home?" She heard herself echoing Joe's thanks as they left, only remembering her sandals as they crunched on the gravel in the driveway. Leaning hard on Joe and giggling as she lost her balance, Elin changed into the flats and managed the walk home in silence, Joe's arm helping her stay upright.

Elin couldn't be bothered to remove her makeup, but kicked off her shoes and fell straight on to their bed. She closed her eyes and was almost asleep when she felt Joe gently pulling off her jeans and removing the rest of her clothes. She didn't protest. Joe didn't stop at taking off her clothes, he stroked her body and she heard his breathing change as she lay there, eyes closed, naked – numb. Joe was insistent without being forceful, his desire was obvious and her degree of drunkenness was such that he expected little response from her. Soon it was over and Elin lay there, dazed. Before long the wine reasserted its effect and she drifted off.

Nausea overcame the desire for sleep sometime late on Sunday morning. Elin groaned. She navigated the pile of discarded clothes and made it to the bathroom. The memory of the previous evening precipitated further waves of sickness. She hoped she could make it safely back to bed. She filled a glass with water and held it carefully as she tottered back. A headache overtook the nausea and became the primary cause for her misery. Who cared about Joe, or Aaron, or marriage, or infidelity, real or imagined? All that mattered was that the pain would subside and she could feel human again. She felt too ill even to doze.

Sleep must have overtaken her, and when she opened her eyes her stomach had settled. She felt that someone had kicked her hard in the midriff but her headache was one notch down from excruciating. She needed a cup of tea. She moved her body tentatively and worked herself into an upright position, then completed the challenge of finding her dressing gown and putting it on. Bending over was out of the question so she shuffled downstairs barefoot.

Through the kitchen window she could see Mutt snoozing in the sun; Alley and Tom were similarly occupied on a garden chair. She noticed an empty cereal bowl and mug in the sink. While waiting for the kettle to boil, Elin moved slowly to the front window. The Mercedes was the only vehicle to be seen. Relief washed over Elin as she flopped into her favourite armchair in the cool of the living room, pulling the blind down to ease her still-aching head. When she finished her tea, her stomach rumbled and she slowly made her way back to the kitchen. She was pushing away Sunday papers to make room for her plate of scrambled eggs when she noticed a scribbled note.

"Gone for drink with Mickey. Mia phoned, wants you to phone her back. Joe x."

Elin glanced at the kitchen clock. Almost three o'clock! Something didn't feel right. Elin struggled through brain fog. She didn't have Mickey's phone number and she had a gut feeling that Joe wouldn't answer if she called his mobile. She tried and she was right.

This called for another mug of tea and some serious contemplation. Was it because she had become devious herself that she now recognised the signs in Joe? Late nights at work; disappearing at weekends; it all added up.

This didn't answer the question of what to do about

Aaron and their arrangement to meet. Tomorrow. Or Tuesday. Or Wednesday. But definitely soon.

Elin was in the bath, almost submerged in bubbles when she heard Joe's voice as he came up the stairs.

"*Pulcino*, how are you feeling?"

"I'm improving, I slept a lot." Elin wondered if he'd volunteer any information about his day.

"I'm glad you took it easy. You drank a lot last night." Joe came in to the bathroom.

"Only myself to blame."

"Happens to everybody now and again." Joe's voice was conciliatory and the focus was still on her. Elin continued to wait. Joe sat on the edge of the bath. "Can I get you anything, some tea maybe?"

"No thanks, I've drunk a lot of tea. I think I'll have an early night."

Still not a mention of Mickey. "Is there anything to eat? I'm famished." Joe looked a little shamefaced.

"There's some pasta sauce; you can make spaghetti if you like, I can't face cooking."

"*Grazie pulcino*, you're the best." Joe dropped a kiss on her damp cheek and went downstairs.

Elin felt sure he hadn't been with Mickey. Avoidance of detail was generally characteristic of Joe and it had grown more marked as time passed. Yet, she had trusted him. Resentment grew as she recalled his annoyance whenever she asked what he had been doing, how she'd tiptoed around his irritation.

Perhaps it would feel different in the morning. As she was about to get into bed, Elin remembered the call from Mia. She dialled Mia's number but it went straight to voicemail.

"It's Elin. Sorry I didn't get back to you earlier, bad hangover. Could we get together soon? Hope you're OK."

Elin woke on Monday exhilarated. Thoughts of Aaron filled her mind and she tingled, all her synapses in overdrive. It was the first day of the summer holidays and she had no job lined up for September, but dreams of time with Aaron and six weeks of freedom took precedence. She'd look for another job, but not today. She pulled on a terry robe and made her way downstairs. Faithful Tom and Alley were waiting. A few dirty dishes lay in the sink and the familiarity of the picture comforted Elin. She hardly recognised her life these days; from contented to contentious, from millpond to tsunami. She would be at the coffee shop at 11 and Aaron would be there if he could, so the only questions in her mind were her alibi and what to wear. She smiled in anticipation. A yoga class would do so she would wear her new yoga trousers and one of her favourite stretchy tops, flattering but not special.

Was that strange feeling in her stomach the death throes of conscience or just hunger? Elin made herself a couple of slices of toast and checked the yoga class timetable stuck to the fridge door. Joe was in the office, working from home today, so she stuck her head around the door. "I'm off to the gym and a yoga class. I might meet Mia afterwards."

She was deliberately being as vague as the past master of deception, who looked up and blew her a kiss. She set off feeling as if the eyes of the world were on her and the mundane business of buying a coffee became fraught with unwelcome possibilities. Perhaps a friend would join her — how would she get rid of them fast? Worse, what if she didn't notice someone who recognised her, one of Joe's many friends from work, chess or Friday nights out?

Elin drove into the car park behind the building, then strolled slowly inside and towards the counter, allowing a woman with a toddler in a pushchair to go in front of her. Ordering a skinny latte, Elin felt her adrenaline seep away when she realised that Aaron wasn't there. She hovered over the sweeteners to eke out the time then headed to the toilet, locking the door behind her with a sigh of relief. She hardly recognised the woman in the mirror: her huge eyes signalled high tension yet this woman also looked vibrantly alive. Elin felt a moment of panic that Aaron might have arrived and left while she was out of sight. She tried to cool her flushed cheeks with a damp tissue before strolling back out. She read every notice on the board slowly. Nobody acknowledged her presence. She wandered back to the car and sat sipping her latte. After another ten minutes looking at her phone, Elin drove away. A bewildering combination of disappointment and relief flooded over her as she grounded herself in the present; an ordinary Monday morning at the start of the school holidays.

Feeling as deflated as a New Year balloon at the end of January, Elin arrived home to an empty house. The overcast morning had deteriorated along with her mood and it was drizzling. Elin prowled around the house in search of something to use up her excess energy. Everything was neat and tidy and in its place. Tuesday was the cleaning lady's day so it would seem very strange if she brought the vacuum cleaner out on a Monday, and she was too restless for job hunting. She decided to cook for the freezer, willing away the hours until 11 o'clock the next day as she chopped onions and garlic.

8

E lin got ready for her second foray to the coffee shop. Flutters of anticipation intensified with each minute and she struggled to keep her movements slow and relaxed. Joe moved in his parallel world. Elin said she might try to see Mia today. Joe told her that he wasn't sure what he would be doing, but it would not include dog walking, which didn't please Elin. Did he think that you could switch a dog off and leave him in the garage like a car? Irritation helped reduce her guilt.

Aaron's Land Rover was in the car park. She pulled in alongside, hopped out and walked briskly towards the door. Perfect timing, Aaron was collecting his coffee. He turned and greeted her openly. "Hi Elin, nice to see you, how's it going?"

"Great thanks. Off to the gym, how about you?"

"Me too, need the caffeine though."

They sauntered out together then stopped, keys in hand. Aaron took the lead, lowering his voice. "Where shall we go? We could try Jubilee Country Park? It'll be quiet and it's not too far."

Nagging doubts jostled with desire. It wasn't too late to stop this before it went any further. Hope and anticipation competed with fear and dread, but with overriding excitement rushing through every part of her body, fear and dread had no chance.

"You go ahead, I'll follow." Aaron took charge again.

Elin ground the gears and her hands shook as she drove off. When she caught sight of the Land Rover in the rearview mirror her death grip on the steering wheel loosened and her mouth softened into a smile.

Very little was said as they walked hand in hand, Elin captivated by the unfamiliar hardness of Aaron's fingers and their steady, possessive pressure. She glanced up at his face and he lifted her palm to his mouth and kissed it tenderly. They found a sheltered spot where the sun broke between the trees. Aaron spread a small travel rug on the rough grass. He pulled Elin close and kissed her forehead, her nose, her cheeks then buried his face in her throat. She absorbed his touch and desire overwhelmed her. They undressed, exploring each other's bodies. He kissed her slowly and deeply, his lips moving from Elin's mouth to her throat then down to her breasts. His hands caressed her body from breast to hip. He paused and looked deep into her eyes, "Are you sure?" Elin's body answered without words, urging him on, her hands guiding him inside her.

Elin had no idea how long they lay together afterwards, his arm around her shoulders and her head nestled into his neck. She breathed in his masculine smell, heady in its unfamiliarity. They caressed each other softly. The enormity of her first act of infidelity hit Elin and she shivered. She felt scared, yet secure in his arms. It was easier to speak when she didn't have to look at his face.

"We shouldn't be doing this," she said, but Aaron didn't

respond so Elin forced herself to continue. "I know better, but I couldn't stop." She pressed on before her courage failed, "We're both married, but can we just meet like this sometimes?"

Aaron murmured in assent and brushed his fingertips over her skin. Elin felt herself being aroused until all that mattered was her overwhelming longing and she reached for him again.

When clouds covered the sun and the real world beckoned their mood became less buoyant; there seemed no point in stretching out the goodbyes. The enormity of what she'd done filled Elin with apprehension and she felt a desperate need to be driving in the direction of home.

"Same next week?" Aaron asked. "Monday morning, 11, and keep turning up?" He opened the car door for her. She got in, shut the door and wound down the window in time to hear Aaron's words.

"Monday can't come soon enough."

As Elin drew closer to home her mood changed. What was her story? That she'd got coffee, gone to the gym and then visited Mia for a long girly chat?

Joe's car wasn't in the drive: first hurdle over. She dashed upstairs, changed and shoved her clothes into the laundry basket. In less than ten minutes, she had thrown together a cheese and pickle sandwich and loaded Mutt into the car. She drove to their familiar park and sagged with relief as the dog ran ahead. She had been terrified. Was it worth putting everything at risk for the thrill of snatched moments? Would returning to a life without complications be possible? Resentment battled with her awareness that cheating was wrong. Where had her decisions taken her? Was she really happy with the picture-perfect life? You name it, she had it, but she wasn't happy with Joe. The realisation was so sad.

She hadn't been looking for an affair, it hadn't crossed her mind, not even for one second.

Thinking about Joe encouraged her anger to surface. He had lied when she confronted him about the lipstick. The complete wall of denial had so frustrated her that she had withdrawn into simmering resentment. If he had told her the truth she might have forgiven him. Was it too late now? Would they become two people living together but leading separate lives? What would be the point with no children? She didn't trust Joe, and after today he had no reason to trust her. Aaron was the catalyst, not the cause, of her dilemma. If her affair with Aaron was to continue she couldn't burden it with her unhappy marriage. She found a bench and sank down, closing her eyes as the last vestiges of adrenaline leaked away.

THE FOLLOWING Sunday Mia was opening a bottle of wine when Elin arrived just after seven with a takeaway curry. "That curry smells good, glad I didn't eat much lunch! Let's have a glass of this Pinot Noir first. Daniel left it for us."

"I'm driving, just give me half a glass."

"OK, if you change your mind you can stay overnight, no prob. I'm not leaving until about 10."

Elin took the proffered glass. Staying over was tempting, but how ironic if Joe became suspicious over an innocent sleepover. "Where are you going?"

"London. Daniel's got an interview; we'll stay with his sister for the week, visit museums."

"Mm." Elin sipped her wine and studied Mia. "So, it's all working out?"

Mia stretched back in her chair and yawned. Something had changed and Elin couldn't quite put her finger on it.

Mia was different these days. She smiled at Elin, "Any teaching lined up for September? I haven't got anything yet, I need to earn something soon."

Elin could barely imagine what it would be like to be in such a precarious financial situation.

"Don't you get anxious? Having to pay the mortgage yourself?"

"Sometimes I do, but Daniel's helping at the moment."

Elin took another sip of wine and relaxed.

"I shouldn't complain, knowing that Joe will pay all the bills. I'll miss Beechwood though."

Mia looked at her quizzically, "You're better suited to teaching than me. I'm thinking about museum curating. I wish I didn't have a house, it ties me down."

This was a surprise to Elin. Mia was on the verge of a major life change with a new boyfriend and no savings yet she still radiated a sense of calm and positivity.

While they ate, Mia told Elin about Chrissie's efforts to get Action Men to turn professional. She wanted to create joy and bring people together in harmony to enjoy dance. Elin was in awe of such boundless enthusiasm.

"Yup, she's an amazing person," agreed Mia. "I'd better send you home, it's nearly midnight and I've got to get up early, my train goes at half past ten."

Elin's ears pricked up at the mention of the 10.30 train. "I can take you to the station if you like?"

Mia was surprised and grateful for the offer.

"Well that'd save me worrying about the bus being late, thanks a lot. See you at 10?"

ELIN BOUNCED OUT OF BED. Joe noticed her good humour and asked what was so good about a Monday morning.

"Nothing really. I'm giving Mia a lift to the train station. She might be moving away."

"Really? Where's she going?"

"Oh, nothing's settled yet, she's going to London tomorrow."

"Hmm," responded Joe, clearly not interested. "What time you going?"

Suddenly Elin realised that an extended alibi was presenting itself. "Her train goes at two, but I'm going over this morning — help her sort out her clothes."

` "OK, *cara*." Joe was already dumping his mug and plate in the sink. "I'll be out at work anyway."

The day was getting better and better despite the rain, a steady drizzle that looked set to last. She stuffed a spare set of clothes in her handbag with passing gratitude to the fashion for very large bags.

Mia was waiting when Elin arrived at ten. She locked the front door, dropped, her backpack into the back of the car and jumped in with a rueful smile. "Why did I drink so much last night? My head is thumping."

As they drew up outside the station, Mia threw her hands up in annoyance. "Oh, damn! Elin, I had a favour to ask you, I forgot and now I'm in a rush. Can you park here for a minute?"

Elin manoeuvred into a space on double yellow lines next to the taxi rank. "What's up?"

"Daniel arranged for a friend to drop a parcel off at the house yesterday, then the friend couldn't make it. He's bringing it this afternoon and I won't be there. Would you mind taking the key and being there when the parcel is delivered? I meant to ask you last night and I forgot – too much wine."

"I'd be happy to help." Elin spoke quickly, grasping the

sudden opportunity, "Umm, well, I need to tell you something too."

There wasn't much time and Elin's words came tumbling out in a rush. "You remember Aaron? Well, I'm seeing him occasionally, it's so wonderful, but we can't be seen together. Would it be OK if we met at your place? Just this week while you're away? Please Mia?"

Mia looked startled, then very doubtful, but after a second's hesitation she reached for her backpack and extracted the key. "Here you are, just leave the parcel in the living room. Gotta go."

As Mia jumped out of the car and disappeared through the drizzle into the crowded station entrance, Elin sat staring at the key in the palm of her hand. She forgot that she was in a no-waiting zone until a horn blast startled her. She drove off in a daze. What an opportunity. She pulled over, parked, then delved into her handbag, pushing the spare clothes that wouldn't be needed to one side. She extricated a small notebook and silver ballpoint pen and wrote quickly: 157 Princess Street. Tearing off the single sheet she folded it and slipped it into her pocket.

Elin saw the Land Rover already parked and walked straight into the coffee shop.

"Aaron, I was hoping to see you! Do you think you could go over to Mia's house and help move some heavy stuff? Here's her address." She handed him the folded paper, "I'm on my way there now."

Aaron mumbled a surprised response as Elin turned away. She drove quickly to Mia's and let herself in with the precious key. She left the front door unlatched and crossed the tiny hallway into the living room. She saw the Land Rover drive past and paced around the room until she heard Aaron push the door open then shut it quietly behind him.

When he realised that she was alone, he crossed the room and pulled her towards him, holding her close. He caught her lips and covered her mouth in a lingering kiss. Elin's arms found their way around his neck; she could feel his rock-hard shoulder muscles and a tingle of arousal ran through her.

Her body urged her to make the most of every second and let nothing spoil this precious time. He put his hands on her face and the kiss deepened. She thought she had never felt such desire. Aaron's hands guided her backwards and they fell in a heap on the sofa, giggling as they pulled their clothes off so that nothing would come between their bodies. He stifled her laughter with kisses, and warm skin to warm skin they melded together, moving as one. Their passion reached its peak and Aaron gasped Elin's name over and over. He lay still and Elin delighted in the sensation of his full weight on her body until he raised himself on to his elbows then lifted a hand to brush her hair gently away from her flushed cheeks. Her eyes closed at his touch and the time they had spent apart melted away.

"Honey, I have to go," Aaron said hours later, nuzzling his mouth close to her ear. "I'll get here as often as I can."

"I know you will." Elin forced a smile and found words to match, adding hopefully, "Can you manage a whole evening?"

Aaron pushed his fingers through his hair and frowned, "Not sure, I'd have to think up a good excuse to give Rachel."

Elin hated to be reminded about Rachel. She answered as calmly as she could, "Can you do lunchtime tomorrow? I'll be here."

"That would be great, but, if not, then Wednesday? I'll try for a long evening too, sweetheart." As he slipped out of the house, Elin stood unmoving, trying to eke out the last vestiges of his presence, then slumped on the sofa and relived the morning. Her brain told her the affair was doomed, but she was incapable of acting on that knowledge. She buried her head in her hands and gave in to tears. Today was different from the previous hurry and subterfuge. It was wrong, she knew that, but equally she knew that she would not be able to put an end to the affair. She needed to exert tighter control over her emotions. It must be possible to enjoy the physical excitement without the remorse and agitation.

She waited until Daniel's friend delivered the parcel. Her watch told her it was three thirty, but if felt much later. After locking Mia's front door, she put the key very carefully in a zipped pocket of her bag and drove home.

9

After three hours, Elin accepted that Aaron wasn't coming. She had paced up and down Mia's living room, wiped down the kitchen surfaces several times, and tidied up everything that was possible in someone else's home. She had picked up some fresh baked Cornish pasties on the way, thinking that Aaron might be hungry. She'd even put a bottle of wine in the battered old fridge and some cans of beer too. Now the pasties seemed to mock her, sitting there cold and stodgy. With a sigh, she recovered their paper bag from the recycling bin and packed them up for Mutt.

Wednesday began and ended as a virtual repeat. She'd brought a loaf of French bread and a large slice of Brie, completing the picnic theme with a pretty pot of pork rillette, its lid covered in jaunty red check cotton. That cheerful look now reproached her as the pasties had the day before. She went into Mia's kitchen and tore off pieces of bread, stuffing the crusty morsels into her mouth. The rest could be thrown to the ducks on Mutt's next outing to the park.

By Thursday there was a tight knot in Elin's stomach. She used her restless energy to make coleslaw and potato salad. Two large containers remained in the fridge at home while two adult sized portions of each had been spirited away in her handbag. Quiche from the bakery sat in Mia's fridge as she settled down with *Vanity Fair*, prepared for a long wait. Suddenly she dropped the magazine, her stomach unclenching as she heard the familiar sound of the Land Rover's engine. She watched Aaron walk towards the house. The way he moved triggered a long-anticipated thrill of excitement. How could she have allowed herself to doubt that he would come?

It was real, it was happening. They wasted no words, Aaron kissed her as if she was the centre of his universe. He drew back and stared at her with such intensity in his blue eyes that everything felt utterly right. The days of separation slipped away and they undressed feverishly. As their naked bodies came together, Elin felt she could have waited forever to experience such rapture.

Afterwards they lay together, spent. Elin ran her hands over the contours of his back and down his muscular thighs then sat up with a smile. She touched Aaron's taut stomach then her own soft abdomen.

"Are you hungry? I'm starving!"

Aaron's eyes following her appreciatively as she rose and walked to the kitchen. They picnicked on the floor, laughing as they fed each other and sipped wine. Elin savoured her food as if she'd been released from prison and had just rediscovered the joy of eating. She lay back and marvelled at how simple pleasures could feel so different in Aaron's company.

"Guess what Elin? I can be here tomorrow evening! I said that I have a rugby re-union. Can you?"

Elin pummelled him with her free hand as pleasure coursed through her. "Course I'll be here!"

Saying goodbye was easy. Elin dumped the well-wrapped remains of their meal in a litterbin on the way home. She hummed to herself; the voices of doubt were quiet for a while. What people didn't know wouldn't hurt them, she was sure of that.

Next morning, after a silent breakfast, Elin watched Joe slouch off to the study, noting that even in his ratty jeans and old T-shirt, he was still a striking looking man. Dark stubble enhanced his masculinity, and his physique, tall and rangy, needed no upkeep at the gym. These observations didn't rouse any emotions. Irritation stirred, nothing else.

"I think I'll get my hair done later," she called to Joe. "Remember I'm going out with Hilary and the girls tonight?"

"Oh, tonight's a girls' night out? Do you need a lift or are you taking the car?"

It was like taking sweets from a baby, Elin thought. All she had to do was put the word 'remember' into her alibi and Joe fell for it. "I'll take the car. It'll stop me drinking too much." The last thing she needed was a lift from Joe. There was no need to get anxious, nothing could possibly go wrong.

For once the timing was perfect. Although the sky was a forbidding steel grey, Elin managed to get in and out of the supermarket with the ingredients for a romantic dinner before the first roll of thunder could be heard in the distance. She dashed into Mia's house as fat drops of rain started to fall and Aaron's taxi drew up outside. She unpacked the food as Aaron paid the driver, but thoughts of eating were driven from her mind when their first kiss set desire shooting through her with a force that took her breath away. She closed her eyes and inhaled the smell of his skin and the scent of his now familiar aftershave. All evening, Elin hardly left Aaron's arms. The thunderstorm outside was a fitting background to their passion. As the sound faded into the distance and the rain began to ease, Elin and Aaron lay with eyes closed, his forehead against hers. Elin's need for him filled her, leaving no room for anxiety and fear. They ate the whole roast chicken while it still hung on to some vestige of warmth, tearing it to pieces with their bare hands, wiping them on each other's bodies, licking off the grease, kindling desire. Elin handed the bottle to Aaron.

"Finish up the wine, Aaron, I've got to drive." Aaron twirled his glass and swallowed a large mouthful of Shiraz then reached for her again. He enjoyed sex and food to the utmost; whatever Aaron did he did with heart and soul, he held nothing back. Elin marvelled at her good luck as she lay back in his arms.

Sooner than seemed possible the magical evening came to an end and with it the knowledge that Mia was due back the next afternoon.

"Just half an hour in the morning, Aaron, sweetheart, you could bring the baby...." Elin begged.

Aaron was firm, "Elin, we can't, it's too risky. If I go out tomorrow morning Rachel will smell a rat. I usually have a clanging hangover after a night out with the lads, I wouldn't be rushing out anywhere."

Elin managed to look away so that he wouldn't see her tear-filled eyes. "You're right. I'm sorry." She managed a smile, but didn't turn towards him. "Mia might let me have the key again; she's away a lot."

"That's my girl." Aaron dropped a kiss on her shoulder then got dressed. Elin slowly did the same, keeping her face averted as Aaron phoned for a taxi. "They'll be here in a couple of minutes." Elin buried her face in his neck as he whispered huskily, "I have to go, sweetie, fingers crossed for II on Monday."

Elin was alone again as a black taxi bore her lover away and home to his wife. The possibility that Mia might offer them her home occasionally buoyed her up. She locked the door and set off for home.

IT SEEMED like a lifetime since Elin had dropped Mia at the station. By Saturday lunchtime she could be quiet no longer. She texted Mia, who answered that there was no rush for the key. The response left Elin in a quandary. Broaching the subject of holding onto her key wouldn't be easy. After some thought Elin replied simply that she would like to see Mia soon. Within seconds Mia had replied, "Come over Sunday afternoon?" After agreeing Elin put her phone away and changed into old clothes, ready to weed the garden. "Joe," she called to the figure hunched over the computer, "I want to work on the garden, could you take the dog out today?"

"Maybe, if I get this done quickly." His eyes remained glued to the screen.

The weeds came out with satisfying ease after the rain. Elin mused that she knew about silent meditation and walking meditation, but perhaps she'd stumbled on another version, weeding meditation. Her shoulders appreciated the pull of muscles in place of continuous tension as she worked steadily through the afternoon. Joe had, with much sighing and his usual difficulty in locating the lead, taken Mutt to the park. Her knees grew sore and her back began to ache with a satisfying tiredness. The thought of a lengthy session in her luxurious bath became more and more inviting.

Submerged in a sea of perfumed foam, she soaked her

tired body and gradually came to the realisation that she did not love Joe. It was so clear, she wondered how that knowledge had eluded her for so long. Subconsciously, she must have seen it as a failure and refused to acknowledge it. She had wanted to rewind the clock and find happiness again with Joe. Was this new understanding caused by, or was it the effect, of her affair?

Examining herself closely as she scrubbed away the grime of the day and soil from beneath her nails, Elin wondered if she knew who she was anymore. Hiding in her bathroom was no longer hiding from herself — it was hiding from Joe. When prune-like wrinkled skin gave Elin a preview of middle age and she stepped out of the bath to rectify the damage with expensive lotions, she decided to pass the rest of the evening quietly, not make waves, and look forward to seeing Mia the next day.

10

Mia welcomed Elin with a wide grin, but it felt strange to be there.

Mia had only been home a few hours, yet already there were piles of papers, books and items of clothing scattered around the room that Elin had left so neat and tidy less than 48 hours earlier.

Mia wasted no time after the two friends greeted each other, she stood and looked straight at Elin. Her expression was hard to read. Elin waited, key in her outstretched hand. Mia put her hand lightly on Elin's arm as she searched for the right words, "I've been thinking about your situation all week. I'm sorry Elin, but I can't see any good coming of your affair. Please don't ask me to be involved again."

Elin looked at her friend, her heart sinking. All her hopes were dashed, yet she didn't feel any negative vibes coming from Mia. Mia meant exactly what she said, no more, no less.

Elin made a huge effort to hide the depth of her disappointment. She swallowed hard and turned away.

Mia continued gently, "I'm sorry Elin, it just doesn't feel right."

They puttered about in the kitchen making toast and carried it into the living room. Elin sat on the sofa coming to terms with the dashing of her hopes. She half closed her eyes and allowed Mia to regale her with stories about the importance of preserving precious artefacts. Mia broke off, "Sorry, I'm going on and on. I've decided I don't want to be a teacher; it's been useful for earning a living, but more than six years marking time is enough."

"You're not boring me. I can't remember when I last felt that enthusiasm. Perhaps when Chrissie came and helped us? Seeing the kids' eagerness revived me."

Then she changed the subject, "How did Daniel's interview go?"

"OK, I think. But my decision isn't dependent on him," Mia said, and lapsed into silence.

"Don't you see a future together?" Elin asked eventually. "I thought everything was great between you?"

"Oh, that's not what I meant. Everything's wonderful! I never think about the age difference anymore. We're enthusiastic about the same things," said Mia with a grin, "and I can't keep my hands off him! The sex is fantastic, but looking in the same direction in life will probably last a lot longer!"

Elin gestured at some of the pamphlets scattered around, "College courses?"

"Yup, I'm looking into the qualifications."

"Looks like you have a lot of research to do, I'll leave you to it," Elin said as she stood and moved towards the door.

Mia followed and hugged her goodbye, "Sorry about the key. Let's get together again before too long, OK?"

Elin pondered as she drove slowly home. Her hopes had

been dashed yet she didn't feel too bad. Mia had made it clear that her decision would not affect their friendship. Elin was surprised to see Joe's car still in the drive. She called out, "I'm home!"

From the office came a preoccupied reply, "I'm in here."

Elin walked through the kitchen, out into the garden, came back, looked in the fridge; there was plenty of food, no need to cook or shop. Everything was tidy and the cleaner was coming on Tuesday. She glanced at the papers but felt no interest in the banner headlines. An idea flitted across her mind and she called out again to Joe, "I think I'll pop over to Hilary's."

"OK. The guys are going out for a drink, so I may go out later."

"There's plenty of stuff for dinner in the fridge if I'm not back."

"OK." Joe still sounded distracted.

She went to the wine rack, selected a nice bottle of Sauvignon Blanc, hesitated, then got a container of homemade chicken cacciatore from the freezer and put it in her bag before making her way to the car.

HILARY WAS PLEASANTLY surprised to see her friend, and the two women were soon chatting over a glass of wine.

"Joe out again?" enquired Hilary as they settled.

"He's actually at home, says he might go out later."

"Perhaps his latest isn't available?" Hilary responded.

"Stop dropping hints! Nothing'll surprise me," Elin sighed, drank some wine and looked closely at her friend. "I've decided I want to know everything about Joe. Give it to me straight, the days of protecting me are over."

"What is there to say? You believed in fairy-tale endings

for longer than most!" Hilary dropped some ice into her glass, settled back and sampled the wine. "What a treat to drink good wine for no reason. Or is there a reason?"

"Don't change the subject," Elin responded. "Come on, Hilary, in words of one syllable. What. Is. Joe. Up. To?"

"Where shall I start?" Hilary sighed.

"At the risk of sounding like Julie Andrews, why don't you start at the very beginning, a very good place to start?"

"Ricky's such an open book, he doesn't realise when I'm pumping him," Hilary said, then paused. "Hmm, let me think, about two years ago Ricky started coming home earlier on Friday nights. I gathered that he'd lost his drinking buddy."

Elin's throat tightened; memories of Aaron's lovemaking protected her, but she couldn't control her gut reactions. She braced herself.

"I don't know her name, just that she and her friends used to hang out at the same bars. It was over in a few weeks."

Elin's heart jolted at the confirmation of her suspicions. It was a blow to her self-confidence and she could feel her pulse racing. She let her breath out slowly. Unexpected tears prickled, "Go on Hilary, I'm OK." She took a fortifying gulp of wine and scrabbled in her bag for a tissue.

Hilary was grim faced, "A few months later Ricky was home earlier again. That was Alyssa: she started 'accidentally' bumping into him in different places, flattered him and he didn't resist. A cracking blonde, according to Ricky, but Joe ended that, she was too intense." She paused. "He is pretty sexy, Elin, women fall over themselves to get near him."

Elin wiped her nose then drank more. The death knell

of her dreams thundered in her ears. Her eyes narrowed and she muttered a terse, "That's no excuse. Keep going."

There was a long pause as though Hilary hadn't heard. Elin sat up straighter and Hilary continued, "There was the wife of a colleague and it didn't follow the usual pattern. Joe was missing some Fridays, but there was a bit more to it." Hilary took in Elin's stricken expression. "Sorry Elin, then either Joe realised it could jeopardise his career or she decided he wasn't worth it. I couldn't find out any more. It was a while ago."

Jess and Finn thundered down the stairs and came to say hello. Elin forced a smile, glad of the break to assimilate her new reality. Her hand shook as she refilled her glass and she used both hands to raise it to her mouth. She turned her face away from the youngsters and gulped. Hilary remembered the chicken dish and ushered Elin in to the kitchen, arm around her waist. As the pasta cooked Elin found her chin wobbling. She swallowed hard and stuck her lower lip out to hold in the tears. Hilary patted her shoulder and mused, "I think that men are wired differently from women. Joe probably doesn't care much about these other women. They don't last long, then he becomes the ideal husband again. He loves you in his way."

Elin's thoughts lurched in all directions as she poked at the chicken, tasted the sauce then pushed her plate away. The second wine bottle was almost empty and she couldn't marshal a coherent response. Instead she slurred, "I should go home."

Hilary was emphatic, "There is no way I'm letting you drive."

"What time is it?" Elin mumbled in response.

"It's not late, only nine o'clock. Let me make some coffee, I fancy an amaretto too." Hilary cleared the table and loaded the dishwasher, banging the plates and dishes unceremoniously into their slots.

Returning to the comfort of the living room, they sipped coffee and the liqueur. An unexpected calm enveloped Elin as she absorbed her new knowledge. She sank deeper into the armchair and allowed herself to daydream about her lover – then Joe didn't matter. Hilary rattled on until she was jolted out of her reverie by the sound of Aaron's name.

"Enough about Joe, c'mon Elin, what about you?" Hilary looked at her expectantly. "Anything you say is safe with me."

Elin felt herself weakening. It would be such a relief to share her feelings. Her eyes filled, she blinked and focused on the curtains behind Hilary, trying to get herself together by counting the lines in the linen fabric. The outright confirmation of Joe's infidelities had hurt more than she had anticipated. She turned to Hilary.

"I feel a fool, trusting Joe for so long. Even after the lipstick on his shirt when he said my paranoia was showing. I thought I was going crazy."

"You're no fool, Elin. I don't know why Joe acts the way he does. Don't blame yourself. I've had arguments with him and he can be extremely assertive, I'm not surprised you doubted yourself." Hilary left to make more coffee; Elin closed her eyes again, jerking them open when Hilary returned and continued, "Do you think you and Joe'll work things out?"

"I don't want it to work out anymore!" Elin felt her face go red as she fought back angry tears, "I'm so mixed up." She was furious with herself for showing weakness. She sniffed, fumbled in her bag for more tissues then giggled hysterically. "I might as well tell you, Aaron and I are having an affair and it's fantastic!" Elin smiled joyfully at the thought, "I'm on cloud nine when I'm with him. Then this..." Her face fell, "What should I do?"

Hilary gave Elin the I-told-you-so look then sat back to listen. The story flooded out, Elin's face lit up and Hilary just nodded and sipped her liqueur. Eventually, Elin subsided into silence and picked up her glass.

"Any advice? Aaron won't leave his wife so I'm stuck, aren't I?"

"How about couples counselling? Might help?" Hilary was pragmatic.

Elin shuddered, "God no, I couldn't, not yet. I need time to think." Elin looked at her phone. "I must go, don't want Joe to get suspicious."

"Let me phone for a taxi," Hilary said, then brought two glasses of water from the kitchen and they both downed them. They heard the cab stop outside. Grabbing her bag, but forgetting her jacket, Elin enveloped her friend in a maudlin hug and slurred a reminder not to tell a mortal soul as she walked unsteadily to the taxi.

Hilary leaned on the front door jamb for support, "Good luck Elin. Birds of a feather!"

Elin collapsed into the back seat and was already beginning to regret her outburst of honesty as her head began to throb.

11

E lin woke the next morning feeling wretched. The three glasses of water she'd forced down and the vitamin C she'd swallowed before bed had not prevented a miserable hangover. She wished she could take off her thumping head and replace it with the one she usually carried around. Her stomach was queasy and she felt generally out of sorts. Even the knowledge that she might see Aaron later that morning didn't help. In fact, it made her feel worse. Suppose today was the only day they could meet and she wasted their time together on a rotten hangover?

Joe had left early so she got another taxi to take her back to Hilary's. She felt a little better; the painkillers she had taken before leaving must have helped. Even after a bath, she was still off colour; her brand-new underwear didn't even help, perhaps today might be more suited to talking than lovemaking. After listening to Mia describe her relationship with Daniel, she wanted to understand Aaron better.

The weather was being no more cooperative than her

aching head. It looked like rain. Her spirits improved as she pulled into the familiar car park all of two minutes early. She forgot her aching head. Aaron's Land Rover was already parked in its usual place. She swung into a space alongside and walked towards the entrance. Aaron was waiting to give his order. An elderly lady in a wheelchair, pushed by an exhausted daughter, held up the queue as she hesitated over her choice, speaking in a voice that carried across the room.

"I just want a nice cup of coffee, dear, instant will do for me."

Elin waited patiently, meeting Aaron's eyes with a smile but not speaking; they ordered separately and waited silently while their coffees were prepared. They didn't speak until they were both ready to leave. He held the door open for her, beaming broadly and making a bow as she walked through.

Suddenly they both stopped. A battered Volvo had arrived and parked on the other side of the Land Rover; a young woman dressed in saggy jeans and a washed out, once-navy sweatshirt emerged and stood surveying them, her arms folded across her chest. She looked familiar and Elin realised with horror that it was Rachel. She glanced across at Aaron; he was ashen faced. He didn't look at Elin, but after a split second's hesitation began walking towards his wife.

"Hi Rach, did I forget something?" His voice didn't match the casualness of his words; he sounded half strangled, but continued walking.

Elin forced herself to walk slowly towards her car, leaving a gap between her and Aaron and trying her hardest to act as if there was nothing amiss.

It was obvious that they had been together, so Aaron continued to try and rescue the situation.

"Do you remember Elin? She was at Beechwood last term?"

There was a decided hush. Rachel didn't speak. Aaron struggled on, "Want a coffee? Or something for the kids?"

Until that moment Elin hadn't realised that Aaron's two children were in the car.

"For god's sake Aaron. Cut the crap, will you?" Rachel snapped. She glanced between Aaron and Elin. "I don't want to upset the kids, but I had to see the latest floozy for myself." She moved away from her car and approached Elin, who took a step backwards. Her words came out with quiet venom.

"Oh, it's you, Little Miss Perfect! Not so perfect now: you made one big mistake messing about with my husband."

Elin took another step back as Rachel came towards her, fearful that Rachel was going to attack her. Rachel's voice became more shrill.

"I bet you think he's wonderful, don't you?" she sneered. "This is the last time you'll ever see him, I'll make sure of that. He'll be far too scared to contact you. Let me tell you, Miss Fashion Plate, Miss Career Girl, you're not the first and probably won't be the last. I'm used to his lies. I feel sorry for you, fooled by a nice body and a pretty face. Let me tell you, if he wasn't a games teacher he'd be as fat as a pig. He's a lazy good for nothing, but he's mine! So, stay away!"

Elin stood transfixed, unable to utter a word. Aware that she was the centre of attention, she tried to mumble a response but nothing emerged. She looked desperately at Aaron, but he wouldn't look at her. He dropped his eyes and moved towards the Volvo as the baby started to shriek, "Dada, dada!" The joyful shouts added a note of unreality to the nightmare.

Elin realised that she was on her own. Her head felt like

lead. Dammit what a day to have a hangover. Pulling herself up straight, she looked directly at Rachel and managed to keep her voice level.

"You've made a mistake, Rachel. I just bumped into Aaron. I'm always in here getting coffee. Please don't jump to conclusions."

"Pff!" Rachel dismissed the idea with a wave of her hand. "Jump to conclusions? You really are an arrogant bitch!"

"Please don't scream at me, I don't know what you're talking about," Elin said; her heart was pounding and she felt sick.

Rachel's voice sank to a hiss and she leaned towards Elin, "You sanctimonious cow, you think you're better than everybody else, Miss High and Mighty. I'll keep it down, you skinny posh bitch, for the sake of my kids, not you. Last Friday my precious husband — mine, not yours — thought I swallowed his story about a rugby reunion. I'm not stupid, I knew something was going on, but you were so devious, so fucking devious: no text messages, no phone calls. But that taxi was a big mistake. I checked with the taxi firm and I know where you were. You're not as clever as you thought, you smug, self-satisfied cow!"

Her face grew red and her voice became shrill again, "You're just a rich bitch who thinks she can have everything she wants. I know your type, scrawny skinny coat hanger, and I know all about you." Rachel paused and her face twisted into a grimace, "Think you've got friends at Beechwood? Think again. You wait and see. I'll make sure everybody knows about you, you vile, snobby, selfish cow."

Elin stepped back as if she had been slapped. Rachel's face contorted as she spat out the words.

"Leave. Him. Alone. Do you get it?" Then she went on in

a rush, "He doesn't care about you. He just wants all the sex he can get, understand? Leave Him Alone!"

Elin looked at Aaron, but he wouldn't look at her. Both children were now whimpering, picking up on the charged atmosphere.

Summoning up all the dignity she could muster, Elin turned away. She felt the watching eyes boring into her back. She managed to reach the haven of her car. She fumbled with her keys, almost dropping her drink and her bag, and struggled inside. Her hand shook as she turned the ignition. She drove away. In her rear-view mirror, she could see Aaron leaning into the car, calming the children as his wife, hands on hips, stood watching Elin's departure.

Shock and humiliation kept her going until she was out of sight. Then horror and disbelief overwhelmed her. Why hadn't Aaron said anything? She was gripped with fear. Untended tears poured down her cheeks and dripped on to her top as a yawning emptiness engulfed her. She pulled into a side street, stopped and sobbed like a child, her body crumpling over the wheel. Where could she go to gather herself? Was Rachel serious when she said she would tell everybody? Would anybody tell Joe? She found herself driving towards the house and realised how short a time had passed since she'd left. If Joe's car was there she would drive past, if not she could collect Mutt and stay out until she'd regained some control.

Hours later she felt spent and defeated. Elin had walked and cried until her eyes were so swollen she could hardly see, and every tissue she could find was balled up into a sodden sludge. As her tears dried, anger welled up: how could Rachel have called her such names? She couldn't believe that her passionate affair with Aaron was nothing more than a diversion, a passing intrigue. The few times they'd been together had been blissful; tears overflowed again at the thought that she wouldn't experience that again. Aaron and Rachel, their names churned around in her brain but sounded wrong; it should be Aaron and Elin. She walked, oblivious of her mud-spattered trousers, and the skin on her face felt tight and drawn. The drizzly rain had soaked unnoticed through her light jacket until the chill made itself felt and Elin glanced at her watch. It took almost an hour to get back to the car. She checked her face in the mirror. Her eyes were puffy, but Joe probably wouldn't notice; if he did she could say she had an eye infection. Her heart dropped even further, home wouldn't be a welcoming haven but another perilous situation.

The thought that something was amiss flitted across the screen of Elin's consciousness when she pulled into the drive. Ricky's car was parked outside. Was Joe's car in the garage?

When she went in through the back door the feeling returned. Something odd was going on. The sound of male voices came from the living room and an unfamiliar grey jacket was draped over a kitchen stool. Empty tonic bottles cluttered the counter top amid blobs of melting ice. She stood transfixed, listening, identifying Joe's angry voice. He sounded loud and aggressively drunk; his voice was followed by a deeper murmur in Ricky's calmer tone. She couldn't move. Had Rachel contacted Joe? As far as she knew they'd never met. Willing it not to be true, Elin raced through the possibilities in her mind. What else could have caused the grim atmosphere and the early evening drinking? The door opened and Joe stood there, swaying, glass in hand, with Ricky, looking anxious, right behind him.

"Well, well, well, if it isn't little innocent Elin home at

last," he smiled derisively. "I know what's been going on." Elin shrank back as he jabbed his fingers forwards and advanced towards her.

"Yeh, I got a phone call earlier. How do you think I felt when this harridan starts screaming at me, telling me to keep my wife under control? Nice, eh, lovely surprise, *cara mia*?" Joe jeered as spittle landed on his chin and he brushed it away roughly. "What've you got to say for yourself? What lies are you going to invent this time, huh?"

"Let's get Elin a drink and we can talk calmly. How's that?" Ricky took Joe's arm. "Sit down mate, there's no rush, Elin's just come in."

"Just come in from where? That's the point." Joe thrust his face towards Elin again. "What've you got to say for yourself?" He turned unsteadily, slumped into an armchair and put his head in his hands. "How could you do this to me, Elin?"

Elin was relieved that Ricky was there. She'd never seen Joe like this. It was hard to believe that he could be this full of rage. She saw the empty bottle of vodka on the coffee table and the new one just opened. Ricky fussed about getting her a drink as she sat down opposite Joe, shrinking back into the depths of the armchair, looking mutely towards Ricky. She took a large gulp of vodka and tonic.

"Joe came over earlier, Elin," explained Ricky. "He told me and Hilary. He had a few drinks at our house so I thought I'd better drive him home. He's had a few more since then," he added apologetically.

Joe's eyes were closed; he shifted in the chair, then with an effort leaned forward and opened his bloodshot eyes. "So what if I've had a few drinks? It's not every day a man gets told his wife is fucking someone else behind his back." He took another swig of his drink. "Didn't believe her at first, but she convinced me. Nobody in their right mind would make up a story like that, screaming down the phone." He struggled but failed to get up. His face twisted, "You're not saying much, Elin, c'mon on, tell me how many others, eh, how many others?"

Elin looked at him with revulsion. She was sickened by Joe's oh-so-righteous anger. He was acting as if he was an injured innocent. How could he reproach her when he was the one who had broken the trust between them, had made her feel crazy, paranoid even, with his supercilious denials?

Elin looked at Joe again, this time she comprehended just how drunk he was. It was pointless talking to him now, he wouldn't hear anything. She made up her mind quickly and firmly. She put her glass down carefully and spoke to Ricky.

"There's no point trying to have a civilized conversation with him now. I have plenty to say, but it's not the right time. I don't feel safe. I'm going to stay somewhere else for the night. I'll be in touch."

Elin stood up and left the room as Ricky restrained Joe; luckily it only took one small push to land Joe back in the armchair. She grabbed her bag, hurried to her car and was gone before they could follow.

For the second time that day, Elin drove aimlessly. Her first instinct was to go to Hilary's, but that would be the first place that Joe would look. She couldn't face going to her parents and hoped Joe wouldn't phone them. If he did it would upset them terribly, but Joe had never had much time for her Mum and Dad so it wasn't likely. Which of her friends might Rachel have contacted? Arriving at a hotel with no luggage was too depressing to contemplate. There were no tears this time. Her earlier desolation festered, side-lined for the moment by her anger. Round and round she drove, worrying more about Tom and Alley and Mutt than Joe. Her life had been turned upside down and she didn't want to think about it. She felt sick; she had to eat or she would feel a hundred times worse. Dusk was falling and she noticed a fish and chip shop, people clutching well-wrapped packages, children munching warm golden chips. She parked outside and went in. The man behind the counter beamed a welcome and chatted companionably as he served her a generous portion. Back in the car, she opened the package and inhaled the familiar aroma of malt vinegar before tearing off chunks of cod and stuffing them into her mouth. After the initial pleasure, she jerked back to harsh reality and the food transformed into sawdust in her mouth. The memory of her breakfast felt like a different existence when the world was safe and everything was under control.

Elin retrieved her phone from the bottom of her bag and scrolled down her list of contacts. Gina and Bobby had no room. Jeannie lived on her own; where were her details? Nothing there, how strange. Then Mia's details popped up. Elin stared at the number. Asking her for help now would be difficult. Elin tried to remember the conversation; Mia hadn't wanted to be a part of the affair but hadn't been judgemental either, she just needed to grit her teeth and dial the number. Would Daniel be there? Would that make a difference?

It was almost 10 pm but Elin went through the list several times before coming to the conclusion that Mia was her best hope. Taking a deep breath, she pressed the call button.

"Hi Elin," Mia's voice sounded warm, "what's up?"

"Something terrible's happened, I can't go home, I need somewhere to stay tonight, can I come to you?" Elin's voice trailed off, she held her breath.

"Of course you can, you OK?"

Elin exhaled, "Thanks a million. I'm on the other side of town, can I come straight over?"

"Absolutely, drive carefully."

"I'm on my way."

Elin was soon knocking on the familiar front door and being drawn inside with a comforting hug. She flopped down and sensed acceptance, offered wordlessly, and felt deep appreciation for Mia's unquestioning support. She recognised, on a profound level, what a good friend she had in Mia.

"Can I get you something to eat?" Mia's face held concern.

Elin closed her eyes and exhaled a sigh of relief, "Nothing thanks. I just had fish and chips."

Mia hovered, "What about some tea? Or wine?"

"No, thanks. Maybe a glass of water, I'm tired out." Elin felt exhaustion seep over her. She felt drained.

"You look knackered, do you want to go to bed? Maybe whatever it is won't seem so bad in the morning?" Mia fetched the glass of water. "Come upstairs I'll show you where you're sleeping. Do you want a bath?"

"No, I'll just fall into bed, thanks."

Elin followed Mia up the stairs and into a small room; the double mattress lying on the floor was covered with mismatched sheets and an old-fashioned eiderdown. The pillow with its cheerful floral cover looked soft and inviting. The only other furniture was a chair. The curtains barely kept out the light from the street lamp outside.

"I haven't furnished this room yet," said Mia apologetically. "I hope the mattress is OK; the bedside table is disguised as a chair and the wardrobe is the hook behind the door."

"I do appreciate this, Mia." Elin felt the tears well up as she turned away. Mia went to the bathroom and extricated a new toothbrush from a basket piled haphazardly with toiletries.

"Here you are. Sleep as long as you like. Daniel's off early tomorrow, but I'm here. See you in the morning."

Within minutes Elin was in bed, safe at last. What a day. She closed her eyes and tried to empty her head. There were sounds of traffic in the distance, but it was the chaos inside her brain that was chasing sleep away. From the room below came an interesting sound, melodic, rhythmic and soothing. It sounded like Mia's voice, but she had never heard her friend sing before. She drifted off; her last thought was that she must remember to ask Mia about the singing in the morning.

12

E lin would gladly have slept the rest of her life away, but when she opened her eyes the thin light leaking around the ill-fitting curtains told her it was still early morning. Her thoughts immediately began circling the events of the previous day like a hawk in the sky, repeatedly diving and imploding at the point when Aaron had scuttled away from her without a backward glance. She heard Daniel get up. She smelled fresh coffee, then heard him let himself quietly out of the house. Everything was silent again. Elin checked her phone: only 6 am. She crept to the bathroom then back to her warm bed, drawing the covers closer around her. Unbelievably, she must have fallen asleep. The next thing she registered was that the smell of fresh toast had replaced the aroma of coffee. Elin checked her phone again, now it was 8 a.m., still too early for people with nothing to do except contemplate their own misery. She heard Mia coming up the stairs then tapping gently on the door.

"Room service! I've left towels and some clean clothes in the bathroom. Take your time."

Elin murmured her thanks as she heaved herself up from the mattress and padded to the door, but Mia had already gone downstairs. She picked up the tray, put it carefully by the bed and sat back down. The large wooden tray was loaded with a full teapot, a jug of milk, a thermos of hot water, a pile of toast, butter in a dish and two kinds of marmalade. She plastered a piece of toast with butter and orange marmalade then propped herself up against the wall. Elin tried to eat but her mouth was dry. As she sipped the tea she found herself shivering, so pulled the sheet up higher and tucked the eiderdown around herself. The mouthful of toast felt like a wad of damp cotton wool, getting bigger with each chew. She abandoned the attempt to eat and poured more tea.

She tried to think about Joe, but she couldn't summon any emotion about her marriage. Elin searched for ways to explain Aaron's behaviour. It must have been the shock of Rachel's sudden appearance that led him to succumb so weakly. Was he suffering as much as she was? The possibility he was not suffering hurt even more. She was certain he still cared about her. What could she do? If Joe wanted to end their marriage that was OK with her, she'd manage somehow. Being without Aaron was unthinkable.

Elin made her way to the bathroom. It was small but inviting. Wicker baskets and cluttered shelves spoke of a household at ease with itself, male and female toiletries mingling, decorative touches showing individuality rather than contrivance. Noticing the clean towels and spare underwear laid out for her, Elin was surprised. The choice was a brand-new thong or a wisp of pink lace that would cover very little. Mia never failed to surprise her. Mia was also large breasted, so Elin was relieved to see a stretchy athletic top: a half empty bra would have done nothing to raise her spirits.

Elin added some bath crème and the scent of geraniums filled the air. She lowered herself into the warmth and rubbed her calf muscles that ached after the hours of walking. She turned off the taps and lay back. The silence was broken by a low murmuring coming from downstairs, just like last night. Again, it sounded like Mia's voice; was she singing, humming, talking? Straining to hear better, Elin wondered who she was talking to. Maybe she was on the phone. The sound became more rhythmical so she dismissed that thought. It was a strange sound for sure, but so soothing. She listened idly for a while, enjoying the cadence, feeling calmer. The longer she listened the calmer she felt, as if the sound was connecting her to something universal, enveloping her in a soft, comforting embrace.

When Elin went downstairs carrying her breakfast tray, she felt fresh and clean if not fashionable. She still wore her own trousers — she had rubbed most of the dried mud splashes off — they looked a little dusty but would do. She had discarded her navy top when she saw the greasy marks from the fish and chips and now wore a baggy, well-washed, white T-shirt and an all-enveloping grey cardigan. Mia called from the kitchen.

"Did you find everything you needed?"

"Yes thanks, here's the tray. I'm sorry but I couldn't manage the toast."

"That's OK. I was just going to make some more tea, or would you prefer coffee?"

"More tea would be nice. Thanks." Elin stood and watched her friend finish her last bite of toast.

"Can I get you something else to eat? Eggs? Cereal? Chocolate biscuit?"

Elin shuddered, "No thanks, just tea, I'll make it."

Elin removed her mug from the tray and rinsed it under the tap, made two mugs of fresh tea and walked into the living room. Mia followed. She studied Elin. "Do you want to talk about it? It's OK if you don't," Mia looked full of genuine concern, "but I won't be shocked by anything. We're all human, bad stuff happens."

Elin couldn't speak. She hadn't expected to hear such calm acceptance. Mia wasn't jumping to conclusions even though she must have a good idea what this was about. Instead, she just sat back and waited. Elin started to tell Mia what had happened; the flow of words increased to a torrent as she relived the dreadful events of yesterday.

Mia sat listening, her presence soothing, "It sounds awful, Elin, what a mess."

"I'm utterly wretched. The only thing I know for sure is that I want Aaron back, that's the only thing that'll help, I know it. I feel so angry with Rachel, she was vile to me, screaming in front of everybody. I know I did wrong, but she can't be making him happy, can she? I hate her and that's awful, I know." Elin paused, part of her knew she was being irrational, but she was too agitated to care. She went on defiantly, "I hate Joe, he's conveniently forgotten about the other women. He's not hurt; he just can't bear the idea of somebody else messing about with his wife – not me, just his wife, his possession. It doesn't matter that he's been unfaithful, probably quite often with somebody else's wife!"

"You're going to have to talk to Joe at some point; he's a human being and deserves that at least." Mia's voice was free from harshness or control, but Elin reacted.

"Joe! I just told you I don't care about him, he brought this on himself. I can't talk to him. Not yet anyway."

Mia said no more, and Elin started pacing around the

room then turned abruptly to face Mia. "I don't know what I would have done without you last night. I know I'm messing up big time, but I can't think straight." Her voice held a hoarse note of despair, "I don't want to outstay my welcome so I'll go now. I'll get your stuff back to you as soon as I can."

Mia protested, "I'm here for you Elin, whenever you want. I've found a new way to feel better about myself and be happy, but maybe now's not the time to talk about it. I'm absolutely certain that things can change for the better. Winter never fails to turn into spring."

ELIN NEEDED PETROL. She found a filling station, pulled into a space and searched for her purse. With her hand poised on the door handle, she looked up and saw Fiona getting out of the car in front of her. She froze, looking down again into her handbag. Did Fiona know what had happened? Had Rachel contacted everybody she knew? Would they be laughing behind her back or, even worse, feeling sorry for her because Aaron had abandoned her? She felt sure the whole world was whispering about them. Pushing her purse back into her bag she started the engine, reversed as quickly as she could and drove away.

"Get a grip, get a grip, get a grip," Elin muttered to herself. She was on the edge of a precipice; at any moment she might fall and be swallowed up into a yawning nothingness. Much of her wanted to fall, to be consumed by blackness so there would be no more pain, no more despair. How could she have come to this point? From the woman who had everything to the woman who had nothing, all in a day. Elin found herself on a dual carriageway. She contemplated the strong buttresses of an overpass and wondered if she'd die quickly if she drove straight into it at speed. Might be better for everybody, especially herself. She was unaware of the warmth of the day and the bright blue sky. Everything was enveloped in a pall of greyness.

A light on the dashboard attracted her attention briefly. Fuel level low, it informed her. Logic reasserted itself, she couldn't continue driving indefinitely. Going home was not an option; she'd head to Hilary's. She didn't want to risk bumping into Joe, so she pulled over and phoned.

"Elin, we've been so worried," Hilary said, sounding anxious.

Elin's eyes filled up again.

"Can I come over? Joe's not there, is he?"

"He's not here, but he's very angry."

"Are you sure he won't come over?"

"His car's still here from yesterday, and Ricky's with him at your house. Ricky promised to let me know if he wants to come here."

Fifteen minutes later, Elin was again in Hilary's kitchen. Hilary bustled around, "Shall I open some wine? Vodka and tonic? Tea?"

"Would a small vodka be OK? I need something to steady myself."

"Coming up," Hilary said as she measured a shot of vodka into a glass, added ice and a splash of tonic before handing it to Elin. "It's a small one."

Elin took a sip while Hilary turned to stir an enormous pot of soup bubbling on the stove. "I thought you said there was no way anybody could find out?"

Elin drained her glass and mutely accepted another. "I feel so worthless, Hilary. Rachel said I'd never see him again, but I know he'll contact me, I just know he will."

"Don't despair Elin, it's such a shock," Hilary said and

took Elin's shaking hands between hers. "You'll feel better soon."

"I don't think so," Elin sniffed. "I feel battered inside and so adrift."

"I can see how much it hurts," Hilary said and squeezed her fingers gently. "Hard to believe that Aaron was so spineless and then Joe so angry, no wonder you're upset. Men!"

Elin didn't respond. Hilary waited a minute before prompting her, "Where did you go last night? I stayed up late thinking you'd phone. You didn't sleep in the car, did you?" Looking at Elin's clothes as if she'd just noticed them she added, "What on earth are you wearing?"

Elin looked down, "Oh, these are Mia's clothes. I finally crashed out at her house."

Hilary gave a sigh of relief, "Glad you were safe."

"Joe was so drunk and out of control. It was awful." Elin's voice trailed away.

Hilary added it all up, "Rachel must have enjoyed telling Joe."

"Dammit, I'm beginning to hate her. That's not right, I know. She ignored Aaron and attacked me as if he had nothing to do with it!"

"Nightmare! There's not much you can do, she's a fact of life and so are the children, poor things. Joe's another story; he's finding out how it feels and he doesn't like it. Do you think he'll come around?"

"Come around? You don't understand! Our old life is over," Elin said, sat forward and repeated, as if to convince herself as much as Hilary, "There's no Joe and Elin anymore."

"Don't be too hasty. You have a nice life with Joe."

"You didn't see him last night. He'll be watching my every move from now on."

"More likely he'll be sorry about losing his temper. He'll want you back."

"Do you think so? I hadn't realised until I met Aaron how far apart we'd drifted. When I tried to talk to him about the late nights, he made me feel I was being stupid. Funny how I often felt stupid around him. I'm not, am I?" Elin's eyes filled up. "I suppose I'm stupid about Aaron, but we felt so good together." Elin started to cry again and reached out for her drink. Hilary put her hand over the glass.

"You're going to feel even worse if you drink any more. Have some soup. We needn't stop talking."

Elin blew her nose, "You sure it won't help? I want to sleep until I'm old, then I wouldn't care anymore."

Hilary ladled soup into two bowls, "Don't worry, you'll have fun again. You'll have no problem finding another man, one who'll treat you better than Joe or Aaron. I'm not fond of Joe but he is your husband and he has his good points. Keep your options open. Now eat."

"Can I stay here tonight, Hilary? I can't face Joe after last night. Maybe I'll feel better tomorrow, I don't know."

"Stay as long as you like. Would you rather be out of the way before the kids come home?"

"They'll wonder why I'm here and I couldn't tell them, could I?"

"My dear, you underestimate the self-centredness of teenagers. You do whatever you like."

Hilary's spare room was large and airy with cream bed-covers on the king-size bed, blackout blinds behind the matching curtains and an en-suite bathroom. Elin cleansed her face with toiletries from Hilary. She heard the kids come in and the hum of voices, then the TV downstairs and snatches of music from the kids' rooms. She flicked through some magazines on the bedside table, but couldn't summon up any interest. She switched off the lamp and closed her eyes.

Another interminable night. She replayed her mental film on an endless loop. She felt battered but had no bruises to show. Elin tried to adopt Hilary's pragmatism but it was impossible. She thought about Mia's optimism and wondered if she would ever develop such a positive viewpoint.

Sounds of the household waking told Elin that another of the longest nights of her life was over. She reached for her phone. Four voice-mails, all from Joe; nine texts, six from Joe. Nothing from Aaron. She deleted everything. She heard Ricky leave, then Jemmie and Finn. Elin wandered downstairs wearing a towelling robe she found hanging behind the bathroom door.

Hilary was sitting curled up watching a morning news programme and nursing a mug of coffee. She heard Elin come in and patted the seat by her side. Elin sat down. "I thought maybe an outing to the Basque Boulangerie for a croissant might help?" Hilary said.

Elin recoiled, "I couldn't face that, I'm not ready. I don't know if I ever will be!"

"Nonsense, you're here with me. That wasn't so hard. You'll have to meet people sometime."

"Really, Hilary. Not today. I know you mean well, but I can't."

"Piddle!" Hilary pouted. "I want an almond croissant, theirs are out of this world."

"I'll make it up to you, I'll buy you a dozen almond croissants, just not today."

Hilary patted her well-padded hips. "Maybe not a dozen,

but I'll hold you to that." She uncurled and led the way into the kitchen. "You'd better give Joe your side of the story soon or he'll make it up for himself and it won't be pretty. He'll paint himself as the good guy and you as the scarlet woman."

Elin nodded disconsolately and Hilary directed her firmly. "Breakfast first then shower and wash your hair, fix your face. I'll find a top of Jemima's that'll look better than that awful T-shirt. Do you think those trousers will do another day? Mine would be too big and Jem's too small." Hilary cracked eggs into a bowl. "Then you're going to drive home and act confidently. It's your home too and you haven't done anything worse than Joe's being doing for years."

Elin followed the instructions and emerged an hour later, makeup hiding the dark shadows under her eyes.

"You look good, Elin. Off you go, there's no point hanging around. You've got to talk to Joe sooner or later and putting it off is going to make it worse."

As Elin made her way slowly to the car she didn't feel at all confident. She would have given anything for the world to go away. Her stomach lurched, but she gritted her teeth and the nausea lost its strength. She felt nothing but emptiness. What was it that Mia had said about winter and spring? It had given her a glimmer of hope, but that was now fading. She sat in the driver's seat, unmoving. Two more texts arrived, both from Joe. With fingers like cotton wool, she managed to insert her key into the ignition and start the car as Hilary waved encouragement from the kitchen window.

13

Joe was in the kitchen with his back to her when Elin entered. He swung round to face her, momentary relief replaced by a hostile stare.

"Decided to come home, did you? Just sail in as if nothing has happened? Boyfriend got no room at his house?" He spat the words out like bullets.

Elin gripped the counter top, Hilary's words echoing in her brain, "Joe, I came to talk to you."

Joe bristled, "You blow my world apart, now you want to talk. What can you say that that harridan hasn't screamed at me already? How could you?" Disdain crept into his voice, "Really? A rugby teacher, all brawn and no brains."

Elin managed to splutter, "If you'd just listen," before she was cut off again.

"Listen to what? I actually defended you, said it wasn't true, I couldn't believe it!" Joe gave a shake of his head. "Don't you know I love you? I've always loved you."

Elin's anger flared, "What do you mean, always loved me? What about the other women? The lipstick on your shirt?"

"Those women weren't important. I didn't care about them!" Joe came towards her.

"Now, at last, he tells me! All the times I wanted to talk about it, you denied everything, made me think I was crazy. You actually called me paranoid and now it's all my fault?" Elin's voice rose to a scream.

Joe regained an icy calm, "I've always done my best to make you happy; what more could you ask for?"

"Joe, you haven't changed a bit. You're not listening. You never have and I'm beginning to think you never will." She silenced him with a wave of her hand and summoned up a note of defiance. "I'm sorry about hurting you, but I refuse to take all the blame. I'm sleeping in the spare room tonight and until we can have a proper conversation about this." Elin's voice suddenly quavered, "Don't try and stop me. If you do I swear I'm going to stay with Mia or Hilary again."

"Hilary, I understand, Ricky's been a good friend these last few days, but Mia?" Joe snorted, "She probably encouraged you!"

Elin swallowed hard, "I'm not getting through to you, am I? I'm exhausted. Just leave it. Maybe things will seem different tomorrow."

Joe had to be content with that crumb of comfort. Elin went upstairs and collected a stack of clothes from their room and took it to the bedroom furthest away. She trawled the internet mindlessly for hours then fell into a doze until evening, when she ventured downstairs. She heard the click of computer keys and crept quietly into the kitchen, but not quietly enough to fool Mutt. She went outside, knelt down, ruffled his soft coat and buried her head in his neck. She gave him his dinner and fed the cats.

Elin dreaded the night. She wanted to be as far away from Joe as possible. She moved quietly, gathering up her phone charger, her laptop and her book, encouraging Alley and Tom to follow as she went upstairs.

The next morning, Joe joined Elin in the garden. "I know we got off to a bad start yesterday, but I've had an idea." He had a hangdog look about him, "Let's go away somewhere; I've looked online, we could go to the Bahamas tomorrow, put all this behind us, make a new start?"

Elin stared at him in horror. The prospect was appalling. She groped for words to convey this without being too harsh. Surely he could understand that if she was sleeping in the spare bedroom, a romantic hideaway wasn't a good idea?

Joe looked at her expectantly, "It would help, Elin, wouldn't it? We could relax, get close again?" He moved towards her.

"I don't think I'm ready for anything like that," she said as her voice trailed off. She avoided his eyes by examining greenfly on the roses. "I'm sorry. I know you mean well. I need to lick my wounds, be around friends."

Joe stiffened. The puppy-dog look was replaced by a scornful half-smile, "I forgot, you're the wounded one, pining after that useless lump of brawn." He raised his voice, "I've got feelings too and I think getting away from here would be the best thing."

Elin yelled back, "Well I don't! I'm not going, end of. Take one of your girlfriends instead!" She turned on her heels and walked back upstairs. The agony of the first few days had turned into a dull, hollow ache. She considered her options. Who of her friends would accept what had happened and still be pleased to see her? Finally she settled on Fiona, and hoped that she had not noticed her strange behaviour at the petrol station,. She hoped even more fervently that Rachel hadn't been in touch with her.

"Hello, Fiona, it's Elin, how are you?"

"Fine thanks. How are you?"

Was that a hint of reserve?

"Are you busy? I was hoping we could get together?"

"Sorry, I've got a lot on today, all this week in fact."

"How about next week?"

There was a short silence.

"I'm not sure. I'll text you, OK?"

"Thanks, Fiona, regards to John. Bye."

Elin closed her eyes. A line had been drawn and Fiona had chosen her side. She watched movies on her laptop until she fell asleep, not hearing Joe arrive home after midnight.

They continued to skirt around each other, and Elin tried not to antagonise him, intimidated by the anger simmering beneath his impassivity. The routine was familiar; Joe's life here; Elin's life there. She trawled the internet for jobs without success, the summer holidays slipping away. Each day she hoped for contact from Aaron, each day she was disappointed. She resisted the urge to find out where he lived.

Mia had been away, but one day Elin received a text from her inviting her over. Then Elin returned to her job search with something close to energy. A teaching assistant's post to cover a year 6 class, suddenly available due to illness, closing date that day. Elin had no experience of children of this age, but completed the application hastily and hit send. She was shocked when a response arrived in her inbox just before 5 p.m., asking if she could come for an interview the following afternoon. She realised they must be desperate, but then so was she. She typed an affirmative response and closed her laptop.

Elin felt a rush of expectancy as she stood on Mia's doorstep, a white cymbidium in her hands.

"Good grief, you've lost weight," gasped Mia.

Elin thrust the plant at her, "This is for you, you can put it in the garden after it finishes flowering. And the clothes I borrowed, thanks again, you saved me that night!"

"It's lovely, but you shouldn't have. How about a milky coffee? You look as if you need feeding up."

"Do I look that bad?" Elin pushed her hair back off her face and peered in the small mirror propped on a shelf.

"I'm exaggerating, but I do detect a certain lack of oomph."

Elin watched as her friend put heaped spoonfuls of instant coffee into two mugs and added frothy milk, boiled in a saucepan. Elin took a mug and carried it to the sofa before sipping gingerly. "Actually, it's not bad. It feels comforting."

"Just thought you needed it. How are you?"

Elin held the warm mug between her hands and leaned forward. "Aaron hasn't been in touch. Oh Mia, I'm devastated. I keep thinking about finding his address and driving past the house, but I know I shouldn't." She sipped some more coffee and went on, "Things at home are awful in a different way. Joe is so angry. Then suddenly he flips and tries to win me back, which if anything is worse. I avoid him as much as possible. Hilary says to stay there and make the best of it." Elin looked mournfully at her friend, "You are so lucky to have Daniel, I envy you, you're both so happy. I don't think I'll ever find that again."

"It sounds as if you and Joe are bringing out the worst in each other," Mia mused. "Joe's had an awful shock. He had no idea that you weren't happy, then all this." Mia waved her hand expansively. "He can't do anything right, can he? Maybe you could do something? Change the way you're thinking? It would be easier than trying to change him."

"Will anything bring back my feelings for him?" Elin sounded confused.

Mia smiled gently, "You were unhappy so you went for excitement with Aaron and security with Joe. But that hasn't worked, has it?"

Elin verged on sullen when she replied, "I didn't realise Joe was playing the field. When I found out it was a shock, but I thought if it worked for him it would work for me too."

"I'm not criticising you Elin, just saying it's not good to be dependent on someone else for happiness. Perhaps if you take more control you'll feel better?"

"Do you think so? Sounds like a self-help book: you read it, you try it, and a week later you've forgotten most of it."

"You sound so cynical, Elin, I've never heard you like this before."

"That's because I've never been hurt like this before."

"I'm sure things will change, Elin. I'm happy now but I've struggled many times."

Elin could feel her friend's support. She exhaled slowly, "I knew I could count on you, Mia. Not always in the way I expected, but thank you." Her eyes filled and she did her best to suppress the tears.

There was a knock at the door. Mia frowned, "Wonder who that is? I'm not expecting anybody." She walked towards the door. "What a nice surprise! Come in, Elin's here."

Then Elin heard Chrissie's voice, "If you're busy I'll just go on home. No problem."

"Elin's feeling down in the dumps," Mia drew Chrissie inside, "Come and help cheer her up."

"Hi, good to see you again." It was painful for Elin to remember the happy times.

"You too. How are you, and Fiona, and Aaron? It was so much fun working with you three." Chrissie curls bounced as she flopped onto a floor cushion.

Mia glanced at Elin, "A lot has happened, I'm not sure that Elin is ready to talk about it."

"It's OK. I'd like Chrissie to know. She knows Aaron." Elin faltered, "But will you tell her? Perhaps that'll help me see things more clearly."

Chrissie's face was a picture of concern, "Sorry I butted in. Are you sure it's OK if I stay?" Seeing assent in Elin's eyes she handed over a paper bag. "Let's share these, hope nobody's on a diet?"

They sat with a plate of fresh doughnuts in front of them. Mia launched into the story, conveying sympathy for Elin as well as concern for the others. It was weird to hear someone else relating the facts. Elin helped herself to a doughnut. Chrissie paid rapt attention to every detail, and when Mia had finished she turned to Elin and hugged her.

"You must feel so hurt and it's awful for everybody, but you are the one right in front of me, so you're the one getting the hug! What a mess. I liked Aaron, he seemed genuinely nice, just like you. I didn't see this coming."

Elin latched on to the positive comment about Aaron and felt validated. Chrissie and Mia rambled on, sharing their hurts, then funny incidents too. Elin contributed the Freudian slip in the Yelverton and felt her spirits lift. Chrissie checked her watch, "Goodness, it's seven thirty already, you two must think I'm never going. Thank you for trusting me with your troubles, Elin. It can't have been easy." She turned to Mia, "How about inviting Elin to a meeting? I think she'd enjoy it."

Once Chrissie was gone, Elin also decided it was time to go home. "Thanks so much, I've enjoyed myself for the first time in ages. You made me laugh again."

"What could be more important than helping a friend through a rough patch?" Mia said.

It amazed Elin that there had been no "I told you so" from Mia since everything had fallen apart. As she walked towards the door she stopped, "What was that about inviting me to a meeting?"

"Chrissie thinks everybody would find it interesting," Mia's voice trailed away.

Elin was intrigued; Mia wasn't usually so reticent, "Just tell me, I can always say no."

"Do you remember when I stopped complaining about teaching? You noticed something different about me? I'm a Buddhist now. Chrissie wanted you to come to a Buddhist meeting."

Elin's jaw dropped; orange robed monks with shaved heads came to mind, not bottles of wine and pink thongs. "A Buddhist meeting? I'm not religious, I haven't been inside a church, except for weddings, for years."

"That's why I didn't ask," replied Mia mildly. "It's not that weird, really. We discuss life and how to deal with difficulties."

"That doesn't sound so bad," Elin said, being polite. Mia had been so supportive, she couldn't refuse outright. "Let me know and I'll see if I can come."

"There's one next week. Maybe we could talk about it and walk the dog together this weekend? We can't sit around and eat doughnuts all the time!"

The mention of a walk reminded her of Mutt and the things she had to do in preparation for the impending interview. As she drove home the sky didn't seem so grey.

14

E lin wanted a job, any job, but in the interview, at the local education authority offices, she failed to project any enthusiasm until questioned about drama. She woke up just in time. Bright-eyed she told the bored interview panel about her recent success and brought the room alive. After explaining the need to fill the vacancy urgently, the chairperson asked her to wait outside. He emerged, smiling.

"Mrs. Petersen, we're offering you the job. If you accept we'll fast track the formalities so that you can start on the first day of term, this coming Tuesday."

It was hard to believe. Elin stayed glued to her laptop: first the website for River Park Primary, then anything about 10/11yr olds. She left the house for a quick drive to find the school, an imposing two-storey red brick Victorian building surrounded by tarmac with not a blade of grass to be seen. Elin felt a flicker of enthusiasm for this new challenge.

On Tuesday she felt as nervous as a new pupil in reception. She was to assist Mrs. Hargreaves, middle-aged, with a cloud of fading auburn hair and a frazzled expression. Mrs. Hargreaves soon recognised Elin's strengths and didn't dwell on her lack of experience with younger children.

The first pay cheque was a shock — about half of what Elin was used to — but she had no marking or lesson plans to do, so it was fair enough. Mutt had benefited and the long evening walks helped Elin sleep, still hiding away in her own guest bedroom. Joe prowled around, angry and resentful or wearily reproachful. Elin was doing her best; when Joe would put his arms around her she had begun to relax, his familiar shape and the well-known toothpaste and aftershave combination lulled her senses. However, Joe couldn't be undemanding no matter how often she explained that this in itself was progress. Joe pressed her for more, demanding sensual kisses, sending Elin back into her protective shell. The days passed, tense, strained.

About a month into the new job, she was walking to her car in the school car park when she heard the familiar ping heralding the arrival of a text on her phone. A number she didn't recognise popped up, but when she opened the message her world stood still. She reached her car, steadied herself and looked at the text again.

"Not my phone. Missing u. Coffee, 120 Commercial St, Newton Sat 11 o'clock? I'll wait. Don't reply. A."

With shaking hands, she unlocked the car and got in. After all this time! She closed her eyes, excitement tingling all the way to the tips of her fingers and toes. Aaron hadn't forgotten her! She leaned back, savouring the moment. Then she remembered that Joe would be watching her and there could be no more claims of accidental meetings. She drew a jerky, stressed gasp. This was why Aaron had suggested meeting in Newton; she had no doubt that she'd be there.

. . .

MUTT SAT in the back of the car on Saturday morning, drool dripping in anticipation of a long walk in unfamiliar territory. He was going to be disappointed. She parked in the Newton Centre's multi-storey car park, opened the windows a few inches, gave him an enormous doggy chew, which claimed on the wrapper to keep a big dog occupied for hours, locked the car and walked away. As she waited for the lift, frenzied barking broke out and she could see Mutt hurling himself against the windows. She headed back to the car as the barking changed to pathetic howling. Minutes later she was walking down four flights of stairs with Mutt in tow. He'd refused to enter the lift, spooked by the automatic doors and small, enclosed space. She made her way through the throng of shoppers, nerves on edge, apprehension seeping into her joyful anticipation.

"What a beautiful dog," a passer-by commented as Elin hesitated outside the coffee shop. Relief flooded through Elin as she heard Aaron's voice. "Yes, he's a beautiful creature, isn't he?" He bent to fondle Mutt's head then turned to Elin, "Coffee?"

Elin nodded, "But I can't take the dog inside." She felt lightheaded, dizzy with adrenaline. Her misgivings were fading fast and she desperately wanted to feel his arms around her.

"I'll get it, what do you want?" His grin made Elin weak as she struggled to restrain Mutt who'd seen a portly little pug scurrying by. Within minutes, Aaron was back and, lowering their voices, they agreed to rendezvous at the car park exit. Elin tossed a casual goodbye over her shoulder and sauntered away slowly, but almost dropped her cup when Mutt spied an apricot miniature poodle and set off in hot pursuit. She didn't see the smile on Aaron's face as he stood watching her, sipping his coffee slowly.

Elin's gut was filled with churning uncertainty, her shoulders were rigid and she rubbed the itchy skin on the inside of her wrists as she followed Aaron through winding country lanes until their cars were parked side by side once again.

"Sweetheart," Aaron whispered as he stepped forward. He held her face between his palms, then slid his arms down her body and drew her close. Elin felt herself softening as they kissed gently, reacquainting themselves, and her tension drifted away like dandelion seeds in the breeze. Their kisses grew more passionate and more urgent. Aaron drew her towards the car and she followed, her pain and disappointment melting away. Seconds later, Aaron pulled a rug from the back seat. Elin froze. His action seemed so calculated it felt tawdry. Her hands fell to her sides. "I can't."

Aaron pulled her to him again. Mouth close to her ear he whispered endearments as he held her close. They stood locked together; Elin felt his ragged breaths, inhaled the faint odour of sweat lingering on his tracksuit, floated in the sensations awakened by the closeness of their bodies. Elin didn't doubt his desire for her, but he accepted her reluctance, understood this meeting was different. Rachel and Joe were constant grey shadows lurking in the outer reaches of Elin's consciousness.

Their goodbyes were not prolonged. Aaron whispered that he would contact her again as soon as he could. She believed him absolutely.

School was a joy and Elin absorbed new experiences like a sponge. The headmaster, Mr. Roberts, was popular – his innovative ideas less so. School assemblies had become stale and Mrs. Hargraves was open to Elin's fresh ideas, eventually suggesting she coordinate the Autumn Concert. However, Elin soon ran into trouble and began to doubt herself again.

She had tried to keep away from Hilary, afraid of becoming a bore, moaning about the state of her marriage and having to keep her own counsel about Aaron again. This development needed tending in silence before bursting out into the spotlight with Hilary or anyone else.

Elin was grateful that, on the occasional dog walk with Mia, the subject of Aaron wasn't raised at all, neither was a Buddhist meeting. Chrissie was busy getting her daughter, Hope, off to college. Perhaps Elin would ask her for advice about the concert once Hope had settled down.

At lunchtime on Friday 6th October, the school secretary, Mrs. Dang, looking surprised, summoned Elin to her office. "There's a call for you, he said it was urgent so I came right over to get you."

Elin followed her ample form down the corridor and picked up the phone with trepidation. Who would phone her at school? What could have happened? "Hello, Elin Petersen here."

"It's me," Aaron said, practically whispering. "Can you get away tomorrow? Same place as before? Can you find it? We could go on somewhere else? Please, Elin."

Elin paused, checking that nobody could overhear. The secretary had realised from Elin's expression that it wasn't bad news and had thoughtfully left the room. Still Elin spoke formally, "I'll do my best, say 10.30?"

"Wonderful! I'll be there at ten. I'll wait. See you tomorrow. Bye."

Elin replaced the receiver and left the room slowly, thanking Mrs. Dang who was hovering outside. Here was that fluttery anticipation again, how she'd missed it. She wanted to laugh and dance and clap her hands, but she had to be practical. What on earth could she say she was doing tomorrow? She racked her brains for an alibi. No way could she ask Hilary or Mia to help. Who else?

She remembered Jeannie, but they hadn't been in touch for months and Elin no longer had her details. How many times had Jeannie turned to Elin, crying over a shared bottle of plonk, bemoaning her love life? Long since divorced, Jeannie's most recent entanglement had been with a married man. Elin grimaced as she recalled how judgemental she had been. The shoe was decidedly on the other foot now. Pulling out her laptop, Elin tried Facebook, but drew a blank. After trying Friends Reunited Elin let out a whoop: there she was! Elin made contact, pleading with Jeannie to contact her urgently. By the time school finished, Jeannie had replied asking what on earth was so urgent. Elin dialled, hoping against hope that Jeannie would pick up the phone.

"It's Elin, still alive! You OK?"

"Hey, good to hear your voice! Didn't you know I moved to Newton?"

After the usual general catch up, Elin gabbled out her story. Every now and again Jeannie interjected a heartfelt "Poor you!" or "I know". Elin felt she'd found the one person who really understood. "The thing is, Jeannie, I need an alibi for tomorrow?"

There was a short pause. "El, I hope you know what you're doing." Another pause. "What do you want me to say?"

Elin knew Joe was watching her like a hawk these days. "I'll tell Joe that you invited me over tomorrow. If he phones, say I'm there with you but in the toilet or something. Be creative, say it's a bad line and get cut off! I don't know."

Suddenly Elin had a brainwave, "How about we're shopping for your new house, maybe a sofa?"

"That sounds OK, Elin, but what if Joe calls you?"

Elin thought for a moment, "I'll 'accidentally' leave my phone at home. Then if he's suspicious he'd have to phone you."

Jeannie sighed, "It could go horribly wrong, but OK."

Elin put her phone on charge that evening, dropping her scarf over it to hide it from view. She made sure the notepad beside the home phone had Jeannie's name and number written down clearly amid other reminder notes. When she told Joe about sofa shopping he gave her a long look but made no comment.

Saturday promised to be a grey day. Elin brewed coffee and made herself a cheese omelette. She wiped the pan with some kitchen roll and put it back in the cupboard before eating quickly, standing at the counter. She was sure Joe was on high alert. After finishing the omelette, she made and ate a slice of toast and left the crumby plate and buttery knife in the sink.

"There's coffee left in the pot," Elin called out to Joe as she went upstairs to get ready, but there was no response. A short while later she emerged in her newest jeans, several layered tops, and carrying a warm down waistcoat in a flattering shade of emerald. Downstairs again, she pulled on her newest Uggs and picked up her smart black raincoat to throw into the back of the car with the waistcoat. She was dressed suitably for a day's shopping, but also for spending time out in the elements.

Elin stood undecided. It was 9.30 and time to go; would leaving a note or calling goodbye be the more natural thing to do? Nothing felt natural anymore. The decision was taken out of her hands when she heard Joe coming downstairs.

She waited until he came into the kitchen, unshaven and bleary-eyed.

"I'm off to Jeannie's. You look rough, late night?"

Joe responded grumpily, "Nothing a shower and a shave won't put to rights." He turned to fill his mug and Elin made her way to the door without another word, brushing his cheek with her lips as she passed.

Aaron was waiting in the Land Rover at their meeting place. She quickly slid in next to him and he kissed her tentatively at first. She was exquisitely sensitive to his touch and as he caressed her, shivers ran up and down her spine. Aaron drew back. Elin looked at him, her eyes large with surprise, her body taut and expectant. He spoke urgently, holding her close.

"Let's not grope around like a couple of teenagers. We want more, don't we?"

Elin looked at him in amazement, had she heard right? Did he just say he wanted more? More than a hole and corner affair involving lies and deception?

"Let's find a hotel room?"

Elin ran her hands over his jawline and through his hair in delight. She murmured, "I've got all day."

"Rachel's taking the kids to her mother's for the weekend; she was stressed, needed a break, so I can stay as long as you can."

Aaron smiled at her. Elin felt a shard of ice penetrate her gut. She drew back and her eyes narrowed. That one throwaway reference to Rachel changed everything. Elin understood for the first time the expression about scales falling from eyes. Aaron transformed in that split second from someone she idolised into a despicable human being, selfish to the core. She'd been deceiving herself all along.

"I'm not going anywhere with you Aaron, not today or

any other day. After all the hurt, the anguish of waiting to hear from you, I've realised you're not worth waiting for. I was willing to put you first, but the only person you put first is yourself. You're not willing to leave your wife and children, but you're selfish enough to carry on lying and cheating. Your wife is tired and stressed, and instead of trying to help her you've just taken advantage of the situation. I've no respect for you. You are utterly despicable."

Elin wanted nothing more to do with him. She got out of his car without a backward glance. It wasn't an effort. It was exactly what she wanted to do and it felt right. She walked calmly to her car, took a deep breath to settle herself before starting the engine, then drove off feeling light and free.

As she drove towards Jeannie's house she laughed out loud: her complete transformation was hard to believe. She felt powerful instead of powerless. She had hurt his ego and had been glad. How had this happened? She realised with a jolt that it had been his willingness to take advantage of Rachel's absence. It was about the solidarity of women. She didn't want anything to do with a man who preferred to let his wife run to her mother for support than help her himself. She was relieved that she still had standards.

She had to admire Rachel, she had fought and she had won. Whatever happened to their marriage, the fault could no longer be laid at Elin's door. An enormous burden had been lifted from her shoulders, one she had not been aware she was carrying. She couldn't be bothered to think about Aaron any more. He so clearly wasn't worth it.

She drove along and contemplated her own marriage. Despite the clarity of her thoughts about Aaron, she couldn't see the way forward with Joe. Maybe it would be easier now? A clear conscience was a good start.

Elin pulled in and rummaged in her handbag for

Jeannie's address. Her phone was still at home so she had to ask for directions several times before she recognised the battered pale blue VW beetle parked outside Jeannie's new home. When she opened the door Jeannie almost dropped the plate she was holding, "Elin? What happened?"

Elin hugged her friend with relief, "The alibi won't be needed after all."

A frown flitted across Jeannie's face. "He didn't let you down did he? That Aaron guy?"

Elin laughed. "I'll tell you while you put the kettle on."

Jeannie bustled about tidying away papers and magazines. She was the divorced mother of Miles and Jonathan, both grown up and independent. She was older than most of Elin's friends, but just as much fun and quite ditzy at times. She gave Elin a quick tour of the house. Upstairs was an office/spare bedroom, Jeannie's own bedroom and the bathroom. Downstairs was a kitchen, old and to be replaced as soon as Jeannie could afford it, and a cosy living room with scented candles flickering in the hearth. Elin flopped onto the battered sofa and looked around taking in the array of books, *objets d'art*, framed photos and mementos of times and places in Jeannie's life.

Jeannie brought in a tray of coffee and biscuits saying, "Don't keep me in suspense, what's going on?"

Elin marvelled at the difference between this morning's telling and previous tearful occasions, even seeing the funny side of her Freudian slip.

Jeannie responded by clapping her hands in glee. "You are so lucky to have come to your senses so soon. I suffered for years thinking I was happy with Gareth."

Elin recalled her frustration with Jeannie as the affair had dragged on, "But it was harder for you, seeing him every day at work."

Jeannie shrugged, "It's over and done with and I'm glad yours is over too. Good on you."

"Do you fancy actually doing my alibi?" asked Elin, laughing. "We could have lunch and look at sofas?"

Just then Jeannie's phone rang. They looked at each other, eyes wide. Jeannie answered. "Hello Joe, she forgot her phone? She's right here; do you want to talk to her?"

Jeannie passed the phone to Elin, "Hi. I hadn't missed it. It doesn't matter, we're just off to look at sofas then lunch and shopping."

She listened again, "No, I don't know how long we'll be. See you later, bye."

They let out a joint sigh of relief. It had been a close call – but a clear conscience was a joy in itself.

15

E lin was struggling with the Autumn Concert. Only Tamsin Edwards, in charge of a year 5 class, and Nathan Protheroe, year 4, supported her ideas, and her position as teaching assistant meant that her influence was minimal. On Friday 13th, Elin was on edge even though she wasn't superstitious. Maybe it was the darker days or the early Halloween decorations, but something about Joe during the past weeks had made her very uneasy. He watched her constantly. He wanted their old life back yet couldn't let things move along gently while they recovered from the recent trauma.

Elin was tired and hurried to clear up after class. She picked up her bag and ran through the rain towards the Mercedes. She was struggling to extricate her keys when she heard Nathan starting his car nearby. It was an opportunity to give him details about the show – the timing was perfect, he'd have the whole weekend to mull over her suggestions. She ran over and tapped on his passenger window. "Glad I caught you, those printouts? For the concert? Won't take a minute to explain," she shouted.

Nathan rolled down the window, "What's that you said? I couldn't hear."

Elin thrust the papers through the window and repeated her request.

"You're getting soaked, jump in. You get precisely two minutes," Nathan responded with a grin and Elin handed him the papers.

"See this article? The exciting bit is this.... "

There was a sharp knock on the window. To her horror, Elin saw Joe's face looming towards her. She wound the window down, "Won't be a minute, I was just talking to Nathan about the concert."

Joe's face was twisted, he ignored Nathan and hissed at her, "You expect me to believe that? I watched you tap on the window of his car and ask him to let you in, don't deny it!"

"It's work! I was getting wet, that's why I got in. You're jumping to conclusions." Elin opened the door and got out; she spoke over her shoulder, "Sorry to embarrass you, Nathan. This is my husband Joe. I'd better go."

Nathan looked shocked, "Will you be OK, Elin? Shall I explain?"

She shook her head, "Thanks, but I'll be fine." She got into her own car leaving Joe standing there like a raging bull. He followed her, bending over and speaking with icy control.

"I'm not as easily fooled as I used to be. Can't keep your hands to yourself, can you?"

"I'm not going to argue here. I'm going home." Her voice shook, but she didn't hesitate before driving off. How self-righteous he was, she fumed. She'd never spied on him. Even when she had her suspicions, she'd never followed him or used apps to check his whereabouts, and now he was stalking her.

Joe shadowed Elin all the way home. She slammed on her brakes, marched into the kitchen and dropped her things on the table. She turned to confront him, "How dare you make a scene at my school? There's nothing 'going on'. I was sheltering from the rain. You embarrassed me and you won't believe my explanation."

Joe slumped into a chair, head in hands, "All this is tearing me apart and you won't let me make it up to you."

Elin sighed and summoned up the last dregs of her patience. She spoke softly, "I keep telling you I need time. I promised myself I wasn't going to pretend anymore. Pretending was what got us into this mess in the first place."

Joe's face reddened, "Time? To get over being dumped by that idiot!" He banged his fist on the table then shoved his chair back and stood. "It's driving me demented!" Elin backed away as he advanced, bellowing, "We had a good life! I don't understand, time for what?"

Elin moved to the doorway, turned and said, "Why does it have to be your way? Some macho pride thing? I stayed! That was me trying, don't you understand? But I can't try any more, I can't." Tears trickled down her cheeks.

"Elin, I love you." Joe held himself rigid, arms by his sides.

"Then why did you lie to me? You said I was crazy, imagining things."

"I'm sorry. Those women meant nothing, nothing at all."

"But you lied to me, over and over. So it felt OK to lie to you. You made me think I was paranoid." Elin's voice trembled, "You were OK with that?"

Joe looked away and muttered, "I thought you were happy."

"You decided what I didn't know wouldn't hurt me, but

when I did the same it hurt, didn't it? Why was it OK for you?"

"Can't we try again, Elin? Let's go to the sun, let's get away from here..."

Elin spoke slowly and clearly, "You're still not listening. I'm going to move out for a while. I'll let you know where I am. I have to do this otherwise I will have a breakdown. I'm sorry."

She walked upstairs to her bedroom and wondered what to do and where to go. What about the dog and the cats? She felt exhausted. It was too much to deal with tonight. She'd figure it out in the morning

Elin got up after a night of fitful sleep. She took the cats on her lap and promised to come back for them as soon as she could. She bundled up in warm clothes, planning on taking Mutt out, worrying how he would cope when she left. Before setting off she checked into RightMove and sent emails to local agents asking about rental flats that allowed pets.

It was still eerily quiet, the misty morning adding to the unreality of her life. She had to do something, go somewhere. Hilary and Mia had busy lives and partners. At last she dialled Jeannie's number. When she heard her friend's cheerful voice, she could hardly speak.

"Elin?" Jeannie's voice was immediately concerned, "You OK?"

"Not really, Joe and I had a massive row last night. Could I stay with you for a bit?" Elin's voice wavered.

"Of course you can."

"I'm sorry to be a nuisance." Again, her voice wobbled, "Can I come today?"

"Of course!" Jeannie continued brightly, "Come whenever you like, I'll make up the spare bed."

. . .

FOR NEARLY TWO weeks Elin enjoyed the holiday atmosphere, cosy nights by the fire in PJs with Jeannie – though space in the house was at a premium. Elin didn't think Joe would remember to care for the animals so she went straight from school every day to exercise Mutt and feed the cats. She spent time with Hilary at weekends, went to the cinema alone and visited Mia when she was available. She looked at a couple of flats, but nothing was suitable. She took fish and chips to Mia and Dan one evening and the three of them settled with trays in the living room. They ate quickly. Daniel stood up and collected the plates, "Sorry to hear about you moving out, Elin."

"The trouble is I'll outstay my welcome with Jeannie soon, though she's too warm-hearted to tell me. Now I'm a gooseberry here."

Daniel put her mind at rest, "Don't worry, I have stuff to do, I'll leave you two to catch up." He picked up his mug and headed upstairs.

"He's so nice, wish I had somebody like him."

Mia was about to respond when the phone rang. Elin couldn't avoid hearing her own name mentioned as the conversation drew to a close.

"That was Chrissie, she sent her love," Mia said after she hung up.

"How is she? I need her help again, but I don't want to be a nuisance."

"It'll be fine, don't worry about it. But before I forget, she wanted me to invite you to a meeting at her house on Thursday evening."

Elin looked surprised, "To her house? Where does she live?"

"She and Jared live out in the sticks, it's hard to find. You could come here? We could eat, then go together if you don't mind driving?"

"A Buddhist meeting? I'm not sure, but I'd like to talk to her and it'd keep me out of Jeannie's hair." Elin wrinkled her nose, "But I take Mutt out after school."

"Don't worry, it doesn't start until 7.30." Mia was smiling again, "You might even enjoy it!"

Elin laughed, "OK, why not? Next Thursday, about six o'clock?" The phone rang again, and Elin reluctantly rose to go.

"Thanks for the fish and chips. See you Thursday." Mia picked up the phone as Elin got her things and left.

As Elin drove back to Jeannie's, she remembered her mother's favourite saying that fresh fish and visitors both stink after three days; she'd been at Jeannie's almost three weeks.

On Thursday they arrived early and had a tour of Chrissie and Jared's house, an old farmhouse even bigger than Joe and Elin's place. Thick stone walls, mullioned windows and massive fireplaces gave an air of stability and permanence, yet Chrissie had brought air and light into all the rooms. There were traditional furnishings, but without heaviness. Chrissie's warm nature shone through in lamps of all shapes and sizes that cast a mellow glow throughout the house. Elin would happily have spent hours admiring every detail, but the antique front doorbell jangled before she had raised the topic of the autumn concert, reminding them of the purpose of the evening.

Elin was ushered into the main living room along with the new arrivals and told to sit anywhere she liked. She tucked herself into a corner and studied each person as they gathered with handshakes and hugs. Young, old, men, women, sophisticated, scruffy: it was difficult to see what brought this assortment of people together. The last to arrive, apologising profusely, was a middle-aged man with full Rasta dreadlocks. The group started chanting. Mia handed Elin a card with the words of the chant but Elin decided just to listen. Later, everyone introduced themselves, then Chrissie encouraged them to share their thoughts on the importance of gratitude, a concept that Elin had never thought about previously. She listened intently, intrigued and entertained. Gales of laughter erupted frequently, once in response to a self-deprecating comment from an elegant young woman called Yoko, yet moments later Elin observed sensitivity towards a young student suffering from crippling anxiety. She was surprised when the meeting ended that most people crowded into the kitchen. Elin took the opportunity to compliment Yoko on her outfit, praise that Yoko laughed off, more concerned that Elin had a ride home from the meeting.

"So, what did you think?" asked Mia as they got into the car.

"It was great seeing the house and Chrissie suggested meeting next week about the concert."

"What about the rest?" Mia persisted.

"It wasn't what I expected," Elin paused, considering her response. "I loved the discussion bit but I'm not sure about the chanting. Is that what you were doing when I stayed with you? I heard your voice, but I thought you were singing."

"I didn't realise you'd heard. Sorry, I tried to be quiet."

"Oh, it wasn't a problem. It soothed me; I was in a terrible state that night." She shuddered at the memory.

"That reminds me, how is Joe doing?" Mia asked.

"I think he's avoiding me, he knows I go to the house every day after school. We text."

"Poor guy, he's suffering too," Mia reminded her quietly, then changed the subject.

The next day a call came from the estate agent about a garden flat newly available to rent. Elin traded playground duty to view it at lunchtime, fearing that something sounding that good would be snapped up quickly.

A miniscule, shared hallway led to a private front door. Inside the flat was another tiny hallway with doorways off to a single bedroom and the bathroom. Directly ahead was a glass door leading to an airy kitchen and living space. Elin glimpsed a walled garden accessed via the little utility room off the kitchen. It was completely dog proof. Elin turned to the agent and said without a second though, "I'll take it."

That afternoon she signed the papers and expedited the move.

16

Joe was shocked when Elin rang to tell him about the flat. He'd thought she'd come home soon. After Mia's reminder about him hurting too, she spoke softly.

"The lease is only for six months, Joe, you knew I needed a break. Let's go for a drink next week, say Thursday? Maybe dinner too?"

Joe hesitated, then said, "I suppose that'll have to do. How about the Red Lion in town?"

Elin appreciated the effort he was making, "That sounds lovely, 6.30 OK?"

"6.30 is fine. I've heard they have a new chef."

Elin gathered up all her courage, "The flat isn't furnished so I'll need to collect a few things on Saturday, is that OK?" She held her breath. Another pause before Joe spoke.

"OK, what time are you coming?"

"I'll let you know, if that's alright?" She hesitated before the big ask, "Oh, I thought it'd be easier if I took Mutt as well as the cats. What do you think?"

Elin waited as Joe struggled. Eventually he responded, "I didn't think you'd have space for the dog?"

"The garden has high walls so it should work."

"If you say so, Elin, if you say so," Joe grumbled.

"I'll see you Thursday, 6.30 definitely."

Saturday morning found her, Jeannie following, walking from room to room, deciding what to take from the house that was still technically her home. She needed a bed and a couple of comfortable chairs, bedding and some towels. She didn't want to upset Joe, especially as he had opted to be out of the house. A blue van pulled into the driveway promptly at 10.30 and two young men piled out. After the van was loaded, Elin made them all sandwiches, including Jeannie who had spent the time putting Elin's clothes, shoes and bags into her VW Beetle, now packed to the roof. They gathered together bits and pieces from the bathrooms and kitchen that Elin would need and Joe wouldn't miss.

The morning had been punctuated by mournful meows from the cats in their carriers and outbreaks of frenzied barking from Mutt in the back garden. Elin took a last look around. She had been happy in this house. Would she ever live here again? Only time would tell. Even now she couldn't bear to spoil the overall effect and had picked only those items whose absence was barely noticeable. Would it register with Joe that she had taken only one or two of her favourite things; an antique chair from her father's old home; two framed abstract prints of no great value and, carefully wrapped, two of each of their collection of modern stemmed glasses? Basic plates, bowls and mugs, two sharp knives, a few place settings of cutlery and three saucepans completed her haul. Her decision felt right. She needed the basic necessities, but she already had the essential element: her freedom.

The van drew away and Jeannie was waiting. Elin loaded the cat cages then made a final tour of her precious garden before bringing a frantic Mutt to join them on the journey to their new home.

Elin felt full of energy. The furniture had been placed in the right rooms and the van had gone. Piles of clothes covered the bare single bed and the living room was jam-packed with boxes. Alley and Tom were still confined to their carriers and voiced their displeasure constantly as Mutt happily investigated every inch of the small garden.

Elin popped out to buy the cheapest kettle, toaster and microwave she could find as Jeannie went in search of food.

When Elin returned she'd added a small TV and a cafetiere to her concept of basic necessities. The cats demanded their freedom and Elin opened a tin of their favourite food, emptying half of it into each of their familiar dishes. They emerged cautiously.

As Jeannie and Elin sat on the window seat, cupping their hands around mugs of tea, Alley and Tom prowled suspiciously.

"Does Hilary know you're here?" asked Jeannie, still drinking tea and now stroking the two cats.

"Oops, no, I've been so taken up with sorting this," Elin waved her hand indicating the whole chaotic scene. "I'll text her now, and Mia too."

Jeannie sat comforting the cats until it was time for more work.

They decided to focus on the bedroom first. Elin had remembered to bring single bed linen, though the cream pattern, elegant in her old house, now looked drab against the grey walls and swirly old curtains. She crammed as many of her clothes as possible into the built-in wardrobe and piled the rest on the floor – fortunately the cord carpet was almost new. A tower of shoeboxes teetered against a wall, and a small table and the antique chair completed the furnishings. The back of the chair was soon covered with sweaters while the table held makeup and hair products.

The same grey cord covered the floor in the living room, except for a laminate square demarcating the kitchen area. The radiators were now cranking out some serious heat with Alley and Tom stretched out on the carpet nearby.

"Let's put my chair where the cats are, Jeannie, it must be the warmest place." Together they dragged the comfiest of the two Ikea chairs close to the cats and placed the other nearby, with a low table between them. They filled the fitted bookshelves and propped up the prints until Elin could decide where she wanted them. She'd forgotten a hammer and tacks anyway, not to mention the necessary permission from the landlord.

They put a slatted wooden picnic table and a couple of folding chairs in the kitchen. Suddenly they were startled by a tap on the window; they could just make out a woman's face by the light of the streetlamp. Then came a questioning voice, "Is that you Elin?"

"It's Hilary," Elin squealed in excitement. "A visitor! How wonderful."

She rushed to the door, remembering to close it behind her to keep the cats inside before opening the main front door.

Hilary thrust a carrier bag at Elin, "Put this in the fridge for later, doesn't need a corkscrew!"

"Champagne! Thank you, Hilary, what fun I'm having."

They took a quick tour of the flat, with Hilary exclaiming that it was perfect, if a tad small, enthusing about the great location. Then Elin remembered Mutt, still outside.

"How could I forget him?" Elin filled his bowl full of

food then opened the back door. Mutt flew in, wagging his beautiful tail and greeting each of the women with great joy. He found his food, wolfed it down then flopped on his bed, which almost filled the utility room, watching them closely, but staying quiet.

"The excitement seems to have worn him out. That's a first," Elin said gratefully.

"Time for the bubbly? I brought snacks," Hilary said as she busied herself in the kitchen, putting olives and nuts into bowls, slicing salami and opening a tray of veggies with hummus. Elin opened an enormous packet of crisps for scooping up salsa. Jeannie cut the Italian bread into large chunks. Finally, Hilary brought in the champagne.

"A toast?" suggested Jeannie. "To good friends?"

They clinked glasses, two flutes and a wine goblet, then sat down, Elin insisting her two guests take the chairs while she settled on cushions on the floor. Jeannie entertained them with her internet dating experiences and Elin consumed most of the champagne. She protested loudly when Jeannie made a move to go.

"Do stay longer, it's Sunday tomorrow!"

"It's been a long day. Shall we clear before I go?" suggested Jeannie, gesturing towards the war zone of dishes and half empty packages.

"I'll help Elin with that," Hilary said as she rose to her feet and gave Jeannie a hug.

Alone at last, Elin walked the few paces to the back door and let Mutt out. She stood, making sure the cats didn't get out, until he scuttled back inside when he heard the bangs of exploding fireworks.

"That's why you were quiet, Mutt! I'm sorry you're scared, but fireworks' night will be over soon." She ruffled his silky head affectionately, "I've missed you and Alley and Tom too."

In the morning, the cats snuggled up, Elin was woken by Mutt whining. It was cold. Where was her warm dressing gown? She peered from under the covers and tried to guess which of the teetering piles of clothes covering the floor was the likeliest. The cats stretched and went back to sleep; not so the dog. The weak light penetrating the thin curtains made no impact on the dreary bedroom, but neither did it make any impact on Elin's high spirits. She located her cosy robe without trouble and her bright pink Uggs weren't hard to find either. She switched the heating on to constant as she made her way to let Mutt out.

After christening her new cafetiere, Elin noticed that the morning was now as bright as her mood and decided to walk to the nearest park with Mutt, a task that took just three minutes. The only people to be seen were a couple of dog walkers, one with a stout Jack Russell on an extendable lead, the other throwing a ball for a Border Collie. Could Mutt be trusted off the lead? Now, while it was quiet, might be best. Making a bold decision, Elin made her way to the centre of the park and unclipped the lead. Mutt tore off into the distance, leaving Elin with her heart in her mouth. She continued walking steadily and soon Mutt was circling her like a bright golden missile skimming over the dewy grass. Elin watched him with joy in her heart.

Once back in the welcoming warmth, she set to work trying to make the flat as warm and inviting as the surrounding temperature. Hunger started to gnaw: she filled a plate with last night's leftovers, reheated the coffee and sat down. As she ate she surveyed the room and came to the conclusion that it was totally lacking in charm. What could be done on a strict budget?

Elin checked her phone, saw a text from Mia, asking if she could pop around later and grinned to herself, already looking forward to the visit. She prowled around trying to make the room more inviting, to no avail. Her energy level plummeted and just as she was depressing the plunger of the cafetiere again another knock on the window made her jump. She hurried to the door, Mutt barking at the window, cats skittering away in alarm.

Mia and Daniel stood there, scarves wound round their necks, noses red and arms laden with an assortment of bags.

"Come in, you look cold, did you walk?"

"We came through the park; it only took twenty minutes," Dan said as Mia looked around enthusiastically. "Great place! These are house warming gifts, not new I'm afraid, but useful." The first of the black bin bags held two enormous floor cushions covered in a muted cotton print, one in shades of orange and brown, the other black and gold, tiny mirrors in the patterns twinkling. Mia apologised, "We were out trawling the charity shops when I got your text yesterday. I hope you don't mind that they're not new? They're perfectly clean."

"I don't mind, they're going to be on the floor anyway. Thanks a lot, these are perfect." Elin could hardly believe she was grateful for other people's rejects, but she was. "What else is here? This is like Christmas!"

"Careful with the next couple of bags, Elin, everything's in there higgledy-piggledy. Alisha and Swati, you met them at the meeting, donated these. Swati's mother bought them when she visited from India. The girls don't cook! Everything's brand new."

"Wow, I can't believe it, a colander, wooden spoons, storage jars, mixing bowls! Please thank them for me."

"They were glad to declutter; maybe you'll meet them again sometime."

Elin was putting the utensils away when there was yet another knock on the window. Dan and Mia grabbed their mugs to safeguard them from Mutt wildly careering across the room demonstrating his newly acquired guard-dog persona, the cats finding refuge under the two chairs.

"It's Hilary!" Elin said, hanging on to Mutt's collar as she opened the door and was surprised to see Finn and Jemmie too. "Come in, the more the merrier!" Elin was as giddy as the teenagers standing in front of her.

"Jem and Finn are here to help. I hope you don't mind, but I looked around and found a few things I thought might be useful. Have a look and don't say yes just to please me."

"Let me put the dog in the garden first," Elin said as she dragged a disappointed Mutt outside then rushed back; sticking out of the boot she could see a wooden chest of drawers with a rolled-up rug wedging it in place.

"That's exactly what I need, thanks so much!" Elin was so excited she was gabbling.

Mia and Elin carried the rug and a couple of lamps as the others struggled to get the chest of drawers into the bedroom. Hilary explained, "Jemmie had new bedroom furniture and the old chest was stored in the garage — it's solid. My parents gave us the rug, but the colour was wrong for our house so it was rolled up and put in the loft, waiting for a home. I'd forgotten we had the lamps, they were in the loft too!"

"They're exactly what I need: look, the rug and the floor cushions go together!" Soon the lamps cast an inviting glow over the revamped room. Dan and Mia stayed on, talking about Dan's new job and Mia's online course. "But I might have to do some teaching soon, our boiler's on the blink and it'll be expensive to fix."

"I'm enjoying being a TA but the pay is terrible," Elin grimaced. "If I'm going to keep myself, I'll have to find a better job."

"Good luck to both of us!" Mia made a move to go. "Oops, I nearly forgot, Chrissie wants you to contact her about getting together."

Elin sent a text to Chrissie. She'd had a fabulous day and the flat looked much better. She filled her new chest, but there was no way order could be achieved in the bedroom. Piles of clothes, admittedly smaller piles, still adorned every available space. Even the gentler glow of the "new" bedside lamp didn't help much.

The bathroom had one major advantage. Everything was no more than an arm's length away as she lay back and soaked the tiredness of the weekend away, her towel warming on the radiator. Elin climbed into her pyjamas, dressing gown and Uggs. She had set the central heating timer, hoping for a warm start to Monday morning when her phone rang.

"Hi Elin, I can hardly believe you have a new place already! How are you?"

"Chrissie! I can hardly believe it myself!"

"What about the concert? Do you want to talk more?"

"Absolutely! You say a time and place and I'll be there! I'm so happy you're willing to help again!"

There was a short pause, "Umm, you know how to get to our house don't you? I'm having a women's meeting on Wednesday, 7.30. If you come earlier, we could have something to eat while we talk?"

Elin hesitated, but only for a second, "I have to walk the

dog first. I could make it by 6.15, maybe earlier depending on traffic. Is that OK?"

"That's plenty of time, see you Wednesday!"

"Bye Chrissie, and thanks."

Elin wondered if she had agreed to go to the meeting. She wasn't sure. She assumed it was a Buddhist meeting. Women only? Groups of women could be on the bitchy side in her experience. She'd check it out with Mia before she made up her mind.

Fireworks exploded, the cats hid and Mutt cowered. Reassuring them that the torture of Guy Fawkes's night would soon be over, Elin prepared for another week at school. There was a lull in the explosions so she encouraged Mutt out into the garden. As soon as he could he shot back into the warmth and safety of the flat. Elin spoke with feeling, "I know how you feel, Mutt, old boy, I know how you feel."

17

By Wednesday, Elin still hadn't decided whether to stay for the meeting or bolt for home after the chat. She couldn't be rude, but possibly there'd be a chance to leave before the women arrived. She reminded herself how generous Chrissie was with her time and decided to keep an open mind. Hurrying to change after Mutt's walk, she couldn't find the outfit she wanted and dislodged precarious piles of clothes into a disorderly heap yet again. She found a bright pink top she'd forgotten about and threw it on over a pair of narrow, dark plum trousers. She slipped a copy of the research paper she had been sharing with Nathan Protheroe on that fateful afternoon into her bag and bought a quiche on her way.

Chrissie held out her arms in welcome, "Glad you found the house! Jared's out so let's eat and talk in the kitchen. Thanks for the quiche, it smells good. I have salad to go with it."

They discussed the children's concert as they ate. Elin couldn't believe it when the doorbell rang and she heard

Mia's voice in the hall. "I got a lift with Celia, we let ourselves in, OK?"

"We're in the kitchen," Chrissie responded as Mia came in with a youngish woman dressed in smart jeans and an amazing red jacket who she introduced as Celia, short for Cecilia.

"Brrr, it's cold out there, could I make a quick cup of tea Chrissie?"

"Go ahead, I'll have some too, what about you, Elin?"

Elin could have gone on talking to Chrissie for hours, but soon they were drinking tea and, as Elin had feared, there was no opportunity to leave without being rude. The doorbell rang again and Elin bowed to the inevitable.

Elin couldn't understand what drew these women together; their ages ranged from young students right through to mature women in their fifties – sixties even. She didn't know what to make of the chanting and was glad they stopped after ten minutes; it had seemed like an eternity but her watch definitely told her it was only ten minutes. They started discussing relationships and Elin paid close attention when a young woman, sitting crossed legged at the front, spoke. Dressed in jeans and a grey sweatshirt emblazoned with Stanford University, which Elin had assumed was a fashion logo until she spoke with an American accent, the young woman ended with a rueful smile, "Still working on absolute happiness, I guess!" That puzzled Elin but she was soon distracted by Cecilia's red jacket, studying the details more closely. However, the mention of Antoine de Saint-Exupery's book *The Little Prince* regained her attention. A skinny woman, who had stylishly chopped blonde hair, was struggling to remember a quote. "I've got it now! 'Love is not two people gazing at each other, but two people looking ahead together in the same direction'," she ended triumphantly. Clapping and laughter greeted her feat of memory.

"I've got the boss from hell," announced a dark-skinned woman with an elegant wrap around her hair. Elin didn't want to hear about work, she wanted tips on lovers and husbands. Her attention wandered as an older lady started talking about finding a long-lost sister. Elin contented herself with giving the speaker an imaginary makeover and restyling her wispy hair.

Elin was about to slip away when Mia appeared with two women, one the wearer of the red jacket. "Elin, you've met Celia, and this is Yoko."

Elin blurted out, "Celia, I love your jacket, it's so gorgeous it distracted me from the discussion." She stopped, covered in confusion.

"I'm glad somebody noticed!" Celia directed the teasing at Mia, dressed in a saggy peasant skirt topped by two layers of knitted garments of indeterminate hue.

"The detailing is exquisite," Elin burbled enthusiastically.

"I got it free at a clothes swap in London," Celia said and then turned to Mia, "Why don't we have one? We're recycling and it's fun."

A picture of her cluttered bedroom popped into Elin's mind, "Great idea!"

Mia looked bored.

Celia and Yoko stood back, sizing Elin up. Yoko spoke this time, "Size 10? Same as me so count me in!"

Celia explained roughly what happened at a clothes swap, finishing enthusiastically, "This could be great."

Elin exchanged numbers with Celia and Yoko and drove

home wondering how soon she could get the clothes swap organised. Who to invite? Jeannie, Hilary, Gina, Mrs. Hargreaves? Maybe not, but possibly Tamsin. What about Beechwood School? Could she face inviting Fiona and risking another snub? Perhaps not. Definitely Mia and Chrissie as well as Celia and Yoko. She came down to earth with a bump. Was there enough room in her flat? It was too late to worry about it tonight though, there was the "date" with Joe tomorrow to think about and that was enough for now.

Elin had silenced her phone at Chrissie's and then forgotten until she arrived home. There were two texts and a voice-mail from Joe. She texted an explanation.

Alley and Tom had grudgingly adapted to their indoor existence, it was cold and often wet outside which helped, but Elin couldn't wait to be rid of the smelly litter tray. As she came out of the bathroom in her pyjamas she heard Joe's text arrive. "OK. 7.30 2moro. Late mtg?"

At precisely 7.30 the next evening Elin opened the door to the lounge bar of the Red Lion. She paused and scanned the room. She located Joe sitting where he could see the door and as she waved to him he rose and came towards her. "Good to see you," he said and leaned towards her to kiss her lightly on the lips.

"Nice to see you too," Elin responded with a smile. Once they were comfortably seated, Joe asked her if she wanted a drink before dinner. "No thanks, why don't we order at the bar and get drinks at the same time?"

"We could go somewhere else if you prefer, how about the Thai Kitchen or The Vintage Inn?"

"This is fine. What are you going to order?" Elin picked up the menu.

"I heard their pies are home-made. I'll have the Steak and Mushroom."

Elin scanned the short list, "Ok, I'll try the Ocean Pie, please, and a white wine spritzer."

The service was prompt and they were soon eating. The food gave them something to talk about until Joe could resist no longer. "Late meeting last night? TAs at staff meetings now?"

Ow! Elin winced and responded mildly, though not without effort, "I asked for that. The meeting wasn't work. It was a Buddhist meeting."

Joe looked incredulous. Elin continued, "I was visiting Chrissie, then it seemed rude to leave. That's why I didn't pick up your messages."

"Not that Chrissie again, she and Mia got you into trouble before." Joe looked ten, twenty years older when he put on his judgemental, portentous look, "I don't know why you're friends with them, Mia always looks scruffy and from what you say she struggles to hold down a job. And a Buddhist meeting, what nonsense."

"Mia is highly qualified. She doesn't have a permanent job by choice, and the clothes she wears are irrelevant." Elin struggled on, "The meeting was interesting, about relationships. I also met some nice women."

Joe launched into a tirade about crazy pseudo psychology, that Elin was being drawn into some sort of cult. Elin distracted herself, clearing her plate and even eating all the bread in the basket. Eventually, Joe paused.

Elin spoke quietly, "If you knew what Mia was really like you wouldn't say such things. The conversation was good; it showed the women were well read. Can we change the subject now, please?"

They made arrangements to meet the following week at

a different gastropub. Elin took the initiative and gave Joe a hug and a light kiss on the lips. As she drove home she congratulated herself on keeping calm. Perhaps things would ease over the weeks and they would get on well again. Anything was possible she supposed, but her heart was heavy.

On Friday evening, curled up with her little TV and the cats, she was caught unawares by a wave of sadness. It was raining, a cold drizzly miserable rain, but the curtains were drawn and she was warm and comfortable. Work had been good; she had a fridge full of food, a good book she hadn't yet started and no need to be in any particular place at any particular time for two whole days. She stared at her phone. It sat there silently. No texts, no voice-mail. She checked emails, Facebook and Instagram. Nothing personal. She read a few pages then checked her phone again. Why didn't anybody phone? She answered herself, "When I was the centre of drama, they were interested, but now they've moved on." Elin felt tears roll down her cheeks and didn't bother to stop them. Was this what she'd fought so hard for? Had she made an awful mistake?

Elin opened a bottle of wine, flipped through the TV channels and trawled Netflix but nothing suited her mood.

Determined not to cry again, Elin washed her dinner dishes and scrubbed the kitchen counter as she sipped her wine. She made another attempt to impose order on her bedroom. She packed summery clothes into suitcases and hoped Hilary would store them in her garage. The room was still a mess. A red jacket jogged her memory and suddenly her spirits rose. She found Celia's number, her finger hovered. 'Oh, what the hell,' she thought, what was there to lose? Within a couple of rings, she heard Celia's voice.

"Elin, I was hoping you'd phone."

Relief washed over Elin, "Do you have a minute? I wanted to ask about the clothes exchange?"

"Ask away, I've got plenty of time."

Elin explained her storage problem and the size of her flat.

Celia laughed, "It's hard to tell if your place is big enough, shall I pop over sometime and see?"

"That'd be great. When? Would you have to come far? I don't want to be a nuisance."

"I live on the east side of the river, where are you?"

"I'm on the east side too, Blue Street, number 57."

They settled on the following evening, babysitter permitting. Elin felt like a different person. She picked up her book and began reading.

The next morning Elin phoned Hilary to share the idea, "Would you like to come, Hilary? It'll be fun. Celia's coming over this evening to plan."

"Celia? Who's Celia?"

"I met her at Chrissie's. I admired her jacket and it went from there."

"What does she do? Is she married?" Hilary was intrigued.

"Hang on a minute! She has children, I don't know anything more," Elin laughed. "I hate to ask, but could you store a couple of suitcases for me?"

Elin put two suitcases of summer clothes in the car to take to Hilary's then jammed the clothes she wanted to keep into the wardrobe, just getting the doors to close. Turning, she surveyed the chaos; skirts, tops, jackets, trousers, jeans, all scattered over the bed and the floor, all to be swapped. A minute or two after 7 pm Celia arrived, simply dressed in dark grey jeans, blue striped sweater and a full length knitted mohair coat in silver. Navy leather boots and a navy tote bag completed the ensemble.

After a tour of the flat, Celia was thoughtful, "You're right, there's not much room. People like to try things on; it's part of the fun." She paused, "We could have it at my house, maybe next weekend, what do you think?"

"I wouldn't mind, but are you sure? We only just met."

"A friend of Mia and Chrissie's is a friend of mine!" Celia beamed. "What night is best for you?"

"Friday's best, but how exactly does it work?"

Celia smiled again, "You give each item stars. Say a dress cost a lot and you still quite like it, you'd put ten stars on it. Something you'd never wear again, only one star, so it's a better bargain for the others."

"What about sizes?"

"That's a challenge, but we can't be size-ist, can we? It helps if people bring accessories and jewellery. To downsize you'll have to resist clothes and focus on small items."

Elin nodded, "I get it, super handbag ten points, quirky earrings one point. If you're not sure about getting rid of something you give it lots of points."

"Exactly!" Celia gave Elin the thumbs up. Suddenly Celia stopped, "Oops! I forgot, a housewarming gift." She brought two pretty mugs, a jar of drinking chocolate and a litre of semi-skimmed milk out of her bag. "It's such a cold night and I have a weakness for hot chocolate!"

Elin was touched, "What lovely mugs. Hot chocolate sounds good."

"As for the swop, next Friday would be perfect, Elin, a few weeks before Christmas, a fashion boost without spending anything. I'm excited."

Elin asked how long she'd known Mia and Chrissie. "About two years, since I moved back from London when I got divorced. I needed help with the girls and my parents live fairly close. It's working out better than I could have hoped."

"Where do you work?" Elin asked, interested.

"Just at the Tax Offices."

"I wouldn't have guessed. You look much too interesting and fashionable."

"That's quite a compliment coming from a fashionista like you," Celia smiled with delight.

"Where did you meet Chrissie?" Elin asked.

"Can't you guess? At a meeting after I moved back."

"You're a Buddhist too; of course!" Elin banged her hand to her head in mock frustration. "It's all new to me."

"You did look like a deer in the headlights, I hope it wasn't too scary. My next-door neighbour invited me the first time. She was quite well known, on TV, so it was cool for me, ordinary Celia hobnobbing with an actor."

"An actor, a tax collector, a choreographer and a teacher. Interesting."

"We're all very different, but we all know life can be a struggle. I was in a terrible state when I went to my first meeting. I think my neighbour felt sorry for me. She knew what was going on. No doubt she heard the monumental rows."

Elin leaned forward, "So, what happened?"

Celia looked at her watch and jumped up, horrified, "I'd love to talk but I have to rush off, babysitter!" Celia took Elin's hands in hers and asked, "Are you free tomorrow afternoon? Gwennan's going to a party so I'd only have Lowri and she occasionally naps after lunch. Would you like to come over?"

"I'd love to, what time?"

"About 2.30?" Celia paused for a moment, then continued, "Just remember the saying 'Winter never fails to turn into spring'." She bustled out with a pat on the head for Mutt and a tickle under the chin for Alley and Tom. A blast of cold air as the door closed behind her made Elin shiver and she wondered about winter turning into spring. Was the winter of her marriage going to turn into spring?

18

The corner shop didn't have much in the way of toys and Elin had no idea what was suitable for a four-year-old. She stared at the meagre selection of dog-eared comics and cheap plastic tat. Finally, she asked the shop owner for his advice. "Mr. Hassan, what should I get for a four-year-old girl?"

"Mostly they buy sweets, chocolate, ice cream. How about some chocolate?"

"I'm not sure if the mother would approve. Maybe a comic?"

"They like if there's a toy with it."

Elin picked up one of the less battered copies. It featured Fireman Sam, Winnie the Pooh and some strange creatures that inhabited a Night Garden. Elin realised how ignorant she was about young children. She was finding out about ten-year-olds at school and here she was dipping into yet more uncharted waters. The comic had a plastic toy in the shape of a mobile phone stuck on the front, maybe Lowri would like that.

"I'll take this one, Mr. Hassan, and the paper and some

cat litter too."

Ringing up the items, the shopkeeper announced, "That'll be eight pounds fifty-six pence please."

Money was slipping through her fingers at an alarming rate. No more procrastination. The pay at River Park School was ludicrous. She was determined to search for jobs, starting today.

Elin walked to Churchill Road. As befitted its name, the terrace had been built post war and looked its age. When Celia opened the door, Elin entered a narrow hallway cluttered with scooters, bikes and an assortment of shoes and small wellies.

"Sorry about the mess, come on in." Tucked under her arm, Celia had a tiny blonde beauty, all straight golden hair and big blue eyes. Once they were in the living room she put the child down only for her to hide behind her mother's skirt.

"This is Lowri, she's tired, she was up too late last night and could do with a nap but she wanted to see you before going upstairs." At this Lowri hid even further behind her mother. "She'll thaw out when she's ready."

Elin proffered the comic to Celia, "I'm not sure if she'll like this, I've no idea what little ones like."

"Fireman Sam is her favourite. Lowri, look, a Fireman Sam comic with a phone as well!"

Lowri emerged, her shyness forgotten, and held her hands out for the gift.

"Shall I read it to you?" Elin asked.

"Mummy read it," announced Lowri firmly, leading her mother to the settee.

"What's the magic word, Lowri?" asked Celia.

"Please, Mummy."

"Well done. I'll read you two stories then you can take

the phone with you when you go for a nap, OK?'

Lowri was happy with the deal.

Elin watched as Celia pointed out words and showed Lowri the pictures.

After hearing the same story twice, Lowri pouted and refused to go upstairs.

"Oh well, nothing else to be done, I'll carry you," Celia said, trying hard to keep the atmosphere positive. "Let's take your new phone up so you can talk to Daddy or Grandma."

Lowri howled loudly before flinging herself on the floor, still screaming. She was scooped up in a trice, Celia throwing an apologetic look backwards at Elin. "I'll be back in two ticks, sorry about this. There's an old *Vogue* on the coffee table."

Elin picked up *Vogue* and leafed through it thinking that if the volume of the screams were anything to go by she was in for a long wait. A gorgeous sweater caught her eye and she was checking the outrageous price when Celia reappeared and Elin realised that the house was quiet.

"Sorry, she was overtired. She'd stopped that god-awful noise before I'd walked down the stairs. I need a cuppa, my ears are ringing."

Elin followed Celia into the kitchen. As the kettle boiled, Celia cleared paints and jars full of murky water off the table and plopped down two mugs and a packet of biscuits. She poured the tea and joined Elin with a sigh, "Where were we last night?"

"I was asking if Joe and I could be happy again after I had an affair and Joe admitted he's had girlfriends? What happened with you?"

Celia listened, absent-mindedly munching on leftover sliced apple, brown and shrivelled. "Do you want to hear my story or dissect yours?"

"You first."

Celia leaned back in her chair, screwed up her eyes and inhaled deeply. "I was married to Pete for twelve years altogether. The first five were good, both of us working for the Inland Revenue. We had lots of friends and a great social life. Work was pretty monotonous but it paid the bills, and nice clothes for me and music equipment for Pete. Pete was, still is, passionate about music. He was in a band and it was exciting, pretending to be a groupie. He loved the whole scene, hoped to make it in the music business, but it didn't happen. I loved him and didn't need to be constantly searching for novelty. I was looking at our marriage from one perspective and he was looking at it from another. These days I can see my part in the breakdown of the relationship, but I couldn't at the time."

"So what happened?" Elin was relieved she didn't have to think about children.

"Pete didn't want to give up his dreams. We still loved each other but we wanted different things. I thought that if I had a baby he'd want to stay home more." Celia gave her head a small shake of disbelief, "But Gwennan cried a lot, I became exhausted and wanted to sleep every chance I had. Pete still wanted to play music, it was his escape from the chaos. I didn't get a babysitter to go out and listen to him, all I wanted to do was sleep. Going back to work helped, and things improved. I was happy once Gwennan stopped screaming. At first, I was OK with Pete going out in the evenings, it was what he'd always done. Then, gradually, it wasn't OK. I felt all the responsibility fell on me. I resented his music." Celia paused.

"I wasn't the most welcoming wife so he stayed out even more. I'm not sure when I became suspicious. I was slow off the mark considering I used to be a groupie... duh! Then the rows really started. He stayed out more and I got angrier. He still had his job, but I was getting promoted and he wasn't. I resented him even more when I started bringing home the lion's share of the money. He was getting gigs but not earning enough to cover his expenses. He always wanted the latest equipment and the band relied on his van for transport. I blamed him for everything and he resented my nagging. He loved Gwennan and was great with her when he was home. It was awful for us and bad for her too." Celia pulled a face at the memory.

"Sounds awful, Celia."

"Yes, it was horrendous. That was when Suzie, my neighbour, invited me to her house. She knew about the rows, she wasn't deaf."

"What happened then?"

"I met a lot of lovely people; nice men — I'd forgotten they existed — and women. They said that there's no point trying to change other people. I didn't get it at first, but when I started to understand, things got better at home. Then, oops, I got pregnant again. Boy, did that put the cat among the pigeons."

"My life was a mess. Pete wanted me to have a termination but I couldn't. I already had a beautiful child by him and we were still married. I love Gwennan so much. I knew I would love another just as much. We had a home and enough money, I couldn't justify getting rid of a baby and I began to hate Pete for suggesting it. I finally realised how self-centred he was. I shouldn't have been surprised; I'd been trying to change him for years and nothing worked."

Elin nodded, her troubles seemed minor in comparison. Celia continued, "Suzie and the others were wonderful. They kept telling me I had the strength to get through it. I didn't believe them at first. My family didn't like Pete and I heard 'I told you so' constantly. Their idea of help was to tell me to give up work and live with them. Can you imagine, a five-year old, a baby, and no job?"

"So how did it all work out, you look happy?"

"I kept the baby, obviously. She's great, you've seen her at her worst." Celia shrugged, "That's what four-year-olds do sometimes. When I decided to keep the baby, Pete threw a fit. It got worse before it got better. I listened to Suzie and I tried chanting. I was desperate."

Elin didn't comment and Celia carried on, "I stopped blaming Pete. My marriage was over and I had to take responsibility. After twelve years, I had got used to being with him." Celia smiled at Elin and threw her hands up in the air, "*Voila*! It was simple! I took charge of my life." Then she shook her head sadly, "But I wanted Gwennan and the baby to be close to their father. It was odd, discussing our breakup while I was still pregnant. I'd go to my check-ups; the other women were excited and had partners with them. I was on my own." Celia stared into space for a moment, "I'm still amazed by the way it worked out. Pete and I got along better. We'd lapse into the blame game once in a while, but I have to say we organised the separation with dignity. We sold the house in London, I got this house and Pete got a tiny flat, so he can have the girls to stay. It doesn't happen often, but that's OK. When I started chanting I saw my marriage clearly and I found strength I didn't know I had.

"I applied for a transfer to Cardiff and got it. They even kept the position for me until I'd taken my maternity leave. Cause and effect: I had worked hard all those years, so they kept the job for me. Since I've been here, I've moved to the Fraud department and it's more interesting. I enjoy the work and I get to wear nice clothes if I want to."

Elin sat back and studied Celia, "Nobody would guess —

you look as if you haven't got a care in the world and you always seem happy."

"That's because I am. You can be happy too Elin, and you will be, I'm sure. Just stick around with us and it'll rub off. We Buddhists are a happy lot," Celia grinned before continuing thoughtfully, "Do you think chanting would help you?"

Elin wasn't too sure. She shrugged and decided to change the subject. "At the clothes exchange, what do we do with the clothes nobody wants to swap? Do people take things home? I don't want you to be stuck with a pile of unwanted clothes."

"We decide on a charity and take all the leftovers there."

"Sounds good. I've almost finished the invitations. I'll print them out later. I'm going to send them by email and snail mail, hopefully they'll catch people's attention that way. It's not long before the swap, so I need to send them first class tomorrow. Could you give me Yoko's contact details? And anyone else you want to invite. I'll come early on Friday to help."

"Thanks, 6 o'clock would be great! I'll have to get Lowri off to sleep before everyone arrives. Gwennan's not a problem, she can get herself to bed."

Elin let herself out through the front door and hoped Celia wouldn't think she was strange, leaving in such a hurry.

That night, Elin tried to print the invitations just to have her printer die on her; after a few phone calls she got hold of Jeannie. As the chirpy requests poured out of Jeannie's printer Elin told her friend all about Celia.

"I'll look forward to meeting her on Friday," Jeannie said and then was suddenly struck with an idea. "Maybe Celia would come out with us on Wednesday? I was going to tell

you about this new place where they have a good singles'
evening. My forays into internet dating haven't been good so
I want to try it."

"I'm not ready for the dating scene yet, Jeannie, I'm still
married and still trying to work out my feelings for Joe.
Celia seems very happy with her life as it is. Why don't you
try it first?"

"I might. A group of single friends hire a room at St
Cato's Country Club. There's a bar and comfy seating, but
no dancing, and they run it like a private party, introducing
people to each other, then you move around naturally. You
pay at the door and you can leave any time if you're not
enjoying it. Oh, do come Elin, I need company. I'm no good
at going places on my own, you know what a wimp I am."

"See if you can find somebody else who wants to go with
you first. If you don't find anybody I won't abandon you, but
I really don't want to go."

"It's hard living on your own. I really want to find a
partner. I'm sure that would make me so much happier. Do
come with me, you never know who's out there looking for
someone just like you."

Elin left smiling; she thought about Jeannie on the drive
home, how she was so competent but so needy. Elin
doubted her own competency when she got back to the flat
and realised she had eleven invitations to be personalised,
eleven envelopes to be addressed and eleven stamps to be
found if they were to be posted tomorrow. The newspaper
was still open on the table, an article on rising
unemployment reminding her that a job was not going to
materialise out of her wardrobe, no matter how clear and
uncluttered, and most definitely not from a singles' night
out with Jeannie.

19

Winter flu caused a staffing crisis at school the following week. The head-teacher was stressed, guidelines were ignored and Elin was generously cooperative, teaching a Year 3 class. At 5 pm on Wednesday she phoned Jeannie, regretting agreeing to go to St Cato's Country Club. "I didn't promise, Jeannie, I said I'd think about it."

Jeannie had come out with a string of reasons, all valid, why Elin should keep her company and Elin was too tired to come up with convincing rebuttals. Jeannie was thrilled.

"Wonderful, Elin, you won't regret it! I'll pick you up at 8. That way you can have a drink, all men look more handsome after a glass of wine!"

Elin shovelled down an omelette, walked the dog, then sank gratefully into the bath, wishing she could get out and climb into warm pyjamas and bed socks instead of dressing for an evening at the Country Club. She hoped that the wine she was set to consume would improve her attitude. The thought of an evening with Joe the next day led to a groan and she sank right under the water before surfacing to shampoo and deep condition her hair.

Jeannie was on time and Elin was ready, "This 'do' had better be good tonight or I'll want to come straight home, OK? I haven't got the energy to make small talk so there'd better be some chatty people there! Left alone I swear I'll make for the nearest armchair and fall asleep."

"Don't worry, I'll make sure that doesn't happen," Jeannie smiled and took Elin's arm. "Thanks for coming with me, you're a true pal."

Jeannie kept her promise, but her efforts didn't change Elin's mood so she eventually accepted defeat; they murmured their goodbyes to the group and left.

"Did you notice that tall man in the black sweater, the one with thick blond hair and nice eyes?" asked Jeannie.

"Can't say that I did," Elin yawned, "why do you ask?"

"He couldn't take his eyes off you, that's why! I think he must be shy. I expected him to ask for your phone number, but he didn't. "

Struggling to keep her eyes open, Elin considered this, "Pity I'm so tired, I'm sure I would've been more aware otherwise. Was he really good looking?"

"Yes, a bit young though, probably in his mid-twenties."

"I couldn't face going back even if you told me Tom Cruise was there and even then, I'd say he was too short," Elin mumbled, and closed her eyes.

"The set up was OK though, wasn't it? Will you come with me next week Elin, if you're not too tired?"

Elin nodded, not opening her eyes.

Elin covered for another teacher and was just as tired when she met Joe the following day. The evening began pleasantly, but over coffee Joe pressed for a decision.

"It's more than three months since my world fell apart,

what's going on Elin? I keep hoping you'll come to your senses and come home. Surely, you've had enough time to reflect? I'm waiting. I need to know. It's hard for me too, you know."

His injured innocence didn't sit well with Elin and led to the display of irritation she had hoped to avoid, "Joe, those first weeks went by in a haze, then I was squashed in with Jeannie. I've only been in the flat for a month. You know quite well that I signed a lease for six months and this is a time for us to work things out. Why do you always have to put pressure on me?"

"I need you to make up your mind. You can't have everything you want Elin. Sooner or later you're going to have to make a choice. Either you stay in this marriage or we go our separate ways."

"I hear you loud and clear, Joe. I thought these Thursdays were to put all that behind us, to remember the things we liked about each other, dig them out, nurture them. This constant pressure defeats the object. I'm sorry I snapped at you, I'm very tired. I'm going home." She pushed back her chair and rose.

"I'm sorry Elin, I can't help it. You hurt me badly and I lash out. Shall we try again next Thursday? Here? Same place, same time?"

Elin plastered on a smile, "I'll be here, same time next week. Bye Joe."

Elin fumed as she drove home. She had to learn how to say no to people. If she'd said no to the teaching, which wasn't her job, she wouldn't be so tired. If she'd said no to Jeannie she wouldn't be so tired. If she'd cancelled tonight she wouldn't be so tired. If she hadn't been so tired she wouldn't have snapped at Joe. She was so tired at this moment that she would happily have cancelled the clothes swap the next day, but the invitations had gone out and the acceptances had rolled in. Maybe she'd feel more like it after a good night's sleep.

She was right. On Friday morning, everything seemed different. The weather turned cold and bright, Mutt cooperated on his morning and evening walks and there was a full complement of teaching staff again at River Park School. She loaded up the car and arrived at Celia's bang on six o'clock.

A shy little girl with short, dark blonde hair answered the door and held it open as Elin staggered in, arms full. Sounds of laughing and splashing came from upstairs. "You must be Gwennan, I'm Elin. Sounds like your Mummy's busy upstairs? Would you help me by keeping the door open while I bring in some more stuff?"

Gwennan nodded silently; she was certainly different from her sister. Once everything was inside, Elin stood there wondering what to do next. "Would you be very helpful again and tell Mummy that Elin is here, please? Would you ask her what she wants me to do?"

Another nod and Gwennan ran upstairs. Elin heard Celia shout a greeting and Gwennan came back proudly. "Mummy says it would be a big help if you could clear up in the kitchen. I'm supposed to put all the toys away in the living room. She says she'll be down once Lowri's in bed and then we'll do the clothes."

"OK, I'll start in the kitchen. Thanks for helping, Gwennan."

Elin surveyed the kitchen and felt daunted. Celia obviously didn't have a dishwasher and the sink was full of a day's worth of dirty dishes. The table was covered with Play-Doh and not a single work surface was clear. She saw an apron hanging behind the back door and put it on; rubber gloves and a bowl were easy to find under the sink. Then Elin set to and scrubbed away at dried-on cereal, congealed egg, toast crumbed plates and coffee stained mugs. The water was hot and it didn't take long. Next, she enlisted Gwennan's help.

"Gwennan, do you want to save any of the Play-Doh creations on the table? Or should I put it all back in the pots? It'll dry out if we don't and your Mummy wants the kitchen cleared."

Gwennan came to the doorway, "We can put it all away, Lowri won't remember what she made."

"Don't be too sure of that, young lady," Celia appeared behind her daughter. "Elin, you're an angel! I'm so sorry about the mess, we overslept and it was a rush to get out this morning. Thank you Gwennan, for tidying the toys away, it was a big help, you can have half an hour on the computer now if you like."

Elin pushed her hair back with a rubber gloved hand, "It was no trouble, I came over to help. We have half an hour before people come, what should I do next?"

"Let's finish in the kitchen first, shall we? I'll clear the table so we can put the glasses out, open the wine, put tea and coffee by the kettle."

Celia was already working as she spoke and within ten minutes they'd moved to the living room. Celia put up a couple of laundry racks for hanging clothes and they made sure there were plenty of flat surfaces for smaller items. Celia glanced at her watch before turning to Gwennan. "Five more minutes on the computer then you can watch us try on clothes if you like, but when I say go to bed, no arguing; it's Mummy's turn for fun tonight. OK?"

Gwennan pulled a face, "I don't want to watch you try on

clothes, Mum, it's boring. Can I take some snacks up to my room and play up there, please?"

"That's fine, I'll come up and say goodnight later. Clean your teeth after the snacks."

Celia turned to Elin, "I sometimes wonder about that child, she has no interest in clothes whatsoever. Her favourite outfit is an old pair of camouflage trousers and a red Hello Kitty top. Winter and summer, that's all she wants to wear. I despair."

There was a quiet knock on the front window.

"Oh, that'll be Yoko, she's afraid of waking Lowri up if she rings the bell. I'll let her in and leave the door on the latch."

Within a quarter of an hour everyone had arrived. Lowri hadn't woken and Gwennan was in her bedroom. Celia brought a cheval mirror downstairs and there was little hesitation in stripping off and trying on new stuff. Hilarious efforts to squeeze into sizes too small were greeted with good-natured jeers. Helpful suggestions for combining separates and new ways of using accessories were shared. It was like having a team of fashion advisors on tap. Elin concentrated on jewellery until Yoko showed her imaginative new ways with scarves. Hilary and Jeannie were busy making new friends, Tamsin had armloads of clothes and Chrissie was pirouetting in the most outrageous outfits.

Mia was the only one out of her element. She was watching the others, chatting and sipping wine. She'd brought a couple of pairs of shoes and some lovely delicate jewellery but made no attempt to join the melee. Chrissie noticed and dragged her to her feet, "Come on Mia, let's help you get kitted out. There's some lovely stuff here that will fit you."

Mia responded with a laugh, "The trouble is I don't

know what to choose, and worse, I don't really care! But go ahead and do your worst."

Mia was soon dressed in a long madras cotton skirt, with a toning vest top. Celia found a light suede waistcoat in faded olive; the effect was even better when Elin suggested a cream linen tunic over the vest and under the waistcoat. It looked good. Then, when Yoko stepped forward with an armful of long scarves and experimented with various drapes and ties the outfit suddenly came to life. The whole effect was quirky and suited Mia's casual lifestyle perfectly.

The evening slowed, Elin was glad she'd made her choices early when there was a superb array of accessories. Chrissie and Elin were the last guests. As they carefully folded leftover clothes Elin said, "Thank you, Celia, you were right about needing the space. It would have been chaotic at mine and not nearly as much fun."

"My pleasure. Not a peep out of Lowri and Gwennan, you saved me a babysitter remember, so we're even."

"It was fun and I've got a super skirt and a couple of tops," Chrissie added. "And didn't Mia look amazing?"

Elin's weariness had disappeared and she could have stayed for hours. They washed glasses and plates and put everything away. Celia turned to Chrissie and Elin with a wide smile of gratitude, "Wow, this place looks amazing, so much better than it did earlier, isn't that right, Elin?"

They laughed and made promises to get together soon. As Elin drove home she sincerely hoped they would.

Saturday again. What was it about weekends and the expectation of fun? She felt a hint of panic; she had no plans except taking the unwanted clothes to the charity shop. By 4 pm the flat sparkled and her clothes were organised for the first time since she'd emptied her beautiful walk-in wardrobe and Jeannie had loaded it into her car back in

October. Getting dressed would no longer be a problem every morning. Not as much choice, but it felt good.

Niggling at the back of her mind all day was the job search issue. No more procrastination. Elin wondered how to get hold of a copy of Wednesday's paper. She liked seeing the opportunities in education together in print, but she'd forgotten to buy a copy. She sent the same text to everybody who might still have one. Tamsin texted back to say she didn't buy the paper; Hilary answered that their copy had already been recycled. Just as she was abandoning hope, Mia replied that she had one and invited her over later to collect it. Mutt went wild with delight as she clipped the lead on his collar before donning gloves, scarf and a woolly hat – all new from the previous night. After the walk, she got large saucepan of Bolognese sauce simmering on the stove, enough for that night and the next day, and enough to freeze a few portions for busy evenings to come. Instead of spaghetti she paired the sauce with thinly sliced steamed cabbage then jumped into the car ready for the short ride to Mia's house.

Wednesday's paper lay on the sofa in the living room as Mia welcomed her. "Are you warm enough, Elin? I'm economizing, but I've got a blanket for you or I can turn the fire on if that's not enough?"

"I'm fine thanks, I have lots of layers on. I pay heating bills too. Thanks for saving the paper."

"I get it out of habit and I might be driven back to teaching; maybe soon."

Elin looked closely at her friend. Something was amiss, "Are you alright Mia?"

"I'm OK, a bit down at the moment. Let's put the kettle on then I'll tell you."

They settled down a few minutes later, mugs in front of

them. Elin waited for Mia to speak. Mia managed a weak smile, "Dan's gone. He came home from the pub last night just after I got home from Celia's and said that he'd been thinking about our relationship for a while. He said he loves me and he's been happy living with me, but the fact that I'm twelve years older has been bothering him. He gets teased about it. So, you're right, I'm not very happy today."

Elin rushed to Mia's side and hugged her, "Oh my God Mia, poor you! What a shock. You always seemed so happy. I didn't think Dan would be so selfish."

Mia considered this, "Not selfish, quite brave really. He thought it was better to tell me rather than hiding it. I was shocked because we were happy. We were planning our lives together. We thought the same things were important and the attraction was there too, the sex was good. We didn't quarrel. If he was twelve years older than me it'd be fine, that's what's so frustrating."

"Did you go crazy? I know I would've."

Mia gave a wan smile, "Yes, part of me did want to scream, but it wouldn't have helped." Mia lapsed into silence.

Elin was quiet too, thinking about Mia's reference that good sex hadn't been enough. Memories of her shame when Aaron abandoned her surfaced. "What other people think can have a huge impact. I remember feeling that everyone was whispering behind my back," Elin said and fell silent again. Eventually she continued, "You're telling me about it so calmly. I'd have been on the phone straight away, crying, wanting sympathy. And Dan only told you this last night? What happened then?"

Mia smiled faintly again, "I couldn't think properly. I asked him what he intended to do and that defused the tension."

"What then? Did he pack his bags and go?"

"He didn't have a plan other than to split up with me, and that hurt. He was also upset about not getting that job in London."

Elin felt a stab of a compassion for Dan, but her loyalty was decidedly with Mia. "What happened then?"

"We kept our arms around each other, saying nothing, for a long time. I knew I still loved him and wanted him to stay. I felt that he still loved me but wasn't sure enough of his feelings. I think he was swayed by his mates' opinions." Mia snorted, the only sign of anger she'd shown. "We decided to go to bed and sort the details out in the morning."

Elin was round eyed, "You mean you went to bed and made love as if nothing had happened?"

"No, that wouldn't have felt right. We lay with our arms around each other until he fell asleep; I think the beer helped. I couldn't sleep, I came downstairs and drank hot chocolate, mulling it over. I did some chanting and then went back to bed."

"And in the morning?" Elin prompted.

"I got up and decided to wear the outfit you put together for me last night." Mia's smile was heartfelt for the first time, "I wanted to be remembered looking my best!"

This attitude Elin did understand. Mia went on, "Breakfast felt like a condemned man's last meal. He packed, which didn't take long. He's left his camping gear here, it seemed sensible. Part of me wanted to beg him to stay, part of me was angry and wanted to yell at him for hurting me. But I worked hard not to say those things.

"What did you say?" Elin was deeply upset on behalf of her friend.

"That I loved him. I said I didn't believe he would find

another woman that he could be happier with than me, no matter how old or young. I left it at that."

"That was it. Nothing else?"

"There was nothing more to say. The taxi came and he went." Mia summoned up a smile, "I'm glad I didn't say anything else. Now I'm going to carry on and be happy with or without Dan. I'm certain that I can be happy again even if it's hard at the moment." She looked down at her ancient sweatshirt, "Oh, and I put old clothes on again!"

Elin pondered; everything Mia had said rang true. "You're so strong, Mia. You have such a positive attitude. I know you'll be OK, but I want to help you stop hurting."

"You being here is good. Don't worry about me. You can be happy too you know, there's nothing special about me."

They sat peacefully until Elin said, "I think you are amazing. And you looked great last night!"

"You think so? All I know is I couldn't pull that look together myself."

"Celia's amazing too, and she's been so helpful."

"Absolutely. If you stick with Celia you won't go far wrong."

'Or stick with you,' Elin thought to herself, in awe of Mia's reaction to the Dan debacle. "Do you want me to stay with you tonight?"

"I'll be fine, thanks. Dan and I never lived in each other's pockets."

Mia changed the subject, picking up the paper. "What sort of job are you looking for? Are you open to moving?"

"I'm not sure, I'm enjoying the younger children, but the money's not enough and staying at River Park isn't good for my C.V.; I'm over qualified. I don't know where my marriage fits into my plans."

"What's important to you, Elin? For you and Joe to be

happy together you need to be happy as individuals. You've organised your life around him. It may have been your choice at the beginning, but perhaps it became a habit?"

"You're right Mia. I lurch from one thing to another, but at least for the last few months it's been my choice."

"You, Elin Petersen, are the one who knows what's best for you," Mia responded with a wry smile. "I'm trying to look at my challenge as an opportunity. Perhaps I'll go back to college, who knows?"

Mia move away? Elin hated that idea.

20

E lin spent Sunday poring over the job adverts and filling in forms on her laptop. She had tried very hard not to phone someone just to hear a friendly voice. Then Jeannie had called her, and in gratitude she agreed to keep Jeannie company at the Wednesday singles night. Was this to be the pattern of her life? Working all week, looking forward to the weekend but when it came feeling isolated and abandoned?

Elin was using the photocopier in the school office on Monday morning when the door opened and she was flustered to see the head-teacher, Mr. Roberts, standing there.

"Hello Mrs. Petersen, I wanted to say how grateful I am that you stepped into the breach last week. I was at my wits' end! I wish I could pay you properly for those days."

"It doesn't matter Mr. Roberts, it's all good experience."

"I'm looking forward to the Christmas show, I heard you have some great ideas."

"It's going to be a challenge, the staff are all working so

hard. Hopefully it'll reflect the talents of all the children, not just the most able."

"I had a feeling I was doing the right thing when we appointed you."

As he turned to leave he hesitated and came back in the room, closing the door this time. "I don't know if you'd be interested, but there may be an opening for a teacher here soon. I can't say more."

He smiled again. She was both surprised and happy. She had evidently underestimated Mr Roberts. But permanent teaching in a primary school? It had never crossed her mind.

Mr. Roberts' words and four completed applications meant that Elin's happy mood lasted into Wednesday. She related all that had happened to Jeannie as they drove towards the Country Club. "It's got me thinking, Jeannie. I assumed that as a science teacher I'd be better off in a secondary school. I'm wondering if that came from not having children of my own, and because of that, feeling insecure around younger ones."

"You don't have to be a parent to be good teacher. Think back to the teachers who inspired you as a child, were they all parents?" Jeannie had hit the nail on the head.

As promised, Jeannie bought the first round of drinks and they joined a knot of adults groping for conversation. Elin got chatting to a lively redhead, who said she was a primary school teacher, until Jeannie joined them accompanied by a tall, youngish man. He looked vaguely familiar. Jeannie kept catching her eye and trying to interest her in him but Elin was content to talk teaching. When the conversation stalled for a moment, Jeannie did not hesitate. "Elin, I wanted to introduce you to Seth. He'd like to meet you." Jeannie turned to Seth with a grin and a wave before making her way across the room, leaving Elin standing there with Seth. He looked very uncomfortable.

"Would you like another drink?" Seth asked, eyeing the empty glass in her hand.

"Oh, um, yes, please, if you don't mind, it's a Chardonnay."

"OK, I'll be right back." Seth took her empty glass and made his way to the bar. Elin watched him, noting that he was quite good looking, darkish blond hair neatly cut but not particularly stylish, even features, nice eyes, a nose slightly too big for him to be handsome. A bit too thin, he obviously didn't work out in the gym and nothing about him betrayed that he took much interest in his appearance. Despising herself for being so shallow, Elin waited until he returned with her glass of wine and what looked like a Coke for himself.

The conversation awkwardly settled on Seth restoring a classic Mercedes. Elin couldn't think of anything to say about cars but Seth looked so uncomfortable she tried to help him out. "So, what do you do when you're not restoring your car?" she asked, hoping against hope that he might be a teacher.

"I've just bought my own plane and I'm hoping to start a business doing charter flights."

Elin brightened up, this was a novelty. "How will that work, what sort of charters?"

"I'm thinking business people needing to get across the country in a hurry. Or maybe carrying light freight, even joyrides at weekends. It's only a two-seater so I'd be limited, but I love to fly."

Elin sipped her wine and acknowledged that she found Seth a lot more interesting now she knew he owned a plane, even a small one. "That's wonderful!"

"I hope it works out. I could take you up at the weekend if the weather's OK — if you wanted to, that is?" Seth's voice was a monotone even when he was offering something as exciting as a joyride in a plane, but she accepted without hesitation.

"That sounds great, you mean this weekend?"

"Saturday, if that's OK with you? I keep her at Winton airport. I could pick you up at ten o'clock?"

Elin realised she would be putting her life in this stranger's hands. He told her a little more about the plane and promised to phone her to confirm early on Saturday morning. Then there was little left to say.

There was an awkward pause so Elin took the initiative and leaned forward to kiss him on the cheek. "Bye 'til Saturday, I look forward to the joyride."

Elin walked over to Jeannie's group who were busy exchanging numbers. She looked up as Elin joined them, "Ready to go? I'm about to call it a night." She gave a general wave to the group and started towards the door.

"What did you think of Seth? He's the one that was watching you last week. Didn't you notice him?"

"I can't say I did, but thanks for bringing him over. Did you meet anybody nice?"

"A couple of the guys in the last group were OK, we exchanged numbers, but maybe I won't hear from them." Jeannie shrugged with resignation, "I'm not sure if I'll bother to contact them either. What about Seth? "

"Sparks didn't fly, that's for sure. He seems shy so I thought I'd be patient. Helped a bit that he has a plane and is taking me up on Saturday!"

"He owns a plane?" Jeannie was opening the car door and nearly dropped her car keys in her surprise. "You jammy devil you, Elin, imagine that, a plane!"

Elin had to admit that Jeannie had been right, it wasn't a bad place to hang out for a couple of hours if you had no great expectations of meeting somebody who would sweep you off your feet. She'd really enjoyed talking about teaching and she'd arranged a plane ride. Not bad for a couple of hours, even if Seth didn't light any fires.

Job applications were the topic of the following evening with Joe. The pub was half full, there a pleasant background hum, and Joe kept his distance, physically and emotionally. He made helpful comments about the job openings and the evening went well. Elin was able to give him a genuinely friendly hug goodbye, although she felt no desire to see him more frequently. She was content with their weekly rendezvous. Was it too late to rekindle their feelings? She simply didn't know.

On the way home, Elin reviewed her decision not to tell Joe about the plane ride. She felt zero sexual attraction towards Seth. Was it still a date or could it be classified as going out with a friend? That was manipulating the truth and she knew it. OK, it was a date, because Seth was, according to Jeannie, attracted to her. He could have fooled her, but she was looking forward to time high above the clouds.

SETH KICKED the tyres as he made a final circuit of the plane; he'd already checked the engine. At least that was what Elin presumed he was doing, he hadn't said. He hadn't said very much on the drive to the small airport either. Elin shivered in the cold morning air and pulled her woolly hat down over her ears. She was nervous, but in a good way and not for a second did she contemplate chickening out of the ride.

In the plane, Seth explained everything she had to do

and then what he was going to do. There were only two seats
and she sat behind him, buckling herself in tightly and
trying to relax. Soon they were taxiing down the runway,
then with noisy and bumpy acceleration they made it into
the air. It felt matter-of-fact and not in the least scary. The
small scale of the plane and the ease with which it took off
surprised her. Seth pointed out places of interest. He was
obviously in his element and to her relief Elin found that
she was having a good time. She felt a calmness that came
from Seth's confidence. Seth suggested they fly over the city
and look out for Elin's street. She watched cars jockeying for
position on the motorway and the doll's house versions of
familiar villages. All those people had their worries, but
from this vantage point they seemed minor in the grand
scheme of things. She could see why Seth was so single-
minded about flying. Seth pointed out the landmarks and
she worked out which was her street as the city unfurled like
a giant child's puzzle.

"Time to go back now, OK?" Seth shouted over the noise
of the engine.

"OK," Elin shouted back.

"You're enjoying it? Not scared?"

"Not at all. I'm having a great time."

Conversation was not easy over the background noise,
but Elin imagined that Seth would have a satisfied smile on
his face. He landed the plane competently and Elin
considered how lucky she was. Seth had proved to be a
more interesting companion than she had expected. It
wasn't yet noon and all was well in her world. Over a pub
lunch on the way home, Seth smiled and chatted about how
he got interested in planes and how he enjoyed not just
being in the air, but looking after the plane and navigating.
They decided to go to the cinema. After the film, they opted

to pick up kebabs and a bottle of wine on the way back to Elin's flat. Once Mutt had been let out, let in again and shut in the utility room, Seth and Elin settled down to eat.

As Elin poured the wine, she asked Seth why he went to St Cato's. It was as if she had opened floodgates. He had been going out with a girl and had wanted to settle down with her and have children. She had suddenly broken it off for no reason that she could explain or he could understand, and now he was on his own. He had decided to give the singles night a try. He looked so sad. She refilled her glass and held the bottle out. "No thanks Elin, I don't drink when I'm driving. I'm usually driving or flying so I don't drink much."

Seth continued eating, eyes down. After a long pause, he tried to explain his feelings, but in reality, he only repeated that he didn't understand. They finished their meal and cleared away. Elin brought her glass and the half empty bottle and sat on the floor, leaning back against his knees as he sat in the comfortable armchair. She half listened to Seth. He was talking about his strong desire to have children. Elin tuned out, she was obviously not the woman for him, but now was not the time to tell him. The bottle of wine was emptied and she felt relaxed and fuzzy. Seth slid down and sat beside her on the rug, giving her an undemanding kiss. They sat in silence for a while. Seth kissed her again and she felt a familiar reaction, she'd forgotten that physical pleasure could be fun on its own. The wine and the warmth of her own flat made any effort to do something other than go with the flow seem pointless.

Sex with Seth was straightforward and soon over. He reached for his clothes then picked up her sweater and handed it to her — to cover herself or to keep warm, Elin wasn't sure — she just wanted to go to bed, already regretting her alcohol consumption. She managed to stand up to give Seth a brief goodnight kiss then staggered off to bed.

The next couple of weeks passed in almost as much of a haze; with Christmas looming, everything at school was taking on a frantic, if festive, air. The much-anticipated Christmas show came and went. Mr. Roberts singled Elin out for special praise in public and dropped major hints about staff changes in private. She looked forward to the holidays, but knew she would miss the structure of school life.

School finished on Wednesday, four days before Christmas Day, and Elin had made no plans. Her parents had invited Elin to spend a few days with them, but she had managed to convince them she would be fine so they booked their usual hotel Christmas break. She'd bought presents for them, a cherry red, full-length dressing gown for her mother and a box of his favourite cigars for her father. They'd been wrapped and posted weeks ago. As an only child of only children there were no cousins for Elin to remember. Joe would have to shop for his family himself.

Seth was still around, as morose as ever and still obsessed with finding a woman to bear his children. They'd been out to dinner and watched films, ending up in Elin's flat, occasionally having unexciting sex. Elin had told him how much older she was, but he didn't take the hint. She decided to end the relationship, such as it was, and realised she'd have to lay it out plainly. On that last day of term, she decided that spending Christmas with Seth was a prospect too drab to contemplate. She texted Seth to tell him she wanted to talk. Most men would realise something was up if a woman asked to talk, but Seth wasn't most men.

Not that she would have to be alone at Christmas.

Although Ricky and Hilary were going ski-ing on Boxing Day, Elin was invited to lunchtime drinks on Christmas Day. She wondered if Joe would be there. Thursday evenings with Joe had continued, he played the part of charming man about town and Elin didn't make waves. She would ask Hilary about Joe's romantic dalliances. It would be nice to know. Joe with his chess playing wiles was not giving anything away.

As Elin drove away from school, loneliness loomed. There had been no response to her job applications and only Mr. Roberts' hints about a possible opening at River Park prevented her money concerns from escalating to panic proportions. She texted Mia, wanting to support her in the same way Mia had done when she was desperately unhappy. Jeannie didn't get much time off work for Christmas and Elin knew that Miles (or was it Jonathan?) would be home for a few days. Elin didn't want to intrude on family time, but needed to put something in the calendar so she fired off a quick query to Jeannie.

Elin sat down and switched on the TV. Better to fill up tomorrow cleaning and the next day she would shop for Christmas food for herself. She'd splurge on *Vogue* and *Hello* magazine and make sure she had some cheerful movies to watch. She was going to be fine by herself for the holidays.

True to form Seth arrived bang on the agreed time.

"Hello Seth, come in." Elin gave him a light kiss on the lips before ushering him towards the comfortable chair and making tea. "How've you been? Busy at work?"

"Yes, selling vouchers for joyrides as Christmas presents, the money's pouring in for no work these days." He managed a faint smile, "But it'll be all work and no money when they book the flights after Christmas."

"Perhaps some will never be cashed in, if a person's too

scared; then you'd have got your money for nothing." Elin tried to create a light-hearted atmosphere as she busied herself in the kitchen.

"Most people don't waste the gift, it's not cheap," Seth responded flatly.

Elin remembered her one and only plane ride. Idly she wondered if it was Seth's standard way of attracting a girlfriend. Once they were sitting with their tea, she steeled herself and took a deep breath. "Seth, I'm not the right woman for you. You want children and it's highly unlikely that I could ever have them. We've had some nice times, but I don't want to string you along when there's no future for us."

Seth stared down into the mug he held in both hands. Elin sat quietly. He didn't seem upset, so that was good. Eventually he realised that Elin was waiting for a response and he made an effort to formulate some words, "Thanks for telling me Elin. You could have chosen a better time than just before Christmas, but I guess it makes no difference." He fell silent and then drank some tea while Elin continued to watch him. He seemed to be thinking intently but she saw no sign of emotion. Eventually he spoke again, "I think I might look up my ex-girlfriend, perhaps she'll give me a second chance."

Elin was surprised but relieved that he wasn't upset. She could watch him go with a clear conscience. She'd had enough dramatic scenes to last a lifetime so it was a huge relief that this wasn't another one.

21

A ping announced a text; Joe wanted to change the time they were due to meet to 5 p.m. instead of 6.

The pub car park was already packed and a wall of sound and food-laden warmth hit her as she opened the door to the lounge bar, full of workers having a Christmas drink and office parties complete with silly hats. Joe spotted her and steered her towards a smaller back room. "I thought it would be quieter earlier, but I was wrong. I reserved us a table but they only just managed to fit us in right at the back."

It was marginally quieter in the small room and they scanned the menu with its predictable Christmas specials. Joe gave no reason for the change of time and Elin didn't ask. Conversation was difficult over the hubbub. Gradually the after-work drinkers dispersed and it was possible to speak and be heard easily. Elin and Joe had finished their meal and there was a cafetiere of fresh coffee in front of them. Joe leaned forward and spoke quietly, "I've got something to tell you Elin, before you hear it from some gossip monger who'd get it all wrong."

Elin had no idea what to expect so she didn't respond. She watched him take off his glasses, clean them and put them back on. He tried again, "It's been four months or more since we've had anything approaching what I'd call a marriage, hasn't it? It's been hard, rattling around in the house with no company, not even the dog. It's been lonely." There was a remnant of accusation in his tone but his usual confidence was lacking. Elin was intrigued; whatever it was, he was having a hard time getting it out. She wondered if he wanted a divorce. Surely, he wouldn't find that hard to say, he would enjoy being the one to reject her. She waited.

"A while back I got talking to this girl, a student from Germany in the final year of her Ph.D." Seeing Elin's raised eyebrows, he added hastily, "She wasn't one of my students. I met her at a seminar and we chatted. No problem about a teacher/student relationship, she was at a different university altogether."

Elin poured their coffee and waited. He had a girlfriend, big deal, there was no way he was going to sit at home alone for four months. What was the big mystery? She sipped her coffee and noted small beads of perspiration on his forehead and that his glasses were slipping down his nose again. He pushed his glasses back into place and took a deep breath, "She told me last week that she's pregnant."

Elin gasped, "Do you want to marry her? You want a divorce? Of course, I won't stand in your way. What would be the point? Just tell me what I have to do and I'll do it."

"My God, no, I don't want to marry her. I don't want a baby. I haven't changed my opinion about that. I just wanted to tell you, it seemed only fair." He blew a breath out slowly then reached for his cup.

Elin added more thoughtfully, "Does she want to move into the house? Is that it?"

"No, not at all. I told her quite clearly that I didn't want a baby. I offered to pay for a quick termination, but she wants to keep the baby. She wants an ongoing relationship with me, but I'm not having that. I think she wants to change my mind about being a father."

Elin listened as Joe developed his poor-me theme, tricked by another untrustworthy female. He couldn't see that he was equally responsible for the mess this girl was in. Elin couldn't believe what she was hearing, she couldn't believe that he could be so callous.

"Stop a minute Joe! Tell me more about this poor girl. How old is she and how is she going to manage?"

"She's twenty-three and her name is Dagmar. She's from Munich and she was doing research in Chemistry. She's going home to her parents and she says they'll help her and she'll bring up the baby in Germany and not ask me for anything. She says she won't contact me ever again."

Elin was appalled. She identified with the young woman, far from home, her career dreams shattered; pregnant and rejected by her lover, an older man she probably expected to protect her. She rounded on Joe and hissed at him, "I can't believe you'd behave like that. How could you treat her so badly? She's twelve years younger than you, she expected you to be responsible. Did you think I'd be jealous because she's pregnant and I can't have children? Is that why you told me? Did you think you'd hurt me that way?"

Elin's voice rose and Joe tried to hush her. He shoved a hand through his long hair, another sign of his increasing agitation. He glanced around, "I don't know why I told you. Now I wish I hadn't."

"I think it's disgusting that you're going to let that poor

girl slink off home and you're going to do nothing. What about her career, have you thought of that?"

Joe flushed, "She's getting a leave of absence from her department. She can have up to two years before she needs to come back and finish."

"I think your behaviour has been despicable! She may never catch up on the years' research she'll miss. The least you can do is acknowledge responsibility and pay maintenance. The child should know who its father is and know that he felt some sense of responsibility."

Joe tried to protest that Dagmar had decided to go back to Germany, that it was her decision.

"I don't want to hear any more. This is the last straw. Not Dagmar being pregnant, but your selfishness. This marriage is a charade so let's call it a day and start divorce proceedings."

Elin picked up her bag and stalked out. She drove home in a lather of anger, her feelings of solidarity with the pregnant girl uppermost. She appreciated the irony that this same feeling towards Rachel had led her to rejecting Aaron. The friendship of women was becoming more and more important in her life.

She woke in a low mood on the second day of her holidays. She chose a firm of solicitors from the Yellow Pages, then was told by a bored receptionist that there were no appointments until the week after Christmas. Elin took the first available slot and immediately felt better. No Joe, no Seth. She felt a surge of energy; the City Centre, the Christmas lights and a festive atmosphere felt enticing.

The covered food market was crowded, yet Elin wandered from stall to stall without complaint as she tried to decide on her Christmas meal. She wanted something special for the first Christmas dinner of her new life. Fresh salmon attracted her, with the suggested accompaniment of mango, roasted red pepper and coriander salsa. She picked up the recipe card, then splurged on the fish and the extra ingredients.

The night promised to be crisp and clear. Shoppers were in a festive mood despite their heavy bags and she heard laughter from knots of teenagers enjoying the excitement of the season. Salvation Army singers and their bells provided a pleasing background as Elin stood under the silver lights suspended across the main street, undecided about her next course of action. The thought of her miniscule pay cheque dented her mood and her energy slipped away. She turned towards the bus stop and saw two familiar figures cross the road. The man's head bent to catch what the woman was saying, then he joined in with her laughter and threw his arm casually round her shoulders as they hurried on. She realised that it was Aaron and Rachel. Elin froze and the man following behind cannoned into her. She apologised effusively, he smiled and wished her a Merry Christmas before walking around her and carrying on his way.

The shock gradually receded as Elin sat on the crowded bus analysing her feelings. She was certain that her obsession with Aaron was well and truly over even if her body had reacted viscerally at the sight of him. There was relief that Rachel seemed happy. She felt a connection between Rachel, Dagmar and herself. But worming its way into her consciousness was the realisation that Aaron and Rachel were together but she was on her own. She shook her head to rid herself of this feeling. Her single state was of her own choosing. She could have been driving home with Seth or Joe, not travelling on a crowded bus by herself, with a Christmas dinner which, gourmet feast or not, was still going to be eaten alone.

Back in the flat, she subsided into the comfy chair with a large glass of wine, allowing a few tears of self-pity to escape and trickle down her cheeks. "Come on Elin, what do YOU want to do?" she asked herself. Unfortunately, there was no immediate answer. Another glass of wine gave way to another until hours later she woke, woozy and with a crick in her neck. She didn't feel good. Groaning she castigated herself for drinking too much; a pick-me-up was one thing, a sledgehammer blow to any conscious thought was another. She staggered off to bed with a large glass of water and wished that Christmas would soon be over.

Christmas Eve passed in a blur. A hangover with added waves of loneliness. The dog was optimistic, but Elin buried her face in her hands to avoid his soulful eyes and took a nap. She was roused by him pawing at her side. At last the day was over and she shuffled off to bed with the unhappy knowledge that the phone had not rung all day and though her email inbox was telling her about post-Christmas sales not a single personal message had appeared.

With the run-up to Christmas over, the actual day wouldn't be so bad. Midday drinks at Hilary's sounded OK. If Joe showed up it wouldn't matter: the knowledge that he was soon to be her ex-husband pleased her enormously. She opened the predictable gifts from her parents, vouchers, a box of chocolates and some expensive soap. Elin wondered if they'd sent a gift to Joe. She had decided not to give him anything and no gift-wrapped parcel from him had arrived. She set off for Hilary and Ricky's, leaving Mutt gnawing an enormous bone and the cats playing with their new feathery toys.

In honour of the day, Elin had dressed to celebrate in a black wrap dress that showed her cleavage to advantage, a necklace from the clothing swap and killer heels. Her arrival was timed so that most of the guests would be on their first, if not their second, drink. The front door was unlocked and she walked into the familiar hallway without ringing the bell. Hilary spotted her from the lounge and called out, "Elin, Merry Christmas! You look great, come in and meet some people." Then turning to her son, "Finn, get Elin a drink please."

"Merry Christmas to you too. Tonic with ice and lemon please." Elin was relieved to see some familiar faces but no sign of Joe – so far, so good. She chatted with Gina and Bobby then other old neighbours wandered over. "Elin, we've missed seeing you around, so sorry to hear about the problems between you and Joe, though we weren't surprised. I don't know how you put up with it for so long."

"We've decided to get divorced. We thought we could work it out, but it's no better after months apart."

Hilary came closer, "You kept that quiet, Elin, why now, at Christmas? I thought it was the season of peace and goodwill."

Elin chose not to share the news of the pregnant girlfriend, "Oh, this and that. There was a chance at first, but it got really bad on Thursday so I decided to call it a day. Time to move on."

"If you're sure?" Hilary sounded doubtful. She guessed there was more so she deftly moved the subject on. "You must come around when we get back from ski-ing and fill me in."

"Course I will," Elin said and then put on her happy-party voice. "Introduce me to some new people!"

Ricky and Hilary threw good parties. Elin endured some conversations, enjoyed some others and had her interest tweaked by one. A retired teacher was holding forth. "Take philosophy, for example. Back in my day we had time to introduce basic philosophy and it helps kids to think, not parrot out facts. Learning how to think, knowing what questions to ask, it's the basis of good education."

There was a murmur of agreement but Elin said nothing and carried on listening. "I couldn't agree more. Have you heard of the Philosophy Café at the Drawbridge Centre? Anyone can go, it's free and I go whenever I can," added Angharad, a youngish woman with beautiful mane of long blonde hair.

"Philosophy Cafe eh? I like the sound of it, very Parisian. When do they have these discussions? I might go along."

"The first Tuesday of the month, you go along at 7.30, buy yourself a drink and sit anywhere. The place fills up, a guest speaker gives a short talk, then there's audience participation, you talk to whoever is sitting near you. There's even a Twitter feed! I'd be glad to take anybody who is interested with me."

Elin didn't even know what constituted a philosophical discussion. It would feel safe to tag along and she would meet new people – and it would not be one of Jeannie's singles' nights. "I'd love to come with you, could I have your phone number so I can get in touch?" Elin asked.

Angharad dug out her phone, "That'd be great! It'll be on the first Tuesday in January. I'll message you nearer the day to make arrangements."

When they exchanged phone numbers, Elin noticed four new texts. She smiled and decided to wait until she got home to read them. Later she found they were all happy greetings and invitations. Mia and Chrissie both invited her to the same New Year's Eve party at Chrissie's and Jared's house, Celia invited her to a New Year's Day Brunch and Jeannie asked if she was free for a Singles event on New

Year's Eve. She began to sing tunelessly as she marinated the salmon and prepared the salsa.

New Year's Eve soon arrived. She wanted to go to Chrissie's because a singles' night didn't appeal and two invitations to the same party trumped one. She talked to Jeannie several times and was relieved that she'd found another friend to keep her company. Elin turned up at Chrissie's at 9 p.m. with a bottle of wine in one hand and a tray of mini-quiches in the other. Jared answered the door, welcomed her with hug and called to Chrissie that Elin was here. Background music came from the front room and the usual buzz emanated from the kitchen.

"Elin, let me introduce you to some friends, some Buddhists, some not." Chrissie took her arm and guided her into the brightly lit kitchen where several men were leaning against the counters. Elin put her tray down, noticing the platters of interesting dishes already set out.

"Hey everyone, this is Elin, she's a friend of Mia's. Elin, these reprobates are Matt, Manuel and Caio. I'm only kidding, they are actually fine upstanding members of the community."

As more people squeezed into the kitchen introductions were abandoned. Matt poured her a glass of wine, commenting that he was sticking to water. Elin asked if he was the designated driver.

"No, we've ordered a taxi for later. We're going to do some special chanting to celebrate the start of a New Year. After that we'll start the real party!" Seeing the expression on Elin's face he laughed and went on, "Don't worry it won't last very long. We'll have a great time."

Elin made her way into the front room; Yoko saw her and hurried over, "So glad you could make it. You look lovely, I love your dress. This is my husband Lucas. Lucas, this is Elin, my new friend."

Lucas held out his hand and Elin took it; he asked, "Are you a Buddhist as well? Yoko has been chanting since before I met her, but I've never got around to it. It does her good though, doesn't it, darling?" He put his arm around her shoulder and squeezed lightly.

Soon Chrissie was clapping her hands for attention and encouraging the guests to get platefuls of food from the kitchen. The buffet table was groaning with an array of food from all over the world; curries, enchiladas, sushi, scotch eggs, and much more. Elin amused herself trying to work out which person had contributed each delicacy.

She found Mia and asked if she'd heard from Dan over the festive period. "I didn't but I had a relaxing time with my family. We don't all get together often, my mother loves it, loads of food and a lot of slumping in front of the TV. It's good to be back with my friends though."

"I'm glad you're back too." Elin explained about Dagmar and the impending divorce.

It was Mia's turn to look distressed, "Poor Dagmar, poor baby, what a start in life. It's sad, but it's good you're taking charge and making decisions."

Again, Chrissie was clapping her hands for people's attention. "OK folks, it's time! Those who want to chant the New Year in please come and sit in the front. The rest of you sit anywhere or head for the kitchen, whatever you like. Lucas has volunteered to get the champagne ready in the kitchen and when it's midnight we'll toast the New Year."

A cheer went up and to Elin's surprise nearly all the guests moved towards the front ready to chant. This time Elin knew what was coming so she found a comfy place and closed her eyes. Soon the melodious sound of chanting filled the air; she relaxed and let it flow over her. A muted TV in the corner showed the crowd in Trafalgar Square swaying and yelling Happy New Year as the camera panned over them. She decided to get ahead of her own crowd and made her way into the kitchen, where Lucas opened the first bottle of sparkling wine and handed her a flute with a flourish.

"You've obviously done this before, Lucas, thanks a lot. Happy New Year!"

"Happy New Year! Yoko brings me every year and I've grown to love it. They're all good people and they have lots of fun." Lucas opened a bottle of sparkling apple juice as well as the wine.

"You don't chant yourself then?"

"I don't go to church either. I leave all that to Yoko. She never pushes me. She's happy that I support her and that I do my barman act here." Lucas filled up more glasses as Jared joined them, ready to carry a tray of drinks into the front room. Evidently he didn't chant either.

Elin wandered back into the front room; it was almost midnight. The beautiful bell was rung and the group chanted three times, slowly. Someone turned the volume up on the TV, the chimes of Big Ben reverberating in unison with the bell. Both sounds faded away and everyone cheered and wished each other a Happy New Year. The sparkling wine and juice was almost an afterthought and Elin was very relieved there was no kissing of random strangers. She felt enveloped by an aura of goodwill and friendship.

Groups were forming and reforming, several people were hunting for coats in the hall and Elin found herself chatting to Bob – known as Rasta man in her head. She discovered he worked for a children's charity and did outreach programmes in schools. Elin filed away information that might be useful in the future. Then Mia joined them and Elin asked about Celia.

"She couldn't get a babysitter. Her parents are out and no teenager wants to babysit on New Year's Eve. She's OK with it, says she'll be fresh to host our New Year's Day brunch tomorrow. Are you coming Elin?"

"Yes, I hope so. I've had a quiet week so two parties in two days will fit the bill. What should I bring?"

"We'll be cooking sausages and eggs so anything breakfasty will be fine." Mia wasn't too concerned about details.

"So fresh fruit salad or croissants or bagels?" asked Elin.

"Anything, but no booze. New Year's Eve is an exception, it'll be coffee, tea and fruit juice as usual tomorrow."

The atmosphere the next day at Celia's was vibrant. Elin took her fruit salad to the familiar kitchen where three frying pans stood waiting on the stove. Elin followed the others into the living room and unobtrusively took a chair. She couldn't believe she was going to listen to more chanting. She closed her eyes, relaxed and let the sound wash over her. Time passed quickly. They talked about the New Year being an opportunity to improve everything in their lives and the importance of determination. She liked that concept. Mia spoke, sounding positive.

When the sound of the bell signalled the end of formalities the atmosphere changed again. Everyone was smiling and laughing. It was infectious and Elin found herself smiling too as they went into the kitchen where the men donned aprons and started to cook. Celia bustled about making fresh coffee. Elin felt the warmth of friendliness and acceptance as she surveyed the chattering groups. People she knew and people she didn't know all seemed equally open. They ate sausages, both vegetarian and meaty, dipped in spicy tomato salsa, and creamy scrambled eggs served straight from the pan to the plate. Replete, Elin sat on the floor in the still crowded living room with a large mug of fresh coffee in her hand, wondering how her New Year would be. In this company, she felt optimistic but she was afraid the feeling would evaporate once she was alone again.

THE PHILOSOPHY CAFÉ a few days later meant another room crowded with people she didn't know and another buzz of conversation. Angharad bought them each a glass of wine and they looked for somewhere to sit. They dragged two chairs towards a group and introduced themselves. Elin leaned back and scanned the room. As her gaze returned to nearby tables she locked glances with a man staring intently at her. She registered his age, roughly hers, and that there was a hint of rakish gypsy about him, but most of all she was drawn to his heavy-lidded, pale blue eyes. She looked away hastily. The conversation at her table swirled, she darted another glance his way and saw he was still watching her. She smiled faintly in his direction and lowered her eyes as she slowly sipped her wine.

Elin was acutely aware of him as he stood there, drink in hand, watching and listening to the speaker. His air of slight dishevelment was sexy as hell and Elin felt a tingle of arousal. She bought a drink for Angharad, hoping her new admirer wouldn't move away while she was gone. As they moved their chairs ready for the debate, Elin heard a well-modulated voice behind her asking to join their group. The attractive stranger leaned on the back of Elin's chair and introduced himself as Chris Summers. Before the evening had finished, with Elin's grasp of philosophy still very tenuous, they had exchanged phone numbers and Elin left, floating on air with the prospect of a new romance lightening her every step.

Before she had parked outside the flat she heard a text arrive. It was Chris, suggesting a pub lunch the next day. Without hesitation Elin agreed. Sleep was elusive; it was a long time since she'd felt such heady anticipation.

ELIN AND CHRIS talked nonstop as they shared a Ploughman's lunch at the Merry Archer. He had studied and lived in London for years, and as Elin had never been part of a creative scene she was entranced by his sophisticated tales. Chris was a writer, which impressed Elin hugely; she'd never met a published author before, but he told her disconsolately that he was stuck on his second novel. He'd got writer's block. He was interested in Elin's life and they realised they shared stalled careers. Time flew by until it seemed natural to hold hands and order coffee and cheesecake to prolong their time together. Elin glanced at her watch then jumped to her feet, "I hadn't realised it was so late, I'm sorry I have to go, my extremely large dog needs a run before it's pitch dark."

"I'd enjoy a walk in the park, do you mind if I come with you?" Chris was already putting on his jacket.

Mutt didn't care who came to the park with him, he hurtled around as Elin and Chris walked hand in hand until the light began to fade. Elin pulled her scarf more tightly around her neck, "Shall we get pizza or something?" They took Mutt back and rubbed him down before ordering and Chris offered to go to the corner shop for beer. Elin found herself with a window of time to freshen up. Her face glowed in the bathroom mirror. She took a deep breath and told herself not to rush headlong into another relationship.

Chris arrived back as Elin was lighting candles and they ate at the rickety kitchen table. They watched the candles burn down before Chris rose to put the leftovers away. "Glass of wine Elin? No more driving tonight!" She nodded and he poured her a glass from the box in the fridge.

They sat down on the big floor cushions and Elin put on some music. It felt as natural as breathing for Elin to return Chris's gentle kisses as they snuggled close for warmth. They talked about life's unexpected detours; Elin felt she had known him forever.

Elin spooned enough coffee for two into the cafetiere the next morning, then beat four eggs ready for scrambling. Judging by the singing to be heard over the noise of the shower, Chris was feeling good. The shower stopped, Elin pushed the lever down on the toaster. She was stirring the eggs in the saucepan when she heard Chris come up quietly behind her. He buried his face in the warmth of her neck; she inhaled the fresh scent of her own shower gel and asked, "Did you sleep OK? Was it cold on the floor or did the cats keep you warm?"

"I had to battle for my share of the blankets. Alley, or was it Tom, certainly knows how to stake his claim and stick to it."

As Chris buttered the toast and Elin served the eggs, she was glad that Chris had elected to sleep on a makeshift bed on the floor rather than walk home in the pouring rain.

A writer with writer's block proved to be the ideal companion for Elin, a welcome distraction from the business of finding another job. She sent off hopeful applications and they spent hours walking Mutt, hand in hand and talking nonstop. Elin laid the ghost of Aaron to rest as they walked along the beach. Chris told her his wife had divorced him a year earlier, saying she was fed up of waiting around for his genius to strike again. Elin thought his ex-wife sounded quite heartless. At the end of the week they popped back to his flat to check the post.

Elin surveyed the sparsely furnished room. "Where do you write? I don't see a desk?" she ventured.

"The laptop is a wonderful invention, I often go to the library, they have Wi-Fi. Saves me paying to have it here."

She said nothing more and they made their way back to the relative comfort of Elin's place. When he stayed overnight she was still making him sleep on the floor and he accepted the situation with good grace. He must have known it was only a matter of time and he was right.

22

E lin dropped into Chris' place on the way home from the first day of Spring Term. He looked cold and miserable, wrapped in a blanket. Elin's buoyant mood was contagious as they walked the dog so both were glowing when they returned to Elin's warm flat. Chris was an attentive lover and by the end of the week Elin's tolerance for driving him home at the end of the evening was waning and by Saturday had disappeared completely. Sharing her bed was a lot more comfortable for Chris than the cushions on the floor, and by the following week there was no doubt that Chris and Elin were a couple. Chris' rent was due at the end of January and it seemed foolish to keep paying for a place merely to store his clothes. Fortunately, or unfortunately, his possessions were few and they joined Elin's without much difficulty.

Elin's days were more relaxed without having to exercise the dog. Chris brought Elin tea in bed in the morning and walked Mutt twice a day. Dinner was prepared by the time she came home and flowers presented on the days Chris' money came through. They took Mutt to the beach or the mountains at weekends, combining their walks with lunches in front of roaring fires in ancient pubs.

The only cloud on the horizon was Elin's job situation. Much as she loved being at River Park, there was nothing to spare after paying rent and bills. Joe had told her that she could no longer take as much as she wanted from their joint account and she feared he was not going to be generous with the divorce settlement. He said it was Elin's choice to get divorced and as they had no children he had no need to worry about her financial plight. Her last interview had been a disaster with no job offer and she was waiting for replies from her latest batch of applications. Mr. Roberts at River Park had said nothing since his hints before Christmas.

Jeannie popped in one evening to meet Chris, but Elin hadn't introduced him to Hilary yet. Elin's new friends had not abandoned her, she received several phone calls from Celia and Chrissie. It was such a relief to Elin that she could honestly say that things were great.

Elin made time for one important person, Mia, because although Mia assured her she was fine, Elin found that difficult to believe. She decided to visit her one Sunday, assuring Chris she'd be back by 1 p.m. to go for their usual pub lunch. Mia was wreathed in smiles as she greeted Elin, "Lovely to see you! Tell me about Chris." Mia listened, smiling at Elin's torrent of superlatives.

Elin stopped short, embarrassed, "Sorry Mia, I got carried away! Have you heard from Dan?"

Mia shook her head, "No, I don't expect to. I know we could be happy together, but he doesn't realise that yet. Perhaps he never will. He's got to work out his own feelings. I have to be happy with or without him, and I'm getting there."

Elin was impressed. Mia was strong. In comparison, she felt like a reed blowing in the wind, sad or happy depending what luck brought her way. They discussed jobs or lack of them, money or lack of it and managed to laugh a lot. They ate mounds of buttered toast and Elin remembered the times she had been consoled by the same comfort food. Elin glanced at the time then gasped and leapt to her feet, it was almost two o'clock. "Oops! We're going for a pub lunch. I said I'd be back by one. Sorry to rush away, Mia, it's been lovely. Come around to meet Chris, how about Wednesday or Thursday?"

"I'd love to but I can't do either, my sister's coming on Wednesday and on Thursday there's a meeting at Chrissie's. Why don't you come, you could bring Chris and I could meet him?"

Elin was scrambling into her coat, "I'll ask him, I did enjoy the party on New Year's Eve."

Chris was waiting at the window when Elin drew up outside the flat. He appeared anxious and came out to the car before she had finished parking. "You're OK! I was getting worried. It's not too late, is it? I was looking forward to trying the Old Mill today, what do you think?"

Elin patted her stomach, "I've eaten so much toast, I'm not ready for a roast dinner right now. Shall we give it a miss today?"

For a fraction of a second Chris looked like a young child refused a treat. He recovered and smiled, "Whatever you say honey bunch. Do you want me to take the dog to the park on my own or are you coming?"

"I'll come, I need the exercise. You and the dog are getting fitter and I'm getting fatter!"

Chris gave her a playful pat on the bottom, "Have you heard me complain?" He popped back into the house to get

Mutt and the lead. They bought the Sunday papers from Mr. Hassan on the way back and Elin settled down to read them from cover to cover.

Chris grabbed a snack, opened his laptop and stared at the screen. He tapped a few keys, stopped, then walked around the room. He sat down again, stared into space, wrote for a while, paced up and down, sat again, scrolled through his work and sighed. Elin didn't look up, she didn't want to disturb his train of thought. Another ten minutes and he put his head in hands. Elin carried on reading but it was hard to concentrate. Chris got up, opened the fridge and stared inside before closing it again with a bang. At this Elin looked up.

"Do you want me to make you something to eat as you're working?"

"Working!" exploded Chris, "I've only managed half a page of rubbish. I'd read it to you if it was any good."

Elin put her arms round him. She could feel the tension in his body, "Do you want to talk about it?"

"Talking won't help. I have to write but it's so hard." Chris returned her embrace briefly then started to pace again. "I need to get away from the computer. Let's go to the pub for an hour then come back and snuggle in."

Elin would have stayed at home happily, but what difference did an hour make? She got up and put on her jacket. "Let's walk, I get fed up always being the driver. When you're a famous author you can drive me round in your Porsche!"

They walked for ten minutes to the Railway Inn where the barman greeted Chris by name. They sat at the bar with their neighbours, James and Philip. Elin had met the young couple but there'd never been time for a conversation before. One hour became two, and two became three; Elin felt hungry but there were only some uninviting Cornish pasties on offer. She tried to get Chris' attention but he was chatting with an elderly man at the next table.

Elin stood, "It's been good to meet you two properly, but I need to go home. See you around." Elin tugged gently at Chris' sleeve while smiling at his companion. "Ready to leave Chris? We've been here three hours already and I'm hungry, aren't you?"

Chris returned Elin's smile, "Mr. Stewart and I are discussing what makes a good read. Why don't we stay a bit longer?"

Elin was undecided. Chris was enjoying himself but she was really hungry.

James and Philip overheard the exchange. "Would you like to walk home with us? We're leaving," James said.

"That would be great, OK with you, Chris?"

"That's fine, I won't be very long." Chris got up and helped Elin on with her jacket.

Once back in her kitchen, Elin decided to make a large pot of pasta sauce so that Chris could concentrate on writing and not have to think about dinner for a few days. Soon it was simmering away and she threw enough pasta for two into a saucepan of boiling water and prepared a salad. Twenty minutes later she was tucking into a steaming bowl and crunching freshly dressed salad. Nicely full, she picked up the papers but her eyelids began to droop so she decided to read in bed. She switched off the living room light and became aware of the glow from Chris' laptop still open on the coffee table. She was overcome with curiosity. In his rush to go out he hadn't shut it down so with one tap his half page of writing was illuminated. Elin hesitated, feeling guilty although Chris had mentioned reading it to her. She tried to make sense of it. Was it a new story or was it the middle of his stalled novel? It appeared to be well crafted but she was no expert and at least he had written something. She padded off to bed and soon fell asleep.

Two rejections arrived for Elin on Monday. She got ready for school determined that if she saw Mr. Roberts she would ask him about any teaching positions. She dropped a kiss on the top of Chris' head, the rest of him still snuggling under the duvet and extra blankets. They needed a bigger bed, there was such a thing as too much togetherness.

When she opened the door after school that evening, Elin was greeted by the aroma of spaghetti sauce reheating, while steam warmed the kitchen as water came to the boil in readiness for pasta. Mutt was lying exhausted in his bed and Chris was typing away.

"Hello, honey bunch, had a good day?" Chris got up, hugged her and lifted her right off the ground.

"Thanks, it was good once I got over the rejections I got this morning. I'm going to see Mr. Roberts this week. How was your day?"

"I've got a few words down at last. I'll show you later? Let me cook the spaghetti first."

Elin exchanged her boots for slippers, still shivering from the cold and wintry conditions outside. Chris opened a bottle of wine, he must have gone shopping as well as walking the dog, they'd finished the box on Saturday night.

"You're spoiling me, shopping, walking the dog and getting dinner started! It's a wonder you had time to write."

"Let's eat and then I'll read it to you."

"Is this a new story or is this a continuation of book number two?"

Chris explained that he was trying a short story before returning to his novel. He brought the laptop over to the table, told her the story thus far and then started to read.

Elin listened, concentrating hard. The words sounded familiar, like the ones she had read last night. She poured another glass for both of them. "It's hard for me to comment, I'm new to all this. There was a certain passage I loved." Elin leaned over to scan the page, then pointed. "Here it is, that's so beautiful. I can't wait to hear more."

Chris beamed, "Enough of me and my book, let's cuddle in front of the TV."

Now that she had met James and Philip properly she noticed them every day. They lived just three houses away. Monday, they all rushed out and off to work at the same time. Tuesday, Philip waved a greeting as he hurried into the house while she parked the car. Wednesday, she and James competed for the same parking space until he realised who it was and relinquished his claim. Half an hour later he knocked on their door.

"Hi, sorry about the parking Elin, I didn't realise it was you! Phil and I have decided to have a little *soiree* tomorrow evening, just a few friends, some nibbles and wine, we hope you can come?"

"Tomorrow?" answered Elin, turning to Chris, "Do you have anything planned Chris?"

"Nope, what time should we come over?" Chris said as he clapped James on the back.

"Seven-ish? Our poet friend is staying on Thursday and we thought that as you were a writer, Chris, you might have something in common. Of course, you might hate each other! It'll go on until about ten, eleven, no later as it's a week night."

"What should we bring?" Elin waited as James thought for a second or two.

"Nothing at all, we're doing fancy nibbles because Phil likes preparing them. See you about 7 tomorrow."

After James left, Elin realised what the niggle in the back of her brain was trying to tell her. "Damn! Mia invited me to Chrissie's tomorrow night and I forgot! Mia asked me first so I feel bad about forgetting."

"Never mind sweetie, it'll be fun and you won't have to drive. Don't worry about it." Elin composed an apologetic text to Mia and sent it off before she did any more forgetting. Just as well she wasn't driving to Chrissie's on Thursday evening, she had an early appointment with Mr. Roberts on Friday.

THE MODERN DÉCOR at James and Philip's house reminded Elin of her old home, scaled down. Elin chatted happily with new people while keeping her eye on the time. At ten she decided to leave, but Chris was listening intently to the famous guest. She whispered, "I'm off now, you stay, I'll be fine. Goodnight darling, see you later." Chris smiled and gave her a sweet kiss goodnight.

Elin emerged from bed aching and stiff the next morning muttering, "Must get that new bed tomorrow, this one's not big enough for two, no more putting it off." Chris stretched out contentedly now he had the whole bed to himself, looking so sexy even with his extra dark stubble and bleary eyes. He mumbled, "Have a good day, hope Roberts comes up with a plan."

Mr. Roberts, however, didn't come up with a plan. He told Elin that he would be only too pleased to have her on the teaching staff once an opening arose. He repeated, "Going through the correct channels, of course." Whatever that meant.

"Of course," echoed Elin and pushed him for more details. She didn't want to waste this precious opportunity, but sorry as he was, he couldn't say anything definite. Everything was extremely confidential. He was sure she understood. She did. She left his room more dejected than when she'd gone in. For the first time since she'd worked at River Park, she couldn't wait for the school day to be over and the weekend to start.

Ikea on a Saturday morning was crowded with families, errant toddlers and screaming babies, so by the time Chris and Elin sank down with a coffee each in the restaurant they were exhausted and bad tempered. Elin stared at Chris, "What do you mean you haven't got any money? You're thirty-four years old and you've had a novel published. I assumed we'd split the cost of the new bed. You like the most expensive one. I can't afford it, Chris! Maybe you should get a job?"

Chris took her hand, abashed, "I'm sorry. I'm no good with money. I was generous to friends in difficulties. I paid for a new bathroom for my mother and I lived well. The novel stopped selling and I got writer's block. That's it." He stroked her hand, "You deserve better."

He looked so disconsolate, Elin softened. "But you're writing now?" She searched his face for some sign of reassurance.

"Let me try a bit longer? I know I can write." He mustered up a feeble smile.

Elin drank in the details of his handsome face, stricken by his despairing expression. In her heart, their troubles melted away. "Let's get the cheapest one, it'll do until you get that bestseller published!" Elin couldn't think badly of a man, especially one with those amazing blue eyes, who gave money to friends and paid for a new bathroom for his mother.

The weeks until Valentine's Day were stressful. Elin

worked, Chris wrote. Most evenings they had dinner, opened a bottle of wine and Chris read his work aloud, phrases he'd fine-tuned and he explained how he spent hours getting a sentence exactly right. Time went by but the plot didn't advance. She wasn't sure if Chris was writing a short story or a novel. She hoped it was a short story; she'd be drawing her pension before a novel was finished.

Hilary was nonchalant about the situation. She could see why Elin had fallen for Chris. "If sex is good, hang on to him! He's useful about the house and walks the dog; he's faithful, even tempered and he loves you. What's the problem?"

Elin couldn't explain her anxiety. She missed taking Mutt out and all the food and wine were settling round her middle.

Joe didn't contact her these days and she didn't contact him. Another few weeks and a court date would be set for the divorce. Life would be easier once the settlement came through; she wanted it as a deposit to buy the flat, but she still needed a good job for the mortgage.

On Valentine's Day, Elin bought a funny card and some fillet steak, asparagus and a bottle of champagne for a treat. She hurried home to set the scene for a romantic evening. Chris was waiting for her with a red rose, smiling broadly, "You remember old Mr. Stewart from the Railway Inn? I saw him today and he helped me with the next plot twist!"

"Great!" They smooched joyfully until Elin leaned back. "Do you want to eat now or later?"

Chris carried two glasses carefully into the bedroom. As Elin pulled her sweater over her head he came up behind her, unhooked her bra and caressed her breasts. Falling on to their new bed, they toasted each other before making love tenderly. They lay back in a haze of contentment until Chris recovered the bottle from the fridge, pulled the duvet around their shoulders and toasted Elin, his muse, again. Their eyes closed. Elin felt the stirring of hunger pangs and leaving Chris to doze she made her way to the kitchen. She made a salad with the expertise of long practice and heated up the oven and grill. Candles sent a glow over the rickety table. As the steak was grilling she leaned over her sleeping lover to kiss him awake but he groaned and snuggled deeper into the duvet. Next, she shook him gently and whispered in his ear, still to no effect. She hurried back to the kitchen where the steaks were done to perfection. Placing a steak on each of the warmed plates to rest, she dressed the salad, calling to Chris that the meal was almost ready. Finally, she put the steaks at their places at the table and garnished them with asparagus in melted butter. She surveyed her handiwork with satisfaction.

She stood looking down at Chris. He hadn't moved an inch and was sleeping heavily. She shook him harder this time and spoke sharply in his ear. Still no response other than a groan. Next Elin pulled the duvet off roughly and shouted his name.

He rubbed his eyes. "Elin babes, I can't wake up. Could I have mine later or tomorrow? I just can't keep my eyes open."

"But it's Valentine's Day, it's a special meal!"

"OK honey bunch, you get started, I'll be there in a jiffy." Chris was struggling to sit up and he reached for a sweater as Elin left the room. She sat at the table, her knife slid easily through the meat but it felt like leather as she chewed. As Chris walked slowly to the table Elin spoke quietly.

"Darling, could you pour me a little wine?"

Chris picked her wineglass from the table and walked towards the fridge; he pressed the tap on the wine-box but only a few drops sputtered into the glass. "Sorry babes, it's finished, is there more in the cupboard?"

"You know there's no more, we agreed to cut back, it can't be gone in two days!" Elin couldn't keep her voice from becoming shrill.

"We had champagne tonight, that's hardly economising, is it? Why the fuss, it's only a box of plonk?"

"The champagne is for Valentine's Day! Maybe I shouldn't have bought such expensive food, but it was our first Valentine's Day together." Elin felt tears prickle.

Chris looked contrite and simultaneously tried to swallow a yawn, "I'm sorry Elin, I just can't keep awake."

"Oh, forget it," Elin gave up, "the food's getting cold." Chris ate a mouthful or two then excused himself and went to the bathroom. Elin finished eating and rinsed her plate. She checked the bedroom, it was only nine o'clock but Chris was stretched out under the duvet snoring ever so slightly.

What was happening? Chris was a wonderful partner in many ways. It was only a meal and Valentine's Day was just a date on the calendar. He loved her and she loved him, so what was the problem? Mutt came and put his beautiful head on her lap, looking at her with soulful eyes.

"If only you could talk Mutt." Elin ruffled his neck affectionately, "You don't understand what's happening, but you know that something's not quite right don't you, my old friend?"

23

Anxiety became the default mood for Elin as the Easter term wore on without a job offer. She felt a growing sense of frustration about Chris' writing despite his assurances that he was getting words on the page, a great improvement on the barren times before they met. He no longer read to her each day, the habit had become sporadic until it finally ceased without comment. She occasionally stole a glance at the screen as he typed but saw nothing to elevate her alarm or give much hope that completion was imminent. She didn't want to nag, but he'd have to get a job soon.

Elin wondered if she and Chris would benefit from a change from routine, a trip away, maybe a festival or a theatre break. She mentioned it to Chris and later that evening opened her laptop to check out bargain theatre breaks in London. She looked at musicals.

"*Mama Mia* or *Phantom of the Opera*?" she asked Chris who was staring at the screen of his computer.

"What's that? "

"Would you prefer *Mama Mia* or *Phantom of the Opera*? Or anything else? It's too early for a festival."

"Sounds fun. You choose, OK?" Chris returned to his screen.

"There are seats available but not at weekends. My goodness, I didn't realise they cost that much!"

Chris murmured an unintelligible reply and Elin continued to look at her screen, trying other theatres and special deals before changing tack.

"We'd have to get a hotel unless we can stay with someone. Do you know anybody we could stay with, Chris?"

"Uh, what's that you said? Sorry didn't catch it."

"Do you know anybody in London? Any college friends still there?"

"No, sorry, we've lost touch. I suppose it'll have to be a hotel unless you know anybody?"

"The ones that come to mind have small children and small houses, not exactly relaxing for us. I'll check to see if there are any hotel deals." Some minutes later, Elin slammed her laptop closed. "I didn't realise how expensive it would be, we can't afford it unless you contribute. Looks like we'll have another couple of weeks stuck here in the holidays."

"Don't give up yet, there might be last minute deals?"

Elin didn't reply. She made herself a mug of tea and headed for the bathroom. "I'm going to have a hot bath, loosen the knots in my shoulders, then have an early night."

Elin lay back in the bath and closed her eyes. What was sailing along under her radar and unsettling her? She loved her work and would surely find a better job before long. The money settlement from Joe would come soon. She hadn't given Aaron a thought for months and Seth had slipped out of her life as quietly as he'd crept into it. She felt secure in her flat with Alley, Tom and Mutt. She had old and new friends and a loving boyfriend who was clearly not out on the town with other women. The feeling had come on strongly this evening and not for the first time.

The water was cooling so Elin turned the hot tap on with her toe and ramped the temperature of the water up as hot as she could stand. It wasn't good for her skin, but she didn't care. She wanted the stiffness in her neck to ease and the tension in her mind to go away. She sank down so that the hot water swirled around her neck, wetting her hair. Even her hair was not pleasing to her these days. She had experimented with a new and cheaper salon, but the results were less than satisfactory.

After working late on prep work for Easter craft sessions the next day, Elin decided to visit Celia. It was gone 6 pm and she hoped that Celia would be home. She bought apples and chocolate biscuits on the way, then stood at the front door and waited for someone to answer the bell.

"What a lovely surprise," Celia said as she opened the door. "Please ignore the mess, we're making Easter eggs and cards for Grandma and Grandpa. Come in the kitchen, we can have a cup of tea."

They sat at the table and made cards until Elin suddenly realised the time. Thanks Celia, for the tea and company, I'd better go, it must be bedtime?" Elin helped sort stickers and stash away paints.

"Why don't you wait and we can have a grown-up chat if you haven't got to rush home?" Celia spoke as she wiped up biscuit crumbs

"I already texted Chris, one of our neighbours has a connection in the writing business and they're meeting up, so he'll be out 'til late."

"Wonderful, it'll be nice to have company after the girls

have gone to bed. I was going to have some soup and a salad, there's plenty for two. Why don't you relax and I'll be down in less than half an hour?"

Bowls of lentil soup steamed on the table alongside crisp salad, and as the two sat down to eat Celia said, "Tell me what's happening, it's been a few weeks since I've seen you."

Elin pondered before speaking, "I'm still enjoying the school but I have to get a better job soon. I didn't realise that my CV wouldn't be good enough. They assume that because I didn't work continuously I must be unreliable. I can't explain because I'm not getting interviews. They're not meeting me, just my CV."

Celia leaned forward and thought for a few seconds. "That must be frustrating. Any opportunities at the schools where you've worked as a supply teacher, so the head teacher would know you?"

"The only one with a job advertised was Beechwood High and I blotted my copybook there. Do you know what happened?" Elin grimaced.

"No, it couldn't have been that bad, surely?"

Elin gave Celia a potted version of the Aaron affair followed by the cold shoulder from Fiona. "I don't think I'd be a popular choice. Mrs. Wilkinson, the head, would have heard the sorry tale from somebody. It's a shame, because it was a great school."

Celia gave a frown of sympathy, "Do you really want to teach at a High School or a Primary School?"

Trust Celia to put her finger on it. Elin responded slowly, "I always thought that having a science degree meant High School. I loved teenagers and didn't think about younger children. Last summer holiday was a bad time and by the end of it I couldn't wait to get out of the house and I fell into this job at River Park. I'm surprised I've enjoyed it as much as I have, but the money's not enough. If the permanent job that the head has hinted about would materialise, I'd seriously think about teaching in a Primary School as a career move. At the moment, I'd take anything that paid better."

Celia looked intently at Elin, "I can see it's difficult, but you're happy with Chris, right? He seems like a nice guy."

"Yes, and he's always there, not like Joe, not a married man like Aaron, and not wanting children like Seth. I'm trying to learn from my mistakes! He's divorced with no children. He helps in the flat and takes the dog out so life goes along smoothly. He's very attentive and good in bed. We get along well, but I wish he'd get on with his book or get something published, start earning money again. I've never been the creative type so I don't understand how creativity can disappear. I'm just hoping his will reappear soon." Elin smiled hopefully.

"Nothing else, no other worries?" Celia probed.

"That's just it, Celia, I'm not sure what's bothering me. I was hoping you might have some advice, you're happy and I know how much you've been through."

"A good friend can help a lot, I do remember that. I don't know how I would have managed without my neighbour Suzie. But she could be strict, quite hard on me for my own good."

"What do you mean 'hard on you'? What good would that do?"

"It sounds counter-intuitive, doesn't it? I was a terrible mess at the time so I needed strong guidance." Celia grimaced, then smiled at Elin. "You're a different matter, despite your problems, you've got a lot going for you. You have a home, a job, a boyfriend, no debts, no dependents. It's not my place to push you in any direction."

"I see what you mean, but I feel directionless. As a matter of interest, what do you mean that Suzie was strict? You didn't have to do what she said, did you?"

"I didn't have to, but somehow in the depth of my crazy life I understood that she was trying to help me. I was a mess, but I listened. You've already heard what she told me."

Elin frowned slightly, "I can remember you said you were fighting with your husband and the walls were shaking with the rows, but I don't remember what she said."

Celia started laughing, "Your face is a picture Elin, you think I'm teasing you but I'm not, honestly I'm not!"

"It does feel as if you're teasing me!" Elin started to laugh too. "Go on, tell me again, please."

"Chanting. You told us you didn't want to do it, but Chrissie, Mia and I have all mentioned how Buddhist chanting has helped us be happier. We've changed, become stronger, since we started. It's up to you, nothing bad is going to happen because you choose not to chant. Good things and bad things happen in life, they happen all the time and they happen to everybody."

"I can't see myself chanting although I'm not as freaked out by it as I used to be. I'm such a realist, but I'm glad it helped you, Celia, I really am."

"I'm not going to nag, let's change the subject. What about another fashion swap? Lots of us are getting our summer clothes out, it would be a great time to do it. I'm happy to host again."

"Great idea! I've put on weight so some of my stuff will be too tight. Let's do it soon." Elin bounced with excitement.

Celia laughed, "Sometime in the Easter holidays? That would suit you teachers, wouldn't it?"

"That would be great, I'm excited. I had nothing to look forward to, you've changed my outlook already."

"Not a problem, m'dear, let's fix a date."

They delved into their handbags to coordinate diaries. "Jeannie's going away in May, so as early as possible for her. How does April 15th suit you? I think a Friday is the best night, isn't it?" They bent their heads together, fixed the date and the guest list.

"Thanks for dinner and brightening my day, Celia."

"I'll be chanting for things to go well for you. Looking forward to the C Swap!"

Elin jumped in the car and Mia's fashion transformation popped up on her mind-screen. She checked the time, then texted Mia who responded immediately, she had big news to tell. Intrigued, Elin put the car into gear and drove to find out.

Mia opened the door, her beaming smile dispelled Elin's hesitation about the late hour. "Come in for a bit, Dan's popped out to get a curry."

"Dan! Dan's here?" Elin was dumbfounded. She embraced Mia then held her at arms' length. "Is he back to stay?"

"Seems like it! He came around earlier, he wants to start over. We talked for hours and he's moving back in. We're celebrating with a takeaway!"

Elin stayed standing, "How wonderful! You were right!"

Mia gestured to the sofa, "Sit down, take your coat off."

Elin shook her head decisively, "I'm not staying, I won't intrude, but I'm so glad I came and saw your smiling face. Tell me more soon. Enjoy the curry."

After enfolding Mia in her arms again, Elin returned home, ecstatic for Mia and happy that she'd have new clothes soon and they wouldn't cost a penny.

24

Chris and Elin sat together nursing cups of tea, the faint spring sunshine sparkling on the mirrored floor cushions. Elin broke the reflective silence, "The last few months have been great, but I'm worried about money. Is there no way you could get a job, maybe part time, and still write?" Elin rubbed the skin on the inside of her wrist until it was red.

"Stop worrying sweetheart, what do we want more money for anyway?"

"There's nothing for emergencies like vet bills or car problems. I don't like it."

Chris put his mug down and patted her hand, "You've put in more applications, haven't you? You'll get a better paid job soon, it's bound to happen."

Elin got up and walked around the room, "It's not bound to happen, can't you see? All my applications, and not even an interview. We may have to give up the flat and find somewhere cheaper."

Chris looked abashed and said nothing. Elin stopped her pacing and faced him. "Come on Chris, say something!

Give me a clue about your book, give me something to hang on to, please?"

Chris looked down, "I thought it was going well, that's why I haven't looked for work. I was getting words down, but they weren't any good." He faltered. "I abandoned the novel, started on short stories, hoping they'd be easier to sell."

Elin gasped. She had assumed the book would be finished though she wasn't so naive as to think it would be a bestseller. "How's that going? Any chance of selling one?"

Chris drained his mug and refilled it before replying, "I've got three on the go so it won't be long."

"You haven't finished a single short story in three months?" Elin sank back onto her seat and put her head in her hands.

Chris didn't look at her. He picked up her mug, "Do you want more tea? I can make more, if you like?"

Elin's voice shook, "No, I don't want more tea." She didn't move. "I need time to process this."

"I was ashamed. I'm so sorry. I'll take the dog out, get out of your way," Chris said. He kissed her softly, picked up Mutt's lead and left.

Elin closed her eyes and saw the image of his stricken face. After a few minutes, she got up and wandered round the flat. She was so disappointed in dear, sweet Chris. She stood in the kitchen but couldn't face more tea. A glass of wine might help, it wasn't often she felt the need to steady her nerves but this was one such moment. A slow trickle made its way from the box into her glass. She paced around the flat, then the garden with its sparse grass and sickly bushes. Back in their bedroom she flung herself on the bed, staring at the ceiling. Her life felt deadlocked. Not a year had passed since she'd felt in the same hopeless state, trapped in her previous life with Joe. Now she was free to do what she liked, but what could she do?

Her life was a tangled ball of problems with no place to start unravelling them. It wasn't as bad as Celia's had been, was it? Celia had suggested chanting to see if it made a difference. She'd said that it would bring out Elin's innate wisdom and courage. Elin needed wisdom right now, but she couldn't remember the words.

Chris was still out; Elin grew restless and decided to tidy the kitchen. Dinner was already made, a casserole of chicken using all the wrinkled vegetables from the depths of the cupboard to postpone the need to go shopping again. She began to feel better, gaining the illusion of control as plastic tubs were arranged by size, lids stacked neatly. She culled takeaway menus and sorted business cards. Here was an unusual one, for an international organisation concerned with peace, culture and education, called the SGI. On the other side in large print were the words *Nam Myoho Renge Kyo*. She turned it over slowly and read both sides again. Where on earth had it come from? These were the words that she had heard chanted. How spooky was that? Had Chris put it there? Elin left the card on the countertop and carried on cleaning, but she couldn't get the coincidence out of her mind. The website was printed on the card www.sgi.org or www.sgi-uk.org so she looked it up on the internet and found that it was movement dedicated to supporting individuals to create a solid foundation of happiness in their lives. Well, that had to be a good thing. It said the chant was to do with the law of cause and effect, part of the practice of Soka Gakkai International Buddhists. She read that there were no priests, just ordinary people and probably because of its belief in the potential of all human beings it was the most ethnically diverse of the many Buddhist traditions. Peace and happiness sounded good to Elin.

It was almost dark when Chris returned with Mutt and rubbed him down with an old towel. He turned to Elin with a diffident smile, "Feeling any better?" He enveloped her in a bear hug, lifted her off the floor and swung her round. "Let's have a lovely evening, shall we? The casserole smells so good and I scraped together enough for this bottle of wine so we can celebrate being together. What do you say Elin?"

Elin was touched, "Sounds great, I'll cook the rice, why don't you pour us each a large glass?" She put water on to boil then picked up the card. "I found this card; do you know where it came from?"

Chris looked over her shoulder, "It does ring a bell." He screwed up his face. "I'm trying to remember where I got it. I think it was the poet at James and Philip's party, the night you went home early. I must have stuck it in the drawer when I came in. He talked about repeating those words to bring out my creativity. Nice bloke."

Elin pushed the card into the pocket of her jeans and returned to measuring rice, "Do you think he was right? Could saying those words help? If you like, I'll chant with you."

"I don't see how could it help. He was successful, but I can't believe that saying those words made any difference."

Elin shrugged; she agreed.

Later, as she undressed, the card fell out of her pocket on to the bathmat. She picked it up, muttering, "If I didn't know better I'd think those words were following me." She propped the card alongside the taps, stepped out of her clothes and into the bath. She lay back and closed her eyes but the words swirled around in her head; she groaned, "I give up! I'll say them out loud!" Hesitant at first, she soon got into the rhythm until it began to sound like the chanting she'd heard. Nobody had said anything about chanting naked in the bath, but she supposed it was alright. She certainly felt calmer, but logic dictated that a warm bath was soothing in itself. The words resonated in her mind as she dried herself. That was interesting but again not unusual, but why not go with the flow and do as Celia had suggested? She sat on the bed and chanted for precisely five minutes then burrowed deep under the duvet. As she drifted to sleep she thought that she'd give Celia or Mia a ring tomorrow, they might be interested in the string of coincidences.

Waiting for the kettle to boil the next morning, Elin texted Mia. A leisurely Sunday lay ahead and she stretched and yawned before re-wrapping her dressing gown tightly round her, shivering in the morning chill. Mutt came charging in from the garden and she knelt to give him a few minutes' complete attention. Her phone beeped; Mia's return message was a light-hearted summons to explain the coincidences. She padded towards the bedroom and got back under the duvet, sitting up against the pillows to drink her tea. Chris's hand stroked her leg and he snuggled up close.

"I thought you were still asleep, do you want tea?"

"My plan right now doesn't involve tea. It's too early, come on back to bed."

Elin laughed, "Patience, Chris!"

Chris groaned, "With your gorgeous body close? Hurry, drink your tea."

Elin giggled and stroked his spiky hair, the only part of him she could reach while Chris reached her centre of pleasure. She gasped with delight, abandoned her mug and slid down beside him, throwing her robe aside.

Later, Mutt nuzzled Elin's face; he'd given up trying to

wake Chris using the same method. Elin shooed Mutt away
and looked at the time. "Ten thirty already! Chris, I'm going
to Mia's this morning, do you want to come? Dan will be
there." Murmurings from under the bedding implied he
would give the visit a miss.

"I'll only be an hour or two. Would you get the Sunday
paper from Mr. Hassan?"

The muttering this time sounding like agreement.

Elin hummed to herself as she drove towards Mia's; her
stomach rumbled in unison reminding her that she hadn't
eaten breakfast. A quick detour to a supermarket that baked
bread had Mia greeting her and the warm French bread
with equal delight. Elin hung her jacket on the bottom
bannister and entered the kitchen.

"French Roast to match the French-style breakfast?" Mia
enquired.

"Thanks, I can visualise the Paris boulevard!" Elin's good
mood matched Mia's. "Black, please. Is Dan here? The
bread's for him too. He'd better hurry before we eat the lot!"

"I'll save some for him. He's upstairs so we can have our
'girly' chat, as he put it, in peace."

"Hope he doesn't feel pushed out?" Elin probed
anxiously.

"Don't worry, he assured me he'd enjoy the quiet before
we go out later."

"Going somewhere nice?"

Mia held up her hand, "Don't laugh, yet another
museum. I'm trying to come up with innovative display
ideas for my term paper."

"You're enjoying your course? Will it lead to a job?"

Mia blew her breath out slowly, "Let's say I may be
teaching for a while yet. How's your job hunt going?"

Elin sighed, "Not very well. Chris came up with a

shocker yesterday." Mia looked concerned and Elin explained about his confession. "I wanted to believe he'd be a famous published author one day, or at least produce work that earned a few pounds. But, he has his good points." She coloured at the memory of their morning's activities.

"That's a blow. He must feel bad about it too."

"I believe he does, he's so moody at times." Elin idly took the end of the baguette and chewed it while Mia watched her. Elin sighed. "I'm trying not to be angry but, you know, he kept saying he was getting over his writers' block."

Mia searched for the right turn of phrase, "Is it his problem or yours, Elin?"

The question surprised Elin, "It's obvious, Chris has the problem." She paused, head tilted. "But I suppose mine is the dead-end career." She thought again. "It helps talking to you, but I mustn't make myself a nuisance now that Dan is back."

"I'm glad to help. Drinking coffee and eating fresh bread with you isn't exactly a burden. I want you to be happy though. Remember when we used to bitch and moan together at Beechwood?" Mia gave one of her irrepressible grins.

"Those were good times. Is it because you are getting out of teaching that you don't complain these days? You didn't even complain when Dan left," Elin asked.

"Not at all! Leaving teaching is the result, not the cause, of the change. Same with the complaining!" Mia smiled, "Can you see the difference?"

"I don't understand; a change is a change, some make you happy and some make you unhappy," Elin pulled a face, "and there's nothing you can do about it."

"Elin, what am I going to do with you? Do you really believe that?" Mia shook her head and laughed as she shared the dregs of coffee between their two mugs. "Shall I make some more coffee?"

"Not for me. Chris'll be waiting, it's pub lunch day."

Mia looked quizzically at Elin, "Before you go tell me about the coincidence, finding the card."

"I was at Celia's after school on Thursday. She suggested I try chanting to help me work out what was bothering me." Elin hit her head with her hand, "I nearly forgot, we're having another C swap in the Easter holidays. A chance to get new summer clothes without spending money. Are you game for another, you looked great last time?"

Mia shook her head, "Do you want me there? Couldn't my place go to somebody else? Nobody would want my old clothes."

Elin laughed, "We want you there, it wouldn't be the same without you."

"I'll think about it, OK?" A thought occurred to Mia, "You know, I could say that I find your interest in clothes weird. Think that's strange? It's true, believe it or not! Perhaps thinking that chanting is weird is in the same category."

Elin reflected, "That's an interesting analogy. Let me tell you the rest of the coincidence." Elin told Mia about the card in the kitchen drawer, the poet, about finding it in her pocket and chanting naked in the bath.

Mia smiled, "Chanting for the first time in the bath! Only you, Elin! The bottom line is that chanting brings out your own strength. It's not magic. Basically, do you trust me? Do you trust Celia and Chrissie? We're suggesting this because it helps us." She paused, then said, "We want you to be happy."

Elin considered this, playing with the crumbs on her plate, licking her finger then chasing them round and scooping them into her mouth. Certainly, Celia was happy after a horrible marriage breakup. Chrissie was kind, helpful and terminally energetic. Mia was, well, she was Mia, and she had been so strong when Dan deserted her. "I have been stubborn. Maybe, just maybe, I'll give it a try. No guarantees, OK?"

Mia accepted her grudging promise, "Fair enough. Shall we do an experimental chanting trial now?"

"I must go, Chris will be checking the time every few minutes, I know what he's like."

Mia pleaded, "Just give me two minutes, humour me for once?" She struck a few notes on a gorgeous deep-toned bell. The sound resonated through the room. "Chant *Nam Myoho Renge Kyo* with me, then go home and make up your own mind. I won't mention it again, it's up to you, Elin."

Elin didn't feel as silly as she anticipated and true to her word Mia stopped after two minutes. "Off you go, don't keep Chris waiting."

Elin hugged her, "See you at the clothes swap. I want you there so if you promise to come then I promise to chant. How's that?"

"It's a deal," responded Mia, returning the hug with interest.

Elin tried not to worry as the days slipped by. On the day of the Easter bonnet parade she woke up with a raspy throat and a curious lack of enthusiasm for the fun ahead. She willed the day over, dodged the parents' praise and staff post-mortem before bolting for home. Chris was out with the dog so there was no need to talk. She forced herself to swallow a few spoonfuls of yoghurt then fell asleep in the chair.

Mutt's rough tongue licking her hand woke her with a start, she groaned, aware that the nap had not helped her mood. After mumbling an explanation to Chris, she gargled with salt water, downed a couple of painkillers for her now aching head and slept again. The sound of the alarm the next morning catapulted her into the awareness that her headache had escalated and possibly she had flu? It was the last day of term, surely worth the struggle to work and to stay in John Roberts' good books? As she laboured through the day her limbs began to feel stiff and sore and she watched the clock on the classroom wall as it slowly crept round to 3.30. Her piercing headache seared up a notch or two.

On the drive home, she wound down her window hoping the breeze would aid her monumental effort to concentrate. She heard the sound of the first lawnmower of spring and smelled new mown grass. As she turned into her street, she began to feel sick and disoriented but registered a parking space right outside the flat. The car door weighed a ton, requiring the last remnants of Elin's energy to open it before she vomited into the gutter, splashing her trousers with foul smelling chunks of undigested tuna salad. She staggered inside, vomited again and sat, exhausted, on the edge of the bath, hands shielding her eyes and wondering what on earth could be causing her to feel so awful. She felt shivery and her head pounded unrelentingly, making her fearful of moving her head even a millimetre.

Chris stood in the bathroom doorway asking what he could do to help. She accepted his offer of tea, stumbled into the bedroom, drew the curtains and sank down on the bed, grateful for Chris's presence. Everything seemed foggy. Her hands and feet were cold, but she didn't have the will to get under the duvet. Minutes later she could barely lift her hand to take the mug from Chris as he hovered anxiously. Her thoughts felt woolly, words wouldn't form and the chimes of the front door bell sounded as if from a far distance.

"Hilary, come in, I'm really worried about Elin, come and talk to her." Chris led Hilary straight to the bedroom.

"Elin, what's the matter?" Elin's eyes were closed, the mug had slipped from her grasp and a pool of hot tea was soaking into the duvet. Hilary's voice trailed off in alarm, she turned to Chris. "She looks ghastly, has she fainted?" Hilary raised her voice and took Elin's hand. "Can you hear me Elin?" Elin's eyes flickered and she moaned quietly. "Open your eyes or squeeze my hand if you can hear me, Elin." Hilary spoke forcefully and when there was no response she turned, eyes wide with fear, to Chris, transfixed by her side.

"Get an ambulance... right now! Dial 999!"

Chris' hands shook as he fished his phone out of his jeans' pocket and punched in the crucial numbers. Hilary held Elin's hand and murmured reassurances. "You'll be OK Elin, we're getting help, the ambulance will be here soon." She righted the mug and Elin twitched, her eyelids fluttered. Hilary felt her forehead then turned to Chris, "Get a wet cloth, a face cloth or something, she's burning up." She sponged Elin's face and hands continually, listening desperately for the sound of sirens as she whispered encouragement to her unconscious friend. Chris waited for help at the front door, oblivious to the birds, the lawnmower, the children shouting, focusing only on the distant wail of an approaching ambulance.

HILARY, Mia and Chris paced the stark impersonal corridors near the Intensive Care Unit or slumped on smooth faux leather sofas in the relatives' small sitting room. They startled each time there was a flurry of activity, desperate for news. Elin's parents, Bill and Glenys, had rushed to her side but Elin lay unresponsive, connected to IV drips and bleeping monitors, an oxygen mask covering her face.

Meningitis was diagnosed, but whether viral or bacterial was still not clear. The doctors spoke reassuringly; they were treating her symptoms with drugs to reduce the pressure on her brain and prevent seizures, as well as sedatives to allow her to rest. It was a matter of time, the doctors said. Her friends waited anxiously; Elin slept on. Hilary and Mia offered beds at their homes to Elin's parents, but they wanted to stay close at hand. Hilary left at midnight to check on her family, the sandwiches Chris brought from the all-night cafeteria for Elin's parents remained untouched in their plastic carapaces on the chipped coffee table alongside a pile of tattered magazines. Chris paced and Mia chanted very quietly in the corner.

Grey light struggled through the dusty windows. Bill accepted the styrofoam cup of coffee Chris brought him from the vending machine and tried the stale cheese sandwich as the noise of trolleys and the banging of doors signalled the start of another hospital day. Cleaning machines hummed as nursing shifts changed. Elin's parents traded places and Mia found herself comforting Elin's mum while Chris planned yet another trek to the vending machine. The door crashed open. Mia and Glenys looked up in alarm only to see Hilary pushing her way through laden with an enormous cool bag. Hilary's heart missed a beat as she registered their shocked expressions as they sat holding hands. Her knees buckled and she lowered herself on to a chair.

"No change," mouthed Mia as Elin's mum blew her nose and sat up straighter. Hilary exhaled slowly and patted Glenys's hand. She was opening the bag as Chris returned.

Hilary moved the magazines to a chair and a sad potted aloe vera plant to the windowsill. She opened a Thermos and the welcome aroma of freshly brewed coffee filled the air. She laid out an array of fresh fruit and still warm muffins. "Jem and Fin wanted to help so they made the muffins." Turning to Glenys she said, "Please have something."

Glenys smiled wanly, "How thoughtful." She picked up a few grapes and stared at them. "Maybe I'll be able to eat when we've had an update. The doctors should be here soon, I'd better get back." She put the grapes down, pushed herself to her feet and left the room.

Every hour of Saturday dragged. Chris left to walk the dog, when he returned Mia took a break to shower and change clothes. Hilary came and went with fresh supplies of food. Chris left again to see to Mutt and the cats. Mia and Hilary huddled over their phones and updated Elin's friends and colleagues. Jeannie was distraught; Celia called frequently; the children's voices could be heard in the background. Chrissie phoned from London; John Roberts and Mrs. Hargreaves from home.

At 10.27 pm precisely, Elin's eyes flickered and opened a fraction, closing again in defence against the glare of the overhead lights. She felt trapped, suffocated, what was that covering her nose and mouth? She struggled to push it away, but she couldn't lift her arm. She heard the whirr of machinery, some bleeps and clicks and then her mother's voice in the far distance, "Nurse, nurse, she's awake!" The smell of rubber and antiseptic filled her nostrils and she panicked. She heard her own garbled attempts to speak as she struggled to move. Again, her mother's voice, far away, "Elin, the nurse is coming, stay still. It's OK, I'm here."

From across a void, Elin heard a calm voice, "Hello Elin,

nice to have you back with us. Just lie still for me, please. You're in hospital. My name's Laura and I'm looking after you." Elin struggled vainly to open her eyes. Her head hurt and her hands moved convulsively. "You've got an oxygen mask over your nose." Laura lifted the mask up briefly and Elin relaxed. "Now that you're awake, we may be able to get rid of that soon, but not yet, sorry." Laura examined Elin's IV line then spoke again, "Let me just check all these machines and I'll let the doctor know that you're awake. Don't try to talk, just rest, your mum is here and your dad and your friends are outside."

From that moment, Elin made a textbook recovery. The diagnosis was viral meningitis, the antibiotics were stopped and the rest of the life-saving medications were tapered down. She slept most of the time and had no opinion about being moved out of ICU to the ward, until she experienced the transfer, with its jerky ride, bed banging into the sides of the lift and the head-splitting clamour of hospital life as she passed through the corridors. Her parents still hovered by her side, encouraging her friends to return to their normal lives while Elin slept the hours away as the ward staff tended to her every need.

After a mere three days on the ward the consultant deemed Elin fit to go home. This news jolted her out of her apathy and filled her with alarm. When the ward round had finished she clutched the ward sister's arm, "I don't want to go home yet, I'm scared I'll get ill again."

Sister smiled and checked her charts, "There's absolutely no reason to think that will happen, you've made an excellent recovery so far. You'll probably rest better at home." She patted Elin's hand, "Your boyfriend and your friends will help once your parents have gone home."

Another wave of panic engulfed Elin. Her parents were

leaving? Elin had been told what had happened before her scary ambulance ride but remembered nothing. With Mutt needing exercise, Chris would have to leave her alone, what if she collapsed again? She bit her lip, knowing how precious hospital beds were, but she was scared.

"You need to make arrangements to be picked up after lunch. I'll get your follow-up appointment made and your medicines from the pharmacy." Sister looked at her watch, "Better say 4 pm to be on the safe side. You can always sit in a chair if we need the bed."

Her parents had gone home for a rest. Hilary couldn't come, she had to take Jem to the airport while Ricky took Finn to his tennis academy. Mia didn't have a car, Chris didn't drive and Celia had the children. Chrissie, freshly back from London, stepped into the breach.

As Elin entered the flat she was struck by how claustrophobic it felt; the small rooms, the dimness, the stale smell. The thought of cleaning exhausted her. She turned to Chrissie, "If you don't mind I think I'll go straight to bed. Thanks so much for bringing me home." The contrast between pristine hospital sheets and the tea stained duvet cover was extreme.

A week later the flat was crammed with flowers, the fridge was full of food gifts and Elin had rested to the max. She sat chatting to Mia as she slathered body lotion on her arms. "I'm glad Celia postponed the clothes swap. I still feel weird. Not sleeping well, bad dreams about being in hospital. I can't remember properly, but I have these horrible images of people looming over me while I lie trapped. I went out yesterday and thought people were staring at me." She snapped the top back on the bottle, "My skin's so dry and I've still got bruises from the drips, and my hair's a mess so I don't need paranoia on top of that." Her eyes glistened, "And I burst into tears at the slightest thing!"

"When's your check up?" Mia munched a chocolate biscuit. "You can ask if all that is normal."

"Tomorrow morning, Hilary's taking me. I need to make a list. I'm forgetful too," Elin sighed.

"I'll pop round in the afternoon, if that's OK, find out what they said? Gotta go now, meeting tonight."

"I haven't done any chanting since we talked, sorry I didn't keep my end of the bargain."

Mia rose and shrugged on her jacket, "At least you remembered we had a bargain! Don't worry we've all been chanting for your recovery. Don't get up, I'll see myself out. Chris out with the dog?"

"Yes, he is. I'm looking forward to walking Mutt again."

Elin reported her check-up excitedly to Mia the following day. "She said I must take it easy and rest plenty, but all those things I was telling you about are quite normal for this part of my recovery." Elin made tea for Mia. "I'm going to start doing more at home for the rest of the week and I've talked to Mr. Roberts about starting back at work part-time." Elin glugged down a glass of water before carrying the mugs into the sitting room. "I've got to drink lots of water to help my dry skin too, and not be surprised by any mood swings I have." She frowned, "That'll be difficult for Chris. He tries hard, poor thing, but nothing he does seems good enough these days."

"Good news. Don't do too much too soon, will you?"

Thanks to Mr. Roberts' flexibility and Mrs. Hargreaves' support Elin's return to work was gradual and free from setbacks. At the end of her first full week, Elin drove home wanting to treat herself to something cheap and cheerful. She had kept her bargain with Mia and although she couldn't pinpoint a huge difference, she was more relaxed about the concept of chanting. Possibly she did feel more hopeful and her recovery had been truly remarkable. She wondered how to celebrate her return to full-time work. These days she shied away from a bottle of wine; it was too easy, too habit forming, and had too many empty calories. Chocolate suffered from the same drawback. She was almost home when the postponed C swap flitted through her mind and she decided to buy a magazine for the latest fashion trends. Curling up with a magazine felt like the perfect zero calorie way to enjoy the evening. She found a parking spot outside the corner shop.

"Hello Mr. Hassan, how are you?"

"Hello, Ms. Petersen, nice to see you again, Mr. Summers has been doing all the shopping, hasn't he?"

All the shopping? That was a funny thing to call the Sunday papers, a last-minute purchase of milk or a few onions. Elin began leafing through the magazines then put her choices on the counter and delved in her handbag for her purse.

"I'll take these please, Mr. Hassan, I think they add up to five pounds fifty pence."

Elin handed over the correct money and turned towards the door.

"Just a minute, Ms. Petersen, would you pay something off your account, please? It's been mounting up recently and we have a policy of not allowing credit over a hundred pounds." Mr. Hassan looked expectantly at Elin.

"Account? I'm sorry Mr. Hassan, I don't understand, what account? Are you mixing me up with someone else? I always pay cash."

Mr. Hassan looked embarrassed, "Yes, of course you do. Mr. Summers, your partner, said he didn't have a car to get to the bank for cash so an account was more convenient. My wife and I, we know you well, we thought that it would be a service. It's hard to compete with the supermarkets."

Elin felt as if somebody had hit her in the stomach. She felt shaky and sick. Whatever had happened it couldn't be Mr. Hassan's fault, he had always been pleasant and helpful. But a hundred pounds? There must be some mistake. "How much did you say you were owed, Mr. Hassan? Perhaps you could give me the bill and I'll get it sorted out with Chris once I get home?"

Mr. Hassan was polite but firm, "I would like you to pay now. Certainly, I will show you, but we have already postponed the first month's payment because you were ill and Mr. Summers said he was expecting a cheque. I really must insist." He looked at Elin's shocked expression and added, "I'm very sorry."

Mr. Hassan evidently was sorry, but equally clearly he was owed money. He made a copy of the itemized bill and handed it to Elin who took a quick glance and felt even more shocked. Almost every item was wine, beer, cider and even vodka. No wonder the total came to one hundred and twenty-four pounds, sixty-two pence. It started on February 15th and the last item had been purchased just this morning.

"I'm sorry, I can't pay it all now. Would you take fifty pounds today? That's all I can manage at the moment. Chris and I will sort this out very soon." Elin's hands were shaking and her cheeks flamed as she handed over her card. Soon Elin was outside the shop, her heart thumping madly. Cold fury replaced embarrassment. How dare he! No wonder she had been uneasy. What a fool she had been to have listened to the sweet talk. All this time he'd been lying to her.

Elin flung open the door of the flat and stormed inside. "Chris, switch that damned laptop off this second! Give me an explanation of what just happened in Mr. Hassan's shop! I can't believe you've lied to me all this time. I knew you like a drink and even need one sometimes, but I didn't know you were this desperate!"

Chris stood up, colour draining from his face. He didn't say a word. Elin brandished the bill in front of him and yelled, not caring who could hear, "I believed you, I trusted you! I can't think of anything you can say that will make this alright, but no doubt you'll try."

Chris moved towards her, a hangdog look on his face, his body slumped, "I really intended to pay the bill, then you were so ill and I never thought you'd find out before I'd paid it."

"Stay away from me! How were you going to pay? Look at it, almost every item is alcohol. We have wine, we go out for a drink. I pay for it all and it's still not enough." Coldness superseded fury in her voice.

Chris held his hands out, pleading, "Please be patient Elin. We're good together, you and I, don't let's lose that. Everything will work out, you'll see."

"There you go again, putting your head in the sand. I've been a fool, believing your grand plans. I don't trust you anymore. Please be quiet and let me think." Elin leaned against the counter, Mutt sat close in mute support. She thought about the highs and the lows of her three and a half months with Chris. The high points at the start had been pie in the sky, talk of Chris getting books published, planning exotic holidays, thinking of the fun they'd have together when the boat came in. The only good thing left was sex and that was ruined now she had lost all respect for him. The low points had been about drinking and money. She folded her arms and stared straight at him, "There's nothing left to say Chris. It's over. I can't bear to have you here even one more night. I want you to leave. You owe the Hassans money and I'd like you to pay them every penny. Can you do that?"

Chris was stunned. "Elin, darling, don't be so hasty. Surely, we can work it out? I'll pay Mr. Hassan, I promise," he whined.

Elin saw him clearly for the first time. "I don't believe you. Why didn't you pay the Hassans last month if it's so easy? You can't, can you? You'll spend it on other things before you pay that hardworking couple. Just pack and go. Now." Elin turned around and picked up Mutt's lead. "I'm going to take the dog for a walk. I want you out of here before I come back and I want my key back too, do you understand?"

Chris nodded, looking utterly miserable. Their eyes met briefly, his still so beautiful yet they had lost the power to move her. She reminded herself that he'd lived off her generosity for more than three months and she didn't owe him a thing. She held out her hand, "On second thoughts, give me your key now, you can pull the door behind you when you leave."

Chris reluctantly pulled the key from his pocket and handed it to her. 'You're wrong Elin, we could have worked something out." He moved forward as if to kiss her.

Elin stepped back and walked out of the door. She hadn't even taken off her coat.

25

"On my own again." The words of an old Country and Western song ran through Elin's head as she opened the door to the empty flat. She hung up her coat and noted that Chris's clothes were gone. There was no sign of him. She was too angry for tears. How could she have been so stupid? Anyone with half a brain could have predicted how the relationship would end but, evidently, she didn't even have half a brain.

She felt so stupid.

She felt even worse about the Hassans. There wasn't a snowball's chance in hell of Chris paying the debt, so was she responsible? She was fifty pounds poorer already, but was the rest of the debt her problem or Mr. Hassan's? She couldn't think straight. She sank into a chair; what on earth could she do? She could economise. She'd go on a healthy diet, salads would be in season and the evenings would be longer to run with Mutt so she'd lose weight. What had Mia said about winter always turning into spring?

Elin thought of her friends. How many more times was she going to cry on their shoulders? She tapped out a general S.O.S. and sat down, hugging her knees, waiting. The phone emitted a string of beeps and the screen informed her that she had five new messages. She felt better even before reading them.

Mia's first: "Cooking 4 Dan's mum, here for w/e. L8r or tomoro?"

Chrissie's next: "Dance show tonite, tomorrow?"

Hilary: "At school mtg, all men are bastards!"

Jeannie: "Poor you, so sorry. On training w/e B'ham. Next week?"

Celia: "Come over."

Five minutes later she was standing on Celia's doorstep. Celia took charge, bustling Elin inside, taking her jacket and settling her at the kitchen table. "Are you hungry? Scrambled egg on toast? Soup?"

Elin smiled despite herself, "I haven't eaten since lunchtime but I'm not hungry."

"Maybe not, but you mustn't get ill again. What can I get you?"

"Scrambled eggs and toast, please, comfort food might help."

"Coming up! So, tell me all about it." Celia cracked eggs and stirred them into melted butter; Elin buttered bread as it popped out of the toaster and brought Celia up to speed. "I'm so stupid, falling for the wrong man again. Now I doubt everything Chris ever said." The skin on her wrist itched and Elin rubbed it absentmindedly. "He was so loving it's hard to believe he was so devious." She looked at Celia, "Maybe I'd be better off single, like you?"

Celia slid the plate of eggs in front of Elin. "You need to eat." She poured tea for them both.

Elin took a bite of toast and a few mouthfuls of egg, then pushed her plate away. "Why, Celia? I don't understand. I started chanting and look what's happened, things got worse instead of better."

Celia removed Elin's plate before responding, "From another perspective things are better, not worse. I didn't realise you'd done any chanting but that would explain it. It's really exciting!"

Elin looked disbelieving. "Exciting? You must be joking!"

Celia thought for a few moments, "Last week something was bothering you. Do you remember?"

"It must have been a premonition," Elin sniffed sourly.

"Exactly! They were only subconscious feelings, then you found out about the lies. Your chanting resulted in an opportunity to change – and you did. You made a good decision. Finding out about Chris was a benefit, can't you see? The situation would have dragged on otherwise."

"You mean this was a good thing?" Elin sounded doubtful.

"Yes, I most certainly do." Celia's smile exuded confidence.

"It could be a coincidence." Elin the sceptic was still alive and well.

"Remember it's about you, not a man. It's about being happy. Make the goal a good job if you prefer." Celia suggested.

Elin paused, "I promised Mia I would chant; her part of the bargain was to come to the next clothes swap. Between both of you I don't stand a chance, do I?" Elin was laughing now.

Celia was disconcerted, "We didn't mean to gang up on you." She fetched two wine glasses and raised her eyebrows, "A drink while we discuss the overdue swap?"

Elin looked at her watch, "Just a few minutes then, no

wine. I should get back to my sad empty flat. Thank goodness for Mutt and the cats."

"No trouble, Elin. Would you chant with me for a minute or two before you go as well?"

"Minute or two? I'll have you know I can do five whole minutes!" Elin gave Celia a playful nudge, "Lead the way and I'll show you."

The two women's voices blended and Elin felt a distinct surge of hope. She would be happy again.

Elin went to bed that night missing Chris less than she would have thought possible. She drank hot chocolate and thought how silly it would be to miss someone snoring beside you when the snoring had irritated you intensely. Alley and Tom appropriated the vacant space and she slept well.

A plan was needed, thought Elin as she nursed her first French Roast of the day. She would clear the vestiges of Chris-type behaviour as surely as she'd cleared out the man yesterday. She pulled a notepad towards her and jotted a to-do list. Clean flat; walk dog; look for job; buy garden plants. Her tight waistband reminded her to add exercise time. She reviewed her schedule: Saturday could be home spa night. She looked again and pencilled in Wednesday papers for job search (Mr. Hassan's or drive to different shop?). She looked again, something was niggling. She remembered her promise to chant every day, that needed to go down or she would surely forget.

She looked around wondering where to chant. She was going to make it a regular habit and now Chris had gone, she could choose the best place without considering his needs. She rejected her bedroom and the armchairs before deciding on a quiet corner by the window in the living room. She put a big cushion on the floor and sat down. She propped up the card. *Nam Myoho Renge Kyo*. Elin repeated the words, stumbling occasionally. She didn't think about Chris or the lack of him, or a good job or the lack of one while chanting.

Next it was Mutt's turn and once through the gates of the park Mutt ran loops around her, barking with excitement. Elin wondered how often Chris had opted for brief sorties to the park to keep his part of their bargain. She walked and ran alternately, attentive to her body, careful not to overdo it. The excess inches that had crept on to her hips would soon be gone.

Now for the garden transformation, to be undertaken on a shoestring. Elin weighed pros and cons at the Garden Centre and reined in her wildest impulses, aware that Mutt and the cats would challenge the survival of all but the most tenacious of species. At the till, horrified at the total, she jettisoned a spade, trowel and kneeling pad, she could get those from the old house. She chose lavender, hardy enough to withstand the animals, with honeysuckle and climbing fuchsia to disguise the fence. The grass would have to stay thin, patchy and weed-filled: paving was way beyond her budget.

A phone call about the C swap led to an invitation from Hilary who gave her a welcome worthy of a war veteran. "You poor thing, come in, tell me what happened with that bastard Chris. And so soon after your meningitis! I'm cooking us a stir-fry. Come into the kitchen."

Tears welled up in Elin's eyes when she saw the table already laid, compete with candles and an arrangement of freesias. "How beautiful! You're so thoughtful, Hilary."

"I wanted to cheer you up. Would you pour the Sauvignon Blanc? I know you like it and it goes with the chicken."

"I'm driving so I'll go slow." Elin poured out both the wine and the tale of the recent disaster, embarrassed and angry in turns.

Hilary stood stirring the contents of the wok. "It was strange the way he always wanted to keep you to himself. You settled down so fast with your long walks and pub lunches."

"He was handsome and so loving. He stayed one night, then two, until it seemed silly for him to pay rent for his own place. We didn't discuss living together, it just happened."

"What's next for you? Speed dating? Being set up by friends like me?" Hilary ended with a smile intended to cheer Elin up – unfortunately, it had the opposite effect.

"No way," Elin shuddered. "I'm off men, don't want one near me. Which reminds me, have you seen Joe? I'm working on my garden and I need a spade and a trowel."

"I think he employs a gardening service now. Do you want me to find out?" Hilary turned off the gas.

"Yes please. I'd like my secateurs and a watering can too. I can't afford to buy them." Elin frowned as she handed the square white plates to her friend.

"Really? I didn't realise it was that bad!"

Elin shrugged, "I've been given a lot of responsibility and I've enjoyed it, but still." Her voice trailed off.

Hilary served the stir-fry and Elin made a list of equipment she needed, all of which would be found gathering dust in Joe's garden shed. As they ate, Elin reminded Hilary about the C Swap.

"I haven't got much to bring, I've just taken lots to the charity shop," Hilary hesitated.

"You must come. Maybe you could bring jewellery? Or some of Jem's stuff?" Elin looked so disappointed that Hilary laughed and gave in.

"OK Elin, I'll be there. Let's go into the living room, it's comfier. Can I pour you another glass?"

"No thanks, I'll be off soon. I'm not the quivering heap of jelly I was after Aaron and Joe. I feel a fool, but I'm not going to mope this time." Elin had felt remarkably good when she set off to Hilary's, but she was fading and Hilary's occasional pernicious comments about men didn't help.

"Want some decaf? There's no dessert, I hope you don't mind?"

"Of course not, decaf's perfect."

As they caught up with gossip Elin wondered if Hilary had always been so jaundiced or whether it was a change in Elin herself? She speculated about what Hilary said about her to others, but dismissed the thought. Hilary was just being her usual acerbic self, she was nothing if not loyal to her friends.

Elin's daily reminders helped her chant regularly and she gradually incorporated an exercise DVD into her routine. Her trousers fitted again and sweaters no longer pulled under the arms.

The second clothes swap was wild, with Chrissie offering to host next time so they could invite more people. Hilary brought an assortment of tiny clothes donated by Jem, which only fitted Yoko. Yoko's usual style being that of a sophisticated business woman, the sight of her in teenage short tops and crotch hugging shorts was highly entertaining, but she refused to take them home and they ended up in the charity shop bag.

At lunchtime on the fourth Saturday of the summer term, Chrissie led Elin into her kitchen where the centrepiece of the table was a huge salad bowl brimming with brightly coloured vegetables beside a platter of crusty bread and butter. A cheeseboard and a fruit bowl of shiny red and green apples completed the array.

"Thanks for inviting me, Chrissie. Do you realise that it's almost a year since we met? I still appreciate what you did."

Chrissie laughed, "That was nothing, I enjoyed myself. You look healthy again, you had us all really scared for a while!"

Elin took a huge helping of salad and confided that her physical state was much better than her financial state. "I've budgeted seriously. Chris has gone and the heating bills will be less in the summer so I'll manage. Heaven forbid that the car breaks down though."

Chrissie clapped in encouragement, "I see a woman dealing with challenges and you look better than ever. That's fantastic!"

"I'm eating better, drinking less. Oh! I chant a bit every day too."

Chrissie looked surprised, "Wow! Do you think it's helping?"

Elin wrinkled her nose, "It's hard to explain. I chant for five minutes and I get a surge of positivity. It's as if my best thoughts grow and fill me up so there's no space left for worry. I promised Mia I'd chant if she came to the fashion swap. She kept her end of the bargain and I kept mine."

"Did you feel silly chanting all on your own?"

"Yes, I did and getting up early to chant as well as walk the dog isn't easy."

Elin and Chrissie reminisced about Aaron, remembering how he was prone to thinking with a part of his body situated a lot lower than his brain. Chrissie became thoughtful, "Elin, did you know that Jared and I have been through some tough times? We have two children but we separated for more than a year. That's when I encountered this Buddhism. I realised that happy comes from the inside not from the outside; then everything felt different. Jared and I got back together and we're happier than ever. I don't blame him for my feelings any more. He doesn't chant, but that's fine with me. What I'm trying to say is that it's perfectly possible to be single and be completely happy."

Elin felt tears pricking her eyes, "Sometimes it feels as if I'm wading through deep mud. I'm trying to keep positive."

"How about aiming for the right job?" suggested Chrissie. Elin smiled but didn't speak so Chrissie continued, "Be determined when you chant! You're a wonderful human being just as you are. Believe in yourself, find your inner wisdom and courage. Gradually you'll understand the wider effects too, like wanting other people's happiness as well as your own." Chrissie paused, watched Elin eating. "Shall we carry on meeting up on Saturdays like this? Bring the dog, there are some lovely walks around here."

Elin perked up, "You sure it's not too much trouble?"

"Not at all, we have this lovely house and I don't ask people round often. I'm out a lot. But Saturday lunchtime is usually OK."

Elin nodded, "But only if you let me bring lunch next time."

"If it'll make you feel better, but no culinary competitions."

Elin smiled gratefully, "It's a deal. I'll bring Mutt next week."

Chrissie paused, "Want to do five minutes chanting before you go?"

Elin stopped in her tracks, "Now? In the middle of the afternoon?"

"I chant any old time," laughed Chrissie. "When I'm

worried it's wonderful. I even chant when I'm happy, feeling grateful for my happy life."

On the drive home, Elin reviewed their conversation. They'd laughed about dance, drama and the drama of Elin's life, but Chrissie had also said things that seemed important and Elin didn't want to forget them.

Elin made a massive bowl of coleslaw the following Saturday morning. Spinach salad with walnuts, pate and a granary bread completed her offering. Mutt's nose twitched as he detected the pate buried deep in the insulated bag.

Shrubs lined the path to Chrissie's front porch. The rain had stopped, the air smelt fresh and Elin admired the glistening foliage as she waited at the front door.

"It looks exquisite, Chrissie; who does the gardening?"

"Mostly me. Jared travels a lot with work. The secret is to have paved areas surrounded by shrubs and ground cover, plenty of green but no lawn to mow. Any development on the job front? It's only been a week, but I wondered."

Elin sighed, "No, nothing at all."

Chrissie squeezed Elin's arm, "Don't get disheartened, it may sound crazy but your chanting will help."

"It does sound crazy, but I can feel something changing. I'm more optimistic. When I chant I feel my troubles are temporary." Elin continued, "It would help if I had some options on the job front. Any suggestions?"

Chrissie shook her head regretfully, "Sorry. Maybe something'll turn up by next Saturday." Then she grinned at Elin, "Let's chant about it after our walk."

There was nothing to report by the following Friday morning. Elin was driving to school after another rainy week and another drenching in the park. She persevered because the dog needed the exercise and so did she. It was a similar story with the twice-daily repetition of *Nam Myoho*

Renge Kyo, but the prospect of lunch with Chrissie helped her stick with it, she trusted her friend's judgement more than her own. Chrissie, Mia and Celia were so upbeat that she wanted to humour them for a bit longer, and she did feel more positive than she had for ages, even though there was no concrete cause for her good spirits.

As she walked into the staff room, Elin felt a buzz in the air. Mr. Roberts wanted all staff members to stay on for a few minutes after the children had left for the day. The staff room hummed with curiosity and an atmosphere of apprehension hovered throughout the day. When the staff made their way to the hall speculation was rife. Mr. Roberts arrived, walked straight to the podium and wasted no time.

"Thank you all for staying, I wanted to tell you all together. I'm sorry to say that Mrs. Wendy Walters, our deputy Head Teacher, is taking a leave of absence for two years starting today. She hasn't been well and has been diagnosed with transverse myelitis, which is a very unpredictable condition. She'll need lengthy treatment and recovery time. She wanted her position filled when she's not here." He paused, "I hope that Mrs. Walters will recover and return. The 2-year temporary post will be advertised soon, but I wanted all of you to know first. I'll be happy to talk to anybody interested in applying. Thanks again. I hope you all have a restful weekend."

Mr. Roberts turned and left the room. Elin was stunned. She didn't know Mrs. Walters well but Mrs. Hargraves, who did, was visibly upset. Elin spoke quietly to her, "You OK, Mrs. H? Did you know anything about this?"

"Nice of you to ask, Elin dear. I'm alright. I knew poor Wendy hadn't been well. I'm shocked, I didn't know it was anything serious. We all thought it was a strange virus. I'm going to look it up on the internet. Transverse what did he say?"

"Transverse Myelitis. I haven't heard of it either so I'm going to do the same. I hope she'll be OK."

"I hope so too. I don't think anyone here will apply, they wouldn't go for a temporary job even if it is deputy head. Poor Wendy, I wonder if she wants visitors?" Mrs. Hargreaves bustled away.

Elin didn't know what to make of it. Was this her opportunity? She decided to call in to see Celia but, evidently, she was still at work, as the babysitter answered the door with Gwennan and Lowri peering round her legs.

"Hello girls, I was hoping to see Mummy, so I'll come back later if that's OK with you?" To the babysitter she added, "Would you tell Celia that Elin popped by and that I'll come back later? Thanks a lot."

As Elin turned to go both girls piped up, "We'll tell her Elin." Then Gwennan added, "When you come back will you read us a story in bed?"

Elin was surprised, "I will if Mummy says it's OK. I have to take my dog for a walk and have something to eat first. I'll phone Mummy to check, OK?"

As Elin jogged she thought about Mrs. Walters' job. From teaching assistant to Deputy Head was quite a leap. Was it a crazy idea? She had to discuss it with Mr. Roberts, he must have known about Mrs. Walters's health problems all along. No wonder he hadn't been able to be specific, but he had been encouraging. Her thoughts ran in circles similar to Mutt's and with similar lack of tangible results.

"Elin, come and play with us, please read us a story!" Gwennan and Lowri jostled for Elin's attention as soon as she and Celia had exchanged greetings.

"Girls, give Elin a chance. Come and finish your supper

and then it's time for bath and bed. Elin, sit in the kitchen otherwise Gwennan and Lowri won't finish eating. They've really taken to you."

"I tell you what, let's play I Spy while you're finishing your supper. I'll change the rules so Lowri can play."

Lowri's face brightened, and Gwennan's curiosity got the better of her, "What are the new rules, Elin?

"I'm a big girl," added Lowri.

Celia broke in, "Eat your supper so that you can grow into an even bigger girl. Finish your banana and drink your milk while Elin explains."

"It's the same as I Spy but instead of letters you use colours. Here we go." Elin looked around, "I spy with my little eye, something that's yellow."

The girls looked around them. "The duck on Lowri's plate," shouted Gwennan.

"Good guess, but no," responded Elin.

"The duck on my cup?" asked Lowri.

"That's not a duck, silly," said Gwennan, "it's a goose and it's white."

Lowri's lip quivered and she looked down at her plate, then back up again, pointing to the fruit bowl.

"I know Aunty Elin, a banana!"

"Very good Lowri, you're absolutely right, a banana. Now it's your turn."

Getting Lowri to play without blurting out her choice straight away was a challenge, but they all laughed a lot. Elin happily read stories until two pairs of eyes were drooping.

"At last!" sighed Celia as the women both sank down on the sofa. "This job prospect sounds exciting."

"I need your opinion about applying. I'm hoping that I might have a chance," Elin said, looking both worried and excited.

Celia was matter-of-fact, "Nothing's impossible Elin. It's about whether you believe in yourself enough to nail this job. Do you think you're capable? If you do, then go for it. You're great with young children, tonight illustrated that beautifully. Look what's happened since you've been chanting, a solution popped up out of the blue."

"I didn't chant for Mrs. Walters to be ill!"

"Everything is connected. When you chant it affects everything. Remember finding out about Chris's behaviour when you started to chant?"

"Mm, maybe... but it's such a different way of thinking."

"Try to clear your mind, just concentrate on saying the words when you chant. The answer will come when the time is right."

"When the time is right? That sounds as if it has some deep meaning. Is it like 'Winter always turns into Spring'? I like that one and I'm beginning to understand it," Elin said smiling thoughtfully.

26

The smell of spices filled the air as Chrissie welcomed Elin and Mutt and ushered them straight into the kitchen the following day.

"Make yourself at home Elin, I just added the prawns, two minutes and it'll be ready."

"It smells delicious, is it prawn curry?" Elin drew up her chair, expressing concern. "But we agreed, no culinary competition."

Chrissie laughed and pointed to the cookery book open on the counter. "Check it out, Elin, four easy steps, only one saucepan, let's hope it tastes as good as it smells."

The Caribbean Prawns met expectations and once they'd pushed their polished plates aside, Chrissie declared, "Fill me in on school politics while we walk, Elin, we can't keep him waiting any longer." She pointed at Mutt who was sitting expectantly at the door, quivering with excitement, ears alert at the word "walk". Soon he was tearing ahead of them as they set off down the tree-lined lane as the sun struggled to break through. Chrissie and Elin walked briskly and Elin summed up, "I'm scared. If I apply they might think I'm uppity. I don't want to spoil any future I have there."

"There are two parts to this." Chrissie held up one finger, "First, you're well qualified." She held up another finger, "Second, you chant and can bring out your courage to influence the situation. It's a win-win solution."

Elin shook her head, "Your confidence is misplaced!"

"No, it's not," Chrissie was firm. "I saw you work at Beechwood. Getting me involved was thinking outside the box, that's what's needed. They'll want new ideas." She grinned, "And being afraid is understandable. Chant so that your courage becomes greater than your fear."

When they returned tired and muddy, Elin reviewed her plan. "I'm going in extra early on Monday to see Mr. Roberts. In the meantime, I know what you're going to recommend."

Chrissie snorted with laughter, "You're getting to know us, aren't you? Do you want to chant now?"

"I was hoping you'd say that, I need to get my courage greater than my fear."

When Elin finally left she took with her a covered dish of prawns and an upbeat attitude.

The following morning, Jeannie looked around Elin's flat with satisfaction. "It's good to see you settled, Elin. Everything is just lovely and the garden's looking better, even with the dog."

"Mutt's good for me, even if he is a lot of work. What do you think about the deputy head job, Jeannie?"

"I can see you're keen, Elin, but you enjoy your job and can manage on the pay so what's the big problem? You'll get the settlement from Joe soon too."

"You're right, it wouldn't be a disaster if I didn't get it. It's a big leap."

They wandered into Elin's bedroom to look through some new finds. Jeannie repeated her mantra of the morning, "Elin, with your flair you don't need more money. Apply for the job and stop stressing." She paused, then said, "By the way, I heard about a speed dating evening. Why don't we try it out next Friday? I think a new love interest might stop you obsessing about this job. You never know, the next one could be the love of your life."

Elin had to smile. Jeannie was incorrigible; constantly searching for a man to complete her life and no matter how many frogs she kissed, she continued her search for a prince. Metamorphosis was just for tadpoles in Elin's jaded opinion.

That afternoon Hilary and Elin chatted, Elin still searching for the magic nugget of advice. Her friend managed to be discouraging and encouraging in quick succession. Finally Elin had heard enough, she was due at Mia's for a visit and would make that her final call. She wanted to get home early to prepare for her chat with Mr. Roberts in the morning.

Mia's home was more untidy than usual. Elin gathered dirty mugs, washed them and made tea for herself and Mia who was hunched over the computer, looking unhappy. "I won't be long; the internet's been down and I've got to get this essay off."

A few minutes later Mia exhaled loudly and smiled, "Done! You hungry? We've stuff in here I think." Mia waved her hand in the general direction of the kitchen but didn't seem too sure.

"No thanks, I've got leftovers from Chrissie for dinner. There's more tea in the pot if you like." Elin picked up the teapot then felt able to ask advice, ending with the same question, "Do you think I have a chance, Mia, given all the unknowns?"

Mia sat back, "The real question is, do you, Elin Petersen, believe you have a chance? It all depends on you. If it's the right thing for your life then you'll get the job." Mia smiled benignly at Elin.

"What, no advice?"

Mia spoke firmly, "Summon up your courage and show it. I don't mean a show of bravado but the calm conviction that you are the best person for the job. First you have to convince yourself, after that it's a piece of cake."

Elin continued arguing, "I can't see how chanting will help get a teaching job. You're joking, right?"

"You're a science teacher so look at the evidence," Mia was smiling broadly. "First there's anecdotal evidence from people you trust. That's me, Celia and Chrissie. Why would we lie to you? Now you have your own experience too. Remember the gibbering wreck you were when Aaron abandoned you? If something like that happened again wouldn't you deal with it differently? Didn't you get a resolution to the niggling doubts about Chris? Do you feel positive and happier? Ask yourself the questions, then ask yourself why are you holding back?"

"What do you mean?"

"Big challenges require big efforts. Celia, Chrissie and I are encouraging you to launch into a big effort."

"I get it. What do I do?"

"When you talk to Mr. Roberts, brim over with enthusiasm. He needs to feel that you, and only you, will fill the requirements of the position, whatever they are. The tone of the meeting will depend on you, not Mr. Roberts. Do you understand that?"

Elin was fired up at last.

Mia grinned, "Remember, it works even though we don't understand why, like apples fell from trees before we understood the laws of gravity."

Elin arrived at school the next morning feeling confident. As she parked the car she noticed that other staff had also arrived early and she felt her self-assurance plummet. She muttered *Nam Myoho Renge Kyo* under her breath as she gathered her bag and locked the car door. It reminded her of the feeling of courage that had welled up last night as she chanted with determination. She walked straight to Mr. Roberts' office and knocked.

"Good morning Elin. You're here bright and early, maybe just a little earlier than usual and maybe even a little brighter if that's possible? I think I can guess the reason for your visit."

There was a genuine warmth in Mr. Roberts' smile as he welcomed her into his office and Elin relaxed in response. "Good morning. I thought it best to get here early so that I could ask you about Mrs. Walters, I wondered if you had an update on her health? Please give her my best wishes when you talk to her."

"Of course, I will, Elin, but maybe you have something else you wanted to talk to me about?" There was a twinkle in Mr. Roberts' eye.

She gathered up her courage, "Yes, there is. I'm very interested in applying for the job. I'm so happy here and I'd love a permanent position. Obviously two years is not permanent, but I want to use my strengths. I'd value your opinion."

"Of course, I understand. I've no idea what'll happen after two years, nobody does, but we have to fill the position and the sooner the better. You know how highly I value your contribution to the school. You're a wonderful TA and the staff appreciate you. I would certainly encourage you to apply. I can't say more, you understand, but yes, definitely, do apply."

Elin smiled, a huge smile that conveyed her immense gratitude. "Thank you for that vote of confidence, I appreciate it hugely. Perhaps you could fill me in a bit?"

Mr. Roberts was happy to describe his plans. His vision was huge and Elin realised why the school, despite its large size and old buildings, was so good. He believed the purpose of the school was to bring out the best in every pupil regardless of ability. His influence made it a happy school.

Noise levels in the playground began to rise as pupils arrived and Elin was forced to draw Mr. Roberts' attention to the fact that she needed to start work.

"Sorry, I got carried away. We'll talk more, the door of my office is always open."

The conversation buoyed up Elin's high spirits, but she was unsure about sharing her hopes with the rest of the staff. She decided to listen to staff room talk and it became clear that a two-year tenure was not attractive to most of the staff. The consensus was that job security was paramount.

That evening, Elin's shoulders released their tension as she ran in the park with Mutt and she felt no vestige of post meningitis fatigue. Mia was on her doorstep when she returned, phone in hand. Mia looked expectantly at Elin, "I've been thinking about you all day, hope you don't mind me coming around?"

"Of course not, let's get the kettle on. Something to eat?"

"No thanks, we're having curry later."

Elin prepared tea while Mia wandered round examining the way Elin had decorated her flat.

"You're so clever, your home looks lovely Elin, it's quite a talent. A talent that missed me altogether, unfortunately." Mia gave a rueful smile, "But, how was the meeting?"

Elin's face lit up, "Mr. Roberts was so encouraging. Now I'm wondering about telling the rest of the staff. What do you think?"

Mia shook her head, laughing, "Why are you asking me? When you're confident the right words will come at the right time."

"I should have known you would say that. Let me show you where I chant."

Mia had already guessed the exact spot. It wasn't difficult, there was a cushion on the floor in front of a coffee table pushed against the wall. The surface of the table was clear apart from some evergreens arranged beautifully in matching copper vases and a pair of candles in pretty glass holders. "It's beautiful! Remember there's no need to feel helpless, no matter what the situation. Chanting kept me going when Dan left, nothing else."

Elin was beginning to understand. They sat together, voices blending, unseen energy pulsing. Afterwards Elin's mind was clear; the best way forward was to be open and honest about her intention to apply for the job. It would show respect to the staff. The thought that she might be deputy head was exhilarating – anything was possible.

Making the decision to be upfront about her intentions was one thing, carrying out her decision was another. She presented a positive, smiling face at school every day and decided to bide her time.

Jeannie, snuffling with hay fever, cancelled the speed dating plan on Friday so Elin paid Celia a visit. Celia led her to the sofa, "So what's the latest, have you told the rest of the staff yet?"

"Yes, just today! Mrs. Hargreaves asked me in front of

everybody, so I answered honestly. It was amazing, Celia, she wished me luck, so did Tamsin and Nathan. I got the impression that most of the others were OK about it, perhaps it's a case of better the devil you know."

"That's wonderful, Elin," Celia bounced with excitement.

"It feels good, it feels right. Oh, I do hope I get the job," Elin said as she tapped her foot and frowned.

"Don't be put off by obstacles," Celia cautioned.

"The other candidates, you mean?"

"Actually I meant worrying too much and losing your confidence."

After her Saturday lunch date with Chrissie, Elin felt thoroughly encouraged. She knew she was on the right track: chanting buddies and constant reassurance were crucial.

The summer term flew by and Mr. Roberts, who Elin now called John, occasionally gave her tasks outside her remit, giving her experience beyond that of a TA, and she hoped there was no critical gossip behind her back. Speed dating with Jeannie was a welcome distraction and resulted in a few dates, but something wasn't quite right about each one and she nipped any romantic attachments in the bud. Hilary helped Elin by suggesting interview scenarios, but Elin knew the school, knew its aims, and didn't want to confuse herself trying to remember solutions to theoretical problems.

The night before the interview, Elin invited Mia, Chrissie and Celia over to chant; when they left she was calm and confident. She slept well and got up extra early to exercise the dog. Anxiety, with its familiar chest tightening and nausea, crept in. She reminded herself that she was a strong candidate and her job was to convince the interview panel that this was the case. She took comfort in the knowledge that John Roberts would be rooting for her. Never before had she chanted with so much determination; she was ready for this challenge.

Elin knew that the successful candidate would be informed first and that with each hour that passed her chances diminished. By late afternoon her hands shook as she continued her workday. The children meandered out, chattering like starlings, and she was alone in the classroom when her phone rang. Crossing to a chair she sat down, was this the call? How would she cope with disappointment? She reminded herself that she would cope no matter what, but the phone still quivered in her hand.

She'd got it! With a whoop of joy Elin danced around the room, hugging herself and shouting, "I did it, I did it!" Relief and anticipation flooded through her in equal measure. She flopped down and wondered who to tell first. She composed a text and sent it to all her close friends; next, a calmer version to her parents. Once back at home, she sat down in front of her candles and greenery and sent a heartfelt chant of gratitude to the universe, to her friends and to herself for having the courage and perseverance to pull this off.

A celebration was called for. She'd have her first party in the flat. She bounced around like a teenager who'd just been given tickets to see their favourite pop star, issuing invitations, clearing and prepping. And what a party it was! Nathan and Tamsin, and even Mrs. Hargreaves from school; Gina and Bobby bearing champagne; James and Phillip with elegant canapés. The flat was packed and guests spilled out into the garden, which was aglow with candles in jam jars and dotted with borrowed folding chairs. Mutt had been banished to Celia's utility room where, according to Celia, he was patiently allowing the girls to groom him with their plastic dolly's brushes. Hilary was reacquainting herself with friends from the C swaps. Meeting Elin's new friends for the first time, Ricky commented quietly, "It's good to see you having fun Elin. After Joe I thought you'd find it hard on your own."

"Thanks, Ricky, I can't thank you and Hilary enough for sticking with me. I was a wreck back then."

Mia and Dan were coordinating the food and Chrissie was in charge of the music. Elin spotted Jeannie with her new boyfriend; she was holding his hand and explaining who everybody was, the poor man looked overwhelmed. Elin decided the kindest thing was to leave him to Jeannie's fond attentions. Chrissie was encouraging people to dance. The vibe was anything-goes-as-long-as-you're-having-fun dancing, until Elin, breathless and laughing, poured herself a glass of water, downed it in one and went outside. As she cooled down, Hilary joined her.

"Do you plan on staying here, now that you have a new job? Don't you want something bigger with more garden?"

"I love living here, the park's so close for Mutt. I'm a bit frustrated by the garden. I might ask the landlord if she wants to sell, then I could landscape it properly."

JOHN ROBERTS HAD BEEN WONDERFUL. He'd welcomed her back in her new role and had taken her under his wing. Sometimes the short time she had been at River Park showed as she made glaring mistakes. Like the time she forgot to inform parents about a school trip and another time she totally blanked a parents' evening. However, other than total embarrassment, no harm was done and she established herself in the new job. The settlement money came through and she completed the purchase of the flat.

Weeks after becoming a homeowner again, Elin looked fitter than ever, digging holes and planting sturdy bushes as well as donations of divided perennials from Hilary. The days were getting cooler and the evenings shorter. Elin wondered if there was a Buddhist saying about summer always turning into autumn and determined to ask Mia about it next time she was back in town. Elin still dropped in to see Celia and the girls most Fridays, and had lunch with Chrissie on alternate Saturdays. She looked forward to the time when Mia would be back from her studies. Chanting was an integral part of Elin's life now, but she would always remember the first time she heard it that night at Mia's when she had no hope for the future.

27

Christmas festivities at River Park were well into the planning stages when Elin began to feel some misgivings about John Roberts. He had been late arriving at school on several occasions and had taken unexpected days off with little warning. He didn't look well. His face was drawn and had a greyish tinge. Elin got to school early one day, noticed his car already in its place and decided to ask him how he was before the hurly-burly of the day began. She walked directly to his room and knocked quietly.

"Come in," he said, sounding tired – and the day hadn't started yet. "Hello Elin, close the door, would you? How can I help?"

Elin didn't want him to think she was complaining about his absences. "I wondered how you were feeling, John. I was concerned in case you weren't well. Is there anything more I should be doing?"

"You're doing fine."

Elin waited. He clasped his hands together, leaned his

head down and rubbed his forehead with the tips of his fingers, then addressed Elin seriously.

"Please keep this strictly confidential. Promise me, Elin?"

"Of course, John, that is, unless there's an issue that affects the children."

"Nothing like that. The fact is I've had a heart condition for many years, but recently it's worsened. I've had tests, changed my medication, but nothing is helping yet. Some days I feel so weary, everything's a huge effort, as you've noticed."

Elin hastened to reassure him, "I'm so sorry you're not well, but I hadn't noticed any difference in your work, you still run a tight ship."

"My wife wants me to retire; she would carry on working but she's worried that I won't make it for another five years as we planned. The doctors are non-committal, they say early retirement might help, but might not."

"What a dilemma, John. I don't know what to say."

Mr. Roberts sighed, "I saw your potential from the start. I jumped at the opportunity to get you on the teaching staff. I knew we'd lose you otherwise. After a few years I hoped you'd be ready to take over as Head, but now..." his voice trailed off.

Elin wanted to put her arms around this kind man who had done so much for her. "I'm so grateful, but I would never forgive myself if you stayed on to train me and something terrible happened. Think about your health first."

"I think about it constantly, that's half the problem." He summoned up a smile, "I think I hear someone waiting outside? Please, not a word to the staff."

Concern for her mentor welled up as she hurried to her office where two pupils were waiting. She hung up her coat and called the first one in. There wasn't another moment to think about Mr. Roberts' news until the end of the day. Poor man, she thought, he loves the school so much. No wonder he was torn between worries about his health and worries about the school. What if it all fell apart under a new head teacher? Elin knew how easily this could happen and she felt troubled about the school, about John Roberts and about herself.

Elin had been warned that life would continue to hold many ups and downs even though she was chanting. Nothing but good things had happened since she'd started and now she was reminded of the precariousness of life. Doubts surfaced: how would she cope if the school changed while she was still learning her new job? She chanted until she climbed out of the sudden funk, then chose to treat herself to her old favourite, a leisurely spa night at home. She told nobody about the development at school until Friday rolled around, but Celia was far removed from the school and its politics and Elin trusted her. She explained about John Roberts' health. "It shook me. Such wonderful things have happened and I was happy. Now summer might be turning into autumn, not winter into spring."

Celia chuckled, "I've never heard it put like that before but life's so changeable isn't it? You've got to make wise decisions and being brave is crucial. You've learned that wisdom and courage are already inside you."

"You make it sound so simple," sighed Elin.

"That's because it is. Remind yourself that you're wise and brave every day. It may be a tremendous struggle, but things will work out in ways you couldn't imagine."

"You're so good for me; seeing Chrissie on Saturdays helps too. Which reminds me, isn't it time to plan a swap, we planned on twice a year?"

"Can we wait until after Christmas?" Celia asked. "I can't face it until this Santa Claus malarkey is over."

Malarkey or not, Elin had to shoulder the brunt of the extra work involved in celebrating Christmas at school. John looked ill and Elin tried to protect him from stress. It didn't surprise her when he asked her to stay behind for a chat one evening. With trepidation, she knocked on his office door and entered at the sound of his welcoming voice. "A good first term, Elin, thank you. I sensed a winner in you. My powers of perception are undimmed even though my body is failing."

Elin appreciated his generous smile, "How are you, John?"

"That's what I wanted to talk to you about. My doctor now thinks it's stress and has suggested I give up my job. My wife agrees. I hate the phrase 'give up work' don't you? It has such an air of defeat." John looked pensive.

"Oh, no! Please don't retire if you don't want to. I'll do more! I don't want you to retire."

"Nobody can go on forever. The staff will carry on and there's no reason why anything should change."

Elin knew he was trying to convince himself as much as her, but her job would be the one most affected. Her face fell.

"Don't worry Elin. I've decided to finish at the end of this term, but I'll have a place on the selection panel and I'm still a good judge of character – I chose you, didn't I? A good candidate will come along and the school will be fine. Try not to worry, look where it got me."

Elin marvelled that he could still joke. She felt a wave of gratitude for the presence of this man in her life. She groped for words, blinking away tears, "Thank you for having confidence in me, John. You've changed my life. Thank you from the bottom of my heart."

"You flatter me, Elin, but thank you. Everything will turn out fine, just fine."

Elin swallowed her tears, sniffed hard and made her way slowly back to her room.

Later, in the park, she could still feel tightness in her jaw as she slowed to a walk, letting Mutt run ahead. She took a few yoga breaths, which helped. Random thoughts about things that could go wrong at school without John invaded her mind. Back at the flat, she settled to chanting and found positive thoughts elbowing out the negative ones. It was possible that this could be a positive move, for both John and herself. By the time she stopped she had lifted her own flagging spirits.

Elin scrutinised the job advertisements, waiting to see the post advertised in black and white, while she considered whether or not to apply. Then she saw it: Head Teacher. River Park Primary School. Permanent. Deadline for completed applications Jan 10th. The knowledge remained a background hum in Elin's head all through the holidays.

As usual, Elin canvassed advice. Jeannie was all for taking the easy road and staying as deputy. Hilary was all for grabbing every opportunity, telling Elin, "The other applicants might be a load of tossers and it could fall into your lap." Elin didn't think that was much of a reason and managed to fit in time for coffee with Mrs. Hargreaves. "It would be a meteoric rise for you, wouldn't it dear? Maybe there'd be just a teeny bit of jealousy going on? This is a permanent job so some of the staff will apply."

Celia was encouraging, "I know you'd stand a good chance but it is a bit soon. You're happy as you are and you're still learning the ropes. The right decision will come to you. You're over-thinking this."

At her New Year's Eve party, Chrissie echoed those words almost verbatim. Yoko and the others listened and didn't comment. They were all leaving it up to Elin's innate wisdom, or so they said. She didn't feel particularly wise.

As the deadline drew closer, Elin made no effort to complete the application and even when she chanted she felt no surge of enthusiasm. There wasn't a clear answer, but maybe her inner wisdom was whispering rather than shouting? River Park school would be guided by hands other that hers.

Spring term came and Elin took on responsibility for the school on a strictly temporary basis. She limited her phone chats with John Roberts to Friday afternoons when total chaos had been avoided for another week. She looked forward to his encouragement as much as hearing that another week had ended without disaster reassured him.

"So, everything's still ticking over OK?" he chuckled and sounded more relaxed than he'd been in a long time.

Elin smiled her response, "The place hasn't burned down, or worse, so far! How are you?"

"Much better, thank you Elin. The doctors are cautiously optimistic."

"I'm so happy to hear that." The interviews for Head had taken place and Elin was on edge. "Any news about who got the job?" She detected relief and optimism in his reply.

"His name is Robert Bhatia and he'll start full-time in September."

"Not until September! Oh dear!"

"There's better news too. He's moving from Birmingham and has to move his family and find schools for his children so he's negotiated with his present school and can spend several weeks here next term. He'll get started quite soon."

"Is he a head teacher already? What's he like? "

"He's a head teacher at a much smaller school. A friend of mine in Birmingham said he'd turned around a failing school already. Very popular with the staff, I heard."

"That's good news. Anything else?"

"He seemed very genuine. I sensed he wanted a bigger school so that he could be more innovative. He wasn't arrogant. He used the word respect, and he wasn't talking about respect from the pupils towards the staff, he was talking about teachers respecting children and their potential."

"I'm not sure if I'm ready for such a paragon," Elin laughed with relief. "I'll feel more ditzy than I do already. I'm always asking for help even though as deputy head I should know the answers."

"I wouldn't worry. I would say, above all, that he is a kind man."

The word kind gave Elin a picture of a grandfatherly type. "How old is he? Does he have a lot of experience? Birmingham's such a big city."

"I'd say he was about your age, Elin, maybe a little older, it's hard to tell. He'll be at River Park the third week of term, mid-May. Don't worry, he's a really nice man. Maybe I'll pop in for a chat that week, if it's OK with you?"

"Of course, it is, we'll try not to stress you out. Give my regards to Mrs. Roberts and look after yourself, OK."

The next morning Chrissie led the three of them into the kitchen. "OK, I have two questions: Celia, did your internet date come up to expectations; and Elin, what news about the new Head?"

Elin urged Celia on, "You first, what he was like? Are you going out with him again?"

Celia gave a Mona Lisa smile, "Nice evening. I enjoyed myself. We're going out again." Infuriatingly she stopped, "That answers all of your questions, doesn't it?"

Chrissie threw a piece of leftover breakfast toast at her; it missed and landed butter side down on the floor. Elin wished Mutt was there to dispose of the mess. Celia started laughing and continued. "For once, the dating site managed to come up with someone reasonable. I've certainly had some disappointments in the past. Remember the guy with the train set, Elin?"

Elin remembered the tale of an internet date with a man whose only conversation had been about his railway set, which apparently filled the whole of the ground floor of his house. Celia had never been to check. Elin smiled but refused to be side-tracked. "Stop teasing, tell us the details or you'll have more than a piece of toast to deal with!"

"OK. We met at a pub in town, the unspoken agreement was that if it wasn't working we'd go our own ways after a drink or two. He wasn't earth shatteringly handsome but conversation was easy. We decided to eat there and stayed until about eleven o'clock. I took a taxi home and yes, he did kiss me goodnight. We'd agreed to meet again so it was nice to get the first kiss out of the way. Anything else you need to know?" Celia looked at them quizzically.

"Do you really like him?" Chrissie asked.

"I'm not sure. I'll see how it goes." Celia hadn't even told them his name but she deflected the conversation neatly, asking Elin about the new appointment.

"He gets the John Roberts seal of approval so he must be OK. He comes with a guarantee of 'niceness' and a family.

He's not starting till September, but he'll spend chunks of time at River Park next term."

"What's his name, how old are his children?" Celia was always on the lookout for playmates for Gwennan and Lowri.

"His name is Robert Bhatia and I don't know about his children."

"Robert Bhatia? That sounds as if he's got Indian heritage. I bet he's tall, dark and handsome," Celia giggled.

"Stop it Celia, one date and you're incorrigible! He's a family man. I imagine him as cuddly, maybe rotund but short anyway, with a big smile," Elin said firmly. She'd have to make a big effort to see everything with fresh eyes and work as a team with the newcomer.

At 4.30 pm on the Wednesday of the second week of term, Elin was still at her desk when the phone rang. She answered without taking her eyes off the computer screen, "Good Afternoon, River Park School, Elin Petersen speaking."

"Hello, Ms. Petersen, Robert Bhatia here. I'm glad I caught you. Do you have a few minutes to talk?"

Elin's regretted the offhand way she had answered the phone and felt flustered, "Of course, Mr. Bhatia, it's nice to speak to you." Instantly she berated herself for the inane response.

Fortunately, Mr. Bhatia didn't appear to have noticed and continued, "You too. I was checking you knew I was coming to River Park on Monday for a week? I didn't want to turn up unannounced and make a bad first impression."

He had a sense of humour and he was concerned about the impression he would make on the staff – that was definitely good. Elin responded more calmly, "The staff are looking forward to meeting you. The children too. Is there anything you'd like me to do by Monday?"

"There is one thing, I'd like to meet all the staff as soon as possible. I don't want to wander around the school until they've met me, it wouldn't feel right. Do you think you could organise something for my first day, or would that disrupt the routine too much? I'm in your hands, whatever you suggest."

"I'll get on to it, I'll coordinate it with TAs or combine classes. Break times would be another opportunity." Elin was thinking as she spoke.

"I appreciate your help. I'll phone again on Friday. I'm hoping to bring my children down for the weekend."

"I'll get it in hand and talk to you on Friday," Elin said, relieved that his request was within her capabilities.

"Thanks, look forward to meeting you in person, bye."

The line went dead and Elin sat looking at the phone, forgetting her task on the computer. John Roberts had nailed it, he sounded... nice. One thing had surprised her, she had expected a Birmingham accent but he sounded like the locals in Cardiff. You should never jump to conclusions, she thought. Also, she had detected a sense of fun, always a good thing in a work colleague. He was also aware that whenever you walked around as a head teacher everyone wondered if you were looking for something amiss. It was a good start.

The next phone call from Robert Bhatia was business-like and brief. Elin told him what she had arranged and he thanked her. He asked what time she arrived at the school and suggested he come to her office soon after that. He would follow her lead. More thanks and the conversation ended. Elin was pleased to note that he didn't waste time and he seemed as efficient as he was nice.

28

E lin hurried to school on Monday. She hadn't slept well and nervousness had taken away her appetite. She arrived in her office and filled the kettle. Before it had come to the boil there was a firm knock on the door.

"Good Morning, I'm Robert Bhatia, you must be Elin Petersen."

Elin's eyes widened and her pulse hammered as she took in the newcomer, the way he carried himself and the curve of his smile. He had that wow factor, sex appeal oozing from his smile. She pushed back her chair and walked round her desk, hand extended, "Good Morning. Yes, I'm Elin. Welcome to River Park School, I hope you'll be very happy here."

The kettle began to belch steam and switched itself off, giving Elin an opportunity to turn away and steady herself. Already imprinted in her consciousness was his glorious, tousled, inky hair and the darkest brown eyes imaginable. She hesitated, struggling to think rationally, then realised

Robert was looking pointedly at the kettle. He delved into his briefcase, pulled out two brown paper bags and smiled his question, "Any chance of a cup of tea? I had a change of plan, and decided to drive from Birmingham this morning with only an apple for breakfast." He held up the bags, "Do you mind? I hope you'll join me, then we can get down to business without low blood sugar."

This unconventional opening only served to increase his appeal. Her hands shook as she made tea then put out plates and napkins, grateful that she had cleared her desk on Friday. He put two almond croissants and two blueberry muffins on a plate, sat down and took an enormous bite of croissant, looking perfectly at home. She helped herself to a croissant and made a mental note to ask her friends what deep psychological hang-up made her associate the word nice with a non-threatening image akin to Santa Claus.

As Robert munched his way through the croissant followed closely by a muffin, they chatted like friends at a coffee shop; the journey, house prices, amenities of the area, anything and everything except school business. Elin relaxed and offered to refill both their cups.

"Thanks, Elin, oh, is it OK to call you Elin? Please call me Robert. Maybe we can find out what would be comfortable for the rest of the staff as we go along?"

"That's fine, err, Robert."

He brushed crumbs off his jacket and grinned, "We'd better get down to business. Tell me about the school, I've so much to learn."

Elin could see what John meant. By making this first encounter casual Robert had put her at ease. She wondered if he'd planned this, then dismissed the idea; he'd probably wanted to stay Sunday night with his wife and family in Birmingham.

She wished John had mentioned Robert's good looks. He was tall and muscular with lightly tanned skin and even features; his arresting eyes were fringed with long, thick lashes and drew Elin like a magnet. She avoided looking directly at him: those eyes would surely melt her brain and render her incapable of intelligent thought. She focused on his hands with their long tapering fingers and neatly trimmed nails instead. She observed him all morning as he charmed teachers and pupils alike. When he decided to eat school dinner in the cafeteria Elin retreated to her office, opened her plastic container of mixed salad and appraised the confusing morning.

At the end of the day she had the same feeling. She liked Robert and had come to the same conclusion as John. He was nice. It was all good and it would be even better if he was not quite so amazingly attractive.

Elin had heard that Mia was back in town and decided to give her a ring. "Mia? How's it going? Are you busy? Do you fancy popping over, it would be great to catch up and I need your advice, again!"

"Dan and I are just making dinner, I'll come over later, if you like?" Mia sounded happy.

"Great! No rush." Elin busied herself cleaning the kitchen until she heard Mia's knock. She rushed to the door, wreathed in smiles.

"It's so good to see you, you look wonderful."

Mia returned Elin's hug, "You look well too, you must thrive on responsibility."

"More the regular pay cheque. But yes, I do love the job. Come outside and see how my little garden has changed." It was still light enough for Elin to explain how the area had become a sanctuary of greenness that even Mutt and the cats couldn't destroy.

"You could set up as a landscape gardener, 'Difficult gardens a specialty. Nothing too big, nothing too small'," Mia teased.

"It makes me happy to watch things grow, it fascinates me." Elin was silent for a moment then turned to her friend. "I do hope you stay in Cardiff, Mia. Maybe I'm selfish, but I can't imagine you moving away for good."

"Which leads nicely into whatever's bothering you," Mia prodded Elin. "What's your ulterior motive?"

Elin realised how silly she sounded. Robert Bhatia was easy to work with and she wished he wasn't so handsome. She summed up her feelings and ended, "For once this is a small problem, in fact it's not a problem because I know what I have to do. I have to be professional at all times and remember he has a wife and family."

"Absolutely right," responded Mia, "but that's easier said than done, isn't it?"

Elin groaned, throwing her hands in the air, "And the answer is, chant and be determined!"

"Easy to laugh, I know, almost as funny as watching your face when you first got trapped into that meeting at Chrissie's, remember?"

Elin over dramatised again, 'You mean I was tricked into going to that meeting? You had it planned? Showing me how to be happy? How could you?"

They cackled in unison before Elin jumped up, "So, let's do it. I'm going to chant for the strength to observe those good looks as dispassionately as if admiring a Renoir painting."

Robert was returning to his school in Birmingham and Elin offered to buy pastries for breakfast on his last day. The kettle was almost boiling as he walked in and threw himself into the chair in front of her desk.

"I need that cup of tea, Elin, thanks a lot." He reached for an apple Danish and took a big bite.

Elin smiled as she handed him the drink. "Here, the way you like it." She cringed inwardly before reminding herself that she hadn't made tea for him since the first morning. She chided herself for being overly sensitive, she would have done the same if it had been Ms. Roberta not Mr. Robert Bhatia.

"I've had a stressful week but nothing to do with the school." He ran long fingers through his already messy hair. "It looked as if the house purchase might fall through. House hunting again would be awful. I want the children settled before they start new schools. They've got a challenging time ahead. We'll be moving the second week of August." A flash of worry crossed his face.

Elin chose not to press for details. "How old are the children?" she asked politely.

"Ashley's thirteen and Tayler's four. She's going to start in the Reception class here on the same day as me, poor kid. Imagine your first day of school and your Daddy's starting his first day as headmaster. I'll be more worried about her settling in than me! It could have been worse, the places in Reception were all filled when I accepted the job. I thought she'd be going to Lakeview Primary up the road. That would have been a challenge, leaving her very early to get here in time. Nightmare!"

Frown lines creased the skin between his striking darkly-sculpted eyebrows and Elin wondered why that would be a big problem. Maybe his wife worked and had to leave even earlier. She didn't ask; property was a safer topic. "Is your house nearby? It's a popular area, mainly because of the school's good reputation, of course!"

"Yes, it's very convenient, by a park. The house is a bit

run down, but once we're settled I'll try to spruce it up a bit. It's on Churchill Road."

Elin's eyes widened, "I live on the opposite side of the park. It's great for walking the dog."

Robert's family had a very old Basset Hound, one of the reasons the house by the park suited them and they exchanged dog stories while finishing their tea. Robert got to his feet and made his way to the door. He stopped and glanced back at Elin, picking his words carefully. "Thanks for all you've done, Elin. I feel a lot better. It's a big move, uprooting the family and it'll be hard with the girls both starting in new schools. It's going to be tough."

He shook his head almost imperceptibly and hesitated before continuing, "And now a busy last day coming up!" His face lightened and he walked off down the corridor leaving Elin wondering about what he hadn't said. She felt he'd been on the brink of confiding in her but had thought better of it at the last moment.

BEACH WALKS WITH MUTT, a picnic and a book filled many of the sunny days in the summer holidays, and gardening the gloomy ones. Jeannie was on to something with the singles evenings, when you met someone face-to-face you knew instantly if you wanted to further the acquaintance, better than wasting time on internet dating sites only to be disappointed by reality. Friday evenings at Celia's fell into their regular pattern and Chrissie managed more Saturday lunchtimes than not. Life was good.

The phone rang late one evening, "It's Celia, sorry to ring so late but I'm in a fix. My babysitter's gone down with a bug. Mum's away and I've got an important meeting tomorrow. I wondered if you could help? Gwennan's spending the day with a friend so it's only Lowri. It's a lot to ask but could you help me out?"

Elin hoped Celia hadn't noticed her split second's hesitation. "Yes of course, what time should I come over, or do you want to bring her here?"

"I could drop her off and leave you the key. Then you can come back anytime she gets bored. I'll leave you the car seat and the pushchair in case you want to go anywhere."

Celia sounded frazzled. Elin reassured her, "We'll manage. The dog and the cats will be a novelty."

"Got paper and pen for the emergency numbers?" Celia rattled off numbers for the doctor and various relatives. "Thanks a million, I owe you, big time. See you tomorrow morning, about eight thirty?"

Bang on time, Celia arrived outside and double-parked. Elin went out and together they unloaded the pushchair, the car seat, a bag of toys and Lowri. "You're holding up the traffic. We'll be fine, won't we, Lowri?" Elin pushed her friend towards the car. "See you later."

Lowri hardly bothered to wave goodbye and once the novelty of playing with Mutt and the cats wore off they read the books that Celia had provided. Lowri snuggled up and it was Elin not Lowri who got bored with Fireman Sam, and who wanted to scream if any more Disney princesses lived happily ever after. "Lowri, shall we take Mutt to the park? He could run around and we could go to the swings?"

"Park! Yes! Come on Mutt, let's go." Lowri was heading for the door when Elin had an idea.

"Shall we take a picnic?"

"Picnic! Can we have tuna sandwiches? They're my favourite. And apples and crisps? And juice to drink?"

"Of course we can have tuna sandwiches, but you'll have to wait while I make them. Why don't you sit here and draw while I get the picnic ready?"

Half an hour later, they were on their way to Bayley Park. Lowri was in the pushchair and Mutt was on the lead. Luckily Elin had found an old backpack so she could carry the food and drink while keeping her hands free to cope with the pushchair and the dog. To think it was this much work to have a picnic in the park with just one child! Amazement at the competence of parents surfaced, followed by new respect for the energy required; she was sure it was easier to face a whole classroom of children. She let Mutt off the lead at the park gates and Lowri demanded her freedom too; Elin hoped they wouldn't run off in opposite directions. The play area was at the far end of the park so they made their way towards it extremely slowly, with pauses to walk along walls, jump off kerbs and examine flowers and insects.

Mutt seemed intrigued by Lowri's presence and did his usual circling but at closer quarters and without disappearing into the distance. He appeared to be guarding the little girl and Elin's nervousness gradually dissipated. She was pushing Lowri on the swing, lulled by the repetitive motion, when she saw a familiar figure heading towards her. Actually, not towards her but towards the swings. She closed her eyes for a moment, marshalling her thoughts. He was also pushing a little girl in a pushchair and an older child followed him, lagging behind with head down, eyes glued to her mobile phone, holding a lead attached to an elderly Basset Hound in her free hand. She kept walking as her father stopped to speak to Elin.

"Hello Elin, fancy seeing you here. Is this your little girl?"

"Hello, Robert." She managed to speak normally, "This is Lowri. Her mother had a babysitting crisis so I'm helping out."

"Hello Lowri," responded Robert gravely. "This is my daughter Tayler. She's four. You look about five, I think."

"No, I'm four," Lowri held up four fingers.

Tayler was installed on the swing next to Lowri and the two four-year-olds screamed with delight as they were pushed higher and higher. Robert chatted easily to Elin, explaining that the teenager was his thirteen-year-old daughter Ashley and the dog was Flopsy.

Suddenly Lowri remembered the picnic, "I'm hungry, Elin, can we have the picnic now?"

Elin looked at her watch, it was almost noon, "OK, let's find somewhere to sit."

Robert smiled, "A picnic in the park on a sunny day, why didn't I think of that?"

Elin unzipped the bag, "We've got enough to share, if you'd like Tayler to have some. We have plenty of tuna sandwiches, crisps and a bag of apples."

"Thanks, that's very tempting but I need to catch up with Ashley, she's having a hard time at the moment and I don't want her to feel left out." He gave a regretful shrug and turned back to Tayler on the swing. Elin could have sworn he rolled his beautiful eyes, just a little, and she guessed that Ashley was giving him a hard time too. Tayler wasn't too happy about leaving and was eyeing the food Elin had taken out of her backpack. Robert averted the imminent meltdown. "Maybe we could take a sandwich and Tayler can eat it as we walk?"

"Of course, here you are Tayler, and have an apple for later too."

"I'll email you about getting together before school starts? Get a few things rolling before the rest of the staff come in?"

"That sounds like a good idea. I like to get a head start on the work too."

They hurried off in the direction taken by Ashley and Flopsy, with Tayler waving goodbye to Lowri as if they were old buddies. Elin took a deep relaxing breath before starting on a tuna sandwich, wishing he was not quite such a nice man. Or if he had to be so perfectly nice, could he not be a little less attractive? She was glad that Lowri was occupied eating her way through a mound of sandwiches; she needed time to process her feelings about Robert Bhatia.

She frequently had to process her feelings once she and Robert started to work together every day. It wasn't so bad when the two of them were alone, then she was on her guard and concentrated on the task in hand, not allowing her thoughts to wander. He was relaxed but business-like, and there was no personal conversation; she took pride in doing her work and was equally professional. It was different when she could watch him interact and charm her colleagues. Then she studied him, admiring his profile, the beauty of his eyes and their compassionate expression. Her glance took in his body, its strength and suppleness, and she studied his mannerisms, the way he pushed his hair back before making his main point and his habitual glance down at his hands before responding to negative comments. She was falling in love with him despite her best intentions, her principles, her past experience and her inward struggles.

This called for a girls' summit. Elin had prepared a pot of vegetarian chilli and put potatoes in the oven to bake. Her friends had been warned that she was in dire need of support and as they arrived each one hugged her warmly. Elin fussed around with the food and after she had served everybody she explained her new challenge, finishing with the question. "What am I to do? I've behaved impeccably this time. I know that he has a family and I wouldn't dream of hurting them. We have a great working relationship and I've done nothing and said nothing to change that. I love my job, it's what I chanted for and I was unbelievably excited when I got it. I thought all my troubles were over. I don't want to start applying for jobs all over again, I've barely learned the basics of this one. It would give the impression that I didn't care about River Park School if I moved so soon. This complicates everything. Do any of you have any ideas, what can I do?"

Elin was on a floor cushion near Hilary's feet. For once Hilary was lost for words, but she squeezed Elin's shoulder in sympathy. Mia sat crossed legged on the floor, her plate in her lap. She spoke first, leaning over and touching Elin's hand briefly. "It's hard, to have to go through this every day. You've done everything right, I'm glad that you're not thinking of moving to another school, somehow this has got to be faced. You've got to be happy again."

"Easy to say, so far impossible to do," responded Elin with a deep sigh.

"We can get stuck in a rut, believing things can't change. The solution isn't obvious, it's under the radar, so to speak," Mia continued.

Elin wrinkled her nose, "Do you mean that there is a solution but I can't get to it? I've been chanting and trying to change my feelings but, so far, no change at all. I'm so frustrated. I don't know what to do next."

Hilary spoke up, "I'd love to know what the solution

would be, I'm stumped." She gave Elin's shoulder another squeeze.

Mia looked at Chrissie and Celia before she responded, "Do either of you want to explain?"

Chrissie shook her head and Celia also indicated that Mia should carry on.

"Sometimes we end up concentrating so hard on the issue that we tie our mind up in knots when we chant. Perhaps that's what you're doing? We've done the same when the worry invades our every conscious thought."

"Yes, exactly," interposed Elin. "It's there when I wake up in the morning and I feel sick at the thought. I've lost weight because I have no appetite."

They all looked at Elin's plate where the crisp jacket potato and chilli lay barely touched. Mia continued, "Empty your mind when you chant. It's difficult. Concentrate on the words *Nam Myoho Renge Kyo*. Trust your inner wisdom. Really believe that there's a solution that's good for everyone."

"Mia is right," Celia added, "the trick is to chant for everybody to be happy, but don't map out how that's going to happen. That's strategizing. But maybe we've emphasised personal happiness and not told you enough about chanting for others too? We don't just want to be happy ourselves. We want a peaceful world."

Elin put her head in her hands, "That kind of explanation doesn't resonate with me, I need proof not mumbo jumbo. The chanting worked in the beginning but it's not working now."

Chrissie pushed her plate to one side and leaned forward. She screwed up her face, struggling to find a way to explain. When her words finally came, they rang with sincerity, "I hear you, Elin, I really do. It's OK to have doubts. Although it works it's not a magic wand and it often takes a long time. It takes effort and perseverance." She groped around for words, "Dancers train hard, practice hard, and suffer for what looks like a flawless, effortless performance. You went to college, studied, worked hard and even then, you struggled to get your perfect job. But you didn't give up."

Elin interrupted, "I still find believing in something I don't understand hard."

Chrissie tried again, "But you started to chant. What happened then?"

"Things fell apart with Chris and I still needed a better job. I suppose I felt a bit better."

Chrissie sat back a smile playing around her mouth., "Elin, isn't that kind of proof? You felt better?"

"Well I feel better almost every time. But not invariably." There was still a vestige of defiance in Elin's tone, "You reckon this situation will change but we don't know the timescale. Right?"

Celia pushed her chair back and stood up, "That's it, Elin. But I haven't had time to chant yet, rushing from work, settling the kids and getting here on time. Who's ready to chant now?"

Hilary smiled, "Not me, but I'm happy to sit and listen."

As the four of them chanted together their surroundings seemed to be ringing in unison with their determination. Later they brewed hot chocolate with marshmallows and picked through a box of chocolates that Hilary had won in a raffle. As they left at the end of the evening, Elin thanked them with absolute sincerity.

"This is going to be OK. I'm going to carry on going to work, behaving properly and chanting for everybody to be happy. Eventually there will be good effects from those good causes. That's all I have to do, no matter how tough it is."

"We'll all support you. If you start to lose heart, give one of us a ring and we'll come over. won't we?" Celia looked around at Mia and Chrissie and they nodded in agreement as Hilary watched them thoughtfully.

29

Either Mia, Chrissie or Celia managed to be available whenever Elin hit a low point – which was frequently. Together they encouraged and cajoled her; urged her forward and reassured her; inspired her and cheered her on. They didn't allow Elin to dig herself a hole of self-pity and jump in. Sometimes Elin found them so irritatingly positive that she wanted to scream, but the alternative was worse. Jeannie and Hilary listened and sympathised. She ate dinner at Hilary's and Jeannie dragged her to yet another singles evening, but what was the point? All the men fell far short of the one she saw every day, spoke to every day, laughed and joked with every day. Even Jeannie gave up after that.

How she got through the months of September and October Elin would never know, but she survived. Thinner and paler, but she survived. As November drew towards December she even found herself feeling happy occasionally.

Towards the end of term, Elin was surprised when she

walked into Robert's office one morning to find Ashley sitting in the corner, huddled over a mobile phone. Her long, straight hair was light brown and hung in a curtain, hiding her face.

"Hello Ashley. I'm Elin. Are you OK? Would you like a cup of tea? I have some biscuits if you like?"

Ashley looked up and Elin could see that her eyes were a beautiful dark brown with sweeping eyelashes, just like her father. "No thank you, I can make my own tea. My Dad's got biscuits anyway," she answered flatly and looked back down at her phone.

Consider yourself snubbed, thought Elin, wondering what to do next. The door had been ajar, which was a sign that she could walk in to Robert's office, but he was nowhere to be seen.

"I'll leave you to it then. Would you tell your father that I was here? I need to clarify a few things." Elin realised that Ashley had tuned her out and was texting away at speed.

Elin turned to leave just as Robert came hurrying down the corridor, slowing when he saw Elin. When he spoke, he sounded decidedly off-balance., "I see you've met Ashley. Her school has an inset day and she was supposed to be spending it with a friend but the friend is ill. It didn't seem like good idea to leave her at home, so here she is. I hope it doesn't start a trend among the staff." He smiled wanly, "Did you need something Elin? Come in, sit down."

As Ashley was sitting in the chair Elin usually occupied, this was not straightforward. Robert asked Ashley to give up the chair. Ashley complied very slowly. Elin said she would fetch a chair from her office. Robert said he would carry it. Elin said she was perfectly capable of carrying a chair. Ashley watched the exchange impassively and Elin felt rattled. Robert had lost a little of his usual self-possession too. Ashley seemed to sense this and even enjoy it, though Elin couldn't have explained why she got this impression and she was glad to escape for the few minutes it took to carry the chair from her office. By the time she returned, Robert had regained his composure. Ashley didn't speak again and didn't interfere with her father's work in any way, but the tension in the room was palpable. Elin couldn't wait to get back to her own office.

Elin told the story to Celia on Friday evening as they cozied up in front of the gas fire. The girls were tucked up in bed, and she was anxious to discuss the encounter, which still preyed on her mind.

"Mm, it does sound uncomfortable. Ashley sounds like a piece of work all right. I wonder what Gwennan and Lowri will be like when they get to that age?"

Elin couldn't imagine either of them changing into sullen, enigmatic teenagers, but what did she know? "There was something going on, I felt hostility in the air. I'm not sure if it was directed at me or at her father. Probably me, but I felt that he was getting flak for something too."

"She doesn't sound very happy. Maybe she's insecure and was reacting to you as if you were some kind of threat. If her father's as... what was the word you keep using? Oh yes, nice, as you say, you'd expect her to be secure and happy." Celia was teasing but the question remained. Celia mused, "It's unlikely that Dad's the problem, it makes you wonder what Mum's like, doesn't it? Sorry to bring her up."

"Nothing to be sorry about," Elin assured her. "It's also strange that he never mentions his wife. He's being very careful to keep his private life just that, extremely private, but when I met the younger one in the park she seemed perfectly normal and friendly."

"I suppose you can't compare a four-year-old with a

thirteen-year-old, can you? Leaving her friends when they moved would be upsetting for a teenager. She probably blames Dad," Celia suggested.

"It's not my business anyway. I'm over the worst of my obsession with Robert. I still think he's wonderful and I still have to make a big effort not to make googly eyes at him and let him know how attractive I find him, but I'm not so miserable. I occasionally laugh and have fun."

"You've been a trouper, battling on. You deserve to be happy. Would you like a glass of wine to celebrate your burgeoning recovery?" Celia raised her eyebrows, "It's Friday night!"

"OK, just one glass, I need to get home, I'm really tired," Elin said laughing. The question about Ashley didn't seem so important anymore.

Celia poured two glasses and they watched the gas flames dance. "By the way Elin, did you know that Chrissie's not having the New Year's Eve party this year and I'm not having the New Year's Day breakfast either."

"That's disappointing, I was looking forward to them. Any particular reason?"

"There's going to be a really big celebration on New Year's Day instead."

"I've only been to our small, chatty groups," Elin said feeling herself withdrawing into a protective shell.

"It'll be just as much fun, I promise. We've booked City Hall for the day. There'll be a hundred people, maybe two hundred there, so you'll meet lots of new people." Celia sounded excited.

"All day? What do you do?"

"You'll see, there'll definitely be entertainment. And food. You will come, won't you Elin?" Celia tilted her head to one side expectantly.

Elin finally grinned, "Now let me see? My oh-so-busy social life, I wonder what I'll have to juggle to be there? Oh dear, I'll have to walk the dog early, what a challenge. And I'll have to eat lunch with a lot of new friends, which sounds problematic. And having to go there with you, Mia and Chrissie?"

Celia lobbed a cushion at Elin; she caught it deftly and threw it back. "OK, you know I'm kidding, right? I have nothing else to do on New Year's Day so count me in."

As she got ready for bed, Elin wondered about the Christmas holidays and the challenge of feeling alone. Her relationship with her parents had improved greatly. From the daughter married to the university professor, through the divorced teaching assistant to the daughter with the excellent job. It was time to build bridges, being proud of their only daughter wasn't a crime and she had been glad of their presence during her illness. She would phone them the next morning and invite herself.

Elin unloaded the car on her return from her parents with mixed emotions, the over-riding one was how glad she was to be back in her own space. It wasn't grand, but it was home. The cats were undecided whether to purr or give her the cold shoulder. Elin shivered as she turned the thermostat up to maximum and returned to the car to unload her small suitcase, presents and Christmas treats. By the time she had put everything away, the flat was warming up and she dared to take off her coat. A slice of Christmas cake and a mince pie were her reward after the long drive and she flopped down contentedly, Alley and Tom claiming a knee each.

The visit home had been good. Something had mellowed inside Elin and she could see that her parents had good intentions, they meant well and they loved her. She would never forget how worried they were when she was in hospital.

Elin was running around the perimeter of Bayley Park on the crisp and frosty afternoon of New Year's Eve when she spotted a familiar, elderly Basset Hound waddling along attached to the drooping caricature of teenage angst that she recognised as Ashley Bhatia. Mutt had registered Flopsy at the same time and bounded over to say hello. Mutt's presence was never ignorable and Ashley pulled Flopsy closer. Elin hurried over, calling out.

"Don't worry Ashley, Mutt won't hurt Flopsy, he only wants to play."

A flash of recognition passed over Ashley's face and she gave an uncertain half smile. Elin drew closer and was able to grab Mutt's collar and talk to him. "Don't be silly, Mutt, Flopsy can't play with you. Her legs are a bit short, she couldn't keep up with you, could you Flopsy?" Elin bent down and patted Flopsy with her free hand.

Ashley spoke, "Flopsy's old, she can't walk fast anymore." Elin detected a note of sadness in her voice. "Is he your dog?"

"Yes, Mutt's only four, he's full of energy."

"We've had Flopsy ten years, since I was three."

Elin was relieved to be having a normal conversation with Ashley. "That's a long time. Do you always take her for walks?"

"I'm supposed to take her out every day. Dad gets mad when I forget."

Elin didn't think it would be a good idea to comment on this revelation. "I'd better be off, Mutt's still wants to run. Nice seeing you again."

Ashley gave the same uncertain smile and a half wave

when Elin jogged away and called Mutt to follow her. The third encounter with Ashley had gone a great deal better than the second. The play area came into view and she saw Robert pushing Tayler on the swings. They were both muffled up with scarves and gloves as well as puffy parkas in contrast with Elin's running gear, which she had topped off with a cheerful red woolly hat and matching gloves. Robert must have seen Elin at the same time because he gave a wave before telling Tayler, pointing in Elin's direction. Her jog slowed to a walk as she approached. Robert spoke first.

"You look toasty! Tayler was wondering if you had your friend's little girl with you, I forget her name."

"Lowri? Sorry, only the dog today, see him over by the big trees?" She took deep breaths, "It's impossible to feel the cold after you've been running for a while. You should try it sometime, Robert."

"Bit difficult with this one," he responded lightly, looking down at Tayler. "Those jogging pushchairs are expensive and she's too old for one really. But she loves dogs."

Elin moved away from the swings and called Mutt; he was definitely a changed dog and came running over at only the third call. Robert extricated Tayler from the swing and she ran excitedly over to Elin and Mutt.

"I can see that. Little ones are often scared because he's so tall. Probably because you have Flopsy. I just saw her when I talked to Ashley."

"You talked to Ashley?" Surprise registered on Robert's face. "She's usually so absorbed with her phone, I doubt she'd notice Armageddon! How did you manage that?"

"It was Mutt, he practically bowled poor Flopsy over so Ashley couldn't help but notice. Now your other daughter is having a love-fest with my dog." Elin's face grew pink, she was glad it could be attributed to the nip in the air. Why had she said love-fest? Why did those Freudian slips always have to happen when she was in close proximity to a man she found attractive?

"I'd better get going. Happy New Year, Robert." Curiosity made her add the next question. "It's big night for parties tonight, do you have plans for seeing the New Year in?"

He shrugged resignedly, "Try to persuade Ashley that it's just another night and there's no need to stay up. I'll probably lose that battle, maybe a Scotch to toast the New Year. That's about it. How about you?"

Elin hadn't expected the same question in return, she struggled for a response that didn't sound pathetic. "Me? Well my usual New Year's Eve party's been cancelled this year in favour of a bigger one on New Year's Day. I'll probably have an early night and conserve my energy."

Elin wondered if it was cheating to call a Buddhist gathering a big party. Oh well. He'd never know and it did make it sound as if she had plans to enjoy herself. Which she did. "Bye both, Happy New Year."

"Happy New Year to you too, Elin. See you at River Park next year."

Elin struggled to contain her chaotic thoughts. She could have sworn he was attracted to her. He had a family but never mentioned his wife. She battled to remember the wife all the time. At school he was purposeful and energetic, but today there had been an air of melancholy about him.

She hurried home, the afternoon was already drawing to a close and the light was fading. Elin drew the curtains and did what she always did to comfort herself, curled up with a mug of tea. After three solid hours of TV, Elin was stiff and hungry. She heated up the last of the turkey curry she'd made with her mother's leftovers then there was only one more thing to do before she relaxed into a New Year's Eve extra-special spa night. She pulled out her special cushion and settled herself comfortably, lighting candles and chanting *Nam Myoho Renge Kyo* with determination to be completely happy and to lead a valuable life, no matter what. As her voice filled the room the two cats nestled closer and Mutt joined them, lying as close as his long legs would allow.

What should she wear to this special event at City Hall? Whenever Elin had been to any gathering of Buddhists she had always been struck by the sheer variety of people and this didn't stop at differences of age and gender, it definitely extended to their clothes choices. She chose her newest jeans, high heeled boots and an aubergine cashmere sweater, old but still elegant. Once the decision was made, she dressed quickly, applied her usual makeup including an aubergine lipstick to highlight her sweater choice. Celia was picking her up so she stood in the window, warm coat in hand until she recognised the silver mini drawing to a halt outside.

"Happy New Year," Celia said with a smile as she leaned over to open the car door for Elin. "You're looking good today."

"Happy New Year to you too, "responded Elin as she jumped in. "Love your jacket, swapping it any time soon? Let's go, I'm intrigued about this 'do'. You did say there was going to be lunch, didn't you?"

Celia drew away from the curb, "Yes, there is. A pot luck with everybody bringing a dish, it'll be good."

"What? You didn't ask me to bring anything! I could easily have cooked something, you know that." Elin wrinkled her nose in dismay.

Celia patted her knee reassuringly, "Don't worry, there'll

be plenty, there always is. Yoko was coordinating the food and if she'd wanted a contribution from you she'd have asked. There'll be Japanese rice balls, Indian samosas, Italian pizzas and good old British sandwiches at the very least."

They parked and hurried through the cold towards City Hall. Elin was overwhelmed by the welcome they received; there were smiling young people greeting each arrival and thanking them for coming as they made their way from the foyer to a ballroom filled with chairs arranged in rows. Bright decorations covered the walls and red, yellow and blue balloons caught her eye at the side of the stage. The hum of cheerful conversations filled the air. One or two men and women were scurrying round with printed lists in their hands as the rest of the throng greeted new and old friends. Elin sat back in her chair, pushed her bag under the seat and prepared to enjoy the proceedings.

Chatting with friends was clearly an important part of the morning; now Elin understood why Celia had insisted on arriving early. As she people watched, Elin felt a tap on her shoulder and was given yet more welcoming hugs by Yoko and her friends.

"Yoko, Happy New Year! Celia just told me that you are in charge of lunch but you didn't ask me to bring anything."

"Don't worry, I deliberately didn't ask you. I wanted you to relax and enjoy the whole day. We have plenty of food, you'll probably be taking some home with you. Have a good time!"

Celia introduced her to so many people that Elin's head was spinning. The seats filled up and the noisy chatter reached hubbub level. The sound of a large bell being rung stopped everybody in their tracks, and the MC for the day stepped up to the microphone and introduced the day's programme. Smiling children performed dances with more verve than accuracy, Chrissie must have had a hand in the preparations. Some encouraging words were read aloud. A small choir sang acapella beautifully. She was fully at ease without a tense muscle in her body when the MC stepped up to the microphone to announce the final presentation before lunch.

Total shock hit Elin like an express train and she gasped out loud. Her stomach did a flip and there was a pounding in her head as her pulse rate increased to Olympic sprinter levels. The MC was introducing Robert Bhatia, who would talk about overcoming challenges in life. She struggled to keep her breathing under control as she watched Robert make his way to the microphone and start to speak. Celia turned to her with eyebrows raised and Elin managed to nod acknowledgement to the unspoken question in her eyes. Yes, this was indeed the Robert Bhatia Elin had talked about, described at length and agonised over. Utter astonishment rolled over Elin in waves and she hardly heard his first words as he introduced himself to the audience. Celia leaned towards her, eyes round with amazement, and whispered.

"You didn't exaggerate his good looks Elin, he's gorgeous."

By the time Elin's heart rate had recovered, Robert had finished introducing himself and was talking about his background. He told the gathering that he had been born near Cardiff but had only returned last August when he had fulfilled his dream of becoming head teacher of a large primary school in his hometown.

"My father's family, who were Hindus, came to settle

here from India. My mother was Jewish so when I was growing up any discussion about religion was interesting, but fraught. I decided I didn't want anything at all to do with any organised religion, that it was all hocus pocus, or as Marx famously said 'the opiate of the people'. I left home for college in Birmingham and stayed there to work after I qualified."

Each fibre of Elin's being was straining to hear every nuance of his words. Celia was listening intently by her side. Chrissie and Mia were somewhere in the room and would have realised this was the Robert who Elin had talked about obsessively since the summer. There would be a girls' summit to end all girls' summits after this.

Robert was smiling as he addressed the crowded room.

"I met Amanda, the woman who was to become my wife, when I was twenty-three years old and we married the same year. Our daughter Ashley was born the following year and I had everything I wanted in my life. We were idyllically happy and I thought that I had it made, that I would be happy like that for the rest of my life."

Tears pricked the back of Elin's eyes at his words; did she have the courage to stay in the room? The idea of disturbing everybody by leaving was worse. She decided to stay, she needed to know the whole truth once and for all.

"We wanted more children but Ashley, my beautiful Ashley, was our only child for nine long years. Just when we had given up on the idea of another baby, Amanda found she was pregnant again and we were overjoyed."

At least Elin knew what was coming next, she knew that Tayler would arrive safe and sound and become a happy healthy four-year-old, the apple of her father's eye.

"But at the same time as we discovered that Amanda was

pregnant she also started to experience unusual symptoms that couldn't be explained by the pregnancy. After batteries of tests, she was diagnosed as having ovarian cancer. She refused treatment because that would have harmed the baby. She put her life at much greater risk by postponing treatment."

Elin was transfixed; she felt shock waves go through her. She had never imagined for a moment that Robert had endured such suffering in his life. This knowledge also put Ashley's attitude in a completely different light. Elin wanted to put her arms round that prickly little being and hold her tight.

"Our second beautiful daughter, Tayler, was born early, very small, but healthy. Amanda was able to enjoy her for only a very short time before she started aggressive treatment aimed at getting rid of the cancer. Unfortunately, nothing seemed to work." Robert stopped speaking for a moment. "Although we had some good times after her diagnosis they were few and far between and our lives were trapped in a circle of caring for out tiny new-born and our nine-year-old little girl, juggling all this with Amanda's brutal chemotherapy."

The room was silent; several people dabbed their eyes and there was a great deal of loud sniffing going on. Elin couldn't have described the reactions pulsing through her body, her responses were visceral while her brain seemed detached from reality. How could she feel anything but sorrow as she listened to Robert's story, even though the ending seemed destined to ease her mind and allow her a glimmer of hope for her own happiness?

"Amanda died when Tayler was ten months old. It was a hard time for me and an even harder time for Ashley. She had lost her mother and had a new, very small sister who was taking up most of Dad's time and attention."

It had happened. His wife had died. He was a widower not a married man. Terror grabbed Elin's heart one more time. She gripped her hands together and leaned forward. He seemed so happy now, so well adjusted, so together. Perhaps he had met someone else and married again. His wife had died more than three years ago – after all and he was an attractive man. Elin came back to reality and listened hard again, never taking her eyes from his face.

"This is the part of my story that I most wanted to share with you today. In the midst of all this chaos, the loss, the grieving, the problems of trying to work as well as look after my daughters, there was one person who was a rock, an 'angel', and I know I wouldn't be here, talking to you today if it wasn't for her."

By now Elin felt as if she was going to faint with tension. Hope had risen in her heart and now that flicker of hope was going to be crushed. This must be the woman Robert had turned to and had married before moving back here. She could barely keep her eyes on Robert now, it was unbearably painful, but neither could she turn away. Celia reached over and covered Elin's hands, twisting in her lap, with her own warm one, giving them a gentle squeeze of understanding.

Robert turned to the side of the stage and beckoned to someone. Elin wanted to look away but couldn't. He walked to the side and held his hands out in encouragement.

"I want you to meet Ambika Narayanan, better known as Auntie, and I will be forever grateful to her."

Robert held both the woman's hands in his as he guided her towards centre stage. Elin gasped. Ambika Narayanan was dressed in a beautiful multi-coloured sari and looked elegant and self-assured, smiling broadly as she hugged Robert in front of the crowd, but there was no mistaking that she was at least seventy years old – her hair was streaked with grey and her olive skin had lost the smoothness and perfection of youth.

"This is the lady who stepped in and helped me. But more important than all the meals she cooked and dirty washing she dealt with, more than the times she cleaned the house and even walked the dog, was the fact that she told me the way that I could deal with my loss, a way that our whole family could deal with our loss and be really, truly, genuinely happy again. This is the woman who introduced me to Buddhism, chanting and the SGI."

The room erupted into a cacophony of cheering and stamping, loud applause that continued until Ambika, looking embarrassed, and nodding briefly, insisted on leaving the stage so that Robert could continue.

Elin could hardly contain herself, but she was determined not to let her mind wander into possibilities until she had heard the end of the story.

"I could tell you a great deal of what happened then, but all of you will be familiar with my journey. That's because you will have experienced it for yourself in some form or other. From the small beginning of trusting Ambika and doing what seemed to me a very strange thing just because I trusted her, my life has changed for the better in a myriad of ways. All of you here will know what I mean when I say that I found hope. No longer was life a depressing, painful struggle all alone. I had friends and people to support me, but most of all I had hope. I began to feel that I would get through my difficulties and be happy again. But it would be up to me."

Elin knew exactly what he meant.

Robert continued, "The multitude of difficulties that confronted me were dealt with one at a time. I began to have gratitude for the life I had lived, but also to understand that it was gone forever. I understood that I would damage the life I still had with my two wonderful daughters if I continued to live in the past. Hope grew in me as I chanted. I became more positive with every day and I realised that the best way to pay tribute to Amanda was to be happy again and make a happy life with Ashley and Tayler. I would never have been able to do it without this philosophy and practice. I moved back here and now live closer to my parents and family who help me with the children and I find myself in a very happy work situation. I am grateful to everyone here today for listening to my story, to Simon here for asking me to tell it and I look forward to getting to know you all, every one of you, much better very soon. Thank you very much."

Robert sat down amid tumultuous applause. People stood up to applaud, stamped their feet and whistled. Elin clapped but her knees wobbled when she tried to stand up and Celia stayed seated in solidarity. His last few sentences rang in Elin's head and she heard them again and again. He had said that he was in a very happy work situation. He had said that he looked forward to getting to know them all better very soon. Very soon could not be soon enough for Elin.

Celia and Elin stayed in their seats as the rest of the throng got up and made their way to the next room to the buffet lunch. Elin didn't want to push her way through the crowd, she was trembling from the roller coaster of emotions and needed time to collect herself. Celia took her hand again and held it as she spoke.

"Wow! Elin, I can't imagine what a surprise that was for you. What an amazing, emotional experience. I feel totally drained after listening, I wanted to cry for him. I imagine you must be in a state of shock. How do you feel?"

"I'm not sure. Shaky, I think, would describe it. My body is reacting as if it doesn't know what to do." Elin made no move to get up.

Suddenly, Chrissie and Mia materialised by Elin's side.

"Oh, my god, Elin, was that a surprise or what?" Words tumbled from Chrissie, "I couldn't believe my ears when I heard his name announced and then I couldn't believe my eyes when he stepped up to speak. What a story! Such a dreadful thing to happen, but such a relief that he has hope now. You were right, Elin, he is very, very sexy. You did not exaggerate one iota. Are you OK? You looked stunned."

Mia was calmer than the others but that was typical. "It was such a sad story. Yet he looked so happy, despite everything. Did you notice he said he had a very happy work situation, Elin? It must have been good to hear him say that."

"Yes, I do remember him saying that, it's something to hang on to. What I'm really amazed about is seeing him here. I had no idea he chanted."

Celia responded to this immediately, "Well, he would be just as surprised to know you were here. I don't suppose you've ever mentioned Buddhism and the SGI to him either. We don't always talk about it in work, do we?"

Chrissie interrupted excitedly, "Does he know you're here, Elin, did you catch his eye when he was speaking?"

"No, I don't think so. He was focusing his attention on people at the front. I saw Ashley there. I don't think he looked over here, I didn't see any flicker of recognition as he spoke." Elin felt a wave of appreciation for her friends. Here they were, oblivious of the splendid lunch awaiting them, more concerned in checking that she was OK and giving moral support. She smiled and tried to hurry them on their way.

"Enough about me for the moment, I can only take so much at once. Why don't you go and get some food before it's all gone? I think I may go outside for a breath of fresh air."

People were wandering back into the main room with plates laden with samosas, empanadas and salads, sitting round in small groups, talking away twenty to the dozen as the smell of spices and savoury delicacies wafted over. Mia suggested, "Why don't we go and get lunch while you get some fresh air and we'll bring an extra plate back here for you? We should be back in ten minutes."

Elin leaned over and gave her friend a hug, "Thanks a lot, you guys, I can't say I feel like meeting a lot of new people right now. I wouldn't be able to concentrate on anything they said. My head's still in such a whirl. Ten minutes out in the cold will bring me back down to earth quickly enough. I'll see you back here."

Elin made her way outside and pulled her coat round her tightly. She stared at the huge Christmas tree decorating the patch of grass outside City Hall without registering a single one of the baubles or the hundreds of twinkling lights. She walked up and down to keep warm, keeping an eye on her watch. Time seemed to be standing still as she deliberated over how her attitude towards Robert could and would change now that she knew he was a widower.

A few smokers emerged from the foyer. She moved further away and stared into the distance. A familiar voice came from behind her and she spun round.

"Hello Elin, your friend Chrissie said I'd find you out here. She wanted me to tell you that she has your plate of food ready whenever you want to go back inside."

It was Robert, jacket collar turned up and hands thrust inside his pockets. He smiled that wonderful warm smile again and for the first time she was able to return it fully. She was oblivious to the frosty air and forgot about the delicious lunch being kept for her inside.

"Hello Robert. I'm so sorry about your wife. It must have been so awfully hard, I can't even begin to imagine. But I'm glad I know about your difficulties now and I'll do anything I can to help and support you at school, I hope you know that."

Elin couldn't believe that appropriate words that actually made sense were coming out of her mouth when all she wanted to do was throw herself into his arms.

"Thank you. I appreciate it very much. I didn't know you were a Buddhist?" Robert's eyes widened and Elin felt weak.

"The same goes for me about you. I had no idea either. I've only been chanting for a relatively short time, since my life went to hell in a hand basket. It's a lot better now." Elin reflected silently that Robert could have no idea how much better it was at this moment. "You look frozen, Robert, perhaps we'd better go back inside. Have you eaten yet?"

"Actually, I was queuing behind your friends when one of them, Chrissie, introduced herself and told me you were outside. I'm glad she did. Your other friends said they would get a plate for me too and we could all sit together to eat." He shivered, "You're right, I'm freezing, let's go back inside."

Elin was very happy to go back inside now that she knew Robert was going to sit with them. They made their way back into the warmth and the hum of conversation. Ashley came rushing over with a boy, aged about fourteen, in tow. "Dad, Dad, this is William. He goes to the same school as me. Is it OK if I go and sit with him and his sister?"

"Of course it is Ashley, I'm glad you've found a friend. Do you remember Elin? From school and from the park?"

"Oh yes, hi Elin." Ashley glanced briefly at Elin then pressed on, "They're planning on going to the cinema tomorrow, can I go with them, Dad?"

"Slow down a bit, Ashley, give me a chance to think. We'll talk later, OK? I'll need to talk to their parents too, make sure they don't mind."

Ashley had to content herself with this as she rushed off without a second glance at Elin. Robert smiled, "The bit about checking with the parents was a bit superfluous in present company, I'm sure they'll be fine. But Ashley can't just assume that tagging along will be OK. She'll go along with anybody at the moment she's so desperate to make friends. It's been tough for her, losing her mother then moving here."

"I can understand that, she's been through a lot. Where's Tayler today?" Elin glanced around.

"She's with my sister, I thought the day would be a bit long for her, especially as I was asked to speak. I didn't want her to distract everybody. I have to pick her up as soon as this is over."

Mia, Chrissie and Celia were already making inroads into plates piled high with food when Elin and Robert returned. They'd been stopped several times by people wanting to talk to Robert about his story. He was courteous and left each one saying he hoped to get to know them better before long.

An enormous plate of food was thrust at each of them and Elin subsided into her seat, happy to let her friends take up the conversation and grill Robert about his plans.

Chrissie started the questioning, "So, Robert, how come none of us had met you before, didn't even know of your existence? Other than Elin, of course, and she didn't know you were a Buddhist. Why have you been hiding?"

"Not hiding, though I can see how it might appear that way. When I moved here I contacted Simon, I'd been given his number by Aunty, and he came around to the house regularly and we chanted together. I had made a decision to stay in with the girls during the evenings, and weekends too, and not get a babysitter for the first six months. I figured they'd been through enough, especially Ashley, and I wanted them to settle, feel secure in the new house and their new schools before I left them, other than to go to work, of course. Six months isn't long for me and it could make all the difference for them."

"So how do you all know each other?" Robert was adept at drawing people out and the conversation flowed with reminiscences from Mia and Chrissie about the early days of their friendship, with Elin and Celia telling him about the regular Friday evenings with her daughters. Elin knew she could trust them not to reveal anything about her obsession with Robert and she basked in the easy chatter. Before he left to find Ashley, Robert managed to convey to Elin that he wanted to carry on the conversation and she knew he meant the conversation with her alone.

The afternoon's singing and dancing were wonderful, but for Elin nothing the entertainment had to offer could top the excitement of discovering Robert's life story. Celia and Elin walked towards the car together; the lights on the huge Christmas tree sparkled even brighter now that darkness was falling, as if it too was happy for Elin. As they stopped and Celia scrabbled in the depths of her handbag for her car keys, they heard a shout.

"Elin, hang on, wait a minute!" Robert was hurrying across the car park towards them, Ashley straggling behind, checking her mobile phone. Elin and Celia waited.

"Sorry I didn't get a chance to talk to you again."

Elin smiled and muttered vaguely in agreement.

"I wanted to say again what an amazing coincidence it was to meet you here today. Maybe we'll bump into each other in the park again. What time do you usually walk the dog?"

"It varies a lot, if it's a nice day tomorrow I'll be there at about two o'clock."

"OK, I'll try to get the kids out and about at the same time, see you tomorrow." Ashley had caught up with him by this time so Robert waved a quick goodbye as they walked towards his car.

Celia turned to Elin with a wide grin but concealed her thumbs up sign until she knew Robert had gone. "I think he's definitely interested Elin. Good for you, telling him exactly when you'd be in the park. Make sure you're there, won't you."

"Wild horses wouldn't keep me away, rain or shine." Elin was smiling, bubbles of excitement were fizzing through her body, "What a day! You told me I'd enjoy myself, but today was something else. Off the scale. No words to describe it."

"You're absolutely right kiddo. Everyone in the room was mesmerized by your Robert's story so I can barely imagine the effect it was having on you."

"It's too early to call him my Robert so don't get ahead of yourself. At the very least I don't have to hold myself back and bury my feelings. What a relief."

"Let me know how it goes tomorrow. I don't want you to get hurt, Elin, and he is very attractive. Now every single woman who was there today knows he's available," Celia pointed out.

"Yes, I'd thought of that too. There's nothing I can do about that. No looking back, only look to the future, right? I'm going to chant and make good causes for the future. And yes, believe in myself. Have I got that right?"

Celia laughed, "My goodness Elin, you've obviously been listening. Keep chanting."

"Oh, I will," Elin replied fervently. "*Nam Myoho Renge Kyo!*"

EPILOGUE

E lin staggered up the path towards the front door of her new home, cat carrier in each hand. She was used to the un-mown grass and weed filled borders and she barely registered the cracked floor tiles in the entry way and the paint flaking off the front door. She stood in the porch and managed to ring the bell with her shoulder. She heard the notes fading away in the distance as Robert opened the door.

"I'm so glad you're here, you've just stopped me blowing a gasket." He ran his hand through his uncombed hair. Stubble sandpapered her chin as he kissed her before taking the cat carriers and making his way back to the kitchen. Elin followed. She watched his retreating form and marvelled at how sexy he was, even unkempt and unshaven, wearing old jeans and a scruffy sweater. There was a smell of coffee overlaid with notes of burnt toast and Tayler was sitting at the table engrossed with her latest colouring book. When she realised what was happening she jumped up and down with excitement. "The cats are here! Are you going to let them out now, Elin? They don't like it in those boxes, do they?"

The sound of piteous meows had been ringing in Elin's ears ever since she had tricked them into entering the carriers earlier, and had grown in volume during the short car journey. Elin hugged Tayler briefly before responding. "I don't want to leave them cooped up any longer either, isn't that noise awful? Do you want to call Ashley, perhaps she would help welcome them to their new home?"

"OK, I'll call her." Tayler ran to the door and shouted upstairs to her sister but couldn't be heard over the music, which was rattling the bedroom door on its hinges. Robert went to Tayler and scooped her up.

"That's enough, she can't hear you. Don't shout again, it's noisy enough already with the music and the cats." He plopped her down again at the table and turned to Elin adding, "I'll go upstairs and ask her, maybe it'll defuse the tension. We had another spat just before you got here." Robert walked towards the door.

Elin took his arm gently, "Hang on a minute, Rob. Give me a heads up, I don't want to put my foot in it."

Robert paused, "She's been nagging me about a tattoo for weeks. She has to have a letter signed by a parent or something to show she's over eighteen. I won't cooperate. Hence the problem."

Elin clapped her hands together. "That explains it! She was asking me what I thought about tattoos, maybe she was hoping I'd be on her side?"

Robert waited, hand on the doorknob, "What did you say?"

"I can't remember exactly, but I pointed out how she might change her mind. That something she thought was important now might not feel so important later, but she would be stuck with it. That it might be embarrassing. I even suggest that a piercing is easier to hide. If you don't want it anymore it heals over."

Robert raised his eyebrows but smiled in understanding, "I'm not so sure about that, though I did say she could have her ears pierced for her birthday."

"Alright, I'll be careful. I hope she comes downstairs soon, the cats are getting on my nerves."

A few minutes later Ashley appeared with Robert following close behind. They were both smiling. Elin slowly opened the cat box doors, Tom and Alley emerged cautiously, eyes wide, before they started to explore their new home, sniffing and rubbing against furniture, on their guard and ready to flee at any sudden movement. The girls watched silently. Elin spoke first.

"Why don't you give them some food, Ashley? I think they might be hungry?" She had purposely not fed them earlier and had brought a tin of their favourite food. Soon Alley and Tom were purring and rubbing themselves around Ashley's legs as she put their dishes on the floor.

Ashley looked at her father, "I need to get ready now so I guess I'll see the cats later." As she moved towards the door she said, "By the way, Dad, I'm meeting my friends in town this afternoon, so I'll see you all tonight. Bye Elin."

Robert spoke quickly, "Just a sec, Ash, who are you going with? I want you back by seven o'clock, OK?"

Ashley frowned, "You know my friends, Dad, the usual ones, Emily and Sophie, maybe Nell too, I don't know for sure. But seven o'clock's really early, Dad."

Robert looked straight at Ashley. His voice was firm, "Let's not go over this again, Ash. Seven it is. If there's somewhere you want to go afterwards, you need to ask permission in plenty of time, OK? Elin and I are taking

Tayler to Celia's then collecting Mutt and the last of her stuff from the flat. We'll see you at seven."

After that final edict, Robert gave Ashley a hug.

Later, Elin clutched Robert's hand as they shut the door of her much loved flat for the last time. They stopped and looked back. Unexpected tears filled Elin's eyes and she searched for a tissue in her pocket. One tear escaped and ran down her cheek. Robert brushed it away gently. "Don't be scared Elin, it's going to work out. I know you've been happy here and now we'll be even happier, together every day."

"I know that too, but I'm scared. I'm worried that me living in your house, in Ashley's home, is going to upset her. If she's upset and angry then it's going to be very hard for us. I don't want our happiness to come at her expense."

"I understand, Elin. I love the way you care about everybody's happiness. I know we'll have to weather some storms with her but we'll get through them together, as a family."

Elin sniffed and managed a smile, "You're right. Goodbye little flat. I hope the new people enjoy living here as much as I did." She reached up on tiptoe and gave Robert a kiss of gratitude. He squeezed her hand in acknowledgement as they turned away.

Finally, Elin and Robert carried in the last four boxes of her belongings. Elin felt shattered. She went upstairs to the family bathroom to wash her hands and splash her face with water. She looked in the mirror and smiled at herself. She liked what she saw, even though she needed a haircut and had developed a few more laughter lines. Today she was happy and her face showed it.

The clouds drifted away and the sun emerged to celebrate her arrival. Elin felt her energy return as they ate a

late lunch picnic style in the back garden. Some rays found
their way through the newly budding branches and Elin
relaxed in her chair as she watched Mutt investigate every
inch of his new environment. When Tayler returned she
transferred her attention from the cats to Mutt, oblivious to
Elin's presence.

Later as Elin and Robert sat together at the kitchen table
Robert lifted her hand and kissed it before saying, "We did
it! We need to celebrate... how about champagne? This is a
big day, definitely needs champagne. Shall I open a bottle?"

"Great idea, and I bought olives and nuts. Why don't we
chant together before opening the bottle? We can make a
determination to be happy together, no matter what."

They had only just finished chanting when Ashley
walked in, early for once. Things were looking good. She
smiled at them and made straight for her room, but Robert
diverted her by asking if she knew that Mutt had arrived.
Even Ashley was intrigued to find out how Flopsy and Mutt
were getting along together, so they trooped towards the
kitchen. Flopsy was sitting in the corner looking bewildered
by the arrival of one dog, even one she knew, and two cats,
who she definitely didn't know. Ashley headed straight
for her.

"Flopsy, lovely girl, it's OK, just a lot of company all of a
sudden. You'll always be my best pal, don't worry." Ashley
bent over to put her arms round the old dog, wanting to
comfort her, letting her know she was still number one dog
in the house.

Elin and Robert looked on benignly, happy that Ashley
was home early and engaging in the events of the day. They
watched as Ashley hugged Flopsy and as she did so her
short, close fitting top rode up from her hip-hugging jeans
and exposed her lower back. Although her skin was

inflamed and sore looking from the tattooist's needle, the words could still be read clearly. Ashley realised what had happened. The room fell silent as Ashley stood up very slowly and turned to face them. She looked from her father to Elin and back again, searching for clues to their reaction. Her expression managed to convey pleading, optimism and a hint of defiance. She gave an uncertain half smile.

Elin hadn't managed to stifle a shocked gasp and stood with her hand over her mouth.

Robert frowned and didn't move. With remarkable control, he finally spoke, "Please turn around Ashley, so that Elin and I can have a good look at your new tattoo."

Ashley turned around very slowly. The seconds ticked by. Even Tayler was quiet. After checking the words again Elin and Robert finally looked at each other, then looked at the tattoo one more time. In beautiful cursive script, it read, "*Nam Myoho Renge Kyo.*"

They let out a joint sigh but could not prevent smiles lighting up their faces. This time they had been well and truly outwitted. They both opened their arms wide, grabbed Ashley and Tayler and held them both tightly. Elin was the first to speak.

"You certainly chose some important words for your tattoo, Ashley. Please don't ever forget them."

The End.

FIND OUT MORE

- www.sgi-uk.org
- www.sgi.org

These websites contain useful information and introductory material for people who want to start chanting.

SGI VIDEOS ONLINE

The SGI YouTube channel:

www.youtube.com/user/sgivideosonline

HOW TO CHANT

Three films about how to start chanting, including karaoke-style pronunciation guides.

www.sgi.org/resource-center/video-and-audio/how-to-chant.html

ACKNOWLEDGEMENTS

There are more people to thank than I can possibly mention, but here are some.

My mother Olive Jones who passed on her love of reading to my brother Mike and me.

My English teacher Miss Roberts whose joy in books was infectious. What a pity I chose to study Chemistry instead.

Librarians, everywhere. How else could I have indulged in my escape into books?

My editor Cherry Mosteshar of the Oxford Editors for her constructive criticism and all-around expertise.

USA:

Terry Beck, Kimberly Pierce and Kimberly Fenter in Napa, California who gave me the book *How to Write*.

Noreen Huffman who kick-started my attempts to write this book at Denny's in Porterville.

Greg Martin Head of Publications SGI-USA for his encouraging comment "We need Buddhist garbage too." I know what he meant and didn't take offence.

Jolene Edwards for her friendship, help and staunch belief in the value of the story.

Carla Gerritsma and the South Valley SGI-USA Arts group who were recipients of my first reading, even if none of that material made it through to the final version.

Nancy Nella for her time and encouragement.

Cardiff UK:

Rachie Williams for her computer support, especially in choosing the cover graphics.

Alison Evans and Jules Twells for their IT expertise and hard work.

Niki Liverton for her ongoing interest and constant encouragement.

Bridget Keenan and James Rourke (the professionals) for practical encouragement.

Megan Phillips Jones for her technical help.

My son Matthew Jones and daughter in law Rebecca Jones for giving up their precious time to right my computer wrongs.

My son Steffan Jones for believing in me.

My husband Larry for his patience and the lessons in perseverance that I learned from him.

And most of all:

President Ikeda, Richard Causton and all the SGI members I have met, worldwide, from whom I learned the lessons in this book and much more.

ABOUT THE AUTHOR

Liz Unser grew up in Wales and after a few years as possibly the unhappiest pharmacist in the UK she changed direction and became a social worker first in South Wales and later in California.

Winter into Spring is her first novel.

She is married, the mother of three sons and is an active member of SGI-UK and SGI-USA.

Made in the USA
San Bernardino, CA
02 August 2020